Praise for Mary Ellen Taylor

"Mary Ellen Taylor writes comfort reads packed with depth . . . If you're looking for a fantastic vacation read, this is the book for you!"

—Steph and Chris's Book Review, on *Spring House*

"A complex tale . . . grounded in fascinating history and emotional turmoil that is intense yet subtle. An intelligent, heartwarming exploration of the powers of forgiveness, compassion, and new beginnings."

—*Kirkus Reviews*, on *The View from Prince Street*

"Absorbing characters, a hint of mystery, and touching self-discovery elevate this novel above many others in the genre."

—RT Book Reviews, on *Sweet Expectations*

"Taylor serves up a great mix of vivid setting, history, drama, and everyday life."

—*Herald Sun*, on *The Union Street Bakery*

"A charming and very engaging story about the nature of family and the meaning of love."

—*Seattle Post-Intelligencer*, on *Sweet Expectations*

The Words We Whisper

"Taylor expertly employs the parallel timelines to highlight the impact of the past on the present, exploring the complexities of familial relationships while peeling back the layers of her flawed, realistic characters. Readers are sure to be swept away."

—*Publishers Weekly*

"A luscious interweaving of a spy thriller and a family saga."

—*Historical Novels Review*

Honeysuckle Season

"This memorable story is sure to tug at readers' heartstrings."

—*Publishers Weekly*

Winter Cottage

"Offering a look into bygone days of the gentrified from the early 1900s up until the present time, this multifaceted tale of mystery and romance is sure to please."

—New York Journal of Books

"There is mystery and intrigue as the author weaves a tale that pulls you in . . . this is a story of strong women who persevere . . . it's a love story, the truest, deepest kind . . . and it's the story of a woman who years later was able to right a wrong and give a home to the people who really needed it. It's layered brilliantly, and hints are revealed subtly, allowing the reader to form conclusions and fall in love."

—Smexy Books

The

PROMISE

of

TOMORROW

OTHER TITLES BY MARY ELLEN TAYLOR

Winter Cottage

Spring House

Honeysuckle Season

The Words We Whisper

The Brighter the Light

When the Rain Ends

Union Street Bakery Novels

The Union Street Bakery

Sweet Expectations

Alexandria Series

At the Corner of King Street

The View from Prince Street

The

PROMISE

of

TOMORROW

MARY ELLEN TAYLOR

 Montlake

Text copyright © 2024 by Mary Burton

Published by Montlake, Seattle

www.apub.com

Amazon, the Amazon logo, and Montlake are trademarks of Amazon.com, Inc., or its affiliates.

ISBN-13: 9781662517822 (hardcover)
ISBN-13: 9781662513459 (paperback)
ISBN-13: 9781662513466 (digital)

Cover design by Ploy Siripant
Cover image: © Ildiko Neer / ArcAngel

Printed in the United States of America
First edition

The

PROMISE

of

TOMORROW

@ThePizzaTraveler

**Lessons learned in
Kansas City, Missouri**

Running away from home is hard.

"Hard to Say I'm Sorry" played on the radio when I pulled into a Kansas City gas station in my 1998 Ford Taurus. The road ahead stretched so far beyond the horizon, and suddenly the journey felt very daunting. Panic fisted my chest. If I turned around now, my full tank of gas would get me back to St. Louis, Missouri, or maybe Louisville, Kentucky. 500 miles closer to Virginia and home.

Signs from the universe aren't bold, daring, or splashy.

The first hint indicating I should keep traveling materialized as a free gas station hot dog.

Condiment free, wrapped in parchment paper, it was the offering of an old guy with a toothless grin and a thin gray ponytail accentuating creviced lines arrowing from the corners of his gray eyes. "Free with a $5 purchase. Take it. You'll need it to keep going forward. Backwards is for the lost."

When the universe wants you to wait, you wait.

Turns out hot dogs can give you food poisoning and engine water hoses break.

After dozing for a couple of hours in my car, a cramping stomach woke me up. I made it to the gas station bathroom and threw up several times.

When I finally stumbled into a nearby diner in search of crackers and ginger ale, I met a nice waitress named Shirley who wore thick blue eye shadow and her white hair in a beehive. Shirley told me about a guy who owned a food truck and needed help. Hank's Barbecue Truck, she added, was parked next to an honest mechanic's garage. I thanked her, got in my car, and started the engine. A mile down the road, steam rose out from under the hood. An hour later, I knocked on Hank's truck.

Do angels wear beehives?

#RUNNING #NEWLIFE #ANGELS #SIGNS

CHAPTER ONE
OLYMPIA

One year later
Saturday, October 26, 2024, 8:00 p.m.
Blacksburg, Virginia

Running away from home never got easy.

That long, winding road that had coaxed me across the western United States last year with promises of freedom, self-discovery, and happiness had circled back to my old Virginia stomping grounds. I was back at square one, smelling faintly of fast-food hamburgers and Doritos chips and wondering if I'd changed enough to resist my old life.

"This is going to be a quick trip. Get in and get out. No drama." My goals were simple. Sign divorce papers, visit the graves of my mother and daughter, and then return to the road.

I'd spent the last ten hours hunched over my van's steering wheel, staring past swabbing windshield wipers into a line of blurred brake lights. The final push along I-81 into Virginia and then the New River Valley had been a grueling pedal-to-the-metal ending to a two-day road trip.

I set my worn canvas bag on a gas station bathroom sink and unzipped it. The restroom space was small, and the black-and-white floor tile was cracked, but there were two functioning, clean toilets, the dented towel dispenser was full, and honeysuckle freshener softened the air. As bathrooms went, I'd seen a lot worse.

I shrugged stiff shoulders. Changing clothes in a tiny rectangular bathroom stall would have been more private, but the confined space required more flexibility than my rigid limbs could muster. An eighteen-wheeler rumbled through the parking lot past the bathroom door, its tires delivering a rush of cold air under the trembling threshold. A horn honked. I didn't bother retreating to the stall. My modesty had become a casualty of living on the road.

I yanked off my purple *What Happens in Bozeman . . .* T-shirt and flinched as frigid air rippled over my skin. A necklace strung with a hagstone, turquoise, and a gold wedding band dangled between my breasts. An Albuquerque roadside vendor had said the hagstone would chase away the spirits circling me and the turquoise would drain the bad energy from my throat chakra. I'd been ready to exorcise a few spirits, so I'd ponied up twenty bucks, unfastened my gold chain, and threaded the ends through the stones until they nestled against my wedding band.

After turning on the hot water, I washed my hands, face, and armpits and then grabbed a wad of paper towels and dried off. From my bag, I dug out a beige bra that I hadn't used in weeks, wangled arms through the straps, and then arranged boobs in the cups.

I pulled a black knit dress from the bottom of my bag, snapped the dress until the synthetic fibers released their wrinkles and it fell into a smoothish drape. I yanked the dress over my head, then tugged the fabric over full breasts, a narrow waist, and a too-flat stomach and let it fall past my knees. I kicked off Converse sneakers, shimmied out of dusty jeans, and stepped into black ankle boots. I shoved my travel clothes into the bag.

Several folks on the road had called me Mary Poppins because I could always reach into this bag or my backpack and pull out whatever anyone needed. Aspirin, hair ties, Band-Aids, pencils, tampons, scissors, and even duct tape. I was prepared for everything and nothing.

As I raised my eyes, my gaze collided with my reflection. I'd lost weight on the road, leaving my cheeks and chin sharper. My thick black hair had grown well past my shoulders and thankfully could go another day or two without a washing. The dark circles under my blue eyes weren't that stark, and hints of a tan still lingered from Wednesday's Montana hike.

I finger combed my hair and then fished red lipstick and blush from my bag. A few swipes of each added pops of color.

Drawing in a few deep breaths, I slid on silver earrings, willing the tightness in my chest to ease. I twisted my lips into a Joker-like grin that missed the genuine mark by a mile. Relaxing my lips, I attempted another smile. Effort number two was a little less cringey but hardly heartwarming or inviting. After a few more failed tries, I stopped aiming for relaxed and confident. Not screaming like a madwoman tonight would be a win. I grabbed my bag.

"Life is what it is, girl," I muttered.

Out of the bathroom, I crossed the lit parking lot to my green Sienna van. Sliding open the passenger-side door, I tossed my bag onto an armless futon covered with a quilt and a half dozen pillows. The folding piece doubled as a couch when upright and a bed when lying flat.

From this futon I'd watched the sun rise and set over desert vistas, sweeping red canyons, and snowcapped jagged mountains. I'd developed an obsession with the sun because in the ruins of my life, its cycle reminded me that this very consistent earth would keep turning in space despite the unexplainable chaos on the surface.

Across from the mattress were two large plastic tubs with lids. One held my clothes, and the other stored my food and cooking supplies. There was a small stack of books I'd bought from used bookstores, jars of rocks I'd collected on hikes, and a battery-operated lantern a diner owner in Santa Fe had tossed in with my small paycheck. All the side and rear windows were covered with red cherry-print curtains that I drew closed when I slept.

I slammed the side door closed and walked around the back bumper, splashed with mud and embellished with stickers from Missouri, Arizona, Colorado, Wyoming, Utah, and Montana.

At my driver's side door, I breathed in cold mountain air.

The temperature had been falling for the last couple of hours and was headed into the low thirties. Inside the van, I started my engine and pulled out onto Route 460.

Seeing so many familiar buildings and side streets was oddly comforting. I wasn't overthinking or checking my location on my phone, as I'd done most of the last year. Tackling so many challenges on the road (food poisoning, tornado warnings, and getting lost in the desert to the point of believing I'd die) had softened the pulsing anxiety that had originally driven me out of town.

At the stoplight, I glanced at my younger sister Eve's engagement party invitation stuck in the dashboard AC vent. I wondered if I'd made a mistake. Maybe it would've been better if I'd stayed away. But I couldn't because running away from home is hard.

Though I'd grown up here, the back mountain roads were a little tricky in waning moonlight that cast long shadows and masked street signs and landmarks. I grabbed the invitation and plugged the directions into my phone (lesson learned in the desert). It was just too easy to miss the mountain side streets, and I was already an hour and a half late. Getting lost would only add to the tension.

When the light turned green, I took a left and drove west. Each new turn took me farther away from city strip-mall lights and deeper into the dark mountains.

I switched on the radio, finding my favorite country and western station, which had always played at Tony's Pizzeria, where Eve and I had practically grown up.

Our mother, Jeanne, had taken the job as Tony's Pizzeria's manager when I was twelve and Eve was nine. Our father had died, and Mom had been forced to sell our small house and move us into a two-bedroom apartment in Blacksburg. With childcare beyond Mom's limited budget, she took us to the restaurant. Tony Sr. welcomed us with open muscled, tattooed arms and told us his house was our house, so to speak.

If we weren't doing homework, we were folding pizza boxes, rolling napkins around plastic utensils, or dragging trash to the alley dumpster. I loved hearing Tony Sr.'s stories from the years he'd worked at the Stockton Quarry, driven across the West on a Harley, and then found love and resettled in Blacksburg. Many of his tales didn't quite add up, date-wise, but I didn't care. He was larger than life, and in those days, I felt so small.

I hated homework and didn't see the point of endless algebra or vocabulary worksheets that didn't pay the rent or put gas in the tank. But I took to the daily restaurant work quickly because it mimicked stability in my very insecure world. The task started, and it ended. It was done right, or it wasn't. And a job well done often meant a little cash from Tony Sr. No gray-area drama. No tears. End of story.

My mom, my sister, and I went on with our lives. For the next couple of years, Mom's paycheck, loaded with as much overtime as Tony would give her, covered the bills. Eve and I wore Goodwill jeans and shirts, and we all ate leftover pizza, day-old bread, or nearly expired produce and turned off lights when we left a room, but we got by.

By fifteen, I had grand plans of marrying Tony's son, TJ, two years my senior. He always wore snug T-shirts that fit a muscled chest and arms. Thick black hair was brushed off his angled face and gave him a pouty bad-boy vibe that I'd loved. I dreamed TJ and I would turn Tony's Pizzeria into a global sensation. I fantasized about beating Bobby Flay or hosting my own pizza-making show featuring TJ and, of course, our adorable kids. The number of our children varied, but all my dreams ended with me having love, a home, and stability.

Eve hated our tiny apartment and working in the pizza shop. Too tedious, too boring, too pointless. She didn't want to fold pizza boxes or wrap plastic utensils. She wanted to read her science books and look at style magazines. Her goals shifted between fashion designer and Nobel Prize winner. Her dislike of the pizza shop had motivated her to excel in high school and eventually earn a scholarship to Virginia Tech.

Ours wasn't a perfect life, but it was good enough until Mom got sick. Mom died of ovarian cancer seven years ago, shortly before my eighteenth birthday. Tony Sr. died of a heart attack four years after her. Eve graduated from Virginia Tech with undergraduate and master's degrees in microbiology and now taught science at Montgomery County High School as she worked toward her PhD. TJ, who had popped my cherry in the eleventh grade, was now married to a former restaurant waitress.

The last dozen years had left me with an odd jumble of assets including mad pizza-box-folding skills, Tony Sr.'s secret sauce recipe, and a GED. I also had no permanent address, a baby I'd only carried in my belly for five months, and a failed marriage. So far, the *L*s overshadowed the *W*s.

My phone alerted me to the next turn. Squinting, I struggled to read nearly invisible street signs. Beyond my headlights, a bouquet of white balloons strained against pink ribbon tethered to a street sign. Eve. My little Pinterest baby. She never missed the details.

Slowing, I turned left and wound up a smaller street that took me up the side of a mountain. I couldn't pinpoint my exact location, but I'd driven up this way before, and I'd hiked many of the trails in this area. Back in the day, if I wasn't slinging pizza dough, I was climbing and exploring the trails in southwest Virginia.

More balloons and a sign that read EVE AND BRAD directed me up a smaller gravel road. It was almost 8:30 p.m., making me two hours late to my sister's engagement party.

I really couldn't blame the rain or heavy traffic outside Knoxville for my tardiness. I'd been slow getting out of Montana, uncharacteristically dragging my heels as I convinced myself I needed one last hike. Maybe I'd been hoping an early-fall blizzard would close the roads. When Mother Nature didn't offer me an out, I started driving east. Travel time would be tight, but I reasoned I'd be on time if there were no bumps along the road. Rookie mistake.

Now as I rounded the final bend, a deer darted in front of the van. I jammed on brakes and waited as two smaller does crossed. Finally, I edged forward up the hill's crest until I saw bright lights winking in the distance.

I had been up here before. This was Stockton family land. The Stocktons were one of the richest families in the valley and had made their fortune mining granite from their quarry and constructing some of the most notable structures at the university and in the valley.

I remembered an old barn and a crumbling stone house. Why had Eve chosen a rustic venue up here? My sister had champagne tastes and dressed, decorated, and posted like she'd inherited a fortune from our mother. A country shindig was not her style.

I aimed my van up the driveway. A man holding an orange flashlight waved his beam toward an open plot of grass next to dozens of other parked cars. Valets were more Eve's style, and this guy was my first sign this wasn't going to be your average country affair.

I slid my van in beside a BMW, shoved my purse under the passenger seat, and grabbed the invitation and a jean jacket from the passenger seat. Out of the van, music and light drifted through the woods as I touched my flagstone, slid on the jacket, and then crossed a freshly graveled lot toward the final curve in the road.

Not only was the old barn still standing, but the rotting wooden roof had been swapped for red tin and the siding had all been repaired. Open double doors flanked by standing heaters showcased an interior decorated with a thousand tiny white lights. Crowded around a bandstand, dozens of nicely dressed couples chatted and danced. To the left was a large display of food, complete with tall glass vases filled with backlit white flowers.

A chilly breeze wafted the edges of my jacket. I tugged the folds closed as I remembered the first time Eve and I had been on this property. We'd not been in the barn but in the Stone Cottage behind this barn.

Meghan Trainor's "All About That Bass" pulsed from a speaker as I gripped Tony Sr.'s Louisville Slugger bat and climbed creaking stairs toward the Stone Cottage's front door. As a couple made out on a porch glider, a rock flew out of a front window, spraying glass. Heart pounding, I opened the front door. The room was filled with a crush of people, the scent of beer, and clouds of pot smoke.

An hour ago, twelve-year-old Eve had called in a panic and told me she was hiding in an upstairs bedroom closet at the Stone Cottage. "Please, come get me."

I'd left Tony's, bat in hand, and taken Mom's car, which I drove routinely now. I was fifteen.

I climbed the stairs, stepping past another couple sucking face, and opened the first bedroom door on the right. There were two teens under the sheets, and given their moans, they were also having sex. I strode toward the closet. The male never looked in my direction, but the gal cut her eyes toward me briefly before she went back to kissing the guy. I opened the closet door. Empty.

In the next bedroom a naked girl was straddling a guy. No one was in the closet.

The final bedroom door was locked. I pounded my fist on it, and when a guy told me to go away, I snapped. Tired, irritated, and scared, I cocked the bat and struck the door. The door's solid oak absorbed the blow, and the impact reverberated up my arms.

"Let me in," I shouted. "Or I'm calling the cops." To make my point I struck the door again, bracing for another vibration to rattle up my spine.

The door opened, putting me face to face with a six-foot, two-inch naked guy clutching his T-shirt over his junk. He had dark ruffled hair and a pissed expression. I didn't know him personally, but I had seen his picture in the local paper. He was a Stockton, which in this town translated into rich.

"What do you want?" Naked Guy asked.

I rested the bat on my shoulder, suspecting if Naked Guy grabbed it, I was screwed. "My sister. My twelve-year-old sister."

The statement was enough to get his attention. "She's not here."

I glanced toward the bed to a blonde sitting up with a sheet clutched to her bare breasts. Taking advantage of Naked Guy's momentary shock, I pushed past him and marched to the one closet door.

"There's no one else here," Naked Guy said. "Jesus, I'm not that sick."

I twisted the knob and opened the door. Huddled in the corner was Eve, with her legs drawn up and her chin resting on her knees. She looked up at me, her red eyes shadowed by melting mascara.

Eve sobbed. "Olympia."

I grabbed Eve, hauled her to her feet, and pulled her out of the closet. She was wearing cutoff jeans that skimmed the bottom of her ass, a T-shirt knotted below her breasts, and dangling earrings taken from our mother's jewelry box.

When Naked Guy saw Eve, he swallowed hard and stepped back toward the bed. "What the hell!"

"You didn't know she was in that closet?" I demanded.

"No. Hell no!" Naked Guy said.

The woman in the bed rose on her knees. "We didn't know."

I tightened my grips on Eve's wrist and the bat. Blood battering my veins, I pulled her past Naked Guy and Girl and out into the hallway. The music throbbed loud. Down the stairs and out the front door, I hurried toward my mother's car.

"Olympia, I'm so sorry," Eve said.

"Me too," I said.

I now gripped the invite tighter as I stood at the edge of the party. It was a sea of black tie and elegant dresses. A four-piece jazz band's smooth melody drifted over conversations and the clink of glasses. I hugged myself close, wishing now I'd dug my black tights out of my bag. If I didn't know better, I'd swear this was an alternate universe.

I reread Eve's invitation. Sure enough, in a tiny script font was *Black Tie Optional*.

"Damn it."

Rolling my head from side to side, I stepped through the barn doors. I stood close to the tall heater and drank up the warmth as I gathered up my nerve to enter the party. Too bad I didn't have my baseball bat.

A waiter carrying a tray of champagne flutes moved toward me. He wore black slacks and a pressed white-collared shirt, and his face had the soft pudge of a younger man. He glanced at my dress and dusty boots.

"I'm not lost or crashing," I said. "My sister is Eve Hanover."

"The bride-to-be." His eyes narrowed. "You work at Tony's."

"Did." Good to be tapping into the local roots again. "Do you know where she is?"

"She's wearing a red dress. But I haven't seen her for fifteen or twenty minutes. Would you like a glass of champagne?"

I accepted a flute. "Thanks."

"Of course." Several couples caught the waiter's attention, and he glided away, leaving me alone. I sipped the champagne, grateful for a task.

To the right of the stage, where the band played, was a long buffet and an open bar. To the left was a collection of round tables for people to sit and eat. In the center was a wooden dance floor. "Eve, looks like you're marrying up."

Her fiancé, Brad, was a lawyer, and once his father, Henry, had helped me out of a jam. But Eve hadn't met Brad until a couple of weeks before I left town. I'd not been at my best, so we'd never been formally introduced.

According to Eve, Brad had taken over his late father's practice. I'd been nine months into my western excursion—in Provo, Utah, making dough in a small pizza shop—when she'd called. I'd been slammed with lunch orders and had only caught every other one of her excited words. It hadn't been the first time Eve was in love.

"Olympia!"

The familiar sound of my sister's voice had me turning. Eve was wearing a bright-red dress that dipped off each shoulder. Her blonde hair (she'd started dying it in college) was pulled into a french twist, and pearl drop earrings dangled by her neck. She looked radiant.

When Eve wrapped her arms around me, the soft, spicy scent of an expensive perfume encircled us. She hugged me tight, which was touching because Eve hated hugs. If the last year had taught me anything, it was to accept the good moments with open arms.

Eve drew back. "You haven't changed a bit."

Funny that the outside could stay the same when my insides had been twisted and distorted into something I no longer recognized. "I did buy new earrings."

Eve laughed. "When all this is over, you must tell me all about your travels. I follow you on Instagram. The Pizza Traveler's pictures in Utah and Montana are stunning."

"There's some amazing country out there."

"Did you hit all the line items on Mom's bucket list?"

"And then some." I looked around the room at people who must have been some of the richest in the valley.

There'd never been enough money for a vacation for the Hanover women, but our mother had been an avid collector of used travel magazines. Mom and I spent hours picking out our favorite pictures and pasting them on our apartment's kitchen walls. Eve had never had a desire to visit the West, but Mom and I had curated an extensive bucket list we'd one day tackle. However, Mom's illness had gutted that dream by the time I was sixteen.

"You have a good following on Instagram," Eve said. "Five or six thousand, the last I checked."

It was twice that. I'd never expected anyone to care about my travels or journals from the road, but I'd caught the attention of a few local newspapers out west who'd written articles about @ThePizzaTraveler when I posted and tagged their town. From there my followers grew.

"People like to live vicariously."

"Are you monetizing the page or becoming an influencer?" Eve asked.

Always thinking about finances. At least my rants about money not growing on trees hadn't gone totally unnoticed. "The thought has occurred to me."

"Maybe you won't have to work part time in all those pizza joints."

"Pizza posts get the highest engagement. People love to see how the sausage is made, so to speak."

Eve arched a brow. "If you say so."

The cool champagne hadn't taken the edge off my nerves yet. "So, am I going to meet this fiancé of yours or not?"

"I just saw Brad across the room with his best man. They'll be right over."

I took another sip of champagne. I'd not eaten since the peanut butter sandwich in a Walmart parking lot this morning. I should've eaten a second sandwich as soon as I crossed the Virginia line, but my appetite had dwindled as the miles to Blacksburg ticked down.

I took another sip. "Terrific."

No sooner had I spoken than a tall man dressed in black tie cut through the crowd. He was lean and had sandy-brown hair and an aging-boy-band-member kind of pout reminiscent of the Justin Bieber and Zac Efron posters that had watched over the chaos on Eve's half of our bedroom.

The looker came up to Eve and kissed her on the cheek. "Hey, you."

Eve smiled. "Brad, this is my sister, Olympia."

Brad shifted his attention to me, tossing a grin tailor made for winning new clients. If he thought I was lacking, he gave no hint of it. "Nice to meet you, Olympia. Eve has told me so much about you."

I smiled. "From what I hear, my sister is crazy about you."

"I'm wild about her."

I sipped more champagne. "This is some shindig. Did you put this together?"

"No. My best friend is throwing the party for us," Brad said.

"Really?"

Eve's face paled a fraction, emphasizing her red lipstick. Before I could ask about this best friend, another man cut through the crowd toward us. I barely noticed his tux as his gray eyes settled on me.

"Spencer." So much for getting in and out of town without being noticed.

Eve glanced at Brad, and both looked as if they'd detonated a bomb.

"You're looking good, Olympia." Spencer's voice was as deep and smooth as I remembered. How many times had that voice charmed the pants off me? Too many to count.

However, right now, I didn't feel charmed. I felt awkward and a little ambushed. Not once had Eve mentioned that Spencer was hosting the party. Not. Once.

Spencer searched my face, his taut jaw muscles pulsing. His left hand flexed, drawing my attention to the gold wedding band. "You didn't know, did you?"

I scrounged a smile, not for Eve, Brad, or Spencer but for me. I might have been left in the dark about key party details, but I wasn't going to let them see me sweat. "That this was your doing? No."

Maybe it would've been easier if we'd met in private. But was there a smooth way to reconnect with your estranged husband?

I doubted it.

CHAPTER TWO
SPENCER

Saturday, October 26, 2024, 9:15 p.m.

Olympia had lost weight in the last year. Wide auburn streaks now tunneled through her thick ebony hair, and her skin had darkened to a rich golden. She was wearing the Black Dress, as she'd called it on their first public date. The sheath was her go-to whenever they had an outing or she worked the odd catering job. He'd seen the dress drying in her shower often enough to remember the *Hand Wash, Air Dry* tag. The dark fabric still embraced full breasts, slid over her belly, and skimmed above her long legs. Her choice of red lipstick almost made him smile. A display of bright lip color, she'd once said, was her way of pretending she cared about makeup.

Olympia wasn't classically beautiful. Her eyes were wide, her nose was slightly hooked, and when she smiled, a twisted incisor appeared. Still, her not being classically beautiful had made her so stunning. She wasn't someone he'd ever been able to ignore.

Looking at her now, it was almost impossible to believe a year had passed. That they'd married at the justice of the peace. Lost a baby. Separated.

But it had all happened.

Olympia had been a damn ghost this last year and had only answered his texts when he'd requested proof of life. She'd always been a hiker and allowed Eve and then him into her Find My Friends network. When she'd left town, the tracker had stayed on. Six weeks after she'd left Blacksburg, his texts and calls had gone ignored, so he'd fired off a message:

Spencer: Respond or I send a sheriff to your location.

Olympia: Alive and well.

Each month, he sent similar texts and received the exact same response. Alive and well. And each time he'd tried to start a conversation, and the communication had ended. But the tracker stayed on, the posts continued, and he remained trapped in a no-man's-land with a woman he did not know how to reach. Separated, not separated.

Olympia had never initiated contact with him. He was always the one reaching out and trying to connect. Finally, his patience had thinned, and his last text, two weeks ago, had been blunt:

Spencer: Alive and Well?

Olympia: Yes.

Spencer: Good. I want a divorce.

He'd thought that declaration would've gotten a rise out of her, but nothing. Radio silence.

So, he'd offered to host Brad and Eve's party, knowing Olympia wouldn't miss it. On several levels he'd wanted their reunion to happen in public. Easier to contain emotions when people were watching.

"Eve wasn't sure if you were going to make it," Spencer said.

"Got caught in traffic outside of Knoxville. Best-laid plans, right?"

Olympia sipped more champagne as she shot a glance toward Eve, now clinging to Brad's arm. Eve's body language confirmed Olympia had been blindsided by this reunion. Eve's deception annoyed him. Olympia might have been distant this last year, but she'd sacrificed a lot for her sister. She'd deserved better than what she'd gotten from Eve, and maybe even him.

He'd been following Olympia's social media posts for the last year and had trailed her over the entire desert Southwest, into the Rockies and finally Montana. How many times had he stared at an image of her and tried to dissect her grin, the tilt of her head or set of her jaw? Her smiles were bright, though the lips thinned in a way that suggested tension. He'd also noted there'd been no genuine warmth behind her eyes. Likely no one else noticed, but he did.

"How many miles have you logged?" Spencer asked.

"About twenty thousand," she said.

"What happened to the Ford Taurus?"

She drained the last of her champagne. "A radiator hose busted in Kansas City. I was able to trade a couple of weeks of work in a barbecue place for the van."

Do angels wear beehives? Her posted words rattled in his memory. "The van has to be more comfortable than the four-door."

"It is."

Christ, he hated small talk. He didn't give a shit about radiators or her van. And this room, filled with too many conversations and music, grated on his nerves. This party had been a mistake. It had been a year, and he and his wife needed quiet and privacy so they could have a real conversation. "Good to know."

A light hand rested on his shoulder and then slid down his arm. The familiar Chanel perfume signaled Caroline Davidson stood behind him. Spencer and Caroline had dated in high school and through sophomore year of college. Then they'd both agreed to a summer break while he'd gone to play on the semipro golf circuit. That break had now lasted seven years. Caroline had become an event planner and in the last few months was often in his path. He'd told himself he'd hired Caroline to manage this party because he hated event details like menus and table-cloth selections. When he'd asked Olympia for a divorce, he'd forced himself to wonder what life beyond this marriage would look like. And if he was honest, he was curious about his ex-girlfriend, who was clearly interested in him.

"Olympia, I'm going to have to steal these three away," Caroline said. "We need to get Eve, Brad, and Spencer up onstage. Spencer, you need to say a few words to the lovebirds, and I think Brad and Eve want to make an announcement."

"Now?" Spencer asked.

"It's on the schedule," Caroline said gently. "Introduction and then champagne toast." She spoke as if a party agenda really mattered.

"Right."

"Sounds like a plan." Eve glanced nervously toward Brad, who winked at her.

"I'm Caroline Davidson." Caroline extended her manicured hand to Olympia.

"And you know I'm Olympia." Olympia shook her hand, staring at her an extra beat. "Sister of the bride."

Caroline's smile didn't slip. "I've heard so many great things about you."

"Really?" Olympia released Caroline's hand and swirled her empty glass. "Like what?"

"You're quite the traveler." Caroline knew Olympia was Spencer's wife, but she had the good sense not to bring it up.

"I am."

"Eve can't stop talking about you," Caroline said. "Hopefully, I'll also be planning their wedding, so I'm sure we'll be in contact a lot over the next year. You'll be maid of honor, correct?"

Eve cleared her throat. "Of course."

Olympia glanced at her sister in a way suggesting if they were alone, she'd have been demanding Eve come clean. Instead, Olympia smiled, tried to sip from a now empty glass of champagne, and then frowned slightly into the void.

Spencer had assumed when Brad and Eve married in June, he'd see Olympia in person again. Judging from what Brad had said, Eve was planning a large wedding at the country club. She adored all the bells and whistles, and he was happy to give them to her. Whatever they intended was a far cry from the ten-minute ceremony Spencer and Olympia had shared at the county courthouse.

"Olympia, I'm stealing this trio." Steel girded Caroline's soft southern accent. "They have work to do tonight."

"Don't let me stop you," Olympia said. "There's a dessert table over there with my name on it."

"Spencer picked out quite the spread," Caroline said.

Olympia nodded slowly as she glanced at the tables. "Too bad I didn't bring zip-top bags."

Brad and Caroline laughed. Eve grimaced. Spencer took the comment in stride. Olympia never had a problem speaking her mind, and a childhood of pinching pennies had left a frugal mark.

Brad and Eve followed Caroline, but he lagged. "I thought Eve told you I'd sponsored the party."

"She's Eve. She dribbles out the right amount of information to get the desired results." For a moment, her shoulders relaxed, and for a split second they were who they'd been last year. But she caught herself and stiffened. "It's all good."

"Help yourself to the food." He'd chosen extra desserts, knowing Olympia had an incurable sweet tooth. She could live on chocolate. "I'm pretty sure the kitchen staff has plenty of zip-top bags."

Olympia's smile was fixed. "Thanks. And thanks for hosting this party. It looks lovely."

"Brad and I go way back. I wanted to do something special for him."

"Nice." Olympia nodded to the stage. "Caroline is giving you the stink eye."

He looked over his shoulder to see a grinning Caroline beckoning him forward. "Right." Shit. "See you around."

"At a lawyer's office?" Her direct stare, reserved for rowdy drunks at Tony's pizza parlor, was a professional, polite, don't-think-I'm-your-friend kind of look.

"Did you read my last text?" he asked.

"I did."

"Why didn't you respond?" He couldn't decide if he was hurt or pissed.

"I knew we'd see each other when I eventually came back to Blacksburg." She glanced into her still empty glass, frowned, and then looked back up at him. "And here we are."

He cleared his throat. "How long are you staying?"

"A couple of days. A week maybe."

Olympia had always been steady under pressure because she'd had to be to keep her family together. But a growing part of him wanted to see her armor crack. He wanted to think their ruined marriage had mattered enough to upset her composure. "We'll visit later."

"Sure. Great."

"Ladies and gentlemen." Caroline's light-canary dress shimmered in the overhead light. A yellow teardrop diamond dipped into her V-neck. "If you see Mr. Spencer Stockton out there, deliver him to the stage."

Laughter rippled. A few of the guys around Spencer nudged him, clapped him on the shoulder, and pushed him toward the stage. His smile was stiff and fixed as he cut through the crowd.

When he climbed up on the dais, he shook Brad's hand, kissed Eve on the cheek, and then leaned toward the microphone. His gaze scanned the crowd and settled on Olympia. "Thank you all for coming tonight to celebrate the engagement of Brad and Eve."

Olympia set her glass down, clapped along with the crowd, and then grabbed a fresh flute from a nearby waiter's tray. She'd never been much of a drinker, but that could've changed in the last year.

"Brad and I grew up together. Hell, I think half the people in this room grew up together, so I'm not going to bore you with a blow-by-blow of the troubles Brad and I have found in boarding school and college over the years. I'll save that for the wedding reception."

Caroline swapped his glass of champagne for a fresh one.

He raised the flute. "To Eve and Brad."

The toast echoed over the crowd as he stepped aside and let the couple take the microphone. Brad cleared his throat like he did when nerves got the better of him before a contract negotiation.

"Thank you all for coming," Brad said. "Eve and I appreciate all the goodwill."

The crowd clapped.

Brad coughed and took Eve's hand in his. "Eve and I have a bit of news," Brad said as he reached in his pocket and pulled out two rings. He handed one gold ring to Eve and then slid a second smaller one on her ring finger. It nestled close to a solitaire diamond engagement ring as if it had always been designed to fit. Eve smiled up at him, her eyes glistening with tears as she glided the thick wedding band on his ring finger.

Shit. They'd already gotten married.

"We got hitched a few days ago!" Brad held up Eve's hand and then kissed it.

The crowd cheered, no one missing a beat at the surprise announcement. He watched Olympia down the last of her second champagne, then grab another fresh glass as she drew in a breath and found a smile. For all the shit that had gone down between Olympia and him, Eve owed her sister better than blindsiding her twice in one night.

A Miracle
On the Road Headed West

Food poisoning aside, I stayed in Kansas City for a month, earned $1000 in cash that smelled like barbecue, and swapped my Ford Taurus (a.k.a. Stephanie) for a 12-year-old Sienna van that I named Gertie.

I could have turned around, but I reasoned logging more miles might break the cold, calloused grip of depression that swirled around me like a ghost.

After two days on the road, I rolled into Santa Fe, New Mexico, at midnight. Not the best time when a girl is running from demons. We all know darkness gives them power, and mine was whispering old fears in my ear.

I made my way to a 24-hour Walmart supercenter, grabbed a shopping basket, and walked past the produce section toward the candy aisle. I should have been loading up on veggies but bought an extra-large Snickers bar and made my way back to Gertie.

One bite into the candy bar, and the sugar, fat, and milk chocolate morphed into crime-fighting ninjas who dispelled the clouds over me long enough to take a full breath.

I was still alive. I was not lost. Tomorrow was another day.

A miracle.

#STILLRUNNINNG #FORWARD #CHOCOLATE

@Momof3 commented on your post:
Your posts are so real.
I walk beside you. Don't stop.

CHAPTER THREE
OLYMPIA

Saturday, October 26, 2024, 10:00 p.m.

The microphone carried Spencer's deep voice over a now hushed crowd as I made my way to the dessert table. My jean jacket caught another woman's purse strap. I stopped, smiled at her frowning face to assure us both I wasn't getting drunk, and jerked free.

Several other people noticed me and whispered to one another. I half expected to see a few cell phones dialing 911 to report a trespasser.

But I kept moving toward the dessert table, and I snagged a third—or was it a fourth?—glass of champagne, knowing there was no end in sight now that I'd blown through my two-drink limit. Soon, I'd not be able to feel my face, and tomorrow would be hell, but I had to survive now first.

Choosing the dinner-size china plate and a cloth napkin rolled around silver utensils, I skipped the protein and vegetable selections and moved straight to the desserts. The collection of confections was almost enough to make this party worth it. Had Spencer chosen these as a peace offering? Whenever I was stressed or upset, he always appeared with a box of chocolate chip cookies. He called them my happy pills.

I selected three large cookies, a square fudgy brownie, and a slice of chocolate cake. When I caught the side-eye of the server, he offered pumpkin pie, and I accepted a thick wedge.

The crowd clapped as Brad and Eve kissed again and the happy groom held up his champagne glass in toast. He said something about love and devotion and a life together. Whatever.

So, my baby sister had run off to the justice of the peace with her man. How many times had Eve declared she'd have a *real* wedding in a crowded church while wearing a glamorous white dress? She would learn, like I did, that a courthouse wedding was very real. My pending divorce testified to it.

As I glanced toward the stage, Eve was blushing. She scanned the crowd in my direction, and I knew then she was holding back on something else. I could wait for the next shoe to drop.

My plate loaded, I found a round table in the corner. Everyone at the table was listening to Eve and Brad gush, and they didn't pay much attention to me. Good. If they had, they would be wondering about my obsession with sugar. But I wasn't here to explain myself or make friends. I'd come to support my sister, see my mama's and baby girl's graves, and iron out divorce details with Spencer next week. I was only remaining at this party now for the cake.

After a respectable amount of time, several desserts, and a couple of coffees, I'd make my escape, drive to a well-lit truck stop or parking lot, curl up on the futon in the back of my van, and sleep. Tomorrow was supposed to be pretty and warm, so I'd hike a few familiar trails. Then I'd text Spencer, and we could set up a time next week to sign papers. Given how much Caroline was smiling at him onstage right now, I suspected it couldn't be soon enough for him.

"How do you know the happy couple?" The question came from a teenage girl with shoulder-length brown hair and thick glasses magnifying a wary gaze. "You don't look like you know anyone here."

"Saying I'm a party crasher?"

The kid shrugged. "Maybe."

I smiled. First bit of honesty of the night. "I'm the sister of the bride. Who are you?"

"Miss Hanover is my science teacher."

"Nice." I stabbed a chunk of cake and took a bite. The tender crumb melted in my mouth, and for an instant I almost forgot where I was. "Is she a good teacher?"

"Yeah. Big fan of experiments and interactive stuff. It's cool."

"What was your last experiment?"

"We made a volcano in the school parking lot."

I remember helping fifteen-year-old Eve with a similar activity for extra credit. "How did it go?"

She grinned. "It blew big time."

"The extra baking powder, right?"

"Exactly." The girl took a bite of a cookie. "Miss Hanover said you travel a lot."

"That's right." I popped in a second bite.

"Why?"

"Why what?" I said, my mouth full.

"Why do you travel?"

I swallowed. "Kid, do you have a name?"

"Sarah. Why do you travel?"

"It's a bucket list," I said.

"Aren't you young for that?"

"It was my mother's list. She died." If I thought the last statement would have shut the kid up, I was wrong.

"How did she die?"

"Cancer."

"My grandmother died of that. What kind?"

Sarah was zeroing in on all the questions everyone avoided. Oddly, it felt good to talk. "Ovarian. Spread to her uterus and bone before it was diagnosed."

"Was she old?"

"Thirty-five."

"Kind of young."

"Yes."

"Are you staying in town or going to keep traveling?"

I snapped a chocolate chip cookie in half. "Do you always ask a lot of questions?"

"I do. I drive Miss Hanover crazy sometimes."

"She was like that at your age. Don't stop asking questions."

"Are you going to continue traveling?"

I did say *keep asking*. "I'm leaving. Definitely leaving."

"I'm leaving town too," Sarah said.

The cookie was delicious enough for me to ask, "Really? Where are you going?"

"I'm like you. I'm getting in a car, and I'm going to just drive."

"How old are you?"

"Fourteen."

No sense pointing out her obvious youth. "Do you have a list of places?"

The kid seemed surprised by the question. No doubt she'd been told her idea wasn't sound, and she'd been dismissed. I had been there and done that. "So far I have a hundred places."

"Excellent. Are you starting local or international?"

Sarah rested her hand on her chin. "I think I want to go to Istanbul first."

"Bold choice. But that's not a drivable trip."

"So maybe I warm up with California."

"Have you ever traveled anywhere before?"

"My eighth-grade class went to Washington, DC, last year."

"I think I took that trip when I was in middle school." I'd not wanted to go, but Mom had insisted. *Be a kid. Enjoy your friends.*

"Did you travel before this big trip?"

"Just to DC."

Sarah swirled her cookie in a bowl of melting chocolate ice cream. "Is that why you didn't go far?"

"My mom wanted to see the West, so I went west."

"What took you so long to go?"

"Life."

"I hear ya." Sarah's eyes sparked with interest. "Were the logistics hard?"

"A few failed starts, including food poisoning, a blown water hose, and getting lost more than once."

"Were you scared?"

I took another bite of the cookie. "All the time. I thought a few times my head was going to explode from the stress."

Sarah laughed. "Looks intact to me."

I was warming up to the kid. "I pieced it back together and kept on going. If you're on the road, you'll have to learn how to adapt."

Sarah nodded thoughtfully. "Good to know."

We both ate in silence for several minutes. "Did Eve invite all her students to the party?"

"No, just me. I'm also related to the host, Spencer."

"Really? How so?"

"A cousin of a cousin. He thought a night out for my parents would be fun. They didn't want to leave me home alone, so here I sit."

"Has it been fun?"

"They made me leave my phone at home."

"Ouch. That had to hurt."

"You have no idea." Sarah flexed her fingers as if she were searching for a missing limb.

"I dropped my phone when I was hiking in Yellowstone. I thought it was lost. But I found it." Never mind I had to scale down a steep mountainside and cling to a scrub tree as I reached for it. "Big crack in the screen now, but it still works."

Sarah's eyes narrowed, and she seemed to regard me with fresh eyes. "I can't believe you and Miss Hanover are sisters."

"I get that a lot."

"I mean, she's so . . ."

"Polished? Pretty? Well dressed?"

Sarah hesitated. "Stiff."

I laughed. "She's just nervous. Good impressions are important to her."

"But not to you."

I scanned my black dress. "I thought I cleaned up pretty good."

"Not bad for a picnic or barbecue."

"Ladies." Spencer's voice resonated directly behind me. The hair on my arm stood. I took a long sip of champagne.

I twisted in my seat. "And a major plot twist."

"I didn't know that was coming," he said, taking the seat beside mine.

I held his gaze, searching for hints of a lie. Unless I had lost my touch, I didn't see one. "It's a night for that kind of thing."

"She didn't tell you either?" he asked.

"Nope." And that admission stung. I didn't require advance notice, but Eve could've texted or called me after the deed was done. My sister had chosen to let me learn with everyone else.

"I liked your speech," Sarah said. "So did Olympia."

Grateful for the save, I nodded. "Terrific job, Spencer."

Spencer shook his head. "You're at least a better liar than Sarah."

"It's our story, and we're sticking to it," I said.

Sarah giggled and nodded.

He drew in a breath. "Do you have a place to stay tonight? Brad said they have a full house, and there are no hotel rooms within a hundred miles. Football weekend."

Eve always assumed I didn't need any help. "I remember those weekends well. Great time to be earning tips at Tony's."

"Do you have a place to stay?"

"I'll park my van and find a nice spot to bed down for the night."

"You seriously sleep in your van?" Sarah asked.

"I do. It's parked outside if you want to see it."

"Can I really see it?" Sarah asked.

Spencer shook his head. "Your parents are saying their goodbyes, Sarah. They tell me you have a soccer game early in the morning."

"Don't remind me," Sarah said. "I'd rather hang around and see Olympia's van."

"Not tonight," Spencer said.

"Maybe some other time," I said.

"When are you leaving?" Sarah asked.

"A few days, maybe a week. If you see my van parked somewhere, knock on the door. It's green, has curtains and Missouri plates. I'll give you the ten-cent tour."

"Seriously?"

"Sure. If you're going to be a world traveler, you might as well start learning the basics."

"Thanks. That's cool," Sarah said as she rose.

"Nice to meet you, Sarah," I said.

"I'll follow you on Instagram," Sarah said. "What's your handle?"

"The Pizza Traveler."

"Where'd that come from?"

"Long story. And you must get going."

"I'll follow you," Sarah said again. "I love travel pictures."

"Thanks."

As the girl walked away, I downed the last of my champagne, grabbed a cookie, and rose. I'd only been half kidding when I said I wished I'd brought zip-top bags.

"Thanks for a nice party, Spencer. I know Eve appreciated it."

He stood. "Sure. Glad to do it."

"I'll say good night then." I shoved the cookie in my pocket. "I'll text you, and we can work out something about the other thing." The D-word caught on my tongue, and I couldn't bring myself to say it out loud.

"Brad's my attorney. I'll have him contact you."

"Terrific."

"Seriously, where are you staying?"

"Seriously, the van."

A slight frown deepened new lines in his forehead. "I renovated the Stone Cottage. It's a hundred feet from here."

"I remember it very well."

His jaw pulsed. "You don't want the hassle of drunks banging on your van."

"Not my first rodeo. I'll grab a big cup of coffee and find a quiet spot." Spencer micromanaged when he was tense. I supposed seeing the wife after a year would rate at the top of the Tension Scale. "Thanks, Spencer. But I'll be fine."

"Just have a look at the cottage." And then, as if he'd remembered my soft spot, he added, "There's a full washer and dryer."

I'd been hoarding quarters for laundromat visits since I was twelve. How many overstuffed laundry bags had I hauled down the apartment stairs to the washer and dryer in the basement? "That's not playing fair."

He looked at me with resolve. "Just trying to help."

Washer, dryer, and bed. The trifecta.

Knowing very well he had my attention, he added, "Stay until Monday. I know for a fact Eve and Brad's crowd clears out then. Wash your clothes. Sleep in a real bed."

"And then we'll meet with Brad at his office on Monday, I suppose?"

He swallowed. "That's the plan."

"Great."

We'd been lovers and then husband and wife, almost parents, but we'd never really had a chance to become friends. Maybe that would be the best note for us to end on.

"Seriously, take the cottage for the next two nights." The music kicked up as red, blue, and green party lights pulsed on the crowded dance floor.

"No argument here. You had me at washer and dryer," I said. "I'm parked in the lot with the rest of the guests."

A very slight smile tugged at the edge of his lips. "Follow the road around the right side of the barn. Fifty feet ahead you'll see the cottage."

"I'll find it."

"It's unlocked."

"Great. Thanks again. Do me a favor and tell Eve I'm cutting out early. I'll see her Monday afternoon."

Spencer glanced toward center stage, where Eve and Brad were dancing. "Sure."

I didn't have to look closely to know their smiles were radiant. "Thanks again for all this. Very generous."

No one other than Spencer noticed me as I walked out the open barn doors. Leaving the music and laughter behind, I made my way to my van. Outside, the cold air had sharpened its bite, and I was glad now I'd have heat in the cottage. I'd roughed it enough times, but that didn't mean I'd loved freezing or sweating my ass off.

The van engine sputtered to life, and headlights on, I backed out of the space and then carefully followed the road around the barn. The party lights slid into my rearview mirror and faded as I drove down crisp, bright new gravel. When I rounded the last corner, my headlights swept over the Stone Cottage. A far cry from the night I'd rescued twelve-year-old Eve and met Naked Guy. I'd ultimately had my first date with Spencer here.

We'd met at the pizza shop the day before. He'd asked me to hike, and for reasons I couldn't explain, I'd said yes. Now, I was waiting outside the pizza shop at 10:00 a.m. on a warm April Sunday. The streets were still quiet, and the brick-lined shops were closed except for the coffee shop on the corner. Standing here felt awkward, and I wondered if the few who'd passed thought I'd forgotten my keys. That wouldn't be a first. When days of back-to-back shifts rolled endlessly into each other, details like keys got lost in the shuffle.

I wasn't sure what kind of car Spencer drove or if he'd even remembered we were hiking. I pictured him slightly hungover after a long night at the country club.

After a few minutes I checked the time on my phone. Ten minutes late. "Well, this is a first. Never been stood up before." Even TJ hadn't left me hanging for a date.

I glanced behind me into Tony's, grateful the lights were still off and TJ had not shown up early for the Sunday lunch. I wasn't interested in explaining why I was loitering in front of the store.

Grabbing my backpack, I glanced up at the clear blue sky. The air was cool, but the sun would quickly warm it, and it was still a good day for a hike, even without Spencer.

I walked down the sidewalk toward my alley parking space. As I rounded the corner, a horn blared, the sound so loud it bounced off the stoic Sunday walls of the buildings around me.

Tire wheels squealed. I turned to see a new white Jeep driving down Main Street. Brakes and tires strained as the driver halted at the curb. The window rolled down. Spencer raised Ray-Ban sunglasses, looking a little wild eyed and apologetic. Stubble covered his square jaw, and his damp hair was brushed back. "I'm sorry. I'm never late. It's really been a morning. Family."

When Mom was alive and Eve was a teenager, life had dished out its share of mornings, and I'd learned to give everyone a pass or two. "No worries."

He got out of his Jeep, lingering as if he wasn't sure he should shake my hand or go in for a quick hug. He did neither. "I'm not used to family drama."

I laughed. "Welcome to my world."

He walked around the Jeep and opened the back tailgate. "What drama do you have?"

"A lot when my younger sister was still in school. She graduated from college early in January."

And suddenly, our apartment, once so filled with activity, noise, and too many discarded shoes, was now very quiet. I'd cleaned the place three weeks earlier, right after Eve had grabbed the last of her stuff, and the apartment had, well, stayed clean. No more random piles of laundry, popcorn on the carpet, fashion magazines strewed on the couch, or empty refrigerator. Suddenly the space grew so large I imagined an echo when I talked to myself.

"It's pretty quiet now," I said.

He nodded. "Sounds like a dream."

Oddly, the stillness made it harder to sleep. Regret and sadness had seeped into the silent, empty spaces. "It is."

"Ready to hike?"

"I am. Have any trails in mind?"

"I do. It's on my family's property."

On a state park trail on a day like today, there'd be enough traffic for me to be seen, so if this date went sideways, someone could either call the cops or at least give a report after the fact. But on private land, I was on my own.

Spencer hesitated. Then, as if he'd read my mind, he said, "If this makes you feel uncomfortable, we can hit the state park."

I had my out. But I didn't really want it. Maybe it was the loneliness. Maybe I sensed life had landed me at a new crossroads. I wasn't sure what this all said about me, but Spencer Stockton was the most interesting, sexiest person I'd met in a while, and well-traveled trails suddenly didn't hold any interest.

"Let's do it." I tossed my backpack into the back and settled into the front passenger seat of his Jeep. The leather was soft, and the interior had a new-car aroma, a scent I only smelled when I picked up gig work parking cars at the country club parties.

Spencer slid behind the wheel. "Again, sorry for the delay."

"Again, no big deal."

The conversation stalled as he drove down the hill and followed 460 West, but I was good at small talk and made a living on the tips it generated. "I have five stock get-to-know-you questions, if you're game."

He threaded fingers through his hair. "I am."

I rubbed my hands together and grinned. "I see a lot of hungry faces here tonight. Who's the hungriest?"

He laughed. "Did you say something like that to me yesterday?"

"It's a good line that starts conversations. And you'd said 'starving.'"

"You noticed."

"I did."

He cleared his throat. "What's your next question?"

"What exciting plans do you have for this evening?"

"After the hike?" he said, playing along. "I might be too exhausted to eat. I haven't hiked in years."

"I'd think a pro golfer would be in prime shape."

An amused gaze cut in my direction. "You've checked me out?"

"It wasn't hard. You're the local guy who's made good." We'd also met before, a long time ago.

"Not sure how much I've accomplished," he said.

Despite cut biceps straining the short sleeves of his T-shirt, I asked, "You're not fit?"

"I'm fit. But golfers don't tend to climb mountains that often. I rock flat and rolling hills."

He looked comfortable behind the wheel, and it was nice not to be in charge for a little while. "Where have you played golf?"

"All over the US and Europe."

"You must know a lot about travel."

"Probably more than the average guy."

"Then I'm talking to the right man. I have one hell of a travel bucket list, but I haven't gotten past the wish list. Now that my sister is set, I'm shifting to logistics. I'm sure you know tricks of the trade that will make the journey easier."

He looked intrigued. "Aren't you a little young for a bucket list?"

"No time like the present. Besides, why wait until I'm old." Talk of travel had been just that for so many years. Talk. I'd never really been faced with making my dreams real, and now that the possibility was close, I was nervous. Though I had no excuses, I knew myself well enough to know that if something better came along to distract me from the road, I'd give it a hard look.

He nodded. "Driving or flying?"

"Driving. All the stops are out west. My big goal is to buy a van that I'll convert into living space."

"Van living? Never had the desire. Something about a hotel room with a soft bed and a flushing toilet has always appealed to me."

I supposed he traveled first class. That wasn't an option for me. Gas and food would wipe out what little savings I had now. Maybe in a couple of months I'd have enough money for a hotel room or two. But slumming it didn't mean I couldn't have fun. "Don't knock the rugged life until you try it."

"I've never eaten barbed wire, but that doesn't mean I want to try it."

I laughed. "Chicken."

The lives we'd lived were so different they didn't even run parallel. This chance crossing between us wasn't likely to happen again. Still, I liked him. "What are your top ten spots for playing golf?"

"There's the golf course, and then there's the city."

Viewing golf for me was like watching paint dry. "The city. Think western United States."

"Any idea where?"

"Starting with Arizona and then working my way north to Montana." *I spoke like I had a solid itinerary instead of a collection of travel pictures torn out of old magazines. Fake it until you make it, right?*

"Discovering family roots?"

"In all honesty, I just want to see the desert and the flatlands."

"It's beautiful in Arizona. I like Tucson and Sedona."

Both cities had been featured in high-gloss magazines I'd bought used for twenty-five cents from the library. "Remember, camping in a van."

"Right. I'm sure there are several camping options."

As if he sensed this simple conversation highlighted what we didn't have in common, he shifted tactics. "Going to post on social media?"

"I am. Already do."

"When do you plan to take off?" *Spencer asked.*

"Likely next year." *I didn't want to admit I had to save every extra dime.* "I need to get a few things on track before I go."

"Sounds like me. I'd like to return to the golf circuit. But now's not the time."

Natural curiosity prodded me to press him for more details, but I didn't. "I propose we talk about now."

Tension seemed to melt from his shoulders. "I second that."

"I like being here. I like that it's a lovely day and that we're going hiking."

He grinned. "I like you."

"Back at you."

He pulled off the main road and drove past green rolling lands dotted with barns and houses at the end of long gravel driveways. He slowed at an unmarked driveway and took a right. The drive looked different in the daylight, but the curves in the road were all too familiar.

"You know, I've been up here before," I said.

"Really?"

"My sister sneaked out of the house when she was twelve and came to a party at the Stone Cottage."

He looked at me, his sunglasses tossing back my reflection. "The twelve-year-old?"

"Yeah. Not a genius move on her part."

"Bat Girl?"

I grinned. Nice to see he remembered me. "Good to see you again, Naked Guy."

He groaned and shook his head. "I want you to know I was very traumatized by that night."

I laughed. "You and me both."

"My girlfriend and I got dressed right away, and I cleared out the party. I checked closets for the next year before I could take my pants off."

"I still have that bat," I said. "Tony Sr. willed it to me. I keep it in my car."

"Good to know."

"The ride is smoother now than it was then. But it could be your Jeep or that I'm not filled with fear and rage."

"I had the roads redone."

"Nice."

He drew in a breath. "How old were you that night?"

"Fifteen."

He grimaced. "And you were driving up here alone?"

"Necessity is the mother of invention."

He frowned. "Tell me your sister wasn't hurt."

"Her ego was bruised. Nothing worse than having to call the big sister for a rescue. She was grounded for a month."

"I never saw her until you pulled her out of the closet."

"Good times," I joked. "Why'd you have the road redone?"

He shook his head. "It needed to be upgraded so the contractors could get to the barn and the Stone Cottage."

"Redoing both? That's a project."

"I've wanted to do it for years but haven't been around to supervise. Now I'm home for the duration."

The duration didn't sound like a good thing, but we'd promised to keep it light.

"By the way, we're hiking up the back-right trail. It leads to the ruins of an old cottage."

"Ruins. I like. Where does the other trail go?"

"A lake."

He had his own lake. "Nice."

He drove past the barn, which now had a new roof, and then parked in a circular driveway in front of the Stone Cottage. I noticed another new roof, and the tall weeds had been cut down. "Looks like it's going to be a big project."

"It's a gut job." He took the Jeep out of gear and set the parking brake. "It's been cleaned out. All the old furniture is gone, and the rose wallpaper is being stripped away. I'm also having all the woodwork and light fixtures refurbished."

"It's got great bones."

"I'd like it to be my home one day. The big house is nice, and I'm enjoying my parents, but the day will come when we'll all need some space."

"I hear you. I shared an apartment with Eve and Mom for years. Nothing worse than three women in a cramped space with one bathroom."

"Your sister moved out. What about your mom?"

I'd told the story enough times now, so I could keep my tone light. "Mom had cancer. She died five and a half years ago."

"I'm sorry to hear that."

I shrugged. "We all have something, right? No family drama today, remember? I want to hike a trail."

"Sounds good."

Out of the car, he opened the back hatch, and I grabbed my backpack and worked my arms through the straps. His pack was large and bloated with more items than he'd need in a week. If I'd known him better, I might have pointed that fact out. But I didn't know him, and odds were, life would quickly pull us in different directions.

For now, it was a beautiful day on a stunning piece of property, and I would enjoy this pocket of time and not worry about tomorrow.

"Has this land been in your family for a long time?" I asked.

"On and off for about a century." He shrugged on his pack and pointed toward a path I would've missed if I were alone. "That's the trail that leads up to the remains of the Mountain House, which is ten or fifteen years older than this house."

"Ruins, remains. What happened?"

"The Mountain House was originally my grandfather's, and then the company used it for employees who needed housing. It burned in the early 1980s. I'm not sure how the fire started."

"Was anyone living there?"

"I don't think so. Likely hikers or trespassers who built a fire in the hearth, and an ember popped while they were asleep."

"Did anyone die?"

"I don't think so. I'd have to ask my father."

The grade of the path steepened, and both of us concentrated on hiking for a half hour before the path opened into a large field covered in tall grass. In the center was the foundation and a hearth made of hundreds of stones. The craftsmanship was stunning, and I couldn't take my gaze off it. Oddly, it felt like home. "Wow."

He shrugged off his backpack and settled it in the grass. "My great-grandfather must have picked this spot for the views. He didn't live here long, but he used it as a hunting lodge for years. My father loved it up here when he was a kid."

I looked out over the mountains dipping into the valley. Familiarity hummed inside me. I shifted my attention back to the scorched stones. "What a shame. This place would've been worth renovating too."

"Maybe I can salvage something."

A breeze brushed my skin as I moved toward the hearth. I skimmed my fingers lightly over the stones stacked so tightly mortar wasn't necessary. "I don't know how you'd begin to dismantle this."

"The right craftsman could do it."

Drawing my hand along the hearth, I closed my eyes. Energy snapped up my fingers. And then my stomach grumbled. I pressed my hand to my belly and laughed. "Breakfast was day-old pizza from Tony's."

"As luck would have it, I brought lunch."

"Did you? Is that why your pack is so full?"

He laughed. "I caught your side-eye when you saw my pack."

"I thought I was being subtle."

He unzipped the pack and pulled out a blanket. I grabbed the other end, and we spread it out on a flat grassy surface inside the foundation under charred rafters. He removed two containers filled with roasted chicken, baked potatoes, and salad.

My mouth watered. "I'll never question your packing skills again."

He grinned, clearly proud of himself.

After lunch, we hiked back down the mountain to the Stone Cottage. Other than the new roof, the cottage was in rough shape. The front porch had rotted in a couple of spots, the mortar between the stones was cracked, and several shutters were missing.

"Want to see the inside?" he asked. "It's structurally sound."

"Is this the murder cottage?" I joked.

"Not lately," he deadpanned.

The sparkle in his eyes triggered more laughter as I pushed open the front door. The interior had been stripped bare save for a few piles of drywall, several sawhorses, and a blow-up mattress made up with sheets, a coverlet, and two pillows.

"The mattress is here for me when I need to get away and spend the night," he said quickly.

"So, it's not for me?" I teased.

A charged silence surrounded us. He smelled of fresh air and sunshine. The possibility of something couldn't have been a total shock to him. I mean, a guy who packs a lunch like that is thinking ahead, right?

"It could be," he said.

I set down my pack. He came from money—played golf, for God's sake—and owned all this land. We were the quintessential opposites.

Light bangs swept over his forehead and gave him a boyish air. I'd bet life had never kicked him in the balls like it had me. But I craved his lightness and optimism. I kissed him, hoping to absorb some of that youthful charm.

When our lips touched, I forgot all about everything but the electricity shooting through me. The charge must have snapped through him as well because he immediately cupped my face in his hands and deepened the kiss. With Spencer, in this moment, an edgy need hummed in me and consumed all logic.

Somewhere along the way, we unlaced our boots and slid out of jeans and shirts. When he lowered me to the soft cotton sheets, the scent of laundry soap and sunshine circled around us. I loved the feel of his broad chest as it pressed against my breasts. With Spencer that day, there'd been no responsibility, no worries, just fun.

Building a relationship on crazy sex was akin to constructing a home on sand. Everything was great until the first stiff breeze or storm.

Now, as I stood before the pretty Stone Cottage, renovated and perfect, I realized I missed the graying granite covered in ivy, the broken windows, and the faint musty smell. Its imperfect, unrenovated incarnation had been the backdrop to one of the best days in my life.

I grabbed my bag and backpack from the front seat and got out of the van. Crossing the slate pathway to the front door, I drew in a breath, pushed it open, and flipped on the lights.

On the north wall, tall windows bracketed a freshly repointed fireplace sporting a mantel made from what appeared to be old barn beams. Silver vases filled with white flowers clustered on the left side, and on the right stood two vintage lanterns.

Two couches covered in distressed linen and displaying white and gray pillows faced each other. Between the couches rested a coffee table made of barnwood. A gray handwoven carpet pulled all the elements together, making it look lived in but chic. This renovation must have cost a fortune.

I took off my shoes before moving toward a kitchen outfitted with long marble countertops and stainless appliances only seen on the pages of design magazines. Beyond the kitchen was a laundry room, and farther down the hallway was the bedroom and one of the most beautiful marble bathrooms I'd ever seen.

I turned on the water, and when the glass shower walls steamed, I stripped and stepped under the hot spray. The heat eased tight muscles earned on the twenty-plus-hour car ride.

I only stepped out of the shower when the water cooled. But freshly cleaned and smelling of lavender, I felt a little more in control. Hair and body wrapped in plush towels, I carried my bag to the laundry room and dumped my clothes into the washer. I'd never bothered with sorting. "Color safe, machine wash and tumble dry" was all I owned, other than the Black Dress. I pulled out the chocolate chip cookie wrapped in the white napkin from my jean jacket and then tossed the jacket in with the rest. Soap and the long wash cycle selected, I pressed start and took a bite of the cookie.

I walked to the hearth preset with kindling and logs. I lit a match and held it to the small brush at the base. Flames danced to life. This place was lovely beyond words, and if the last year had taught me anything, it was to enjoy the good moments because they could be very rare.

"Don't kid yourself, Olympia. You tried Spencer's world, and it didn't work out well. Take care of your business in town, and then get the hell out of Dodge."

@ThePizzaTraveler

Bucket List Stop #1: Bandelier National Monument Near Santa Fe, New Mexico

One of the oldest national monuments, it celebrates the Pueblo Indians, who lived over six hundred years ago in small spaces carved in rock.

I sit in a hollowed-out cave and look out over the green scrub brush and trees in the valley below. I picture a tired mother cooking over a firepit, not realizing she'll be dead by her midthirties, as well as two little clueless girls giggling, playing with handmade dolls or drawing pictures in the dirt.

Six centuries has changed everything and nothing.

#LANDMARKS #BUCKETLIST #TIMEMARCHESON

CHAPTER FOUR
OLYMPIA

Sunday, October 27, 2024, 7:15 a.m.

I woke to the sound of a baby girl crying. The little girl sounded angry, as if she'd been ignored for too long. The loud wail plucked at my sympathy and stoked a fierce drive to protect. My breasts ached with unsuckled milk.

"I'm coming, sweetie," I mumbled while I tossed the navy blue comforter aside. My head pounded as my feet touched the cold carpet; the last remnants of sleep fell away. The child stopped crying.

The silence was jarring, and I opened my eyes as I struggled to get my bearings. The cozy bedroom didn't make sense. It wasn't my apartment on Main Street or my van. And where was the baby?

I glanced at my naked body, my full breasts ribboned with faint stretch marks, and the C-section scar at the base of my flat belly.

There was no baby.

She'd never lived.

Never drew a breath.

Never cried.

Blame struck my chest above my heart, as it did every time I remembered my lost child. A year ago, I'd absorbed more guilt and shame than I could stomach. But this morning, I deflected it. And when it came at me again, I shoved back. If I let it continue to hammer me, I'd break down, my knees would buckle, and I'd be lost in darkness for hours, if not days.

Straightening my shoulders, I fought off the pounding headache, glanced at the hagstone on the bedside table, and moved to the bathroom. I peed and then went to the laundry room, where I pulled clean clothes out of the dryer. I tried to thread my leg into my pants but nearly lost my balance as my stomach flip-flopped. Leaning against the wall, I tried a second time and succeeded. "I'll never drink again."

Finally dressed, I packed up my clothes in my bag, grabbed two aspirin, and then moved into the kitchen. I located coffee, creamer, a mug. I poured hot water into a french press and willed the water to turn into coffee quickly.

At the front window, I crunched on aspirin as I stared out over the misty lawn toward the hills. My memory reminded me that beyond the stand of trees were two paths. One would take me to the remains of the mountain cabin, and the other went to the lake.

It was tempting to lie down, but this hangover was not going away, so I thought I might as well get moving and break up the tension in my body. The drying-up lake bed it would be.

Minutes later, with my jacket and boots on, phone tucked in my pocket, and coffee in hand, I crossed the front porch and the lawn. When I reached the outer rim of the trees, cold, crisp air burned my nostrils and skimmed down my spine. Air puffed faster as I quickened my pace. I was suddenly very curious to see the lake Spencer and I had visited last year. This wasn't my land, and though I was Spencer's guest, I wasn't sure if that invitation included wandering the property.

Up until a year ago, I'd always followed the rules. I showed up to work on time. Helped my sister with her homework or, later, when she was short on funds, money for college. I would sit with my mother after a shift at Tony's for hours talking about travel-magazine pictures and planning trips that I knew we'd never really take. I put my life aside so

I could keep Mom's and Eve's dreams alive. I never made waves. I was the good girl. Almost all the time, anyway.

But every so often I broke little rules. Like having sex with TJ in the pizzeria's back room. Like driving Mom's car long before I'd received a driver's license. Like swapping Coke for Diet Coke when the drunk skinny students got a little bitchy. Like hiking on private property. Like sleeping with a rich guy who would never settle for a girl like me.

I didn't smash the rules. I just bent them.

Until Spencer, it had been no harm, no foul. Just little moments that reminded me that I had control of my life. That the decision not to go to college was mine. I liked slinging pizza in a college town. Staying had been my choice.

But when I crossed the line with Spencer, it had been impossible to get back to who I was. I'd seen what life could be, and returning to the past was too miserable to consider. After Spencer, my old life had shrunk five sizes and no longer fit.

As I broke through the forest, I caught sight of a large lake. Mist hovered over still waters and edges that had receded at least fifteen feet from the shoreline. The dock that used to float on the water now hovered close to the mud like a deflated balloon.

There'd been drought in the region last fall when I'd left, but rains came and went, and everyone was sure the skies would open soon. I'd read a few notices in the online local paper reporting on historic rainfall lows. One night in Yellowstone, I'd even dreamed of drought turning the land to kindling. Cookie, an ex-con in a Yellowstone diner who worked as a line cook with me, said that dreams of drought meant prosperous times ahead. I'd not seen it that way. As far as I was concerned, the land had fused with my DNA, and as I suffered, so had it. Honestly, I was glad. We were both in our own kind of purgatory.

Immediately, I was sorry I'd wished ill on my homeland. It hadn't done anything to me. If anything, it had given me sanctuary when I needed it.

As the sun rose higher over the trees, the past and future faded, and there was only the cold air, the warm travel mug in my hand, and the solitude. Unable to resist, I pulled out my phone and snapped pictures of the morning sun.

As I glanced at a few pictures, I noticed what looked like a perfectly square stone about twenty feet to the left of the dock. With a swipe of my fingers, I zoomed in and realized whatever was out there was hand carved. Was it a weight for the dock or an anchor for a small boat? Narrowing my eyes, I imagined I saw words and some type of design on the stone.

Staring out over the thick mud, I took more pictures, but no amount of enlarging was going to tell me more about the stone. I gulped the last of my coffee, set the cup on a tree stump, and removed my boots. Rolling up my jeans, I stood wriggling my toes against the cold ground. Last year had taught me that curiosity was a good thing.

I stepped into the cold mud, which squished between my toes seconds before it sucked my feet into the mire. "What's the worst thing that can happen to me?" I asked the lake bed.

Stepping into a massive sinkhole or quicksand came to mind.

Yanking my foot up, I kept walking and struggling to keep my balance. *Slurp. Slurp. Slurp.* Rude noises followed me all the way to the stone. When I stopped, it took me a moment to catch my breath.

Phone in hand again, I snapped pictures and took video of the surrounding lake and then aimed the lens at the stone. There was a figurine on it, and etched words trailed over the top and bottom edges. I leaned over and brushed aside the mud, wiping until the face was exposed. Images of a hammer carefully hitting a fine chisel flashed in my mind.

The etching was of an angel who stood about ten inches tall, with expanded, graceful wings stretching the length of the stone. Delicate and fine. I marveled at the precision such fine lines required. This would have been slow, careful work.

Block lettering along the angel's wing read, *Tomorrow, I do. 1982.*

CHAPTER FIVE
SPENCER

Sunday, October 27, 2024, 8:00 a.m.

Spencer was nervous when he approached the Stone Cottage. He blamed his ragged nerves on fatigue, too much booze, and a night filled with endless small talk. He'd fallen into bed about 2:00 a.m., but sleep came in clustered minutes. It had been a long night.

The party had gone as expected. Eve and Brad cooed over each other and moved from guest to guest, talking, laughing, and accepting congratulations on their marriage. Everything about them felt new, fresh, and full of hope. Good for them. He trusted the euphoria would last for a while.

Caroline managed all the party details like a pro, and several times she slid close to him and told him the party was a lovely gesture. She'd done that when they were in college. She never made huge displays of affection, but her brushing against him or tossing him a smile reminded him of what they'd shared when they were alone. Last night, he'd gotten the vibe that she was ready to pick up where they'd left off.

And then Olympia had arrived almost two hours late. She'd appeared at the barn doors, looking a little frazzled as she'd grabbed that first glass of champagne. Hovering close to the edge of the party, she was clearly getting her bearings.

All the words left unsaid between them had sucked the oxygen out of him, and he'd found it impossible to expand his lungs and speak. Brad had clapped his shoulder. "She's talking to Eve. Take a deep breath."

At the end of the party, as the waiters picked up glasses half-full of watery booze, Caroline had hugged him and proclaimed the party a success. He'd agreed. She hadn't missed a detail.

And then Caroline had kissed him, and he hadn't pulled away. His hand came to her waist as if his muscles remembered exactly where she liked to be touched. When she'd deepened the kiss, he'd grown hard. She was a beautiful woman. Sharp. Sophisticated. Smart. He and Olympia had been apart for a year now, and the resolution for whatever it was between them was long overdue. Maybe kissing Caroline for the first time in years was his way of finally moving on from Olympia.

Caroline had leaned into him, wrapping her arms around his neck. He'd hugged her close, praying sensations would override his brain.

But the bottom line was Caroline was not Olympia. She was thinner and shorter, and he realized he preferred the scent of sunshine over Chanel. Pulling back, he thanked Caroline and left her standing as the clean-up crews collected the trash.

He'd walked around the barn and looked toward the Stone Cottage. The lights were off. Satisfied Olympia was asleep, he'd driven home.

Now, after a shitty night's sleep, he was back at the Stone Cottage, carrying a large Styrofoam container full of food.

As he passed Olympia's van, he looked inside the front passenger window. Maps, pamphlets, a peanut butter jar, a sleeve of bread, and a Blacksburg coffee travel mug.

A curtain separated the front cab from the back, and a circular dream catcher dangled from the rearview window. The back windows were covered with cherry-print curtains. Curious, he tried the back sliding door, and to his surprise, it opened. She'd always been security conscious, but maybe up here she'd felt safe. Or she was too tired to notice she'd forgotten to lock the van.

The back was organized. But Olympia had always been very orderly. He'd teased her about it often, but she'd only laugh and keep straightening or cleaning. The futon was covered with a quilt he remembered from her old apartment. On the desk sat an electric teakettle, a few clean mugs, and a stack of paper plates. He'd seen several pictures of canyons, rolling hills, and mountains taken from this van.

"I stayed in the house last night, if that's what you were wondering." Olympia's voice emerged from the woods.

When he turned, she was carrying her boots and wore only socks. Her legs were caked in wet mud up to her knees.

Straightening, he shut the door. "I wasn't sure you'd take me up on my offer to stay here. Just making sure you were okay."

"Alive and well." Her socked toes wiggled.

"You bought this in Kansas City?"

"Bought/traded."

"You fixed it up."

"I did."

"Nice work."

"Thanks."

"It has to get cold in the winter."

"And hot in the summer. That's van living."

"What's it like living in a van?" he asked.

"Better than a car and tent, but it's not suited for the long term. No soft beds or bathrooms. Do you have a garden hose?"

"There's an outside shower on the side of the cottage. You're in luck. The water hasn't been shut off yet."

"Terrific."

He followed her around the side of the cottage and watched as she walked into the wooden shower stall. The interior had a dressing area and then beyond it the shower. She sat on a wooden bench in the dressing section and peeled off muddy socks.

"Why are your feet muddy?" he asked.

"I was in the lake."

"It's thirty-eight degrees," he said.

"Yes, very cold. I would've stayed out there longer, but frostbite is nobody's friend." She stepped into the shower section and turned on the hot water tap. As steam rose, she put her feet under the spray. Water beaded against mud, sending it trickling along her calves, over her toes, and then down the drain.

If the reason behind the lake walk was obvious to her, it wasn't to him. "Just for chuckles, why did you walk in the lake?"

She worked the mud out from between her toes as if he hadn't spoken, then said, "I'm amazed how much water has vanished from the lake in the last year."

"We've been in a drought most of the year, and it turned severe in the last month. There's talk of rain in about a week, but we've had next to none since you left."

"Explains why the lake level is low."

He leaned against the stall door. "Still waiting for why you walked into the lake bed."

She tucked a strand of hair behind her ear. "There was a square stone about twenty feet to the left of the dock. It looked so perfect I knew it had to have been shaped by someone."

"This is stone country. We've seen our share of stonemasons in the region over the last century. Likely one tossed it in the water."

"Why throw a stone in the water?"

"I don't know. Maybe it was a castoff. Maybe he wanted to leave his mark on the world."

She sniffed. "This stone dates back to 1982 and has a chiseled angel on it."

"The stonemasons carve their mark on the world in stone. Stands to reason one might have been practicing and, like I said, then dumped his castoff."

"Again, why put the stone so far underwater?" She shut off the tap, wiped the excess water off her skin, and shoved her feet into her boots.

Her casual questions about a damn stone grated on his nerves. Why did she care so much about it? They had been in this cottage almost a year and a half ago, and he'd had the best sex of his life. Now their marriage was all but dust, and she was talking about rocks. "I don't know, Olympia."

"You always carry your breakfast around?" She nodded to the container.

"I brought you leftovers from the party." He handed her the Styrofoam box.

She accepted it, studying him with a mild mixture of annoyance and curiosity. "Thanks. You didn't have to do that."

"We had a lot of extra."

She seemed to forget the food as she stared at him. "I thought you'd know about the stone, since this is your land."

"It was family land, and I just repurchased it two years ago. My father knows its history better than I do." His anger was churning. Why did the damn stone matter?

"That's right, you said once he hunted up here with his father when he was a kid." She drew in a breath. "But I don't think I'll be lobbing any questions at your father. He was never in my fan club."

This was not supposed to be complicated. At this moment, he didn't give a shit about the stone or his father's opinions. There was a divorce lingering between them, and she was pretending that it didn't exist or matter.

"Thanks. For the food. I'm sure it's great."

"I didn't want it to go to waste." He shook off his emotions like he did when faced with a critical putt or drive. He'd asked for a divorce, and she was here to give it to him. End of story, right?

A breeze blew a lock of dark hair over her forehead. "The Stone Cottage had just gotten a new roof, the last I remember. Renovation must have cost a fortune."

More like a king's ransom. His mother had called it good money after bad. "I thought it was worth saving."

She glanced back at the house, but he couldn't tell if she was remembering the last time they were here alone. "You did a terrific job. I never thought you were much of a project guy."

"I can only play so much golf."

"Said no golfer ever."

He spent plenty of time on the local course, but he couldn't travel like he used to, and he didn't enjoy wearing a suit and tie and playing executive. So, he'd diverted his pent-up energy and spare time into the house. "I'd think you'd be glad I found something other than golf. You hate it."

"I don't hate it. I just don't understand the purpose. I like having something to show for my time."

Maybe that was why he'd directed his attention to the cottage. He wanted something good to come out of the last twelve months beyond a low golf score. "Are you ever satisfied?"

Olympia shoved out a sigh. "I'm not trying to stir shit up, Spencer. I'm just making polite conversation so we can get out of this marriage with as much dignity as possible."

They'd tumbled into the marriage recklessly and with little thought. But wasn't that the way it was with disasters? Easy to trigger, but a bitch to repair the wreckage.

When he looked at her now, he saw the promise of what they'd once shared flaring into cinders. It wasn't his or her fault that their baby had died or that the subsequent anvil of grief had smashed into and irrevocably cracked their marriage. All the moral and indignant outrage churning inside him would never resurrect what had crumbled to dust.

"I talked to Brad," he said. "Our meeting is scheduled for Monday morning at eleven. Feel free to stay here until then."

@ThePizzaTraveler

Flagstaff, Arizona
Can pizza erase loss?

New city, surrounded by strangers in a campground on the edge of the desert, I'm missing the littlest things today: my old lumpy twin bed, the hiking trails of southwest Virginia and the nowhere job that raised me.

Scrounged store-bought pizza dough, fresh feta cheese, and zucchini nestled in a grocery store sack that sits on the passenger seat of my new-to-me van. I'm making pizza on the campground grill in a thrift store cast iron pan. The goal is to chase away the homesickness.

I've made thousands of pizzas in my life and there's something comforting about kneading the dough, sprinkling cheese, and biting into something freshly cooked.

I'm a hostage freshly escaped from captivity. I hated where I was, but it was at least familiar. Without confinement I'm a little lost.

What gives you comfort? I'm asking for a friend.

#COMFORT #PIZZA #NEWLIFE

@ThePieGuy commented on your post:
Looking for a cook

@ThePizzaTraveler:
DM me.

CHAPTER SIX
OLYMPIA

Sunday, October 27, 2024, 10:15 a.m.

Spencer drove off as Styrofoam warmed my fingers. Dust kicked up from his back wheels, but I never once saw him glance in the rearview mirror. Okay, so this marriage was going to end. And unlike the celebrity pairs who uncoupled with ease, I suspected we'd be left with torn, jagged edges.

Back at the cottage, I made a second cup of coffee, found a clean pair of socks, and slid them on my feet. I opened the food container and was surprised to see a couple of bagels, scrambled eggs, three slices of bacon, and a big piece of chocolate cake on the side. These weren't leftovers. I dug a fork from the drawer and took a bite of cake. The chocolate-raspberry filling and buttercream frosting melted in my mouth.

Being mad at Spencer should've been easy. So many nights I'd railed against him when I'd been lying alone in my van. I'd begged him to leave town with me, but he'd refused. But I'd still dreamed that he'd find me and knock on the van window, and somehow, we'd fix this mess. But he'd never come. And the truth was we'd shared more losses than wins.

"I'm pregnant," I said to Spencer when he picked me up at the pizzeria. I'd been so nervous I hadn't even waited for him to pull out of the parking

lot. He'd jammed on the brakes so quickly we'd nearly been rear-ended by another car.

A horn honked behind us, but he ignored it. When it honked a second and third time, he pulled out onto Main Street and found the closest parking spot. He shut off the engine and twisted in his seat toward me. "Run that one past me again?"

"I'm pregnant."

"How?"

"Seriously?"

"I mean, we were careful."

"Not careful enough. Remember the broken condom on the second date?" I pulled the white stick from my pocket and showed him the double pink lines. "This is my third test."

He ran long fingers through his hair and stared out over the steering wheel at downtown Blacksburg. I'd been absorbing this shock since yesterday morning, but it was still fresh and still stinging for him. I gave him a moment, trying not to take his silence personally.

Swallowing, he looked at me. "Have you seen a doctor?"

"I have an appointment at the clinic with an OB." Regardless of how this played out for him, I wanted him to know where I stood. I'd been raised by a single mother, and I'd turned out okay, for the most part.

"I'd like to go to the appointment with you."

"Really?"

"Yeah."

"Okay."

"And then we'll get married."

"Seriously?" I asked. "I mean, that was not my endgame. I'm telling you because you have a right to know."

"I was there the night the condom broke, remember?"

"I'll never forget the look on your face."

That teased a small smile. "We played rock, paper, scissors. I win, no baby. You win, baby."

"I won." This moment had been hanging over me since that game, but I'd refused to believe it. I'd been so good at convincing myself I was in the clear that the test's double lines were a total shock.

"We won," he said softly.

Tears welled in my eyes, and the breath I'd been holding since yesterday leaked over my lips. "I appreciate that."

"We can be married by Saturday."

His family would be mortified. His parents, who I hadn't met yet, were going to declare him insane. His friends and mine would be taking bets on the divorce date.

"Okay," I said. "Let's do it."

Now, I glanced at my stomach, resenting that it looked so normal. I should've been seven or eight months postdelivery and my belly a little puffy or my waist a little thicker. There should've been a tiny girl person with my nose and Spencer's long fingers babbling and trying to crawl.

A bone-deep exhaustion slid over my limbs. This fatigue had hit me several times over the last year. Whereas my mother had closed her eyes and slid peacefully toward death, my little twenty-week pup had been cut from my body during an unexpected preterm C section delivery.

Up until the day I lost my little girl, she'd been moving inside me, as she always did. My little busy alien invader had taken over my body and had made herself right at home.

That night, she'd suddenly gone still, and I'd finally fallen asleep. I remembered feeling grateful she'd settled. And then the painful cramps had squeezed my belly so hard that they'd yanked me from sleep, taking my breath away in the process. I woke up Spencer and told him something was wrong. He dressed quickly and threw a coat over my blood-soaked oversize T-shirt.

As Spencer rushed me to the hospital, I was bleeding heavily. I clenched every muscle in between contractions, willing my body to hold on to our little girl. When we pulled up at the emergency room and the nurses rushed out with a stretcher, I thought we'd somehow made it. The doctors would fix this. But my daughter never once drew a single breath.

Four days later, Spencer pushed me out of the hospital in a wheelchair. A cold wind swept over the parking lot. Empty handed and hollow, I had no words to comfort Spencer, who was clearly grieving.

It had taken almost a year to climb out of that hole inch by inch, but the journey had left its mark. I was more reserved now, and the idea of loving anything like I loved my little girl terrified me still.

I stabbed another large piece of cake and ate it. The trick with grief was to outrun it. Never stop moving because it was always trailing close behind. Stop and think too long, and it would eat you right up. So, each day I kept moving until I was exhausted.

Time to move.

I opened my photos, zooming in again on the stone. It was a mystery, and, in this moment, I needed one to distract me.

"Who would toss a stone in the lake? What's the point?" The date 1982 gave me a starting point. When I was in town on Monday, I'd ask Eve. An almost PhD in science might have contacts in the history department.

I finished off the cake, filled my water bottle, and suited up for a long, long hike.

@ThePizzaTraveler

Mundane. Boring. Ordinary. Yes, please.

Once upon a time, there was a woman who grew to hate her daily routine. She decided to leave it all behind and get on the road. But during her travels, she discovered she missed some of what she'd had. So, she recreated bits of the past in the back bed of her van. A familiar comforter, favorite books, a PIZZA QUEEN black coffee mug, and six small, framed photos that hold her heart.

#ROUTINE #EVERYDAY #PRECIOUSMOMENTS

CHAPTER SEVEN
OLYMPIA

Sunday, October 27, 2024, 12:15 p.m.

By the time I arrived at the top of the mountain, I was barely winded. I'd always been active, but the last year had magnified my stamina as I hiked the higher western peaks.

In Kansas City, I'd worked for Hank, who not only owned a barbecue truck but was also a bodybuilder. When I knocked on the side of his truck and offered to work for tips, Hank hired me on the spot, and within a half hour, I was dishing out barbecue on buns. At the end of the shift, he'd dropped and begun doing push-ups. Watching his biceps and triceps pop, I asked if he could show me a couple of moves to firm up. He'd given me ten exercises, including squats, push-ups, Russian twists, and kickbacks.

The first run-through had been easy enough, but the next day every muscle in my body ached. Feeling the discomfort in my muscles had been oddly comforting, though, because the stiffness was a welcome distraction from my thoughts. The next day, I doubled up the routine.

Now I had muscles. Not the Arnold kind, but when I flexed my bicep, it popped a little.

The clearing at the top of the mountain offered a stunning view of the surrounding peaks and the wet gray clouds that hovered over the valley, shadowing orange and yellow trees and the ground below.

Up here, staring at the rock formations millions of years old, I faced the fragility of human lifespans shoehorned into blips of time the earth never noticed. People came and went, time marched on, and the earth kept turning. All my worldly problems that I'd mentally etched in stone felt like a spectacular waste of time.

I drew in a cold breath, expelling all the negativity and hurt in a cloudy puff of air. This feeling of smallness, the *Why worry, because we all die?* feeling, was why I'd kept traveling. There was hardship on the road, but there was also freedom. Freedom from all the pain whittling away at my time on this earth.

I turned from the ridge and walked toward a stand of woods. Dry leaves crunched under my feet. I picked up a stick and twirled it as the morning sun burned through the clouds and warmed my face.

Ahead in the woods was an overgrown path that had almost been consumed by the earth. It was as if Spencer and I had never walked this trail.

As I followed it, brambles and sticker bushes caught the fabric of my jeans and snagged my woolen socks. The path was waiting to be followed, but it was also testing me.

I'll let you pass, but there will be a price, the path whispered.

I laughed. *What's your point?*

Stepping over a log, I kept inching forward. I vaguely remembered the hike with Spencer on our first date. I'd been staring at his ass more than the landmarks on the trail. Now, I wished I'd been paying closer attention to the land. I didn't need to get turned around. Several times I stopped and looked back, trying to remember where I'd come from. But the path behind me felt as if it were closing ranks.

Twenty minutes of walking, and I considered turning around. I'd memorized a half dozen landmarks, but they all looked enough alike that confusion was inevitable. But additional steps kept tempting, so I kept moving, until suddenly the path opened into a small clearing.

In the center were the ruins of the Mountain House. Many of the charred rafters had fallen in on themselves, but the foundation and hearth remained strong. Last year, this place had felt like it was infused with magic. Now it was just ruins.

I noted singe marks ringing the fallen timbers and fingering up the gray stone hearth. Without Spencer or raging hormones to distract me, my focus settled on the fireplace.

The cobbled stones emanated a strong sense of sadness. This fire wasn't intentional but rather the result of a sparking ember. On a windy, dry day, fire would've picked up the small flame and fanned it into a blaze. The fire would've consumed this place in minutes. I knew most disasters didn't happen in slow motion. They were quick, furious, and devastating.

I pulled out my phone and started videoing the area as I walked around the edges of the remains and toward the hearth. "The stones are local," I said as I recorded. "The rocks are stacked so carefully, and there's no mortar. I'm trying to imagine this cabin when it was healthy and whole, before the fire roared through it. This place, for as long as it did last, must have been fantastic."

Smoothing my fingers over the stone, I studied the hearth for any sign of a craftsman's signature. In my short time with Spencer, I'd learned that stonemasons often left small clues to their identity. Double *T*s, triangles, or stars—or the angel on the square lake stone. The signs were as varied as the craftsmen.

As my fingers skimmed the hearth covered in soot and dirt, I felt symbols etched in the rock. I wiped away the grime. Numbers and then the shape of an angel appeared.

1982. The year the lake stone had been carved.

Homes came charged with energy, and this one felt awash in loss and sadness.

"What happened here?" I asked aloud.

My phone rang, cutting through the silence. Annoyed by the intrusion, I glanced at the number. Eve. The girl had radar for the worst time to call.

"Eve."

"Where are you?" My sister's voice sounded raw and congested, likely the aftereffects of too much wine and cigarettes she didn't think anyone knew about. When our mother had been so ill, fourteen-year-old Eve often vanished for a "walk" and came back smelling of mints and perfume.

"I'm hiking," I said.

"Hiking." She groaned. "That sounds like a fate worse than death."

I smiled. "Little hungover, are we?"

"You could say that. I'm on my third coffee, and I'm starting to come back to life."

Something about her words didn't ring true. "Why are you even up so early?" I scanned the horizon. This was Stockton land, but I wasn't familiar with the family history. Spencer and I had been too overwhelmed by our present to consider the past or the future.

"Brad and his buddies got up for a run. He flipped on all the lights as he was looking for his running shoes and woke me up. A touch passive aggressive. Anyway, he said the best way to deal with a hangover is to sweat it out of your system. He's out there somewhere sweating red wine and whiskey all over some poor unsuspecting street, if he's not throwing up in a bush."

"That's a nice image."

"It's how he deals after a night of drinking. He'll be fine when he gets home. He'll be restored. Ready to take on the day. He always rallies. Whereas I only want to crawl back into bed and die."

"Why don't you? Crawl in bed, I mean."

"No. I'm headed to the shower, hoping the heat will restore my soul. And I need to make breakfast for my guests."

"Who's staying at the house?" In all the confusion of last night, I hadn't bothered to ask.

"Friends of Brad's from college."

"All out running now too?"

"Yes. Very intense." A cabinet opened and closed, and a frying pan banged against a stovetop.

"Did you have a good time last night?" I asked.

"Oh, yes. It was magical. Spencer didn't cut one corner. I'll write him a note and thank him for hosting."

"Nice."

"I feel bad I couldn't put you up last night. Where did you end up staying after you vanished from my party?"

"The Stone Cottage. Remember it?"

She groaned. "Don't remind me."

"Spencer said I could use it."

"He did?" Eve dragged out the last word, suggesting she was reading more into Spencer's gesture. A refrigerator door opened and closed. "Brad said he's spent a fortune renovating it."

"He did."

"Are you staying there tonight?"

"Yes. I'll be in town tomorrow and will find your new place."

"I'm teaching until three, but I'll put a key under the mat."

"There'll be plenty for me to do in town tomorrow," I said. "It'll be at least three before I can stop by."

"What's the deal with you and Spencer?"

"What do you mean?"

"I noted an intense vibe between you two last night."

"There's nothing between us. I came back to town for your party and to sign my divorce papers."

"I got the feeling that he was very glad you were there last night."

"We don't hate each other. And it would be nice if we could be friends. But that's it."

"Very efficient of you to celebrate my marriage and get a divorce."

"Speaking of marriage, when did that happen?"

Silence lingered between us. "I'm sorry I didn't tell you. But it all happened quickly. Getting the club and church would take over a year, and we didn't want to wait."

"You turning down a lavish party? That doesn't sound like my baby sister."

"My heart grew a little while you were gone. I'm almost sentimental."

"And?"

"And what?"

I knew what the answer was, but I wanted to hear it. "You aren't hungover. It's morning sickness. How pregnant are you?"

Eve was silent.

"We Hanover women seem to find ourselves single, pregnant, and in need of a husband. Mom, me, you."

"Are you mad?" she asked quietly.

Eve and I had had a similar conversation when she was sixteen. We were barely keeping our heads above water when she told me she was pregnant. The light bill was late, old pizza and peanut butter sandwiches were a dietary mainstay, and I had just repaired the water hose on the Taurus with duct tape. We were hand to mouth. When she'd told me she couldn't do it, I'd applied for a new credit card, made an appointment at the clinic, and driven her. Afterward, we'd both cried.

And now she was pregnant again, and she was thrilled.

Hot tears glistened in my eyes. "No, I'm not mad. Is Brad excited?"

"He's over the moon."

Spencer's delight over my pregnancy had eased all my fears. "That's good. That's good."

"I'm due in early summer."

A tear slid down my cheek. My little girl would have been a winter baby. "That's amazing."

"You sound upset."

"Not upset." I glanced up through the remaining charred rafters to the blue sky.

"But it hurts."

"It does. But I'll be fine." I rubbed the back of my hand over my wet cheek. "I'm always fine."

I turned toward the stone hearth, wondering how much it had seen over the years. What had the stones absorbed in the fire? Screams? Cries? The thud of feet toward the door? Silence?

"I'm sorry it's not you," Eve said.

"Don't be. It is what it is. We'll have dinner tomorrow night."

"I'll pick up takeout."

"Pizza?" I said, teasing.

"God, no." Eve had not touched a slice of pizza since high school. Too many carbs.

"You pick. I'll eat anything. And I remember how unsettled my stomach was in the early days."

"It's a date. Oh, and don't forget about the key under my front doormat. I can't guarantee your bed will be made, but I'll have the sheets in the dryer."

"Perfect."

"How long are you staying?"

I stepped over the foundation. "A few days. The road calls."

More silence. And then a front door opened to male laughter. "We'll talk about that tomorrow. When I'm human."

"Right."

I hung up, slid the phone in my pocket, and drew in a deep breath. The cold air was ripe with ancient cinders hinting of restless souls.

I checked the time and realized I'd been up here for over three hours. By the time I walked off the mountain toward the Stone Cottage, the sun was high in the sky and the air had warmed.

Time was racing today, and I was glad for it. I wanted this trip over and done with. If I could wish away anything, it would be tomorrow. The pain was going to happen one way or another, so better to be over and done with it.

@ThePizzaTraveler

Can ghosts hike mountains?
Yes, but not very well.
Flagstaff, Arizona

Hiking in the Grand Canyon changes perspective and perception. Moving my legs, pumping my arms, and breathing hard summons endorphins.

This simple human chemistry awakens my angels, who remind me to stop and enjoy because life is so short. Also, hard climbs dispel ghosts, who tend to wheeze like chain-smokers at high elevations.

#PERSPECTIVE #ANGELS #GHOSTS

@SarahTheHiker mentioned you in a post:

Yes, @ThePizzaTraveler, the world is clearer, more peaceful from the top of a mountain.

CHAPTER EIGHT
OLYMPIA

Monday, October 28, 2024, 10:30 a.m.

I slept until seven, and after coffee and a long shower, I forced myself to dry my hair and apply a faint shade of pink to my lips. I dreaded this day. No endings were easy, but this one stung.

As I stood in front of the mirror and wrestled with the hagstone necklace clasp, I couldn't quite get ahold of my nerves. My hands shook as I struggled to hook the fastener, and, in the process, I snapped the thin metal. The hagstone, the turquoise, and my wedding band hit the floor. "Shit."

Frustrated, I collected the stones and my ring and tossed them all in my bag. I stripped the sheets on the bed, loaded them into the washer, and hit start. I paced the house, ate cake, walked the grounds, and switched the clean sheets into the dryer, and after all the delays I could find, I summoned my courage and got in my van. The slow drive into town took less than thirty minutes, and I still managed to arrive with a half hour to spare before my appointment at the attorney's office.

I parked in downtown Blacksburg in front of Tony's Pizzeria. As I stared at the historic building painted cerulean blue, so many memories rushed me. All that Eve and I had become was because of this place and a mother who'd never panicked or cried when life served her a plate of shit.

"Don't you want to play with your friends?" Tony Sr. had asked.

It was a Saturday morning as I set out the last of the salt and pepper shakers on a tray. Mom was home with a headache, and Eve was at a friend's house. "I like this. Work makes me feel good."

"But it's work, honey. It's no place for a fifteen-year-old on a beautiful Saturday morning." Tony Sr. *was wearing his trademark black Tony's T-shirt, which showed off bulging tattooed biceps. Thick gray hair tied back in a ponytail accentuated the deep frown lines radiating from his mouth.*

"It helps me stay calm." The extra money also helped now that Mom wasn't working, and I liked being here and around Tony Sr. Like his place, he felt stable and solid.

"You're here even before my son," he grumbled.

"He has an early football team meeting."

"My point exactly. He's doing kid stuff."

I smiled. "I'm an old soul, Tony."

He reached for a vat of flour and set it on the counter. "What are you going to do with your life, Olympia?"

"My life?" I chuckled as I pulled out the dough-mixing bowl. "I'm fifteen. My goal is to make it to next Wednesday and to survive my algebra test."

"Then you should be studying."

"I will. Tonight."

"You can do better than this place," he said.

I scooped out ten cups of flour into the mixing bowl. "What's wrong with this place?"

"Nothing for a bum like me, or even TJ. But you need more."

"I don't know how much more I can take."

He slipped into a moody silence, and then finally, "How is your mother?"

"Doctors don't know why she gets sick."

"Doctors aren't as smart as they let on."

"I hope you're wrong."

He sprinkled yeast over the flour. "I know you're taking the extra shifts to cover for her."

"Work's got to get done."

He regarded me with a raised eyebrow. "You sound like me."

I took it as a compliment. "What's your point?"

A smile played at the corners of his lips. "You can do better, Olympia. TJ, this place—you can do better. I love my boy, but he's not for you."

He could've been right about TJ. But the rest, I didn't understand why he cared. He'd always been kind to us, and it had never made sense to me.

"Why did you take us in?" I asked.

"Your mother said she was a hard worker, and I took her at her word."

"But two kids hanging around is a lot. We did not make your life easier."

He slipped into a silence. For a moment, I thought he wouldn't answer, and then he said, "Your mother and you girls remind me of someone."

"Who?"

"My wife. She and my daughter were killed in a car accident when TJ was five. When you three Hanover women came into the shop, it felt whole. My girl would have been about your age if she'd lived."

I stilled. "Tony, I'm sorry. What were their names?"

"My wife's name was Meredith, and my daughter's name was Susan."

The memory triggered tension, twisting the muscles between my shoulders as I rose out of the car, only to be stopped short by the cold whipping over the brick sidewalk. Wind was a constant in Blacksburg from fall into spring.

I burrowed my hands in my pockets and noticed that Sylvia's, the dress shop near the pizzeria, was opening early. Football weekends guaranteed solid sales that often drifted into Monday. Many of the ladies visiting town made one last stop at Sylvia's the Monday after big weekends because the 10 percent storewide discount tempted them to buy that Vera Bradley bag, cashmere sweater, or hand-painted silk scarf they'd eyed on Saturday.

My eyes watered in the cold wind as I approached the clothing store and opened the front door. "Sylvia."

The tall, lean, salt-and-pepper-haired woman turned, pausing for a moment before red lips widened into a grin. Kitten heels clicked as she hurried toward me and wrapped me in a hug. Sylvia was from Blacksburg and had opened her shop six years ago to combat the boredom that overtook her when her twin daughters had left for college. My mom had been dead a year when Sylvia opened her shop, and her daily stops at the pizzeria for a garden salad with grilled chicken became so routine that I had her to-go order ready for her when she arrived. We had become unlikely friends. The poor pizza girl and the upper-middle-class mom / shop owner had discovered we had a similar sense of humor. She'd felt a little mom-like to me, and I was probably a bit of a stand-in daughter for her.

"You did come back for Eve's engagement party," she said.

"I made it. Here for a week, give or take."

Grateful for the refuge, I followed Sylvia into her shop. It wasn't a very large space, but all the clothes were neatly organized, and regular visitors to Blacksburg knew Sylvia was the woman to see if a special outfit was needed. She could make any woman feel beautiful. She'd even helped pick out a white sheath for me when I told her I was marrying Spencer. The elegant fabric had hidden my doughy belly and glided over my skin like butter.

"Did you make it in time for the party?" Sylvia asked. "Eve came in for a dress last month."

"Her red dress was amazing."

Sylvia raised a brow. "Did you wear the Black Dress?"

I smiled. "I did."

Sylvia scoffed. "You should've texted me. I would've found something suitable for black tie."

I shrugged. "I was running late."

"A woman is never so late that she can't spruce up her appearance."

"Unless that woman is me."

A brow arched. "You are impossible."

"Did you hear? Eve and Brad announced that they eloped."

"Did they?" Sylvia shook her head. "So much for the big church wedding and country club reception. The farther we run from our roots, the closer we get to them, no?"

No truer words. But I'd let Eve spread the word about the baby. I smoothed my hand over a leather clutch and circled the gold H-shaped clasp. "And I saw Spencer."

Sylvia regarded me closely. "Did Eve tell you he was sponsoring the party?"

"No." I grinned. "It was quite the surprise."

"I should've known that girl was going to pull a fast one. She was always a little sneaky."

"She wanted Spencer and me there, and I guess she thought I'd bail if I knew I'd see him."

Sylvia waved red-manicured fingers bent with arthritis. "She doesn't know you that well, then."

I smiled. "Happy ending. She got her wish."

Sylvia motioned me toward thick curtains, and pushing them aside, she led me into the back room, where a fresh pot of coffee brewed on the work counter. Like the front of the store, the back office was neat and organized.

Sylvia filled two white mugs with coffee, splashed creamer in mine, and handed it to me. Sylvia always took her coffee black.

"How did it go with Spencer?" Sylvia motioned for me to sit at a small round table. She took the seat across from me.

"It was civil." I shook my head. "But Spencer and I are always polite. We're not the dramatic people who raise our voices."

"That was your first mistake. You should've yelled, cried, and slammed doors. Maybe thrown a few vases." Her southern accent made the statement sound a little comical. "Fighting clears the air, keeps the men on their toes, and leaves room for the very juicy lovemaking afterward."

"Sometimes I wonder if it would be different for us if we'd yelled and screamed even a little." Whenever Spencer and I weren't in bed, I always sensed he was holding back a piece of himself. At the time, I blamed his silences on the pressures of taking over and learning the family business, my unexpected pregnancy, and then our new marriage. But after the baby died, the stony silence that had settled between us led me to believe he was likely regretting our rushed marriage.

"What are your plans?" Sylvia asked.

"Spencer and I are going to meet this morning at his attorney's office. Papers to sign to end it all." I shoved out a sigh. "Then I'll stay with Eve for a few days, and then back on the open road."

"Where to next?"

"I haven't seen the Northeast. And I've got my sights set on Europe. But with winter coming, the desert Southwest calls."

"I never understood your obsession with Arizona. I know you said your mother talked about going there, but it's so dry. Bad for the skin."

I laughed. "But I got an awesome tan."

Sylvia shook her head. "Gallons of sunscreen, I hope."

"Mostly."

"You're hopeless." She arched a brow. "Now, tell me, what is your dream destination? What motivates you to get out of bed in the morning?"

"Good question. Now that the next step is mine, I'm not so sure."

"Just decide that whatever you do is all yours. Don't share anyone else's dream."

"I'm not. If the last year's taught me anything, it's that."

"Good for you. If you should find yourself in France, let me know. My daughter Robbie is living in Toulouse."

We'd been at the same high school, but I'd been MIA so much during those years that I didn't really know anyone. Both of Sylvia's girls had left for college, then graduate school, and now both worked overseas. The one time I'd met them at the shop, they'd struck me as so young and free. But then maybe they were normal, and I was just old beyond my years. I had envied their lives and their freedom.

"I'll keep Robbie in mind when I travel overseas. I'm better at getting around to visiting new cities now. The next hurdle will be dealing with a foreign language."

"Which is why you'll allow Robbie to help you. She always asks about you when we speak."

I doubted that. "Thanks, Sylvia. I'll keep that in mind."

"How is Eve?" Sylvia asked.

"Happy. Ready to build a life very far from Tony's pizza shop."

"She's never satisfied. I hope she doesn't outgrow her new husband."

"She adores him."

"She's adored *all* her boyfriends, from what I remember. Just as I did."

"Fingers crossed that this relationship takes." I sipped my coffee.

"Was Spencer's mother, Barbara, at the party?"

Barbara had never liked me, even before we ever met. My working-class background was my biggest strike. Spencer, to his credit, had never cared about my upbringing. "No. Maybe rumors had reached her I was going to attend."

Again, Sylvia scoffed. "She's always been very stiff. And if you tell anyone, I will deny it. She's a very good customer. But I never sensed she was happy." Sylvia had once said a woman's dressmaker knew more about her than her husband.

"I can't waste any energy," I said.

"Good for you." She raised her cup to her lips and paused. "But remember, money does not make a family better. They have their little secrets, like all of us."

I laughed. "Sylvia, I've never heard you breathe a word of gossip."

"Maybe I'm older and don't worry so much about what anyone thinks of me. I'm considering selling the store. My husband's retiring next year, and he wants to travel. And I do miss my girls."

"I can understand that." I glanced at the round clock on the wall. "If I don't get moving, I'm going to be late for the meeting at the lawyer's office."

"Don't be in such a rush. Finish your coffee. They can wait."

"It's tempting."

"You must give in to temptation more often. Find that inner teenager who never got to live."

"Last time I gave in, I got pregnant and ended up married."

Sylvia nodded thoughtfully. "Perhaps a little less drastic. But do take time for yourself."

"I've been traveling for the last year."

"That was for your mother. You wouldn't have taken that trip for yourself. Now you've satisfied your dear mother's list. I wouldn't want my daughters giving up their lives for the sake of my memory. Take time to ask yourself what you want for you. Not what your mother wanted. Not what your sister wants."

I reached for my only rebuttal. "I did submit proposals to several travel shows."

A slender brow arched. "Did you?"

"I sent them a reel, but that was two months ago, and I haven't heard back from them."

"Still, I'm proud of you. It's a step in the right direction. It's a step toward your life."

"We shall see." I took one last sip of coffee. "I really must go. I'll be late."

"If you hurry, you'll be just a little late. Don't hurry. Let them wait. You've served everyone else all your life. Now it's your turn."

I kissed Sylvia on the cheek. "When I grow up, I'm going to be like you."

"You grew up a long time ago. I think you have more wisdom than me."

I kissed her on her cheek and shrugged on my jacket. "I'll take that as a compliment."

Sylvia rose. "I will be speaking to Robbie. I'll ask her advice about your travels."

"Excellent." For the second time since my return to Blacksburg, I felt good.

Out the shop door, I hurried up Main Street, past familiar stores that were slowly waking up, hoping to catch the last of the lingering weekend visitors. Soon, cold weather would settle on the mountaintop, the winds would pick up, and the students would leave for fall break. The bustle of academic life would quiet before finals and the rush to leave for winter break. I enjoyed this town most when the streets were teeming with students, who brought with them frenetic energy that was as fun as it was exhausting.

On the corner, I spotted the embossed sign that read **HARPER AND SON**. Leveling my shoulders, I climbed brick steps and pushed through the thick door painted a forest green. Inside, warm air rushed my chilled cheeks. I rubbed my hands together.

I'd passed by this building a million times, but I'd only been inside once before. I was seventeen and four months, and Tony Sr. had called in a favor and set up a meeting with Henry Harper.

I was terrified when I pushed through the lacquered front door. Adjusting my gray backpack on my shoulder, I pretended to study one of the painted landscapes hanging on the reception wall. This office was only a few blocks from the pizzeria, but it might as well have been a million miles away. Rich people like the Harpers couldn't relate to scraping money for the light or grocery bill.

"Olympia?"

Turning, I found a short, thin man with thick white hair. He wore a charcoal gray suit, a red tie with a gold clip, and polished wing tip shoes. "Yes, sir."

His smile was kind, soft. "Come in my office. Tony said you have a question."

I crossed the Persian rug, rich with bold reds and blues. The paneling on the walls was a polished mahogany, and the walls were papered in a beige grass cloth.

In his office, I perched on the edge of an upholstered wingback chair angled toward a long wooden desk supported by sturdy round legs engraved with pineapples and palm leaves. He sat behind the desk in an upholstered chair, which squeaked when he leaned forward.

"How can I help?" Mr. Harper asked.

"Yes, sir." I knitted my fingers together. "Tony told you I don't have much money."

"There'll be no charge."

A slight sigh leaked over my lips. "This conversation will be just between us, right?"

"Of course."

I cleared my throat. I didn't know this man, not really, and I was trusting him with a worry that had kept me up for months. "I don't know if Tony Sr. has told you about my family."

"I understand your father passed away."

"Yes, sir. When I was twelve."

"How old are you now?"

"I'll be eighteen in eight months."

"So, seventeen." He reached for an ink pen and jotted a note on a yellow legal pad. "And your mother is sick, correct?"

"Cancer. It started in her ovaries and spread to her bones before it was diagnosed," I said. "It's now pretty bad, and the doctor said she doesn't have much time."

"How much time?"

"Weeks."

A frown deepened, etched creases in his forehead. "And you have a sister?"

"Eve. She's fourteen. Almost fifteen."

He scrawled down more notes, but it was impossible to read his script without standing and really studying it. "You work full time at Tony's?"

"I do. Forty hours a week."

"And you're in high school."

If you could call it that. I'd been scraping by for a couple of years, and if I passed my senior year, it would be because my teachers felt sorry for me. "Yes, sir."

"How are your grades?"

"Fair. But Eve makes straight As, and even though she's a freshman, she's in all AP classes. She's on track to get a college scholarship."

"What can I do for you?"

I'd known this fact for months, but saying it out loud stoked emotions I kept buried very deep. "Mom is not going to make it to my eighteenth birthday."

"And if your mother dies before you're declared an adult, Eve and you will have to go into foster care."

"I am the adult in the house," I said. "I have been for a couple of years. I take care of Mom, I pay the bills, and I get Eve to school."

He tapped the edge of his pen on the pad. "But the Commonwealth of Virginia doesn't see you as a legal adult."

"I'll be eighteen soon."

"Do you think you can really look after a fifteen-year-old?"

"I've been looking after her for three years. That's about the time Mom had to quit work and go on social security."

"How long have you been working at Tony's?"

"Since I was twelve, but I became full time when I turned fifteen. Mom signed a waiver."

"What did you do when you were twelve?"

"I folded napkins and pizza boxes and handed out menus. Nothing big. Mom worked, and Eve did her homework in the back room."

"Tony paid you in cash?"

"Yes." *My back was to the wall, and confessing to breaking labor laws was insignificant now.* "It really helped a lot."

"Tony's a good guy. We're in Rotary together, and he's always ready to help with fundraisers."

"I helped him at the Labor Day event last year to raise money for the fire station."

"I remember you at his tent. You sold a lot of pizza."

"I'm good at selling."

"I can see that."

I wasn't sure if I'd asked my question directly enough. *"Is there any way I can keep Eve after Mom dies? Can I keep her out of foster care, and when I'm eighteen, can I get real custody?"*

"There's no one else who could help you?"

"No family, and Tony Sr. wouldn't know what to do with Eve. But I get my sister. I understand why she's so high strung and so worried about appearances." *I leaned forward.* *"She's lost Dad; soon Mom will be gone, and I don't want her to lose me."*

His gaze was unwavering for a long beat. *"I can make that happen,"* *he said quietly.*

"How?"

"I'll start the paperwork now so I can take temporary custody of you both. I know a judge who'll sign the paperwork. When you turn eighteen, I'll turn Eve's custody over to you. Her life or your life wouldn't change. It's just a matter of paperwork."

For the first time, the edges of my shrinking world eased off. *"You would do that?"*

"Like I said, it's paperwork, and that's easy for me." *He removed his reading glasses.* *"Tony told me I wouldn't regret helping you."*

"You won't."

The second and last time I'd stood in this lobby was seven years ago, on my eighteenth birthday. Mom was dead, and Mr. Harper signed papers transferring Eve's custody to me. My sister never asked how I managed to keep her home, and I never offered.

Henry Harper passed away three years ago. His funeral was held at St. Matthew's Episcopal, and when I arrived at the church, it was so full I'd been forced to stand in the back.

Now, as I stood in the reception area of his office, I could almost smell his citrus aftershave and picture the frown lines furrowing his brow.

I'd always known Henry had a son, Brad, but he'd attended boarding school and then left for college and law school, so I'd never met him. And as Eve had said, he'd returned home as I was leaving.

I glanced in the office and spotted Brad sitting behind Henry's desk. The space was almost the same, but now Brad's diplomas hung on the walls beside his father's. And on the credenza was a picture of Brad and Eve. His arm was around her, and she leaned toward him, her hand resting over his heart.

"Hello?" I asked.

A chair rolled over carpet, and steady footsteps moved toward the office door. Brad appeared, dressed in a gray suit, blue tie, and polished wing tips. His light-brown hair was brushed back and his face clean shaven. At the party, he'd been relaxed and smiling, but now his demeanor was more measured.

The formality of his attire added weight to this meeting. He wasn't grinning and sipping champagne, but his expression was now sober and cloaked. The weight of my marriage's dissolution settled squarely on my shoulders.

"Brad, nice to see you again. And congratulations. I guess, welcome to the family."

He extended his hand as he crossed to me. "Thank you, Olympia. It means a lot to Eve and me that you made the party."

Didn't families hug at moments like this? Maybe normal ones did. I shook his hand. "I wouldn't have missed it. It was a lovely wedding reception."

"We should've called you and told you we were getting married. But it was just the two of us. I didn't even tell my mother." He stopped as if he'd said something wrong. In this office he was my soon-to-be ex-husband's lawyer and not my brother-in-law or friend.

"If anyone understands a quick wedding, it's me. I get it." I looked toward his open office door. "Is Spencer here?"

"Not yet. He's running late. Something at the office came up."

Ah, the standard excuse. "Running the quarry keeps him busy."

His gaze lingered on me a beat. "Can I offer you coffee?"

I tightened my hand on my backpack strap. "No, thank you. Just had a cup."

"Right." He nodded toward his office. "Why don't we have a seat? Spence will be here soon."

Spence. I'd heard his mother call him that, but the name had always conjured images of a young boy, not a man.

My attention shifted to his diplomas, to a large painting of the mountains, and finally to several golf trophies. "You played golf with Spencer?"

"I tried, but I could never keep up with him. He was always head and shoulders above the rest of us at school."

"From what he's told me, he had some success on the tour." Spencer had rarely talked to me about golf or his years touring. I'd always sensed he'd missed that life and Blacksburg was not where he wanted to be. That had been something we'd had in common.

"He was doing great." Brad tugged at his jacket cuff and glanced toward the door. "He had a couple of top sponsors looking at him, and his game was never better."

And he'd left it all behind to be here. He'd said it was to take over the family stone quarry, but I'd sensed there was something more.

The front door to the office opened and closed in a rush of cold air. I turned to see Spencer cross the outer office to Brad's. He also wore a charcoal gray suit, and the soft scent of citrus aftershave hovered around him. His hair was wind tousled, which usually made him look younger, more accessible. That lighter, happier guy was the man who had wooed me into his bed. But there was no sign of that person today. His expression was grim, his gaze guarded.

"Sorry I'm late. Work." Spencer directed the comments at me. "I hope I didn't keep you waiting."

I smiled and shrugged. "Just getting to know my new brother-in-law."

Brad, in a too-buoyant voice, said, "We were just chatting about your golf days."

Spencer's brow arched slightly, but he said nothing, as if talking about the days before his Blacksburg return was akin to rubbing salt into a wound. "Ready to get started?"

Brad motioned for each of us to take a chair in front of his desk, and he moved behind it. His fixed smile told me he wasn't sure how to handle this. The guy was caught in the middle, and for his late father's sake I felt sorry for him.

I perched on the upholstered chair, just as I had when Henry sat behind the desk. I'd lived through much worse, but the scars left by those battles remained tender.

My mouth was dry, and a dull headache pounded behind my eyes. I visualized yesterday's hike in the mountains and the burned cabin. Up there, standing in the ruins, I'd felt normal.

Spencer took the chair beside mine and tugged at the edges of his jacket. He crossed his legs and then quickly uncrossed them. Brad settled behind his desk, reached for a manila folder, and glanced at the papers inside.

"Olympia," Brad said. "At Spencer's request, I've drawn up divorce papers as well as a settlement agreement."

"Settlement?" I asked.

"A cash settlement," Brad said.

"Why?" I asked.

Spencer drew in a breath. "It seems fair."

Fair. We'd lived together as husband and wife for only four months. We'd shared a child who never filled her lungs. And we hadn't seen each other in a year. "I don't need a settlement, Spencer. I'm getting by just fine."

"This settlement will allow you to do more than get by," Spencer said. "You can keep traveling, go to college, or buy a business."

I uncrossed and recrossed my legs. Was this about me or releasing some of his own guilt? "Thanks, but no thanks. I'm here just to sign divorce papers."

Frustration etched Spencer's features. He knew me well enough to know when I said no, it stuck. "I know you're accustomed to being independent and the person who takes care of everyone else. But there comes a point when you must be practical."

Before I could respond, Brad cleared his throat and restacked a neat pile of papers. "It's a very generous dollar amount, Olympia. Now you can travel first class."

"I like the way I travel," I said, shifting my attention to Brad. "I'm here just to sign the divorce papers."

"Olympia, take the check," Spencer said.

"No. Thank you." And then back to Brad: "Where do I sign?"

Brad glanced at Spencer, and when it looked like Spencer was ready to argue with me, he shook his head. "I have two documents for you to sign, Olympia. The first covers the divorce, and the second is a post-nuptial agreement."

"*Post*, meaning *after*?" I asked.

"By signing this document," Brad said carefully, "you would relinquish all claims to the Stockton company and estate."

"As if the marriage never happened? As if the baby never happened?"

"No," Spencer said.

"Money for time served?" I pressed.

"No. It's not like that. This is a legal formality."

"Signing divorce papers feels pretty formal to me, Spencer." I shook my head. "It was never about the money for me."

"I know."

"Then my word should be enough, right?" My gaze was aimed at Spencer. His face was blank, but the fingers on his left hand fidgeted with his wedding band.

"Brad wants it all in writing," Spencer said. "It's not personal."

Personal? We'd lost a baby. It didn't get any more personal than that. "That doesn't answer my question. Is my word good enough?"

"Not exactly," Brad said.

My mouth filled with bitterness. "I came here to sign divorce papers and leave this marriage with dignity. Not to be paid off. But you clearly expect me to double back at some point, leverage the loss of our child, and make a claim against Stockton, Incorporated."

"You're misunderstanding this," Spencer said. "I would never expect that."

My jaw clenched. "But that's exactly what you are saying, Spencer. I married you to give our child a stable home with the hope we'd grow into something strong and good."

"I know."

"Do you? Your mother thought I married you for the money, and clearly you do as well now."

"I don't think that," Spencer said.

"Does this settlement money soften your guilt?" Tears welled in my eyes. Brad was sitting right there, but I didn't really care. A year's worth of anger bubbled. "I heard you and your mother talking in the hospital. You said, 'Maybe it's all for the best.' You were relieved that you wouldn't have the responsibility of a marriage or child."

"That's not what I meant," Spencer said through gritted teeth. "You misunderstood what I said."

"Sounded pretty clear to me."

Spencer drew in a steadying breath. "No one's done anything to feel guilty about. The money is to help you."

Anger crawled through my body, kicking muscles banding my chest. I could barely pull in a breath. Slowly, I rose, hoisting my backpack on my shoulder. "I had hoped we could end this marriage with as much dignity as possible. But you've both managed to call me untrustworthy as you were buying me off." Feeling tears rising in my throat, I paused and drew in a breath. "And now I'm so pissed off that I can barely think."

Spencer's fingers fisted. "It was not my intention to make you angry. I want you to take the settlement check and live your best life."

Brad rose. "Olympia—"

I silenced him with a raised hand. "I'm beyond pissed, gentlemen. This day has weighed on me for two weeks, but I've kept manifesting a calm, graceful ending. However, you two have screwed up. If I don't leave now, I'll say something we will all regret."

I was halfway across the reception area when Spencer caught up to me. His fingers brushed my arm, and I whirled around. "Don't."

"Olympia, don't be like this." The look on my face was enough to make him drop his hand. "Two signatures, and you can be free, have a good chunk of cash, and move on."

My hand tightened on the front doorknob as I shook my head. "And you can be free, too, right?"

"I want the best for you."

"Spencer, I suggest you shut up because at the rate this is all going, I'm going to punch you in the face."

My anger seemed to startle him. "You wouldn't hit me."

My fingers clenched into fists. "Don't test me."

"Come back into Brad's office. Let's talk."

I shook my head. "You fellas burned the bridge to me. Maybe in another year I'll cool off enough and we can try this again. But not now. *Not* now."

I yanked open the door, and the cold air blasted my flushed face and ruffled the edges of my hair. My heartbeat pounded in my head and deafened the sounds of Main Street filling with hungover students, blurry-eyed parents, and a few locals who looked as if they wished it were already Friday.

I marched down several blocks not thinking about where I was going or what I'd do. Finally, the cold wormed its way into my jacket, and I realized I needed to find my van. However, when I walked to the spot where I thought I'd parked, it wasn't there. Had the van been towed? That wasn't possible. I knew the parking rules in this town better than anyone. Fishing keys from my pocket, I pushed the unlock button on my remote, hoping to hear the van beep. In the distance I heard a faint honk.

Turning around, I walked north again on Main Street, pressing my damn unlock button like a tourist lost in a Walmart parking lot and doing my best not to cry. The *beep, beep* grew louder and finally motioned me down a side street. When I spotted my taillights blinking, I teared up.

I slid inside and laid my head against the cold steering wheel. "Damn you, Spencer. You're such an asshole."

Of all the ways I'd expected this day to go, this was not it. I'd thought Spencer and I could part without anger, but apparently consciously uncoupling had been oversold.

Finally, I started the engine. The heater blew cold air for nearly a minute before warmth kicked in. I tried to absorb it all, hoping to chase away a bone-deep chill I hadn't felt for over a year.

Toes and fingers still cold, I put the car in drive and wound through the backstreets until I reached the cemetery on the outskirts of town. As I pulled through the iron gates, I sat a little straighter and swiped the tears from my cheeks. "You've had a bad morning, but you'll get over it. Time to buck up and stop feeling sorry for yourself."

I followed the small road that trailed past gray tombstones and markers until I reached the back section. The plot I'd been able to afford was not the fanciest and, as my mother would've said, not in the high-rent district. Henry and Tony Sr. had offered to buy a better spot, but my pride refused. I maxed out Mom's credit card and bought the budget funeral package. Mom and I had taken care of each other for years, and we would see it to the end. It took me five years to pay off the funeral bill.

Past a familiar oak tree now vibrant with oranges and yellows, I took the right fork in the road. When the road stopped, I parked. For a moment, I didn't get out of my van but sat and closed my eyes. The whir of the heater filled my ears and warmed my skin until I began to sweat. Finally, I shut off the engine and eased out of the van.

Burrowing my hands in my pockets, I crossed to my mother's grave. It was adorned with a simple brown marker. Embossed lettering read *Jeanne Hanover, 1981–2017.*

The funeral director had suggested a phrase or two. *Loving Mother.*
Most Beloved. Or *Cherished and Forever Missed.* But extra letters cost
money that I didn't have, and even if I could have afforded an additional
twenty characters, how could I sum up Mom's life with so few words?

"How's it going, Mom?" I knelt and brushed the leaves from the
nameplate. The urn was turned right side up, but the flowers in it had
wilted and died. I removed the brittle blossoms and pushed the urn
back into its resting place. "I should've brought flowers. But it's been a
day. I promise to come back with some soon."

I visited this spot daily soon after my mother's death, but once I
met Spencer, weeks could pass before I'd stop by.

I crossed my legs, the cold leaves rustling under me as I searched
for a comfortable spot. Drawing in a breath, I shifted my focus to the
gravestone next to my mother's. This was the first time I'd seen this
grave. I should have come years ago, but I'd lacked the reserves.

This marker was larger, and the brass plate was adorned with angels
and the words *Adelaide Hanover Stockton, 2023, In Our Hearts Forever.*

When I was in the hospital recovering from the emergency
C-section, I'd heard Spencer and his mother, Barbara, arguing in the
hallway. Barbara had wanted my daughter near their family graves
because the girl was, after all, a Stockton.

When Spencer told me this, I'd insisted that *my* girl be near her
grandmother. In my mind, the two would have each other, and neither
would be alone.

Spencer had backed me up and told his mother it wasn't her decision to make. He had paid for our daughter's gravestone, never showing me samples. Looking back, I realized he was being kind. I was too
broken, and seeing our daughter's name embossed in brass would've
shattered the last of me.

An unspent breath hung in my chest, but as hard as I tried to draw
in more air and exhale the sadness, I couldn't. My voice was barely a
whisper when I spoke. "Baby girl. I miss you every day."

I traced the script *A* on the stone and thought about the monogrammed blankets, onesies, and Halloween costumes that I'd never buy. I imagined first words, tottering steps, giggles, and open-mouthed kisses on my cheek. I had mourned all the lost moments that I'd never share with my daughter so many times, I'd stopped counting. Tears filled my eyes as I raised my hand to my cheek.

When I was about sixteen weeks pregnant, Spencer pressed his palm against my stomach and said, "I'd like to call her Adelaide."

"Adelaide?" Never on my growing list of possible names had I scribbled Adelaide. "Where did that come from?"

"My father's mentioned the name several times. He said he had a sister-in-law with the name."

"That's a little random."

A furrow etched between Spencer's eyebrows as he waited patiently for the baby to move. We went through this each night. So far, she hadn't moved. "It's not like Dad to make suggestions."

I'd met my father-in-law a couple of times. As tall as Spencer, he had hair as thick as his son's, and they shared an olive complexion that soaked up the sun.

Frank didn't smile when we first met. His posture was stiff, and when I asked him about the travel books in his home library, he had nothing to offer. He clearly wasn't happy about his son's courthouse marriage to the pregnant pizzeria girl. Spencer's mother was courteous, but I sensed Barbara's icy manners were a battle shield.

After a couple of awkward lunches, neither Frank nor Barbara called to ask how I was feeling or how the baby was doing.

So I was a little put out by Spencer's name suggestion, which felt like an intrusion by two people who hadn't given me the time of day. "I'll add the name to the list. We'll see if it makes the final cut."

Spencer lowered his lips close to my belly and said, "What do you think, my girl? Do you like the name Adelaide?"

And in that moment, I felt what could have been a gentle kick.

Spencer laughed. "Adelaide. Adelaide."

My stomach tumbled again. It was too early for the baby to move, but I sensed I'd somehow been outvoted. From that moment on, we stopped talking about "our baby girl" and called her Adelaide.

"Adelaide," I whispered.

Wind rustled through the remaining dried leaves clinging to oak branches and brought with it an energy that buoyed my mood. An old man in Arizona who worked at a gas station had told me people didn't die, really. Their energy just changed. I'd clung to those words.

"I didn't bring flowers, ladies, but I did bring a few rocks."

I fished in my backpack pocket and removed a handful of stones and pebbles collected in Arizona, Utah, Wyoming, and Montana. I counted out eight stones and lined my bounty single file on my mother's marker. "You wanted me to collect rocks for you, and that's what I've done. And to be clear, they were all gathered by me. None are store bought. The ones in the gift shops were polished and prettier, but you deserve the real deal."

For as long as I could remember, Mom talked about the trips we'd take. I'd always bought old vacation magazines when the library sold them for twenty-five cents. Some of the pictures were so stunning that they didn't seem real.

"We don't want to junk up the place," she'd said. "Only classy travel for the Hanover women."

When I was fourteen, I'd found a used United States map at Goodwill. My plan was to chart our trip right down to the routes and hotels. I'd suggested we buy a van, but Mom had insisted on places with a soft bed and a hot breakfast.

As my finger had trailed over Tennessee, old questions about my father swirled.

"Is Daddy buried in Tennessee?" No funeral was ever held, so I'd never seen the place where he was laid to rest.

"Why do you want to know that?" My mother was sweeping the floor of Tony's. It was after ten in the evening, and Eve had already fallen asleep on the cot in the back room. I never slept well while my mother was still

working, no matter how tired I was. I always believed being at my mother's side lightened her load.

"I guess when you talk about traveling, I think of him. He was always traveling."

Nodding, slowly, she smiled. "Yes, he was."

"I don't remember where he's buried."

Mom had collected the last of the salt and pepper shakers and carried them to the main counter. "He was cremated. I didn't know what to do with the ashes, so I told the funeral director to keep them."

"Didn't you want to know where he would rest forever?"

"He's gone, honey," she said, her head ducked. "His restless spirit is finally free, and he's in a better place. That's all that matters."

I twisted off the tops of the saltshakers and wiped them until the silver coatings shone. "Why was Daddy restless?"

"He was an impatient soul. Never content to stay in one place." Mom sounded tired, as if that old weight was too much to carry.

"You said he worked because he loved his girls."

"He loved us in his own way."

"Am I like him at all?"

"There's a lot of me in you, kid. We're the practical ones who do the work and keep it all going."

After Mom died, there was no money for any kind of trip. Paying off the funeral expenses ate up all my extra money, and whatever I scraped out of my tip jar at Tony's went to Eve: books, a used computer, or summer school courses. Smart kids weren't cheap.

Now, as I stared at Adelaide's name, I wondered if she'd have been like me or Spencer. When she was inside me, she'd moved all the time, and the ultrasound showed long fingers that mirrored Spencer's. But the shape of her nose was all mine.

I would've traded all my experiences on the road—and I had more good ones than bad—for my baby. I gladly would've lived my life in this town. Losing my baby, in any universe, would never have been for the best.

I'd never had a restless spirit until I lost Adelaide. I always accepted what life had tossed me, put my head down, and got to work. But after this loss, I'd fled to the road, praying I could escape the pain soaking every square inch of this town.

What I discovered was that grief could be tricky. It was mobile and could track me for thousands of miles. The faster I drove, the quicker my grief moved. Each time I thought I'd lost it around the last curve in the road, I found it in the passenger seat, weeping. No matter how many days or months I logged on the road, it kept pace.

After a few months of traveling, the constant needling in my belly eased a little. Five months into my trip, I woke up in the Arizona desert as the sun rose. Gold and amber light greeted me as I opened my van door. Mother Nature had found me, and she was showing off. I sat up and smiled for nearly an hour. And then I remembered, and my insides pinched. How could happiness ever be possible again?

Maybe that was why I was back here now. Maybe instead of running from my grief, I needed to embrace it and allow it to become a part of me.

A cold wind blew over the dried ground, riffling the brittle edges of uneven grass. The town was entering the doldrums of winter, and the cold would drive everyone inside. "Cold and carbs," Tony Sr. used to say "Money in the bank." But I hated the cold, gray days.

I touched each of the pink stones on Adelaide's marker, rose, and shoved chilled hands into my pockets. This town was charged with too many tough memories, which would only worsen with the coming snow and ice. Better to hit the road soon, before they overtook me.

If I'd harbored any faint hopes of a resolution with Spencer, they'd vanished when he asked me to sign those papers.

CHAPTER NINE
SPENCER

Monday, October 28, 2024, noon

"Was it possible to fuck that up any worse?" Spencer asked.

Brad came around his desk, hands up in surrender. "We knew it was going to be a difficult conversation. It's not personal. It's business. As acting CEO of the Stockton Quarry, you could be held liable if you don't clean this up now. I like Olympia and will always be grateful for how she cared for Eve. But you and I know there's a lot of money at stake. And money changes people."

Spencer stabbed fingers through his hair. "What happened here this morning was very personal to Olympia. And it was never about the money for her. She's not like that." He shook his head. "I never realized she'd heard Mom and me talking."

"Explain to her why you said it."

Spencer shook his head. "She has enough shit on her plate. She doesn't need all my baggage."

"Talk to her. She'll understand what's motivating you and sign the papers. She's not a heartless woman."

"She'd never go after the money."

"Maybe not, but you need that guarantee in writing for the new owners of the company."

Spencer had wanted to follow Olympia and escape with her. But staying with Dad and the company last year had been nonnegotiable. The financial mess Dad had created within the company had taken months and several accountants to unwind. He'd finally realized selling the company was the best option. Now he finally had a buyer interested, so soon, he'd sign away the business that had been in the family for generations.

"This is bigger than the company and the money," Brad said.

"We're not going there right now," Spencer said.

"You're going to have to."

Spencer refused to think beyond the sale of the company and the divorce papers. "I should've spoken to her privately first. We blindsided her. Shit, I'm not any better than Eve."

Brad slid his hand into his pocket. Change rattled. "Do you want me to reach out to Olympia?"

"No. She's pissed. And when she's angry, the best thing to do is let her work through it. No amount of texting or calling will get through to her."

"She's been gone for a year. Is this confrontation going to drive her away for another one?"

Spencer glared at Brad. What had happened here today sucked, but it wasn't equivalent to losing a child. Crushing pain, not anger, had driven Olympia out of town last year. "I love you, man. I know you're thinking like a lawyer right now, but you really are pissing me off."

A muscle pulsed in Brad's jaw. "Lawyers aren't always popular. A hazard of the trade."

Spencer shook his head as he swiped Olympia's check off the polished mahogany desk. Carefully, he folded it and tucked it in his breast pocket. "I need to get to work. I'm already late."

"Call me if I can do anything."

He shook his head. "Two years ago, I was on the tour and riding high. Now look at me. I'm running a company I hate, living in a house that's not mine, and my wife just might run me over with her van if she catches me in her crosshairs."

"Let me help you."

"No," he spit out. And then, after a ten count, added, "Thanks. If anyone is going to untangle this cluster, it'll have to be me."

"I'm sorry Eve didn't tell Olympia about our wedding. I asked her to talk to her sister a dozen times, but she told me not to worry."

"Eve thinks Olympia can take any hit, get right back up, and keep swinging. It's not true. Especially when Eve lands the punch."

Frustration chased Spencer to his car. He started the engine, angled the vehicle south, and drove the two blocks toward Tony's. As he drove by, he glanced inside, half expecting to see her there, like he had so many times in the past. Olympia had all but grown up there, and it made sense she'd run to it at a time like this.

He could still remember the first time he'd really noticed Olympia. He'd been in and out of Tony's for take-out pizza a dozen times but had never bothered to look at who was behind the counter. But eighteen months ago, the sound of Olympia's wicked, throaty laugh had caught his attention. She was ringing up a customer, grinning as she doled out change.

When he sat in his booth, he watched her moving from table to table with an ease he envied. Her ease in Tony's reminded him of how he felt on the golf course. More than anything, he'd wanted to tap into that feeling of belonging.

Now, he could see that TJ was setting up for the lunch crowd, placing salt and pepper shakers on each table. Since Olympia left, Tony's had been through several managers, and none had quite worked out for very long. No wonder. Olympia had worked in that shop as if her life depended on it. Which, of course, it had.

He'd known nothing about her backstory when he first saw that red *Go Hiking* T-shirt that skimmed over her full breasts and tucked into the narrow waistband of her faded jeans. She'd worn Converse sneakers, and her dark hair was swept into a thick ponytail that emphasized high cheekbones and full lips.

"I'll take the TJ special." He didn't bother to look at the menu.

"Someone is hungry," she said.

"Starving."

"That's what I like to hear, hon. What can I get you to drink?"

"Beer."

"Excellent choice."

As he placed his order, she wrote nothing down and moved on to the next table, where a mom was corralling three boys. While Mom read the menu, Olympia showed the boys a magic trick, pulling a sugar packet from her pocket and pretending to lose it in the oldest boy's ear. By the time she produced the sugar packet from the second boy's ear, losing it again and finally finding it in the youngest boy's collar, Mom was ready to order. When Olympia moved to the next table, the boys were all plucking sugar packets from the holder. He couldn't stop staring at her.

When she brought his beer, he asked, "What's your name?"

"Olympia."

She didn't ask for his, but he couldn't resist offering. "I'm Spencer."

"Good to meet you, Spencer." She was polite, but he sensed her attention was already wandering to the next task.

"How long have you worked here?"

"I've been here for about twelve years."

"Unless I'm off my game, that meant Tony broke a few child labor laws."

She shrugged. "Maybe I'm older than I look."

"I'm guessing younger."

She winked. "Slick, Spencer. Always underestimate a lady's age."

"Am I wrong?"

"My mother used to manage this place. I helped. And they put me to work because I kept pestering Mom and Tony Sr. for something to do. Let me get your order."

"Thanks, Olympia." He liked the sound of her name. Enjoyed saying it.

He watched her walk away, admiring her long legs and the rounded shape of her backside. He sat back in his chair, rolled his stiff shoulders slightly. For the first time since returning home, he didn't feel angry or resentful over lost dreams or backtracking over old territory he'd never loved in the first place.

Olympia brought his order out, along with extra napkins for the kids. She set the pizza on his table and asked him if he needed anything, and when he didn't, she turned to the kids. She never wrote anything down and didn't miss a detail. When she handed him his bill, he took his shot. "I'm going hiking tomorrow. Want to join me?"

"Bold move, Spencer."

She didn't look impressed. Nerves needled his belly, but he refused to picture himself going down in flames. "Life's short, right?"

"That's very true, Spencer."

"Is that a yes or no?"

She tucked her pencil in her ponytail. "A yes."

Now, as Spencer drove down Main Street, his annoyance grew. He should never have let Brad talk him into the postnuptial agreement. A player didn't rise in semipro and then professional sports without being logical and calculated. And then he'd met Olympia, abandoned logic, and paid dearly. Had he really thought a very rational business decision would fix spontaneous choices he still couldn't bring himself to regret?

He hooked a right at the corner and turned onto the street that guided him out of town.

Twenty minutes later, he was on Stockton Quarry land and walking the stone pathway into the central office. His great-grandfather had started the company and built it into a success and then had passed it to his son, his grandson, and now him. Each generation of Stockton men had made the business more profitable. And now he was going to liquidate.

His mother was waiting for him in his office, standing at the large picture window overlooking the metal sheds, equipment, and piles of rocks and the quarry beyond. His grandfather had built the corporate offices close to the moneymaking center so no one would ever forget that their prosperity was mined from the earth.

He shrugged off his jacket as he moved to the desk that had passed through three generations of Stocktons. He loosened his tie. He hated ties and in the last two days had worn more than he had all last year. "Mom."

His mother wore black slacks, a silk blouse, and heels. Shoulder-length salt-and-pepper hair was pulled back into a neat ponytail. The faint scent of the perfume she was always known for drifted around her. Barbara Stockton was a perfectionist, and she didn't appreciate anything that fell short of her ideals.

Slowly, she turned, crossed the room, and kissed him on the cheek. "Spencer. I was worried about you. You're always here at lunchtime."

"I had an errand in town." He'd needed a break. He'd craved fresh air and time to process after his meeting at Harper and Son.

"Olympia?" his mom asked. "How did your meeting go with her this morning?"

He drew back. "Is there anything in this town you don't know about?"

That teased the ghost of a smile. "Not much."

Moving around his desk, he picked up a stack of pink message slips and shuffled through them. "What do you need, Mom? Is Dad okay?"

"Your father had a good morning," she said. "We had a nice breakfast."

Spencer's father, Frank, had been diagnosed with early-onset Alzheimer's. Frank had been the head of this company and their family forever. His father had always had a sharp mind, and he had a phenomenal ability to recall numbers, names, and every golf statistic Spencer had ever put up. He'd been a rock.

And then, two years ago, he'd forgotten where he'd parked. No big deal. It happens. But he'd wandered the parking lot for a half hour before he found it ten feet behind him. Two weeks later, he had planned to drive to the airport in Roanoke, but he couldn't remember how to get there. He'd looked the directions up on his computer and studied the route before entering the address into his phone. Two months after that, he forgot his wife's name and defaulted to calling her "honey." After a few days of that, Mom had demanded he say her name. He couldn't. That was when she'd started calling doctors, because she'd remembered how her late father-in-law had become very forgetful in the months before the massive heart attack that killed him in his early sixties.

Spencer had been on a golf course in Palm Beach, Florida, when his mother called him. He'd let the call go to voice mail and finished the next three holes. He should've taken her call immediately, but he'd thought she'd wanted to chat, as she did each week.

When she called the second time, he was on the sixteenth hole. That call was the red flag. His mother laid out the facts of his father's diagnosis as if she were talking about someone else. She didn't cry, and her words didn't falter. He told her not to worry and then finished the eighteen holes seven under par. To this day, he wondered why he'd stayed on that damn golf course.

"What do you need, Mom?" Tension snapped under the words.

"Did Olympia sign the divorce papers?"

"No."

"Why not?" Mom always cut to the chase.

"That's none of your business."

"Don't take a tone with me."

"Don't press."

She sighed. "Did you have Brad draw up the postnuptial agreement along with the divorce papers?"

"Mom, I have a lot of work to do today. You need to leave."

"She didn't like the postnuptial, did she?" She shook her head.

"I'll work it out with Olympia."

"Should I call her?"

"No." The words were clipped. "Stay out of it."

"I'm remaining here until you have a plan of action."

"Then take a seat, Mom, and get comfortable because I'm not talking about my marriage with you." The last time she'd tested his stubborn streak was in middle school. He'd refused to eat the broccoli on this plate, so she announced that until he ate it, she wasn't cooking anything new. He didn't eat for most of the next day and was ready to go until he starved; then she brought a sandwich to his room. Without a word, she set the plate on his desk and left. He ate the sandwich, and she never put broccoli on his plate again.

Mom squared her shoulders as she arched a brow. "You've got to settle things once and for all with her."

"I'm well aware, Mom."

Her gaze lingered on his before she seemed to remember that pressing him never ended well. "See you at home tonight for dinner?"

"Of course."

She crossed his office and hesitated at the door. "I really appreciate you, Spencer. I don't know where we'd be if you hadn't come home."

Those words teased tension from his shoulders. "I'm always going to be here for you and Dad."

When she closed the door, he sat in his chair and slumped over his desk, resting his head in his hands. Was this what a wild animal felt like when its leg was caught in a hunter's trap?

@ThePizzaTraveler

Bathroom stalls are philosophers.
I-17, Exit Unknown

Service station bathrooms confirm these 3 sacred truths . . .

• If the exterior looks bad, so will the inside.

• The cleanest stalls are on the ends (generally).

• Lasting lessons are written in Sharpie.

Scribbled on an Anonymous Arizona Stall:

Time makes room

for going and coming home

and in time's womb

begins all endings.

Ursula K. Le Guin

#TIPS #LESSONS #BEGINNINGS

@MikeS789 mentioned you in a post:
@ThePizzaTraveler:
"No matter how fast you run,
you can't go around a broken heart."

CHAPTER TEN
OLYMPIA

Monday, October 28, 2024, 12:30 p.m.

I parked behind Tony's, just as I'd done a million times in my life, but for the first time, I hesitated as I stared at the back service door. It was a portal to my past, and I wasn't sure I could manage that trip.

"When you're rich, you can worry about that kind of shit," I muttered as I gripped my keys.

Out of the van, I crossed to the door and tugged. It was locked. A year ago, I would've had a master key to the shop on my ring. But I didn't have that key anymore, so like a customer, I walked down the alley and to the front door, which was locked.

As I raised my hand to knock, TJ emerged from the back room carrying a tray of parmesan cheese jars. He looked at least ten to fifteen pounds heavier, and his hair was swept back into a salt-and-pepper ponytail. Dark circles hung under his eyes. He was turning into his father.

The pizzeria had been open seven days a week from eleven to eleven when I was in charge, but when TJ took over full-time operations, he'd decided the staff needed Mondays to recoup from the weekend.

I rapped my knuckle on the glass. He looked up, his face tense, as if he was ready to shout "Closed." However, when he saw me, the tension melted from his handsome features, and his lips split into a wide grin. It wasn't the boyish smile that had coaxed me into the back seat of his truck nine years ago but the expression of a man who'd been given a reprieve.

He set down the tray and hurried to the door, flipped the lock, and opened it. Immediately, he pulled me into a bear hug that smelled of Old Spice and basil. "Tell me you're moving home and want to take over managing this restaurant."

I patted him on the back, chuckling as I pulled away. "I thought maybe I could pick up a few hours over the next week while I'm in town. I could use the cash."

He hugged me tighter. "That's the sexiest thing I've heard in months." He held me at arm's length, taking a hard look. "You look good. Maybe a little thin, but travel agrees with you."

Smiling, I glanced around the space, which had not changed at all since Mom, Eve, and I had moved into town thirteen years ago. The framed pictures of Virginia Tech students dated back to the late nineties, and team pictures featured football and basketball teams who'd long since graduated. There was also the collection of TJ images that went back to his elementary school days and first communion days. Same chairs, same menu above the counter, and same crack in the black-and-white-tiled floor by the booth closest to the door. However, the tables were new, and the artificial green ficus behind the register needed dusting. Overall, Tony's Pizzeria was a time capsule.

"Place looks good," I said.

"We did a deep clean before school started in the fall." He sounded proud, as if that equated to redecorating. "I'm still not sure about the new tables."

TJ, like his father, didn't like change for change's sake. The new tables, I'd bet, were his wife's idea. "I don't know. They look sharp."

"That's what I tell Gina, but she wants to change more."

His wife had started working at the restaurant about five years ago. She'd never loved waiting tables, but she quickly noticed that Tony's Pizzeria was a moneymaking machine. When TJ and Gina married three years ago, she'd started talking more, and eventually fighting about, changing the place. The fights in the back kitchen had been epic.

"Business been good?" I asked.

"Great. I've had a hell of a time keeping up. Working eighty hours a week."

"Where's Gina?"

"She's on vacation."

"Vacation?"

"A long vacation, like the one you took."

As much as I didn't like Gina, this news gave me no pleasure. "I'm sorry."

"Fingers crossed she comes to her senses and comes home like you."

"I'm not staying. I came back for Eve's party. But I'll work here while I'm in town."

He winked. "Maybe I can coax you to stay longer."

I grinned. "Not likely." I'd worked sixty-plus hours right out of high school. I wasn't up for that kind of grind again. "What do you need for me to do?"

"Wait tables. Buddy and I can keep up with the cooking, but I'm having a hell of a time getting help. Thought about automating the checkout process, but that takes time and computer know-how I don't have."

I'd tried to get him to switch three years ago, but he hadn't seen the need. "I'm here for a week."

"Can you give me forty hours?" The question rose on a hopeful lilt.

"I can't work that much."

"I really need help on the Friday and Saturday dinner shifts. I'm going to be slammed."

"It shouldn't be a football game this weekend, right?"

"It's always packed these days. Pizza never goes out of style."

"Can't beat pizza."

He touched the thick gold cross hanging around his neck. "From your lips to God's ears."

"I'll see you back here Friday."

He nodded. "About four p.m.? Help me prep for the dinner crowd."

"It's a date."

He hugged me again, this time a little tighter. "God, it's so good to have you back. You're a miracle, Olympia. A miracle."

Took a little prying to free myself. "No miracle, TJ."

"Can I make you something to eat? You look skinny."

"No, thank you. I'm good."

He eyed me. "Have you seen Spencer?"

"He's some of the unfinished business I'm taking care of."

"Rich boy." He shook his head. "I told you he was no good."

I didn't point out that my relationship with TJ, the pizza-shop heir, hadn't worked out well either. "Live and learn. See you Friday at four p.m."

"Friday?" He said the word as if he were flipping through a mental calendar. "Can you do lunch tomorrow too?"

"Sure, I can do that." As I agreed so easily, I realized I'd slipped a fraction closer to the old life that had felt like a trap at the end.

There'd seemed no way out. Until there was. And now here I was, on the highway to the past.

"It's just for this week, TJ," I insisted. "I can't stay. I'm back on the road next Monday."

He grinned. "We shall see. Everyone will be so thrilled to see you. You'll be swarmed with so much love, you'll never want to leave."

Hungry people loved anyone with a sharp memory and the ability to fill their orders quickly. I'd generated that kind of love sixty to seventy hours a week for years. Sustaining real love was a different, more difficult story.

"See you tomorrow."

He hugged me again. "It's so good to see you!"

Out the door, the cold air hit my face and chilled the heat that had left my cheeks flushed. Drawing in a deep breath, I checked my watch. It was nearly one.

Eve wouldn't be home until three, but the key was under the mat. If I arrived early, I could at least make my bed and log on to the Wi-Fi. I had videos to upload and honestly wanted a neutral quiet spot that wasn't choked with memories.

I found Eve's bungalow easily. It was tucked in one of the neat neighborhoods where many of the faculty lived. It was two levels, banded by a wide front porch, and painted slate gray with wide windows bordered in white trim. The front door was black with a transom above. There was one tall oak now sporting bright oranges and yellows, a small green front yard, and a brick sidewalk laid in a herringbone pattern. Neatly trimmed shrubs rimmed the porch.

Eve had always wanted a house with a yard. Our small apartment had been too cramped for her, and she'd often cut out magazine pictures of houses and pasted them over the travel photos on our apartment walls.

She'd texted pictures of this house to me three months ago, when she and Brad purchased it. No doubt Brad had been the one to make good on the down payment. Eve had an expensive vision for what she wanted but never the bank account to support it. If I knew anything about my sister, this place would one day be too small, and she'd have her eye on the next residence.

I grabbed my backpack, locked my van, and walked to the front porch, where I found a key under the mat. "Good thing thieves never look here."

Inside, I was greeted by a small living room furnished with over-stuffed couches covered in white slipcovers. The modern art on the walls looked original, and most had been done by one of Eve's college art-student friends. A few empty beer cans and bottles were scattered around the room, and the gray area rug and hardwood floors looked in need of a good vacuum. Must have been one hell of a party weekend.

I set down my backpack and picked up the cans as well as random wrappers and discarded napkins. I carried them all into the kitchen and found a sink filled with unwashed dishes, and underneath, an overflowing trash can. Without thinking, I removed the bag and carried it outside across a neatly cut back lawn to the bins by a shed.

Back inside, I refilled the can with a fresh bag. I filled the sink with hot soapy water and began cleaning glasses and plates, which I neatly stacked in the dish drainer on the counter.

It wasn't until I'd grabbed a section of paper towels to dry my hands that I realized I was doing it again. The old Olympia had sneaked out from the shadows and slipped behind the steering wheel. That version of me couldn't resist volunteering for shifts or cleaning up after my baby sister. This was not a good sign.

I finished wiping off the counter, and then, spotting the coffee machine, I found filters and coffee in the cabinet and set the pot to brew. I opened the refrigerator and found what remained of the desserts from the party. "Score."

I wiped off the kitchen table, set my laptop on it, poured myself a cup of coffee, and made a plate of desserts. As I took my first bite, I glanced toward the clean dishes and savored the rush of satisfaction I'd felt when I left a clean restaurant after an evening shift.

"I need a new job."

I sat back in my chair and checked messages on my phone. Most were junk mail, several were from an employer in Tucson asking me to return, and a few were from folks commenting on my posts. The likes and comments had been sparse in the beginning, but since then I'd been featured in a Tucson newspaper about gig workers and digital nomads. The article's title was "Have Pizza, Will Travel," and it cited my social media. After that, my reach had doubled.

I'd taken several bites of cake and had drunk half my coffee before I spotted an email from a production company in LA. I'd reached out to a few when one of my @ThePizzaTraveler reels went viral. The reel had featured me cooking pizza in a thrift-store cast-iron pan over an open fire next to the Snake River. I presented the white pizza with wild mushrooms to the camera, as if I owned pizza cooking.

I'd kept making videos of me cooking in various spots, and I started tagging production studios with as much bravado as the Ford Taurus–driving fifteen-year-old who'd signed her little sister's permission slips. I never really considered that someone from LA might be paying attention.

Dear Olympia,

I run a small production company in Los Angeles, and I've been a dedicated follower of your account for six months. I even tried cooking pizza on a hot rock. After dusting off the dirt, it was amazing. I'd like to discuss a production deal. Call me. We could make money.

Best,
Pete

I reread the message a half dozen times. Flattering to think there was really a company that was entertained by my adventures. As exciting as this was, the chances of this offer being real felt distant. Still, my mind kept circling back to making money.

I typed back. "Pete, tell me more."

After pressing send, I scrolled through my photos for images to post today. One option was the stop at a pizza truck in Nashville, but freezing rain and an overcast sky had dulled the image. Nothing hugely inspiring, I had a few decent older videos of myself bundled up in a hunting jacket, carefully serving up a hot slice of pizza. I created a reel and typed in the hook, "Cold Weather, Hot Pie."

As I scrolled forward in time, I came to the stone I'd found on the muddy lake bed. With a swipe of my finger, I enlarged the photo and studied the neatly carved stone. *Tomorrow, I do.* The phrase had summed up most of my life until I'd gotten on the road last year. For twelve months, I'd lived for myself, done what I wanted and when I wanted. I wasn't letting obligation and grief swallow me. I was saying yes, and I never lingered long in any one place for fear I'd get mired down.

1982.

Over forty years ago, and someone's chiseled thoughts were reaching out to me. "Why toss the stone in the lake? Why hide it?" I asked myself.

Keys jangled in the front door, and Eve appeared. She looked a little breathless and tired. When she saw me sitting at the kitchen table, she grinned. "Good, you found the key."

"Right under the mat."

"I brought us Chinese food," she said, holding up a white bag. "I consumed more calories than a human should this past weekend, and I'm fairly sure I drank my body weight in ginger ale, and here I am, starving."

I nodded to my dessert plate. "I can always eat."

Eve set her bags on the marble countertop and stared at the clean sink and counter in awe. "I love you."

"What? I didn't do it. It was Snow White and her woodland helpers."

"I love those woodland helpers." She stacked the white paper containers on the counter. "Would you like a glass of wine?"

I glanced at the clock. It was 3:00 p.m. But it felt like I'd been up for days. "That's a yes."

Eve opened the refrigerator, grabbed a ginger ale, and popped the top. She took a long sip, then poured me a tall glass of white wine and dropped in a couple of ice cubes.

"The ice is sacrilege," Eve said, handing me the glass.

"I held back at your party. Not the zip-top-bag or ice-in-wine kind of group."

"They're all good people. They have the same problems we did."

"Except with money."

She opened a white container of beef and broccoli and quickly turned her face away.

"Smells hit me hard when I was pregnant. I felt sick the first three months," I said. "The nausea passed in the second trimester." I'd been thrilled when the sickness passed but had wondered ever since if that was a warning sign.

"Good to know. Did Mom ever say what it was like to be pregnant?"

"She never said. She was seventeen when she had me, and I think she was too shocked to notice."

"I don't know how she did it. She was always on the move. She never sat down until she got sick." Eve's shoulders slumped. "You're the same."

"Trying to fix that."

"I should've taken today off."

"Why didn't you?"

"I'm angling for a position in administration. More money, no grading, and more time for my graduate studies. And the baby is due in the spring, so I need to bank all my vacation time."

I swiped chocolate icing with my finger and sucked it off. It tasted flat. "I know it seems like forever, but the time will fly."

"That's the hope." Eve set paper plates, forks, and napkins on the table and then lined up paper cartons of food beside them. "We're hoping to have a church wedding next summer. I want to feel really married."

"I always felt really married."

"But it didn't last."

I opened the container of white rice and dished some on her plate and mine. "Expensive church weddings aren't a guarantee."

Eve kicked off her heeled boots and sat. "You sound just like Mom. Always worried. Never want anything fancy for yourself."

"That was her reality. And mine for the most part." I thought about Pete's email and his promise of making big money. Wouldn't that be nice?

"How did it go at Brad's office today?" Eve grabbed a plastic fork and poked at the white rice.

I went for the broccoli and beef and three packets of duck sauce. "Didn't Brad tell you?"

"He never, ever talks about his cases to me."

"Good for him." I supposed that counted for a few points.

"So did it go well?" A fork loaded with rice hovered below her lips.

"It went. To be determined."

"What does that mean?"

"Paperwork to iron out." Too humiliating to say *postnuptial, a.k.a. I-don't-trust-you, agreement.* Why the hell would Spencer be such a dick? Even if Brad had put him up to it, Spencer should have said no. In the beginning, money had not been a thing with us. We had a lot of simple, cheap fun. Laughs. Hiking. Great sex.

And then I got pregnant, and he asked me to marry him. I'd said yes more out of fear because I didn't know how I was going to raise a baby alone and hold down a sixty-hour-a-week waitress job.

Even the first weeks of marriage had been simple. In fact, it was kind of like we were still dating. For the first few days, he lived with his parents, and I stayed in the apartment. Telling his parents, he'd said, was going to require great timing. Finally, three weeks into our marriage, he showed up at my apartment with one suitcase.

"How was your timing?" I'd asked.

He kissed me gently on the lips. "Not great."

I closed the door behind him and watched as he set his suitcase by the worn green couch. "A bit of hysteria."

"Seriously?"

When he faced me, he found a smile. "They'll get used to us. And when the baby comes, they'll be thrilled."

And now Spencer was back at home, and money had bellied up to the bar next to all the other shit that had stood between us.

"I don't like that look on your face," Eve said.

Shaking my head, I chased away the moody cloud. I reached for my phone and opened the picture of the stone. "What do you make of this?"

"So, we're not talking about Spencer?"

"We are not."

"Okay. I'll let that stand for now." She accepted the phone and looked at the picture. A frown furrowed her forehead. "Where did you take this?"

"On the Stockton land on Sunday morning. I was hiking by the lake up there. I didn't realize the water had gotten so low."

"Very, very dry year. I'm hearing the rains are expected in the next week, but it's going to take a lot to get us back to normal."

"What do you make of the stone?"

Eve sat back and really looked at the picture. "Two other stones like this one were found early last summer, near the New River. I can't remember the messages, but they were also dated 1982." She took a bite of an egg roll, wiped her hand on a paper napkin, and reached for her phone. After scrolling texts, she opened a link. "Have a look at this."

She turned her phone around as I took a bite of broccoli and beef. The image was of a square stone almost exactly like the one I'd found. As Eve had said, it was dated 1982, but the message here was *Choose Hope.*

"Looks like we have a stone philosopher, don't we?"

Eve scrolled through more images and then flipped the phone around again. "This one read *Even With No Path, 1982.*"

I considered all the phrases. "*Tomorrow, I do. Choose Hope. Even with no path.* They look like they were made by the same person."

"There are stones like this in Europe. They've shown up multiple times in the last five years when water levels drop. Some date back to the 1500s. *If you see me, weep* is a popular one carved into the stony banks of the Elbe River. Drought equaled famine, so it was the fast track to widespread starvation back in the day."

Spoken clearly, like a science teacher. "But this stonemason isn't warning of bad times."

"This stonemason was living in difficult economic times. We were in a recession, and drought was a real problem then too."

"You know a lot about this."

"Easier to teach kids about weather patterns if you can thread in a little mystery."

I studied the angel carved on each stone. They were all very similar. "The angel is a kind of signature, I guess."

"Many stonemasons have a trademark symbol. This guy chose an angel."

"What makes you think it's a dude?"

"Because I don't know of any stonemasons in this area who aren't." Eve studied the picture. "The other two stones are underwater again, but I'd love to show this one to a few of my students."

"Then call Spencer. The lake is on his land."

"I don't want to press my luck. He hosted the party for Brad, not me. They've always been good friends."

"I'm sure he likes you just fine. He can be quiet, is all."

"He thinks I let you down."

"Did he say that?"

"He didn't have to. I saw it when he looked at me after . . ."

The unspoken words rattled in my head. "You can say it. When the baby died." My throat tightened, but I forced myself to bite into a spring roll.

"I also wasn't super supportive when Mom was sick."

This was the first time she'd ever brought up Mom's death. And the admission felt small. "You were busy with high school. It was important you stuck to your studies."

"You were supporting us all."

"When Mom got sick, it was hard on everyone."

"I wasn't around as much because I was so scared. And when she died, I thought we'd fall apart."

"You were a kid."

"So were you."

Mom's death had altered Eve's life, but I'd helped her course correct and kept her on track. I'd been too busy shouldering death, child-rearing, and financial debt to do anything for myself. But that was a burden I'd gladly accepted.

I cleared tightness from my throat and shifted my attention back to the picture of the stone. "Of all the people on this earth, I never would have expected you to know about these stones. I still can't get over that you're on your way to a PhD in microbiology. Not the road to financial success."

"There are plenty of private or public entities that need a PhD on staff. I met Brad when I was lecturing about droughts in the valley."

"Why would Brad attend a lecture like that?"

"He said drought is more exciting than bankruptcy law."

"Really?"

"He loves this kind of thing. In fact, he's the one that told me about the first stone. *Choose Hope.* He read about it in the paper."

"Wrap history and science in a sexy package, and you've got magic."

Eve grinned. "I know, right?"

"Are you curious about who made these stones?"

"It would be nice to know, but it doesn't keep me up at night."

"I'll post it and see if anyone knows anything. You never know what will turn up before I go."

Eve set down her fork, rose, and grabbed a fresh can of ginger ale from the fridge. "You haven't touched your wine."

I lifted the delicate glass and took a liberal sip. "It's good."

"Have you considered staying around?"

"I've discovered that I function better on the road. Blacksburg is no longer my happy place, if it ever was."

"You were always happy when we were growing up. I could never understand how you could be so upbeat."

"What was the alternative? Mom was sick, I was working all the time, and I had to keep you in school." I swirled my wine. When I'd taken custody of Eve, I'd picked up more shifts at the restaurant.

"You should have chosen yourself."

Annoyance pestered me. "Where do you think we'd have ended up if I had?"

"We would've found a way."

We. Our well-being had been on my shoulders, not *ours.* "I never saw it." A sad smile tugged my lips as I pushed aside an unexpected stab of resentment.

"I always wondered why you didn't want more than that pizza shop."

"I wanted more, but I didn't see a way clear. Pizza kept us going for years."

"You shouldn't have given up so much for me."

"I raised you when no one else could," I said. "It was me or foster care, kid."

She sighed. "It wasn't my fault."

"I never said it was." I took a long gulp of wine. "And now you have your Prince Charming, and I'm figuring out my life."

"Why do you have to figure it out on the road?"

"If I stay here, I'll end up back at Tony's. And trying to fix your problems."

"It would be different this time if you stayed."

"I don't trust myself to break old patterns." When Spencer took me out on our third or fourth date, I'd vowed that one day I would quit Tony's and do what I wanted to do. Spencer had nodded thoughtfully, as if I'd struck a nerve in him.

"I can lend you money," Eve said. "You can go to college."

"When do you have extra money?"

"Brad will help."

"No, thank you. Brad has already helped enough today."

Eve cracked a fortune cookie in half. "What's that mean?"

"Never mind. He's Spencer's attorney, and it's not right for us to talk about it."

"You're my sister. Brad's my husband. You can talk to me."

"And Brad is still Spencer's attorney. I don't want what happens in that office to spill out into our life. After this is all settled, I'll be able to think of Brad as family."

"Is Brad being mean?"

"He's being a good attorney." Maybe in another life or even in the distant future, Brad and I would become good buddies. But in this world in the here and now, he was a bit of an asshole.

"I'll talk to him." Eve's direct tone made the statement sound like a done deal.

"Do not."

"Why not?"

"I need you to butt out of my business."

"I'm your sister."

"Really? I've shared everything with you, *everything*, over the years. But you neglected to tell me that Spencer was hosting the party, or that you got married, or that you were pregnant."

Color rose in Eve's cheeks.

I glanced at my food and realized I was no longer hungry. Once we'd been so close, when we were younger, but after she left for college, she started to keep me at arm's length. I tried to bridge the gap, but nothing worked. Now, I could see the divide between us was wide, deep, and maybe permanent. "I'm going for a drive."

"Where to? I'll make your bed, and then you can just close the spare bedroom door behind you and crash until the morning."

"Might be better if I leave. This is Brad's house."

"It's mine too."

I wasn't debating ownership percentages of this structure. "I'll call."

"Hey, I'm sorry for not telling you about the baby. I just didn't want to piss you off."

"I wouldn't have been mad."

"You're mad now."

"I don't like being lied to."

Eve rose and followed me to the door. "I didn't lie."

"Not telling is a lie, Eve."

"The last time I told you something like this, you were furious. You didn't make it easy."

I had yelled when sixteen-year-old Eve had come to me with her positive pregnancy stick. But I was barely keeping us afloat, and I was as terrified as she was. "Don't put that on me. I stood by you every step of the way. I always have."

Eve raised her chin. "It didn't always feel that way."

"Is that why you didn't help me when my baby died?" The words slipped from my lips before I could stop them.

"I felt the loss. And I felt your hollowness like it was my own, and I couldn't face it."

The admission cut as deep as Spencer's postnuptial agreement. Why couldn't others sacrifice for me? "We do the best we can, right?"

"I'll never fail you again."

"Maybe. Maybe not."

"Sorry, I made mistakes. Maybe in my next life I'll be a better kid."

"And I'll be a better instant teen mother to a teen sister."

Eve blinked back a tear. "I didn't mean . . ."

"What are you trying to say?"

"I'm trying to build a better us."

"Then why do I feel so alone, Eve? So excluded?" Searing misery seeped between the words as I moved toward the front door.

"Where are you going?" Her voice pitched higher.

"Like I said, I'm going on a drive." I had a half tank of gas, so this trip wasn't going to be far. Until I worked a shift at Tony's tomorrow and had cash in my pocket, my traveling options were limited.

Frustration stormed inside my chest. I snatched up my backpack and tried not to hurry to the front door. Only when I was halfway down the herringbone sidewalk did I draw in a breath. TJ wanted me to slip back into my old life. Eve wanted me to be the mother she'd lost. Brad wanted my signature. And Spencer wanted me to wipe away last year.

They all wanted the impossible.

On the road, those random Olympia fragments had started to coalesce into a real person. Now those barely tethered fragments were unraveling.

Inside the van, I started the engine as Eve opened her front door. She called out to me, but I simply tossed my sister a wave and put the gear in drive.

I reached for the hagstone, remembered the clasp was broken, and drove miles beyond the Pinterest neighborhood, toward the adjacent town of Christiansburg, which was near the I-81 exit and my truck stop. It was familiar, and the tiny bathroom was clean. I'd park and bed down for the night and do my very best not to cry.

CHAPTER ELEVEN
SPENCER

Monday, October 28, 2024, 6:00 p.m.

Spencer stood on the back patio of his parents' house. Cold, crisp, and clear air sharpened a medley of yellows, oranges, and reds blanketing a distant mountain reminiscent of a reclining woman.

This time last year, he'd barely noticed the change in the season. Deep in mourning for his child and his marriage, he'd had no desire to watch sunsets or savor the cool mountain air.

"Spence."

His father, Frank Stockton, stepped out onto the patio and joined him.

Shaking his head slowly, his father said, with awe softening his words, "It doesn't get much prettier than that, does it?"

The scent of fall was dense with musky-sweet decaying leaves, mulch, and moist grass. "No, I guess not."

"Take these moments whenever you can, kid. They don't come along often."

He studied his father's deeply lined face and thick gray hair. His dad still rocked the statesman look even at sixty-five. His body was lean and wore the dark suit pants, collared shirt, and cloth jacket well. "What happened to the guy that raised me?"

His dad's confusion quickly gave way to a smile. "I was driven. I was chasing my father's legacy and was determined to outdo him."

"I never realized you were in competition with your dad."

"He and I didn't get along."

"I didn't know that. I thought you were best buds."

"Maybe when I was young, but we entered our cold war in my early twenties."

"Why?"

His dad frowned. "I'm not sure. But I've thought a lot about that wedge between us lately."

"And?"

"I'm not sure." His frown deepened, and tension crept over his limbs when he couldn't remember.

"It'll come to you."

"Maybe. But in the end, I'd become good at my job."

"I got to admire that. I don't have your knack for business."

His dad frowned. "Being good at something doesn't mean you love it. Guys like me went to work in the family business. It's what was done. I wanted you to have more options and do what you loved."

His dad had put in long hours at the quarry, but when Spencer had shown real interest in golf, his father had had a driving range built on the property. The two would wake up early, and as the sun rose, they would carry drivers and a bucket of balls out onto the back lawn. When they needed to up their skills, his dad hired a coach. They'd drive balls under the coach's watchful eye for at least an hour. They did this until Spencer left for college.

"I do love golf. I've got you to thank for that." It had been Spencer's life until two years ago, when he'd had to step up. He was twenty-five when he'd left the tour and come home. Olympia had been taking care of her family since she was fifteen.

His father's mood sank. "And now you're here doing what you don't love."

"Dad, running a family business is hardly a fate worse than death. I like the challenge." That much was true. It required drawing upon all the strategy he'd learned on the links. Patience, anger management, grace in the face of failure. And now he was selling the family business, making him the first Stockton in eighty years to tap out.

His father's frown deepened as he nodded. "I always said you were smarter than your mother and me put together."

"I don't think either of us is smarter than Mom."

His dad chuckled. "You're right."

His mom walked out onto the back deck. She was wearing black pants and a fur-lined jacket; her hair was styled and her makeup perfect. He doubted he'd ever seen his mother without makeup. Her smile was warm when she slipped her arms around her son's and husband's fit waists. "What are my boys doing?"

"We've decided you're the smartest Stockton," Spencer said. "Right, Dad?"

He chuckled as he stared lovingly at his wife and then kissed her gently on the lips. "That's right, son."

His mom always said her favorite moments were the simple ones; she loved the men in her life, and she was fiercely protective of them. Spencer resented that his mother had seen Olympia as a threat to their little pod, which only had room for three. He had no doubt his mom would've accepted his daughter, but Olympia would always have lived on the edges of his mom's life. She gave her volunteer time freely to the church, and there was no charity she'd said no to. But that generosity didn't apply to Olympia. Maybe it had been the unplanned pregnancy or Olympia's background, or maybe his mom would have treated any woman in his life like this. Hell, she'd never been fond of Caroline.

"Dinner's ready," his mom said. "I hope you two are hungry. I bought out the deli today."

"I'm starving," Spencer said.

"Yeah, me too." His dad was starting to forget to eat, and so now his mom was making a production out of dinner. All three sat at the table together, and it was Spencer's job to engage his father in often one-sided conversations.

"What's on the menu?" Spencer said as he and his father walked inside the house.

"Roast chicken. Mashed potatoes and rolls."

They were all Dad's favorites, and she served them at least four times a week. His mom settled her husband at the head of the table, she sat to his right, and Spencer took the chair to his left.

"How was your day, Spencer?" his mother asked.

"Good." Spencer cleared his throat. "Olympia is back in town."

"Very nice," his dad said. "How is she?"

Spencer's mother was serving his father, but Spencer sensed she was paying close attention. "She's good."

His mother smiled at her husband as she buttered a roll for him. "She's been living in a van, from what I hear."

Spencer cut off a large bite of chicken breast and popped it in his mouth. He was chewing when his mother chipped the next question.

"Any word from Brad?" Mom asked.

"Not since this morning."

"What's that mean?" Her tone was so light that it sounded as if she didn't mind either way. She only shared her true opinions of Olympia with him when they were alone.

"It means he'll work out the details, okay?"

His dad tore a piece of buttered bread. "We haven't had Olympia to the house in ages. Where has that gal been?"

"She's been traveling, Dad," Spencer said. "Her mother had a travel bucket list that she needed to fulfill, remember?"

"That was months ago," he said.

Twelve months and four days ago. "That's right."

"When did she get back?" his dad asked.

"A couple of days ago," Spencer said. "Her trip took longer than she'd expected. She had more places to see."

"Where did she go?"

"We didn't get into specific destinations." Though he'd become familiar with every city, park, or mountain range she'd posted.

"Why not? She's your wife."

"You're right, Dad," he said, hoping it would be enough to halt the line of conversation.

"You'll have your details ironed out with her by the time she heads out?" Mom asked.

"Don't worry, Mom. I've got this." Spencer figured if he said it enough, he'd believe it. A simple set of signatures should've been a cut-and-dried task and accomplished in under twenty minutes. But the signature lines remained blank.

He should have been pissed. He was damn sure what he wanted when he'd asked Olympia for a divorce. But as the temperatures in the valley had cooled, the hardness in his chest had softened. Each time he saw her, everything sure became unsure.

"I don't like that look," his mom said.

As his knife cut through breast meat and scratched against the porcelain plate, chicken juice oozed. "What look, Mom?"

With a slightly raised brow, she checked off every one of his doubts. A memory floated into his head. His mother packing his suitcase for his first tournament when he was sixteen. She'd included extra toothbrushes, new socks, and, at the bottom, a laminated picture of the three of them, as if she'd feared a week on the road might make him a little homesick.

She knew her son as well as he did or (maybe didn't) know himself. The unsimple truth of now was that he had no idea how he was going to untangle this marriage.

@ThePizzaTraveler

Colorado Springs, Colorado
Bad Luck Doesn't Come in 3's

The polar vortex caught up to me in the Colorado mountains. White-out conditions. Too dangerous to travel. Unless you know exactly what you're doing. I do when roads have guardrails. But there are none to be found here.

A tarot card reader's neon Open sign caught my eye, so I ducked into her storefront, more to get out of the cold. She smiled. Told me to sit. Today's reading would be free. When she drew the Tower card, she said, "The snowstorm will clear in three days. The storm in my life isn't finished playing out."

But if bad luck comes in 3's, haven't I filled my quota?

Silver earrings jingled as she shook her head. Bad luck comes as often as it wants.

#LUCK #POLARVORTEX #TRAVEL

@Randibutler mentioned you in a post:
@ThePizzaTraveler
"When shit goes sideways . . . keep bobbing and weaving."
You inspire me, girl.

CHAPTER TWELVE
OLYMPIA

Tuesday, October 29, 2024, 9:15 a.m.

Even a trap can be comforting.

I stepped into Tony's, drawing in the scent of oregano, basil, and garlic, which still blended into a comforting mix. From the first slice of pizza Tony gave me when I was twelve through the countless slices after, each piece tasted like love, security, and hope. Those feelings had anchored me here for so long and had maybe overridden my better judgment. Tony's couldn't guarantee safety, security, or happiness; in fact, it had the power to drain my youth and rob me of a better future. But my programmed cells kept humming the Rolling Stones: "Wild horses couldn't drag me away."

Maybe this was what an alcoholic felt like. Quitting made great sense in the morning, but by night, it had morphed into an insane, terrible idea.

When I'd worked here full time, I usually arrived right after school and I'd close the store most nights. I'd spend the final hour untangling the register, refilling saltshakers, or inventorying the supplies for the next day.

Getting here early and staying late also got me away from the apartment and Mom. I loved her, but watching her crumble had been too much most days. I'd allowed the hospice nurses to do the heavy lifting, justifying it all with the knowledge I was helpless to fix Mom, but I could show up here and log in several extra hours. And even after she was gone, the habit continued. Easier to be here than in an empty apartment.

I walked to the battered gray lockers and opened the top-right slot, which had always been mine. Inside the narrow metal space, which still smelled of old times, hung a pair of shorts, a T-shirt, and beat-up running shoes. For an instant, I thought the clothes were mine and the last year had magically been erased.

I opened the next locker and shoved my backpack inside; I dug a small lock from the side pocket and secured the door closed.

As if no time had passed, I grabbed a clean white apron hanging from a hook, dropped it over my head, and tied it around my waist. "Yo, TJ!"

"Olympia!" His joy radiated. "Thank God! No one else has shown."

"Someone a few inches shorter than me with wider hips has staked a claim on my locker. Where is she?"

"Not here," he grumbled. "Don't ask."

Pushing through the swinging doors into the kitchen, I found TJ mixing a large pot of red sauce. TJ, like his father, always made his pizza sauce from scratch. The Mancini men also special ordered their flour and farm-sourced their vegetables as much as possible. The ovens, Tony Sr. had said, weren't magic boxes. If you put crappy ingredients in, you got crappy pizza out.

The tomato and garlic smelled good, and my stomach grumbled. Last night, I'd parked in a truck stop between two eighteen-wheelers, locked my doors, and closed the van's window curtains. Temperatures dipped into the low thirties, but I'd burrowed deep into a subzero sleeping bag. I hadn't expected to sleep well, but I'd fallen into a dreamless sleep. I'd woken at 6:00 a.m. to the blast of a truck horn. Wondering for a moment what state I was in, I'd risen, peeked out the curtained window. Sunlight rose over the Blue Ridge Mountains. I was home-ish.

I'd shrugged on a jacket, laced up my boots, crossed to the diner on the lot, used the restroom, and then bought a large cup of coffee. I'd skipped breakfast, knowing I had to make my remaining hundred bucks last.

"Any extra pizza from last night?" I asked.

"In the refrigerator," TJ said. "Extra cheese and onions."

"My favorite. I love you." I dug the pizza slice out of the double-wide refrigerator and popped it in the oven for a minute. When the machine dinged, I blew on the bubbling cheese and took a bite. Some people said smell transported memories better than any sense, but for me the best memory enhancers were the taste buds. They were time-travel machines.

This flavor of pizza reminded me of high school, when TJ and I were dating. He'd make me the onion-and-extra-cheese special and then, smiling, sit back and watch me devour it.

When I glanced over, TJ was watching me with that same satisfied smile. "Just like high school."

"Yes and no. We've come a long way."

He stirred the pot. "Ha! I haven't gone anywhere, and you've traveled in one big circle."

"You're married. That's a massive change." I picked off a long, thin ribbon of sweet onion. "I had a husband and almost a baby, but you're right: I'm back at square one."

"You and me both."

This looked and smelled like that old boat, and just like before, it was rudderless. But this time, no amount of wishing would ever turn our battle-scarred selves into those fresh-faced kids who'd thought they loved each other. "We're still aboveground, so that counts for something." Coiling up the onion strand, I popped it in my mouth.

He shifted his stance; his gaze dipped briefly to my chest before he cleared his throat. "Why are you here early?"

"Starving, and I know there's prep work to be done." In truth, I didn't know where else to go. Eve had texted a few times last night and this morning, each time asking me how I was doing. I'd simply sent her the thumbs-up emoji. We'd always be sisters, but our paths now went in opposite directions.

"There's always work," he grumbled. "The kid who closed last night didn't even dump the trash."

"Let me finish this slice, and I'll get it. Unless the drill has really changed, I'll do what I do."

He closed his eyes, pressed his hands together in prayer, and tipped his face heavenward. "You're an angel sent from God."

"No, just a gal in need of cash."

Once I finished eating, I collected the trash and hauled it out to the back dumpster. Next, I washed my hands, refilled the salt and pepper shakers, rolled napkins, et cetera, et cetera. The routine had not changed a bit, and it was a little frightening how easily I slid back into the old pattern. Though riddled with holes, this life soothed me like an old soft sweater.

By eleven, when I flipped the CLOSED sign to OPEN, the kitchen was prepped, the restaurant floor was mopped, and all the tables and chairs wiped down. I was in the zone.

Patrons, mostly students, piled into the store quickly. The baby-faced freshmen, most of them glancing at their phones, barely noticed me, and the ones who did had no idea who I was. A few college seniors paused, pointed at me, but, par for the course, struggled with my name. Olive? Olivia? Ophelia? Even the variations on my name were comforting.

I didn't have to double think once or wonder what was around the bend. At Tony's, I purred.

I set down a deluxe pizza with pepperoni and extra cheese at a table with three young guys. "You fellas need anything else?"

As they shook their heads and reached for steaming pizza, the front doorbells rang, and another chair scraped against the floor. Another new patron sat. On autopilot, I pivoted and grabbed menus and was halfway through "Welcome to Tony's" when I realized my new customer was Spencer.

He wore his dark formal overcoat and dress shirt, but the tie was gone, likely tucked in the coat pocket of his jacket. He had tugged off leather gloves, sat, and now studied his phone.

When I approached, he looked up, his gaze a mixture of sadness and resignation. "I thought I heard wrong."

"What's that?" I asked.

"I heard you were working here again."

Which patron or passerby had texted or called him? Small-town living. "Only for a few days."

"I thought you might have left town."

"Don't worry. I will. Soon. But in the meantime, I'm making a few bucks." I handed him a menu. "Want to hear the specials?"

"No." He flicked the edges of the laminated menu. "You don't have to work here."

"And why is that?"

He reached in his jacket pocket and pulled out a white envelope. "Because of this. Take it."

"What's that?" I knew what it was, but I refused to make anything easy for him right now.

"The check."

I tucked my order pad in my apron pocket. "Is there also a postnuptial agreement in there as well? I hear they go hand in hand?"

He shook his head. "No. I want you to take the check free and clear."

I couldn't tell if this was a concession or a shift in tactics. "I've always taken care of myself, Spencer. I don't need the money."

He dropped his voice a fraction. "You're working here."

I leaned a little closer. "It's a good, honest living."

Our faces were a foot apart. He stared as if my thoughts would magically decode. Finally, he sat back, clearly realizing brick walls weren't that flexible. "Consider this money an insurance policy. You can put it in the bank and hold on to it. Life happens, and it's nice to have a little extra cash."

Yeah, life had a way of coming at me sideways, frequently, but I'd grown used to the random giant waves, avalanches, and floods. "Do you want to order something to eat?"

The conversations of patrons buzzed around us, utensils clanked, and the door opened and closed. Without glancing down, Spencer said, "The number thirteen."

"The meat lover's special. Nice choice." I didn't bother to scribble it down. "Beverage?"

"Soda."

"Terrific."

"Take the check," he said.

I turned, wove between the full tables, and slipped behind the counter, grateful for the barrier and space now separating us. I was pissed, feeling so angry that my hands shook. I'd said no yesterday, and I'd meant it.

"What's he doing here?" TJ asked.

I punched the order into the computer. "A number thirteen."

TJ barely glanced at the dough round as he smoothed sauce up to the edges. "I haven't seen him in here once since you left."

I shoved a clear plastic cup under the ice dispenser and pressed. Crushed ice cascaded into the cup. I moved it to the Diet Coke dispenser. He hadn't said, but I knew he liked reading golf journals, eating grilled salmon, and snuggling after we'd made love. "He must be hungry."

TJ grabbed a handful of cheese and sprinkled a thin layer over the sauce. "I don't like that he's here."

I was a little touched that TJ was glaring at Spencer. Team Olympia didn't feel so much like a solo act. "He's fine, TJ. I'll feed him, then he'll leave."

"I'll put his pizza in a to-go box, just in case."

"I like the way you think. But put it on a pizza pan. I can survive this just fine."

"There isn't going to be any drama between you two, is there? That's not good for business."

"I've already snapped. I should be fine for a little while."

He eyed me. "Okay."

I wove through the crowds and set the soda down in front of Spencer. "Order will be up in a few."

"You think TJ is going to poison me?" Spencer asked.

"Maybe. But the pizza will taste good regardless." In the corner of my eye, I caught several patrons looking my way. Refills, to-go boxes, and checks awaited. "I've got to keep moving. I'm the only waitress today."

"Sure. Go ahead," he said.

As I moved from table to table, the hair on the back of my neck flickered as I thought about Spencer sitting there. I couldn't tell if he was looking at me, but when I glanced over, he was studying his phone and shaking his head. Such a far cry from the young man who'd sat in that very spot eighteen months ago.

When Spencer's order came up, I picked it up and decided I wanted him to leave. I slid the pie into a to-go box and closed it. I set the box in front of him, along with a napkin rolled around plastic utensils. "Can I get you anything else?"

"Take the check." He slid it toward me.

"Other than that?"

"I want to help. What can I do for you?" Frustration etched around his mouth.

"Nothing. We're good. Even Stephen." I tore off his ticket and set it in front of him.

He turned his phone face down. "You aren't making this easy."

"I didn't think divorce was supposed to be easy. I've heard it's awkward, painful, and hard. Be grateful we aren't in a full-on war."

"I don't want that."

"Neither do I."

"What can I do to smooth the waters between us?"

I nearly turned and left without answering. I didn't want anything from anyone. But then, feeling like I needed a peace offering for my sister, I said, "Eve wants her science students to see the stone at Stockton Lake before the rains cover it up. She wants the kids to see what a drought can do."

"That's it?"

"Yep."

"When?"

"Tomorrow at eleven." The time was random, and if Eve couldn't come through, I'd text Spencer and cancel. In all honesty, I wasn't sure why I'd even brought it up.

"And you'll take the check if I do this?"

"No, I'm never taking the check."

He shook his head and cursed. "Fine. See you tomorrow at eleven."

"Great."

"Terrific."

I didn't parse the extra meaning wriggling under the word and kept moving. That was the good thing about being crazy busy: there was never any spare time to think or worry. Life got shoved to the side, and I never had to pause to think about anything beyond caring for my mother, Eve's education, paying bills, work, or traveling.

Before Spencer, there were times in the middle of the night when I'd lain in bed at my tiny apartment and stared at the cracks in my ceiling. In those moments, some of my biggest worries slithered out of the cracks, brushed a strand of hair off my forehead, and then danced around me and sang. *How am I going to make the rent payment? The cost of Mom's medicines is beyond the Medicaid benefits. How am I going to keep Eve out of trouble and in school?* It was a stupid, rusty song, but it fueled all my fears. I always followed up nights like that with longer, tougher days, knowing if I didn't keep grinding, everything would fall apart.

But no amount of hustling prevented bad things from happening. Mom died. I lost my baby. Spencer admitted her loss was for the best. And the night demon's songs grew so loud I couldn't breathe. So I hit the road, hoping enough miles on the open road could distance me from my darkest thoughts.

When I glanced over at Spencer's table, I discovered he was gone. He'd taken his to-go lunch and left a few twenties under the saltshaker. I moved to the table, took the twenties, and noticed the white envelope. I peeked inside. The check had more zeros than I'd ever seen.

I gave the bill and twenties to TJ and shoved the check in my back pocket. The lunch rush continued until after three, and when the pace finally slowed, I set the last of the dirty dishes in the kitchen sink. My back ached, and my legs had turned to lead. Normally, a day like today wasn't eventful, but Sunday's hike, plus divorce stress, had drained my reserves.

As I peeled off my apron and tossed it in the dirty clothes bin, TJ handed me $200 in cash. "No sense getting technical about paychecks. Besides, I bet you need the cash."

Shoving it in my pocket, I felt it graze the folded envelope. "Always."

"See you on Friday."

"Will do."

I grabbed a can of soda and a pizza (rejected because it had too much cheese) and then headed to my van, parked out back. Silence hummed as my body sank gratefully into the seat. I ate the pizza, not caring that the cheese had cooled and was slightly rubbery. I popped the top on the soda and gulped down half before I put it in the cup holder.

The envelope crumpled and pressed against me, reminding me that it hadn't gone anywhere. "Shit."

I removed the envelope from my pocket and opened it. I'd busted my ass today and made $150 in tips and $240 from TJ. TJ's forty-dollar-an-hour rate was twice the rate I'd earned last year and generous by any table-waiting standards. But at this rate, I'd have to work twenty-five hundred hours to make Spencer's kind of money.

I held the check up to the light. Would I have taken this money if Mom were still sick? I wished I could have said yes for her sake, but I had always been so determined to make it happen on my own. Maybe I understood even then that I was the most consistent person in my life.

As I studied the numbers, I allowed myself to dream. I could buy a new van with AC that worked, install built-in cabinets that didn't rattle when I hit rough road, and wire electrical outlets so I wasn't always running an extension cord to pirate the juice.

Hell, with one hundred grand, I could plan a trip overseas to Africa, Asia, Australia, and Europe. With my talent for budgeting, I could make this kind of money stretch around the world twice.

Spencer and I were going to divorce no matter what. And he clearly had the money to spare. It would be so easy to take the check. So easy.

Grabbing the check's center between my fingers, I tugged until the paper started to slowly rip, one millimeter at a time. I didn't marry Spencer for his money, and I intended to leave this marriage with exactly what I'd brought to it, which was basically nothing.

I stacked the torn pieces on top of each other and ripped them again. And again. I kept going until the check was confetti. Carefully, I dribbled the torn pieces back into the envelope.

Maybe I was stupid. Pride came before a fall, right? But no one had ever accused me of being short of pride. I counted out the bills I'd received from today's job and then shoved them in my wallet.

I texted Eve.

Me: Spencer said you and your students can visit the lake tomorrow at eleven.

Eve: SO, you are alive.

Me: Do you want to go or not?

Eve: I do.

Me: I'll meet you at the entrance to the Stockton estate at 10:30 a.m.

Eve: Okay. Where are you staying tonight?

Me: Don't worry about me.

Eve: Why not?

Me: Because I'm the one that worries. CU tomorrow.

My phone rang. It was Eve.

"Yes?" My tone was clipped.

"Stay at our place tonight. I've made the bed up, and Brad will be home early from work. I know you got off to a rocky start, but I want you two to get along."

I brushed check confetti from my lap.

"Pleeease," Eve asked.

"I'm fine on my own."

"You don't have to be alone. Let me take care of you for once. Seriously, please." Eve's tone softened.

"Okay. Only if we keep dinner topics far from the divorce."

"I swear. No one will say a word. I won't even talk about the baby."

I sighed. "You can talk about the baby. Don't ever hold back on that because of me."

"Okay," she said softly. "I want her to know and love you."

My throat tightened. "The baby is a girl?"

"Yes. We found out last week."

I tipped my head back as unshed tears stung my eyes. "That's nice."

"You're still coming here, right?"

I cleared my throat. "I'll see you in a couple of hours."

"Where are you going?"

Starting the engine, I glanced toward the sky. The sun had yet to set. "There's still time for a hike, and I need fresh air and sunshine."

"What's wrong?"

"Nothing beyond the ordinary."

"You always run to those mountains when you're upset."

"I like to hike. It's no big deal."

"You'll be here at six."

Four hundred dollars would buy me enough gas to get me deep into Nevada. But then what? "I'll be there."

@ThePizzaTraveler

Cold Weather, Warm Holiday, Jingle Bells Rock
Breckenridge, Colorado

The weather broke on Christmas Day. The sun came out. The air warmed. The shop was open, and we were slammed. "Pizza cures loneliness," my boss said as he lent me his hunting jacket, so I could serve pizza to all the holiday expats sitting on his heated patio.

Do I know any Christmas songs? Jingle Bells, sort of. Would I sing with him to the crowd? Sure. He handed me a song sheet. Phone in hand, I pressed record as my boss, a big bear of a man, and @ThePizzaTraveler started singing.

His voice was deep, rich. Mine sounded like a strangled chicken. But the louder I belted, the lighter my soul felt. In darkness there is always light.

The crowd clapped. We had a second performance at the dinner hour.

#HOLIDAY #SINGING #LIGHTERSOULS

CHAPTER THIRTEEN
OLYMPIA

Tuesday, October 29, 2024, 5:45 p.m.

My legs were spent when I climbed the few stairs to Eve's front porch. I'd been on the Huckleberry Trail for a couple of hours, but the walking combined with six hours on my feet was enough to wring out every drop of emotion.

The house was lit up, and as I approached the front door, soft jazz music played in the background. When had the pop-star princess fallen for jazz? I supposed that the music was for Brad's sake.

Backpack on my shoulder, I moved to the front door and rang the bell. I raised my sleeve to my nose, sniffed. Tomato sauce, garlic, and sweat. I couldn't remember a time growing up when I didn't smell like all three.

Footsteps thudded on the floor, and then the door opened to Eve. She was in her sock feet, wearing jeans and a white button-down tied at her waist. Her blonde hair was swept up into a thick ponytail. "Why did you ring the bell? You should've just walked in like before."

"Didn't feel right."

Eve's nose wrinkled. "You smell like pizza. Have you been at Tony's today?"

"I worked an extra shift. Quick cash." I pulled off my hiking boots and left them by the front door.

"Where did you hike?"

"The Huckleberry."

"Easy enough for you."

"Not looking to break a big sweat. I didn't go that far. Just wanted to stretch my legs."

"It was a beautiful day." Eve took my jacket. "And cold. It's still radiating off you."

"It was brisk."

Eve hugged me. "I'm glad you came."

I relaxed a fraction. "Thanks for asking."

"I'm making spaghetti and bread. More Italian food."

"Never gets old."

"Take a hot shower and change. There's a bathroom attached to your room at the end of the hallway."

"Okay." I made my way to the small room and, closing the door, stripped. I turned on the hot spray, and when I stepped under the water, my body soaked up the heat that had continued to abandon me ever since I'd arrived in town. When a chill finally shuddered over my body, I shut off the water and toweled off. Fifteen minutes later I was dressed in clean clothes.

I found Eve standing at the stove. The sink and countertops had been cleaned to the point of sparkling. There were fresh flowers in a vase, two wineglasses, and an opened bottle of red next to a small meat-and-cheese platter. This was her version of an apology.

"Can I pour you some wine?" Eve asked.

"Sounds good." I walked to the sink and stared at the dark backyard. A ghost of my reflection caught in the glass. Sprigs of escaped hair haloed my face, and my cheeks looked slightly chapped. I was no great beauty. A hard seven / soft eight, as I'd often joked. What the hell had Spencer seen in me eighteen months ago? I smoothed out my hair.

Eve handed me a glass. "What was it like working at Tony's again?"

The glass felt delicate, light, and awkward. I was the kid who could break stoneware. "Very, very familiar. Weird."

"How many years did you log in that place?"

A sip of wine told me it was good, very good. "A lot."

"Did TJ tell you he and his wife separated?" Eve asked.

"He said she'd gone on a long Olympia-style kind of vacation." I swirled the wine in the glass.

"He's a little desperate since she left. Staff shortages, from what I hear. And Gina wasn't exactly you, but she handled the finances of the business."

"Gina put in as many hours as TJ. But I guess she had her limit. And you know TJ is TJ."

I remembered well the morning I dropped Eve off at high school and drove straight to Tony's. Tony Sr.'s health was declining, and TJ was feeling the pressure of the business.

I put in extra hours for the money but also to help him. And when his finances ran tight, I told him to make it up next month. He'd done that for a few months, but he'd sworn yesterday he was on the verge of turning a corner financially. There was no reason the business shouldn't be making money, and lately, I'd wondered if TJ was screwing up the books. I'd offered to look at the accounts, but he'd insisted everything was fine.

I entered through the back door, placed my backpack in the locker, and slid on a clean uniform. Threading my fingers through my hair, I secured it with a rubber band. Thursdays were generally busy, but they weren't insane. I half hoped that, with the thunderclouds gathering outside, rain would chase away a few customers. Sure, it would mean less tips, but it would be nice to get home before midnight.

I pushed through the swinging doors and surveyed the dining room. The chairs were turned upside down and resting on the tables, the floor was neatly swept, and everything was in its place, as I'd left it last night. "Another calm before the storm."

I moved into the kitchen and realized the ovens were off. What the hell? They took at least an hour to heat up. I switched each on, knowing they'd barely be hot enough when the first orders were placed.

The prep stations were as clean and organized as I'd left them, but the counter should have been covered with the meats, cheeses, and veggies I'd prepped.

The silence in the shop was suddenly troubling. TJ was always here when I arrived. Rock and roll music should've been blaring from the sound system, and pots should've been steaming on the stove.

I peeked in his office and saw his jacket slung over the chair angled close to his small desk, covered with receipts and product catalogs.

My worry growing, I moved across the main restaurant and looked around, half fearful I'd find him lying in a pool of blood. Shop owners got robbed all the time, and he was never good at locking the back door. But there was no sign of TJ.

Maybe the pressure of running the place had been too much for him. Maybe he'd dropped his coat off and then turned around and left, deciding it was all too much. I'd been tempted to do the same so many times.

Grabbing a kitchen knife, I opened the door to the back staircase and climbed. I avoided the fifth step, which always creaked, because if trouble waited, I didn't want to give it fair warning.

When I pushed into the storage room, I heard TJ moaning. Again, I imagined him hurt, injured by an attacker who'd forced him up here, to the company safe.

I peered around a wall of boxes and saw TJ lying on the floor, face down, no pants. And on top of the naked body of the woman who'd one day become his wife. He was pumping inside her, gripping her breasts and kissing the side of her neck. He called this combination his triple play, and I knew it well.

The irony of it was that I wasn't mad or upset. Whatever this was, it paled compared to the troubles I had on my plate.

"Thank goodness," I said. "I thought you'd been killed."

The sound of my voice broke the erotic spell, and he rolled onto his back, seamlessly grabbing the woman's discarded blue skirt to hide his junk. A light glinted off the knife in my hand. "Olympia. You're so early."

"Are you saying the only thing odd about all this is my early arrival?" I asked.

The woman grabbed the folds of her shirt and began buttoning it. "Who is this?"

"Good question, isn't it, TJ?" I asked.

TJ glanced at the knife. "Olympia, I know this looks bad."

"Not bad. And oddly not shocking." My lack of rage was puzzling. TJ and I had been together for nearly four years, and we hadn't had much time for each other lately. Now I knew how he spent his nights.

My first thought was, Good, now in sixty years we won't be the longest-living pizza-making couple in the Mid-Atlantic. *Not seeing my personal life mapped out ahead was oddly a relief.*

"I turned on the ovens." I pointed the knife toward the door. "I better get to prepping, or there won't be any pizza today."

TJ glanced at Gina and then opened his mouth, then closed it. At least he was smart enough to know there was nothing to say at this moment.

I walked down the stairs, washed my hands in the kitchen sink, and started cutting the onions. I hated cutting onions and garlic, so I always did them first. Sure, my hands would stink of onions for the rest of the night, but the way I saw it, life was always a little better when the hard stuff was done first.

I put on the music, choosing Harry Styles's "Sign of the Times," and was peeling off garlic skins when TJ appeared with Gina. He prompted Gina to leave, and as she passed me, she paused to say, "I'm sorry."

"I'm sorry I interrupted," I said. "I'll get TJ to put a bell on the back door so the next time, everyone knows I'm coming. Until then I'll stomp my feet and clang pots."

Gina ducked her head and left.

TJ was dressed now, and as he washed his hands, he said, head bowed, "I'm sorry. That was not fair to you."

"You owe me nine hundred and two dollars," I said. "It's the back pay I said you could wait on, but I'm tired of waiting."

"I don't have it." He dried his hands.

I didn't raise my gaze as I swapped a skinned garlic for an untouched one. "If I don't have my money in the next half hour, I'm quitting. You can run this place all by yourself."

His chuckle sounded nervous. "Where will you go?"

I shook my head. "I'll have another job in two days. You might find two or three people that'll do the work I've done, but it'll take time, and in the meantime, you'll lose a lot of business. You can explain to your father, or I can, that I quit because you were screwing that chick in the storage room."

"Dad's been sick. He doesn't need to hear this."

"I like your dad. I do. But he would remind me I need to do a better job of sticking up for myself, and I can do better than you." TJ opened his mouth, but I held up my hand, silencing him. "I'm not feeling very generous right now. You two have kept me around because I outwork everyone."

He sighed. "Deal."

Eve shook her head. "You were so cool about the whole thing. How did you do it?"

"I didn't love TJ. What we had was more habit than anything else." I could be loyal to a fault, and I wasn't sure I'd ever have tried anything new if I was with TJ.

"But you stayed. And you're back at Tony's now."

"For a few days. That's it. I need the cash. And TJ will always be short staffed." I drew in a breath. "And because I felt connected to Mom there. She was the heart of Tony's."

"Yeah. Not the same without her."

"No."

Eve's brow furrowed. "Seems Spencer could help you out," Eve said.

Had Brad told Eve about the check? The postnuptial deal? Eve had insisted she and Brad didn't discuss his work, but I wasn't so sure. "I've got this covered."

"But why not take a little help?"

"I couldn't before, and I can't now. Who knows? Call it a personality flaw."

"Maybe you can't accept help from Spencer because you still care about him."

I straightened as if she'd tweaked a nerve. "Who told you that?"

She shrugged. "Brad could see you two are suffering."

Ah, so the happy couple had discussed me. "This isn't anyone's business."

"Spencer has so much money. Let him help you. He owes you."

What did he owe me? He'd married me, tried to be a good husband, and, when it had all fallen apart, in a moment of honesty had expressed his relief it was over. Could I hate him for his feelings? "I was never Spencer's employee, Eve." I sipped my wine and shifted topics. "Do you have any students who are up for the field trip tomorrow?"

"Four kids. They're my best students, and all earned As on the midterms. The other students will have a sub and a study hall. I spent the afternoon emailing parents to get their permission."

"Great. Learn anything more about the stones?"

"Funny you should ask. I spent the morning going through the digital files of the local newspaper. I keyed in on the date 1982. As I said before, there was a big drought that year. There was also a local stonemason, Hans Bauer, who was recognized for the work he'd done on the Stocktons' main house addition. There's one picture of him where he's holding a cornerstone with an angel etched in it." She found the picture on her phone and showed me.

The tall man had broad, muscled shoulders. As he stared unsmiling into the camera, he gripped the stone in large, rough-looking hands.

"Grim-looking man," I said.

"I guess that's the way it was in the old country," Eve said.

"Clearly whoever did the work was skilled. What happened to Hans?"

"He died in a construction accident in 1982."

"Back to 1982. A lot turns on that year." I sipped my wine. "I posted pictures and video of the stone. Received a DM from a guy who said he might know something. He was just cryptic enough to make me doubt him. People say all kinds of crazy shit to get your attention."

The front door opened, and Eve moved toward the hallway. "Babe, glad you're home."

"Thanks."

"Olympia is here."

"Nice." Brad loosened his tie as he walked into the kitchen with Eve. "Olympia, glad to have you."

I smoothed hands over my jeans. "Hey, Brad."

He shrugged off his jacket and draped it over the back of a kitchen chair huddled around a table set for dinner. "How was your day?"

"Good. Worked at Tony's for a few hours and hiked. How was your day?"

A slight frown creased Brad's forehead. "Pushing lots of papers." He bit into a piece of cheese.

"Tomorrow, Olympia and I are taking four of my students to the Stockton land to look at the stone I told you about," Eve said.

"Spencer said something about that," Brad said.

They'd been talking about me. No doubt they'd discussed the amount on the check I'd shredded. Had Brad lowballed the first offer when he'd told Spencer to push the postnuptial agreement? I imagined them wondering how much it would cost to get me to sign the papers and leave town.

I sipped my wine, knowing all the quips I had at the ready were too razor sharp. "Should be a fun field trip."

Eve grinned. "I hope you both are hungry. I made a massive pot of sauce." A pot of water bubbled on the gas burner stove. My sister had outdone herself. The question was, Why?

"Thanks," I said.

Brad unfastened his cuffs and rolled up his sleeves. "When you were traveling, what place was your favorite?"

Brad had shifted from lawyer to brother-in-law. For Eve's sake, I decided to play along. "Hard to pick a favorite. They were all unique. The Grand Canyon was amazing."

"The pictures on your account are stunning," he said.

"You're on social media?" He didn't strike me as the digital-entertainment type.

He shrugged as if he'd confessed to a dirty little secret. "Sure. I had grand plans of seeing the four corners of this country, but graduations, internships, law school, and the job haven't given me the time. I've been trying to convince Eve we should rent a van and drive west during our honeymoon."

Eve wrinkled her nose. "Darling, you lost me at 'outdoor bathrooms.'"

"Eve and I tried camping," he said.

"I can only imagine." Picturing my prim sister roughing it in the woods conjured a slight smile.

"We'll be busy next spring," Eve said.

"Congratulations, by the way," I said.

Eve held her hands up. "She guessed it."

Brad's smile softened. "I'm glad you know. I want you to know your niece."

I refused to imagine my niece fully formed. I couldn't do that right now. "Before the baby is born, you could travel. They do have nice hotels on the road. Vans aren't mandatory."

"But in a van, you're right in the center of a national park," Brad offered. "What an exciting honeymoon."

"But is it safe?" Eve asked.

"Sure," I said. "You can do as much or little as you want."

Eve turned toward her stove, grabbed a handful of pasta, and snapped it in half before she dropped it in the water. I recognized the tension in my sister's shoulders. Time to tread carefully and not mention that breaking pasta is a no-no. "I thought we agreed to go to Paris on our honeymoon."

"We've talked about it," Brad said.

"I'm sure wherever you go, it'll be great," I said as I sipped my wine. Amazing how easily I slipped into the peacemaker role, just like I had as a kid. Eve and our mother had butted heads almost daily. "This is great wine, Eve."

"Thanks," Eve said.

"Yeah, thanks, babe," Brad said.

They'd stepped on two land mines in the last five minutes, and we hadn't even sat down to eat. Why not go three for three?

"There was a place outside of Provo, Utah," I said. "Remember the picture Mom kept in the center of her collage?"

"Stewart Falls," she said.

"I picked up a handful of rocks when I was there." I hurried to my bedroom and fished out a jagged gray rock. Back in the kitchen, I handed it to Eve. "I picked this up for you."

Eve accepted the rock, turning it over in her hand. "I never really thought you'd get there."

"When I visited Mom's place yesterday, I left one of these rocks with her."

Eve curled her fingers around the rock. "You always looked out for us."

I did. Always would. No matter how mad or frustrated I was with Eve.

"Where to next?" Brad asked.

"I'm headed south for the winter. And then in the spring maybe Europe."

"My baby is due in the spring," Eve said.

"I'll swing through after she's born."

"I thought you'd want to be there when she's born."

"That moment is for you and Brad. Not me."

Eve blinked, drained the pasta, and dumped it into a large shallow blue bowl, which she set down hard in the middle of the table. It was all so Pinterest. We all took seats, Brad and Eve at the ends and me in the middle. I could picture Eve and Brad here at this table next year with a highchair and baby between them. Eve had wanted her perfect nuclear family, and so had I when I allowed myself to dream.

Eve was on her way, but despite what I'd just said, I didn't really have a clue what I was going to do with my life beyond heading south for the winter.

@ThePizzaTraveler

Provo, Utah
Fixing the Unfixable and Other Myths.

There's a three-legged dog that lives in the alleys at the edge of town. He knows where I park at night. Knows I can't resist feeding him. I've tried to coax him into the van at night where it's warm. But he won't hear of it. He takes the food I give him, nods, and leaves. I understand pride, and when charitable offers come my way, I always say no. I remained in town a couple of extra days hoping he'd come by my van one last time. I was going to sell him on van living with me. But he never came back.

Even if he accepts my offer, he'll still be missing a leg, and I'll be yearning for my baby.

Kind offers can't fix either of us.

But we are beholden to no one.

#DOGS #PRIDE #KINDNESS

CHAPTER FOURTEEN
OLYMPIA

Wednesday, October 30, 2024, 5:15 a.m.

I woke to the sound of my baby crying. I sat up, tired, but my arms ached to hold my little girl. I'd lain in bed and was so tempted to roll over and pull the covers over my head. Finally, my bare feet touched the cold floor, and when I took a step forward, I bumped into a chair that wasn't in my tiny apartment or my van. Pain radiated up my leg as I rubbed my knee and looked around the strange room. Panic tightened my chest as the baby's cries faded.

In a blink, the room went silent, and I realized I wasn't in the apartment or the van. I was in my sister's spare room. I closed my eyes, tears spilling down my cheeks. I drew in a breath as my hands slid to my flat belly.

Why had the dreams returned? Certainly, being back in Blacksburg must have been the trigger. I walked to the window and stared up at the stars. My fingers flexed, and I rolled my shoulders. It was too cold and dark to hike right now. I'd have to wait until sunrise, a few hours away.

I slid on my jeans and pulled a sweatshirt over the T-shirt I'd slept in. Grabbing my phone from the charger on the nightstand, I opened the door and tiptoed down the hallway past the closed door of Eve and Brad's room.

In the kitchen, I switched on the lights and moved to the coffee maker. I made a pot, pressed the start button, and opened the refrigerator in search of milk. Instead of creamer, I found only oat and soy milk.

Eve had wanted the fancy milks ever since she was a kid. Now, after years of hearing "too expensive," she'd found her fancy vegan milks.

I picked the one with the most calories. I found the largest mug in the cabinet and filled it with coffee and the milk-ish substance. One taste told me I needed sugar. I was rooting through the pantry when footsteps sounded behind me.

"Sugar is in the cabinet to the right in the back. Eve's not a fan of it, but I keep my own stash."

I found Brad showered and dressed in suit pants and dress shirt. No tie yet, but the day was young. "Thanks." I reached for a fresh cup "Can I pour you one?"

"That would be amazing."

"How do you take it? Sugar and . . ."

"Doesn't matter which milk you pick."

I dressed a cup of coffee for him and set it on the island.

"Thanks." He took a sip. "You're up early."

"Some nights I sleep like the dead, and others I don't."

"You're under stress. It makes sense."

"I've lived with stress since I was twelve. 'This too shall pass,' as my mother used to say."

"Don't dismiss the stress that goes along with a divorce. I've handled a dozen in the last year, and even the best ones are tough."

"We were barely married. It hardly counts, right?"

"They all count."

"Why do you handle so many divorces?"

"The firm needs billable hours. It's going to take time and more experience to earn the respect of Dad's old clients. Some stayed out of loyalty to Dad, most left, but a few of those are returning."

"I liked your dad. Very cool guy."

"You knew Dad?"

"He helped me get custody of Eve when Mom was dying. I wasn't eighteen, so he took custody of Eve and me until my birthday."

Faint lines flickered on his smooth face. "I didn't know that."

"You have a lot to live up to," I said.

A humorless smile tipped the edge of his lips.

"I know."

"Family, right?"

Spencer had rarely spoken about his family to me. I'd met Barbara and Frank, but I really knew little about them. I'd tried to get Spencer to talk several times about his parents, but he always deflected or would say, "Dad's just slowing down. Mom's too busy to meet us for dinner. It's just time I learned the business."

It was tempting to tease a little Stockton family information out of Brad, but that would suggest I cared. And I didn't. As much as I'd never wish Spencer ill, I didn't need any more attachments to his family.

"Do you always get up this early?" I asked.

"It's supposed to be nice weather this afternoon. I'm going to leave a little early and play a round of golf with Spencer."

"He as good as I think?"

"Better." He peered over his cup. He hadn't forgotten he was talking to Eve's sister, just as I hadn't forgotten I was talking to Spencer's attorney.

I smiled. "We never played."

He rolled his head from side to side. "I should get to the office."

I held up my cup. "The divorce factory doesn't tolerate slackers."

Brad grimaced. "Harsh."

"The kind of work that will eat at your soul, man."

A half smile tugged his lips. "You a psychologist now?"

"No, but I spent a day with a reiki master in Breckenridge, Colorado. I was seeking peace and clearing of my chakras." I circled my hand above my chest. "My heart chakra was very faint. No surprise."

"And now?"

"I'd need to ask the master."

"In Colorado."

"I would say so. Stands to reason you'd stick with the same reiki master so you get consistent results. Like using the same bathroom scale." I drew in a breath. "The big takeaway is that peace is a journey, not a destination, or so I was told. It's like a butterfly that flits in and out of our lives. Some energies attract the butterfly, and others chase it away. The trick is to notice when those fluttering wings appear because the butterfly never lingers very long."

Brad shook his head. "I'll keep that in mind."

As he reached for his briefcase, I felt a need to bolster Eve. "Eve is the bravest of the Hanover women. I'm a grinder, and so was Mom. Nose to the grindstone. We focus on work, but we weren't the risk-takers. But Eve knew from day one she was going to swing for the fences. She needed a world beyond the pizza shop and our two-bedroom apartment, and she wasn't afraid to tell everyone about her dream. I was always jealous of that."

"She was able to chase that dream because of you."

"Many kids get family support and don't go anywhere. I'm guessing your dad helped you."

"It was easy for him. You took hard hits and kept putting one foot in front of the other. Hats off to you."

There was a tension in his face I couldn't identify. Maybe seeing me was tangible proof that Eve really wasn't from the world she'd carefully curated. "Thanks."

He paused at the doorway. "Take the money Spencer is offering. There are no strings attached. The postnuptial agreement was his mother's idea and mine. I drew it up and pushed him to include it in the paperwork. It's off the table now."

"Spencer is a big boy, Brad. He could've said no to putting it on the table."

A frown knotted his brow. "He wants to make it right for you."

"I don't think he can."

"He lost a child too."

Mention of the baby felt like a strike to my face. My throat clogged with unshed tears. "On that note, Brad, go to work."

"I didn't mean to—"

"I know. Just go."

He hesitated, nodded, and left.

When the front door closed, I sank onto a barstool and laid my head on the island. Tears filled my eyes and spilled down my cheeks.

"Olympia?" Eve asked.

I sat up, swiped my damp cheeks, and smiled. "Good morning."

"Morning." Eve's blue silk robe fluttered around her as she moved toward the coffee maker. She eyed me. "You okay?"

"I'm terrific." I found a lopsided grin.

"You look upset."

"I'm fine."

Eve's eyes narrowed. "What were you and Brad talking about?"

"Just shooting the shit," I said. "We barely know each other, and so we were just chatting."

"Why are you upset?"

I wanted to make a joke but wasn't quick enough this morning. Instead, I poured her a coffee, splashed in oat milk, and handed it to her. "I'm not. Really."

"If I had a nickel for all the times I saw that pained smile on your face."

"Hey, it's a smile. Better than the alternative."

"Not if it's fake."

I'd been faking for so much of my life, I didn't know what genuine looked like. "Tears don't fix anything. So, I choose to keep grinding, even if I look like the Joker."

"It's sad."

"It's worked. You're thriving. I'm still standing."

"How much money did Spencer offer you?"

I arched a brow. "You do know about the check."

She shrugged. "I overheard Brad. He didn't tell me."

Mom and I had always been careful when we were having a difficult conversation, knowing Eve always lurked close. "It doesn't matter. I didn't take it."

"Why not?" Eve set her cup down and stood in front of me. "The family has more money than anyone can spend in a lifetime. It wouldn't be a bad thing if you had a little bit of something for yourself."

"I'm not taking the money." My tone punctuated each word. "I can take care of myself."

"It doesn't always have to be so hard, Olympia. Not anymore."

"It'll always be hard," I said. "That's the nature of life."

"God, you sound so much like Mom. I loved Mom, but she gave up her dreams long before she got sick."

"She did her share of dreaming."

"That was all for you. She wanted you to dream, so she pretended she still had a few."

"That's not true."

"Think back to all your travel conversations. She never decided on a location unless you approved it."

I thought back to the piles of periodicals that would sit on the kitchen table untouched until Mom suggested I look through them with her.

"Don't roll over. Make life your bitch, Olympia."

That teased a smile. "I thought that's what I've been doing."

"You completed the bucket list you made with Mom. But now it's time to write your own list. It's time to start living for your own dreams."

I was trying to, but breaking old habits still wasn't easy. "I will."

She leaned forward. "Find your dream, Olympia. And use Spencer's money to get yourself moving."

CHAPTER FIFTEEN
SPENCER

Wednesday, October 30, 2024, 5:00 a.m.

"Dad, where are you going?" Spencer rose from his bed when he heard his father's heavy footsteps in the hallway.

He switched on the light, and when he opened his door, his father's expression shifted from intense to startled. He wore his pajamas and overcoat. "Spencer. What are you doing up right now?"

His father had taken to wandering at night, and both his mother and he now slept with one eye open. He'd spoken to his mother about hiring help, but she'd refused because she was determined to handle this within the family.

"I've never been a good sleeper." Spencer stepped out of his bedroom and nodded toward the keys in his father's hand. "Where are you going?"

Dad tightened his hand around the keys as if reaching for his reason why. Had he forgotten he'd lost his driver's license last year? "I thought I'd go for a drive."

"Where are you going?" Amazingly, Spencer was utterly calm.

His father looked baffled and annoyed. "Just out for a drive. I like driving."

"You have to be going somewhere."

His father's brow furrowed. "Do I need an answer to justify why I want to take *my* car out for a spin?"

"Where are you going, Dad?"

"The Mountain House, if you must know. I used to go there a lot as a kid. It occurred to me that I haven't been there in years."

"The Mountain House? That burned decades ago."

"It burned?" Worry drew his brows close. "What are you talking about? How do you know that?"

"I hiked up there last summer and saw it for myself."

"Frank?" His mother emerged from her bedroom, securing her robe as she moved. "What's going on?"

"I'm going for a drive." He looked to his wife as if she'd understand what his boneheaded son could not.

"The car is in the shop," she said calmly. "We can't pick it up until later today."

"In the shop? Why?"

His mother gently took the keys from her husband's hand. "The alternator or something like that. You know cars better than I do."

His father nodded. "The alternator. Right."

"Come back to bed," she said softly. "We'll worry about the car later."

"I want to go for a drive."

"We will once the car is fixed."

Spencer watched as his mother led his father back to their room. When the door to their bedroom closed, he tipped his head back. Energy raced through his veins as he stared at the ceiling. Realizing sleep was not going to happen, he moved into his bathroom and leaned on the sink as he stared at his reflection in the mirror. Dark circles hung under his eyes, and thick morning stubble carpeted his chin. He looked like he'd aged a decade in the last year. He dressed in his workout clothes.

The house was silent as he walked to the kitchen. He made a cup of coffee and scrolled through the news on his phone before descending to the basement gym. Before Dad got sick, he'd worked out daily. He'd always been a fitness nut and, like Spencer, was always on the go. If he wasn't running, lifting, or swimming, he was on the golf course. However, in the last year, his father hadn't used the gym once. This fucking disease didn't have the courtesy to kill his father outright. No, it had to take him one painful slice at a time. Looking back, Spencer wondered how Olympia had managed her mother while supporting her family and raising her sister.

Spencer climbed on a treadmill that angled toward the basement windows to the rolling green yard. He plugged in earbuds, cranked the music on his phone, and pressed start. He kicked up the incline, and the speed quickened until the pace was so fast that he didn't have time to think about anything else. His feet pounded the treadmill while his arms pumped hard and fast. Sweat beaded on his forehead and soaked his shirt.

After forty minutes of running, he slowed his pace to a walk. Physically, he was back. He was in the best shape of his life, and he could be on the golf circuit by spring. There'd be phone calls to make, strings to pull, and hoops to jump through, but he could get back on the tour by summer. He could, but he wouldn't.

He grabbed a towel and wiped the sweat from his face and chest. After yanking on a sweatshirt, he grabbed a putter and a few golf balls and stepped outside to the putting green his father had installed for him when he was fourteen. He dropped the ball fifteen feet from the hole and then lined the club up beside the ball. He drew back and tapped the ball. It rolled over the dewy grass, circled the hole, and landed in the cup. Pleased, he dropped a second ball. The endorphins had kicked in, and a sense of well-being flowed through him as he practiced his putting for the next hour. This was the golden hour, and for these sixty minutes, he felt like himself.

After he'd sunk the last, then gathered up his balls, wiped down his club, and returned it to his golf bag, he climbed the stairs toward the kitchen, where he heard his parents talking. It was almost seven.

"Frank, you look quite handsome in blue." His mother's cheerful tone sounded forced and heavy with fatigue.

"Thank you, dear." His father's tone was light, as if his unexpected attempt at a morning drive had been forgotten.

"Remember when we met? You were wearing a blue shirt very much like this one." She played memory games these days. Most of her questions dipped into the safe waters of the distant past because anything new was too fragile.

"We met on campus," Dad said. "You were teaching English, and I was there inspecting the stones the quarry had delivered. You were wearing pink."

She chuckled. "You remembered."

"How could I forget the day I met my best girl." His old man sounded smooth, as if he were still at the top of his game.

When Spencer was a kid, whenever he was around, his parents rarely showed affection to one another. There were polite kisses on the cheek and subtle smiles, but they never held hands, hugged, or gushed flowery words. However, the connection humming between them had been as stable as bedrock and had been the foundation for all their lives.

He'd wanted that for his daughter. Olympia and he had both wanted to build a solid marriage that would give their child the gift of a stable family. Yeah, they'd had their differences, but when it came to their child, they were a united front.

Spencer cleared his throat, giving them a subtle warning of his approach. When he entered the room, they were sitting at the kitchen table, both dressed for the day. Dad was reading the paper's sports section, and Mom was frowning at the political page.

This moment had played out a million times over his life, and he'd always thought it would last forever.

Spencer sat at the table and poured coffee. "You two look ready to tackle the day."

His father touched his red tie, which his wife now tied for him each morning. "Fall's my favorite time of year."

"I love it too."

"I saw you out on the putting green," Dad said. "Glad to see it's getting used. You're always talking about how much you love golf, but you never know with kids."

"I use it every day, Dad."

"Good to hear."

"Spencer, what do you have planned this morning?" his mother asked.

"I'm headed to the lake near the Stone Cottage. Eve is bringing several students from the school to look at the lake. The drought has revealed an artifact."

"What artifact?" she asked.

"Apparently it's a stone that was left on the dry lake bed during the last big drought, in 1982," he said.

"How did Eve find it?" Mom asked.

"She didn't. Olympia did." He braced. "I let her stay in the Stone Cottage the night of Eve and Brad's party. Olympia found the stone while she was hiking the next morning."

"A stone?" his dad said.

Before Spencer could answer, his mom set her fork down carefully on the side of her plate. "Do you think it was wise to let Olympia stay at the cottage?"

"Better than her staying in her van."

"She's been doing that for the last year." Her sharpening tone caught her husband's ear, and he looked up.

"Temperatures were in the low thirties on Saturday night," Spencer said.

His mother drew in a deep, slow breath. "The sooner you two sign the divorce papers, the better. There's no way a poor girl like her couldn't have been influenced by your money."

"You're wrong, Mom."

"Then why did she leave you?"

Rising to Olympia's defense came naturally. "She'd just lost our daughter. She was in pain, and I didn't handle it all that well."

"Because you were grieving too," she said quietly. "We all were. The difference is that you didn't run away. You stayed."

But he'd wanted to run away. Several times—especially after his own sense of abandonment was so sharp that he could barely breathe—he'd packed his suitcase and loaded it in his car. "She didn't run away."

"Will Olympia be at the pond?" she asked.

"She arranged the meeting but didn't say anything about joining the kids."

"If I had to put money on it . . ." She let her words trail off.

"I'd like to come to the lake and see this artifact," his dad said suddenly.

His father had wanted to drive to the Mountain House two hours ago, and the lake was less than a half mile away from it. "We won't be going to the Mountain House."

"Why would I want to go there?" his dad said.

Spencer had stopped reminding him of what he'd forgotten.

"It's a pretty day for a drive," his dad said.

"Why would you want to do that?" his mom asked.

"Why not?" he countered.

"Sure, Dad," Spencer said. "It's a beautiful morning. I'll be leaving at ten."

"Are you sure you're up to it, Frank?"

He waved away her worried expression. "I'm not gone yet, Barbara."

Her face paled. "Of course you're not."

"Then don't baby me," he said.

A slight grin tugged at Spencer's lips. He liked seeing the fire flicker in his father's eyes. Most days it was dim, as it had been early this morning. But sometimes, his dad's brain cranked the pilot light's knob and he returned to them.

"Dad, you know anything about the stone?" He wished he'd paid closer attention to the image Olympia had shown him. "Apparently, there's some kind of saying on it."

"There was an artist in the valley about forty years ago," his dad said. "She left stones everywhere she could. Said she was sending a message to her future self."

"Why would she do that?" Spencer asked.

"I have no idea. When I was a young man, all I wanted to do was get laid and make money."

His mom coughed.

Spencer smothered a smile. "What would you have said to your future self?"

"Stay hard."

Spencer laughed. One of the more refreshing things about his father's thinning filters was the pure honesty. And after a lifetime of his father's silences, Spencer enjoyed the candor.

"Classic."

His mom cleared her throat. "Gentlemen."

His dad winked at his wife.

"I'm a little curious about the stone," Spencer said.

"And Olympia," his dad said. "I'd like to see Olympia."

"I don't know if she'll be there, Dad," Spencer said.

"Bet she will," he said. "That lady always had a curious mind."

"Why do you say that?" Spencer asked.

"She was fascinated by my travel pictures in the study. Asked me dozens of questions about what I liked best about each place." A frown furrowed his brow. "I didn't share too many answers."

"Why not?" Spencer asked.

"Because I didn't think she'd last, son. Not your type, from what I could see."

His father was right. Spencer had a type, as Brad had once said. Blonde. Easygoing. No big life plans. Enjoyed the finer things. Caroline.

When he married Olympia, he couldn't have married a woman further from his ideal. She was intense, driven, a scrapper, and hungry for life.

Spencer checked his watch. "I need to jump into the shower and then get dressed. I have a few emails to wade through, but I'll be ready to leave at ten."

His mom raised a brow. "Don't you want breakfast?"

"I'll make a protein shake after I shower."

"That's not breakfast, son," she said.

"It does the trick, Mom." He'd maintained the workouts, the nutrition regime, and, of course, playing golf, all in the hopes that a miracle would strike, and he could get his life back.

"There's fresh fruit and spinach in the refrigerator," Mom said.

"Stop babying the boy," his dad said. "He's a grown man."

Spencer kissed his mother on the cheek. "Thanks, Mom."

His father's mind hovered in a no-man's-land that bordered on both clarity and oblivion. But for right now, they were enjoying a rare normal day. Most of the dots were connecting, and Spencer was not going to squander these hours.

@ThePizzaTraveler

Bozeman, Montana
Mundane. Boring. Everyday. Yes, more please.

Once upon a time, there was a woman who hated
her daily routine. She got on the open road, stopped
looking in the rearview mirror, and began the work of
reinventing her life. Mingled among her old posses-
sions now are the spoils of her new travels: a Hank's
Barbecue mug, rocks from her travels, fly fishing
gear, and jerky. This new life isn't perfect, but it's all
hers, and she kind of likes it.

#MEMORIES #FAVORITETHINGS #LOVESTORIES

CHAPTER SIXTEEN
OLYMPIA

Wednesday, October 30, 2024, 11:00 a.m.

I followed Eve's white school utility van up the winding driveway toward the barn where the party had been held and around it toward the cottage.

There were four kids in the van with Eve. I hadn't spoken to any of them because when I'd arrived at the school, they were already loaded on board. Suited me just fine. I wasn't up for a lot of chatter.

The van rumbled over the gravel road that wound toward the Stone Cottage. Eve parked and shut off the engine. If you'd asked me eight years ago if I'd ever see Eve driving a school van full of kids on a science field trip, I'd have laughed. Eight years ago, I was the one driving Eve and her buddies to the mall or picking them up from a school field trip.

Today, I was nosing my van in beside the bus she'd driven.

The kids piled out, and Eve gathered them around and introduced each one. First was Mark, tall and muscled, sixteen and a basketball player. Then came Jeff, lean, with glasses and a thick crop of mousy-brown hair. Next there was Kathy, who had long auburn hair and wore faded jeans and a new Tech sweatshirt. And finally, Sarah, Spencer's relative, my dessert-sharing buddy at the party.

"Hey," I said to Sarah. "You enjoy the party?"

"Not bad," Sarah said. "A lot of old people, but the chocolate cake rocked."

I laughed. "Sounds about right."

"I've started planning my around-the-world trip. I think my first stop is Marrakech."

"Bold. I like it."

"Mom smiles when I tell her my plans, but it's the kind of grin that tells me she's not serious."

"My van is here. Want the grand tour?"

"Yeah!"

I looked at all the kids. "Anyone else want to see my traveling van?"

Eve faced the other three students. "Everyone, this is my sister, Olympia. She's the one that found the stone."

"I want to see the van," Mark said.

I led the group to the van and opened the side door. My futon was arranged like a couch, and my neatly folded comforter was draped over the back. The curtains were open, and the books, pots, pans, and clothes all tucked in their bins.

Sarah leaned past me. "This is so cool."

"Do you really live here?" Mark asked.

"For the last year," I said.

Kathy wrinkled her nose. "It doesn't look very comfortable."

"More comfortable than you'd think," I said.

"Don't you feel cramped?" Jeff asked.

"When the weather is bad," I said. "But on a beautiful morning, I open the van door and get a ringside seat of the latest view."

"Enough of the tour," Eve said. "I have to have the school van back by one."

I closed the side door. "I hope everyone's ready to do some hiking. The lake is not super far, but finding it will require some walking."

Heads nodded as they all glanced at their shoes, a collection of sneakers not designed for hiking, but on a dry day like today, they would work.

"Is Spencer coming?" Eve asked.

"I don't know. We just left it that you could have access." I checked my phone but didn't see a message from Spencer. Was I disappointed? Relieved? "We'll see."

As I hoisted my backpack on my shoulder, a dark Mercedes rolled up. Tension rippled down my spine as Spencer and then his father, Frank, got out of the car. Frank looked thinner than I remembered, but his shoulders were straight. He and Spencer resembled each other so much. Frank was a snapshot of Spencer forty years from now.

Forty years. Where would I be in four decades? Still traveling the country or the world, a wandering spirit with no home, ties, spouse, or children? Or would I be working at Tony's, still slinging pizza, just as my mother had done until she was too sick to work? Both scenarios were deeply unsettling.

Sarah approached me. "You found this rock?"

I drew in a deep breath. "I did. The morning after the party."

Sarah looked toward the path in the woods. "What were you doing up here? Were you just walking around?"

The kid must've known my history with Spencer, and she was fishing for details. "Basically. You like science?"

"It's okay," Sarah said. "I mean, I won't get rich as a scientist, but I like it okay. And maybe I can travel the world as a visiting zoologist or marine biologist."

This kid had terrific dreams, and I was jealous. Marine biologist versus aging Pizza Traveler. I needed to up my game.

As Spencer and Frank approached, Sarah smiled. "Hey, Spencer, Mr. Stockton."

The tension in Spencer's face faded into a smile. "Sarah. Not surprised to see you here. Your mom tells me you're making straight As."

Sarah shrugged. "It's easy. No big deal."

"Said no C-minus student ever," I said.

Frank stepped past Spencer and wrapped his arms around me, hugging me closely, as if we were old friends. At first, I stiffened and resisted the contact, astounded that the man who'd barely acknowledged my presence last year was now holding me so close. Still, almost against my will, I melted into his embrace, which smelled of citrus aftershave and mints. His muscle mass had softened, and his bones felt fragile.

In the few months I'd known Frank, he had never said much, even when I'd quizzed him about his travels. He and Barbara had included Spencer and me in a couple of Sunday family dinners after we were married, but to say those meals had been easygoing and friendly would be a stretch. As a parentless kid, I wasn't naive enough to think Frank and Barbara would take my parents' place, but I'd hoped they might fill a small part of that void. But they'd both been so aloof. Cool politeness. No warm welcomes. And then the baby was gone, and my "family" completely crumbled.

"You're looking well, my girl," Frank said.

I drew back, wondering why a simple hug and a few kind words would make me emotional. My throat clogged with tears that I cleared with a cough. "Thank you. You look as handsome as ever, Mr. Stockton."

"Mr. Stockton? When did we become so formal?" he asked.

"Like, forever."

"You must call me Frank."

Frank stuck to the tip of my tongue, and it took effort to knock it free. "Frank."

"That's more like it," he said, grinning.

"How is Barbara?" I half expected a lightning bolt to strike me down at the mention of my mother-in-law's first name.

"Got to stay on my toes to keep my bride happy," Frank joked. "Hasn't changed a bit. She's a rock."

I felt Spencer's attention and shifted toward him. He wore worn jeans, a faded black pullover sweater, and hiking boots, which didn't quite jibe with the neatly combed hair and his freshly shaved face. The cost of his casual outfit topped what I'd earned in a month. The Stocktons had always been formal, and even when they kicked back and did things like hike, they really didn't relax. I couldn't remember a day I'd seen Spencer unshaven.

As Sylvia once said as she was folding up one of her dresses, "Money talks. Wealth whispers."

It was nice that Spencer had brought Frank, but why? Spencer had barely listened when I'd tried to show him the pictures of the stone on Sunday.

"Spencer." I was on Spencer's land, his turf, but his presence felt like an intrusion.

"Olympia."

Eve nudged her kids toward the path. "Thank you for having us. This is very generous."

Frank grinned. "Happy to help shape young minds."

Eve's smile hinted at confusion. "Olympia, ready to lead our parade?"

"Sure." I shifted my attention to the kids and the path that led them into the woods. "I'll go first, and the kids can follow."

"We're joining you," Spencer said. "Dad wants to see the stone."

"The more, the merrier," I said.

Without glancing back, I took off toward the path, as if I'd hiked this trail a million times. I was sure where I was going, but when I reached the fork, I hesitated. An energy pulled me left, toward the Mountain House. Crazy. I'd just been there. The kids slowed behind me.

"It's to the right." Spencer's voice coasted over the kids' heads.

I didn't look back but took the right path. A breeze drifted through the woods, cooling my flushed cheeks. My feet crunched against dried leaves and brittle twigs as I kept going. I rounded a final bend, the woods opened, and the lake appeared before me. I paused at the dried bank that ringed the entire lake.

The lake was as low as it had been on Sunday. The dock dipped toward the mud and tilted slightly to the right. When Spencer and I had walked this path last July, the lake had been full of glistening water, and two floating kayaks were tied to the dock. It was a hot day, and the scene was so inviting we'd gone skinny dipping.

"It hasn't been this dry in a long time," Frank said. "I heard about the low rainfall, but seeing so little water now brings it home."

Eve stood beside me and shaded her eyes from the sun as she surveyed the lake. "What are the chances that you'd end up here when you did?"

"Slim to none," I said. "Do you see the stone?"

Eve pointed. "There?"

"Yes. The lake bed looks dry, but it's very muddy," I said.

"The kids are all wearing shoes that can get dirty," Eve said. "I made sure their parents understood this could be a one-way trip for the shoes."

"Good." I stepped onto the mud, and my foot sank deeper than it had the day before. As I pulled my foot up, the motion created a sucking sound, and the mud tugged at my boot. I wobbled a little and nearly toppled forward. "Everyone, watch your step."

"Move slowly," Spencer said. "There could be places where the bottom sinks farther than you think."

"Like quicksand?" Mark asked.

"Not quite that bad. But I don't want anyone twisting an ankle," Spencer said.

I kept moving forward, my feet sinking, the mud sucking as I pulled up. Sarah was behind me, trudging and slogging forward. When I reached the stone and looked back, the other students had ventured into the mud, but Eve and Frank remained onshore. Eve was talking to him, chatting easily, as she always did with everyone. A flicker of movement caught my attention, and I realized Spencer was almost shoulder to shoulder with me.

He knelt by the stone. "This is it?"

"My big discovery," I said as the kids gathered around.

"'Tomorrow, I do.' What does that mean?" Sarah asked.

"What do you think it means?" I asked.

"I guess don't wait until tomorrow to try stuff," Kathy said.

"That sounds pretty good," I said. "Tomorrow is not guaranteed. So, if you're saying you'll do something tomorrow, it might not get done."

"Then shouldn't there be a question mark and not a period?" Kathy asked.

"The carver is leaving it up to you to decide," Spencer said.

"That's profound," Sarah said.

He shrugged. "I have my moments."

"Any ideas on who carved it?" I asked Spencer.

"None," he said.

"According to Eve, there are two others like it," I said. "All have the same date, an angel, but different sayings."

"A poet and an artist." Spencer swiped the mud off the angel's wings. "It takes real skill to carve such fine points into stone. Whoever made this was talented."

"Frank would know the stonemasons in the valley thirty or forty years ago," I said. "Would he know about this artist?"

"Dad said there were several, and he mentioned one was a woman."

"A woman?" I asked. "That is unusual."

"It is. Frank might not have answers off the top of his head about the older stonemasons, but I know a few working now, and I can reach out and ask."

"That would be cool," Sarah said.

"Should I remove the stone?" Spencer asked. "We've got a good bit of rain headed our way soon. It'll likely be covered with water in the next couple of weeks."

Kathy looked at Sarah, and both girls shook their heads. The boys shrugged.

"If we leave it," Sarah said, "it won't be seen for a long time, right?"

"Correct. It could be another twenty years or more," Spencer said. "If I remove it and put it in the garden by the Stone Cottage, it can be seen and studied anytime."

"Then it won't be special," Kathy said. "People might notice it at first, but then they won't see it at all. It'll become invisible again."

"All those in favor of leaving it, raise your hand," I asked.

Each child raised a hand.

"The group has decided," Spencer said. "No need to remove the stone. But my offer to move it stands until the rains come."

"Olympia, do you always find weird stuff like this?" Sarah asked.

"It's my superpower," I said.

CHAPTER SEVENTEEN
SPENCER

Wednesday, October 30, 2024, 12:30 p.m.

Spencer followed Olympia and the kids across the muck and mud and was the last to reach the shore. He hadn't expected to enjoy himself. In fact, on the drive over, he'd dreaded all this. But he liked being out here with Olympia, his father, and the kids. Even Eve, who was usually selling cheer and happiness, had added interesting content on the average rainfall in 1982 versus 2024 (twenty inches then versus nineteen inches now).

This day was all Olympia's doing. She'd created this moment. She could do that. When they'd met, she'd brought laughter and wonder into his world.

When he reached the shore, Dad laughed when he saw the mud covering everyone's feet and pant cuffs. "You're all a sight to see."

When was the last time Spencer had heard his father laugh? He couldn't remember.

Sarah showed her pictures to his dad. "Do you know who could have carved this? Spencer thinks the carver might be a woman."

His father studied the picture closely. For an instant, recognition seemed to flicker, but just as quickly it vanished. "I don't know. But there's a stonemason at the plant. Henry Bradshaw. He might know. That guy has forgotten more about stone than I ever knew."

Eve scribbled down the name. "Thank you, Mr. Stockton. Would you mind if I called him?"

"I'll call him," his dad said. "He knows me and is more likely to talk."

"Thank you." Eve pulled out her phone. "I need a group picture. Education in action. Come on, everyone, gather around and let me snap a picture."

Spencer and his dad stood behind the kids as Olympia moved to his dad's side. His father wrapped his arm around Olympia and tugged her toward him. She glanced up at him, her eyes wide. Her body remained stiff and her smile a little fixed, but she didn't pull away.

Eve handed her phone to Spencer. "You have the longest arms and are the tallest. Do you mind taking the picture?"

"Not at all." He took the phone and held out his arm, Eve squeezed in, and the kids, his father, and Olympia smiled. He snapped several pictures and handed the phone back to Eve.

Eve quickly typed into her phone, and his phone, along with Olympia's, dinged with texts. "Kids, we've got to get going. I need to return the van."

"It's been fun, kids," Dad said. "Come back anytime you want."

Eve's smile was saleswoman bright. "Thank you for having us, Mr. Stockton."

"My pleasure."

As the kids moved toward the car, Olympia followed.

"Olympia, do you have to leave?" his dad asked.

She turned, not hiding her shock. "Me?"

"Yes, you," he said, chuckling. "Unless there's another Olympia in the group."

"Just me," she said.

"I know Spencer would like you to join us for lunch."

Olympia glanced toward Spencer as if waiting for the excuse that would nip it all in the bud. "I don't know about that, Frank."

Spencer had spent the last year giving her an out. He'd given her space. Allowed her to avoid all things uncomfortable. Suddenly, all that fruitless patience annoyed him. Today, there'd be no easy excuses. "We'd love to have you."

"Does your mom know I'm coming?" she asked. "Probably not a good idea to surprise Barbara."

"She'll be fine," he said. "I know she's missed you."

Olympia navigated the next few seconds with two deep breaths. "Spencer, should you call your mother and give her a heads-up?"

He'd been tiptoeing around his mother for over a year. "She'll adapt."

Olympia shook her head. "Playing with fire, boys."

"You afraid?" Spencer asked.

She drew in a deep breath, straightening her shoulders. "Nope."

"Great. You know the way, right?"

"I do."

"See you in a few."

"Right," Olympia said.

"Excellent, it'll be fun," Dad said.

Spencer guided his father toward the car, half expecting Olympia to get in her van and drive as far away from his parents' house as she could get. Odds were fifty-fifty she'd show for lunch.

@ThePizzaTraveler

Jackson Hole, Wyoming
Hagstones, roadside venders, magic.

The folding card table was set up on a street corner near a cowboy-themed bar. It's high season.
Lots of snow and skiers. The crowds pass by an old
woman with the stone display but don't notice her.
The woman has a rich brown face, lined with five or
six decades in the sun.

I cannot resist stones. I have a box full of rocky sou-
venirs in the van that are the bridge between my past
and present.

My gaze skips the polished stones and settles on
a small box filled with unfinished rocks riddled with
holes. I pick one and ask how much if I pay cash.
Twenty bucks, she says. Steep for a rock, but I
pay up.

"They are called hagstones. They ward off spirits," the old woman said.

"Good, maybe the demon in the back seat and the other riding shotgun will find a new ride."

#MAGIC #HAGSTONE #MOREGHOSTS

CHAPTER EIGHTEEN
OLYMPIA

Wednesday, October 30, 2024, 1:15 p.m.

I took my time driving. Halfway to the Stockton house, where the lone country road intersected a bigger secondary road, I took a left, knowing I needed to take a right. Yep, the idea of having lunch with Barbara, Spencer, and Frank was alternate-universe territory.

Frank's invitation had been heartfelt, but did I really need to mingle with the Stocktons now? Maybe in five years, after all the emotions had cooled.

I drove for a good five minutes past the rolling green farmland before second thoughts called me every version of coward. My annoyance grew. With no food poisoning or busted engine hose to redirect me, there was nothing stopping me but me.

Why was I running from Barbara?

What had I done wrong?

What would a lunch hurt?

And Frank had asked me. I'd known from the moment I hugged him that he was sick. If Frank was ill, I could at least sit down with his son and wife and break bread. No, I didn't owe him anything, but I wasn't so far gone that I couldn't be kind.

I turned my van around.

When I pulled up into the Stocktons' stone circular driveway, I parked behind Spencer's black sedan.

The gray stone house, reminiscent of a medieval fortress, stood silent. Unwelcoming. The first time I'd seen it, I joked about watchtowers, moats, and dungeons. Spencer had promised me the dragons were in their crates.

Forest green shutters flanked each of the twelve windows on the first and second floors. The glittering glass softened the facade and reflected sunlight. A large wreath on the front door celebrated the fall season with bright oranges, yellows, and hints of green leaves. Planters by the door burst with trimmed boxwoods and winter pansies. Barbara's *Architectural Digest*–ready home always looked inviting to the layman.

But looks could be deceiving.

Frank's friendly smile and invitation, and Spencer's acceptance of this, was all just a little too easy. I wasn't sure why I was here. Who was opening the dungeon-cell door?

Call it stubbornness or morbid curiosity, but I wanted to see this house one last time. I wanted to look Barbara in the eye and see her reaction to me. I almost hoped the woman would be rude. Nothing like a good old trailer park fight to work out the excess tension.

I swapped my muddy hiking boots for my white Converse shoes and glanced in the side mirror. Smoothing flat strands of flyaway hair, I pursed my lips several times, hoping to add a little color. Finally, accepting that I wasn't going to flee, like a sane person should, I climbed the steps and rang the bell. Determined footsteps clicked inside the house toward the front door. I wanted Spencer to answer it, but his feet rarely struck any floor with that kind of pointed intensity.

The door opened to Barbara. She was dressed in black slacks, a white silk top, and pointed kitten heels. Her salt-and-pepper hair was styled back in a sleek ponytail accentuating lips painted a bright red and diamond studs winking from her ears. "Olympia."

"Barbara."

"Spencer said you were joining us for lunch. The boys have been here fifteen minutes. Did you get lost?"

I adjusted my backpack on my shoulder and ignored the question. "I know Frank's invitation was spontaneous, so I'd understand if you don't want me here for lunch."

"Nonsense," she said, smiling. "It'll be nice to catch up."

"With me?"

"Yes, of course you."

"This is too easy, Barbara. Are you going to poison my soup?"

A delicate brow arched. "As you said, the invitation was spontaneous. There was no time to mix up the right poison, so you're safe today." She stepped aside and motioned me forward.

My mother-in-law wasn't known for a biting sense of humor. Barbara made polite conversation about the weather or the latest Virginia Tech football game and did not drop suggestions of homicide.

I stepped inside, greeted by a warm burst of air, black-and-white-tiled flooring, and a circular iron chandelier with eight electric candles.

"You've lost weight," Barbara said.

This was a compliment, right? "No more twenty-four-seven access to Tony's pizza will do that."

"Whenever I travel, I gain at least five pounds."

Doubtful. But the stony silence had dropped, and she was making small talk. "I learned pretty quickly to cook for myself on the road."

Nodding, she kept moving down a long center hallway toward a kitchen at the back of the house. "It was nice of you to make Frank feel so welcome at the lake."

"Of course. Why wouldn't I?"

"As you said, it's been a rough year."

"Is Frank okay?" I asked.

Barbara didn't break stride. "Why would you ask?"

"Just a feeling."

She met my gaze. "He's fine. Nothing to worry about."

I'd noticed that whenever people went out of their way to make a point, they often made the opposite one. Translation: Frank was sick. It explained his slighter frame and less stern manner. "Okay. Good."

We entered the glittering kitchen outfitted with a bank of windows overlooking the rolling mountains in the background. A large round table displayed four place settings. No sign of Spencer or Frank.

"Can I get you something to drink?" Barbara asked. "Still like seltzer water and lime?"

"I do, thank you." I lowered my backpack to the floor, feeling certain I'd be leaving behind a trail of dust on the clean floor.

"Frank tells me you found a stone in the lake." Barbara sliced a lime into quarters with a very sharp blade. She ruthlessly squeezed every drop of juice into a glass filled with ice.

"I saw it on Sunday morning when I was hiking."

"Hiking up here? That's right. Spencer let you stay at the cottage." Ice clinked in the glass. "That was nice of him, wasn't it?"

There was a hint of a bite. "It really was. Eve had overbooked her home, so no room for me at the inn."

"New brides. They can be very scattered." Seltzer fizzled in the glass as she poured it over cubed ice. "Though you were not. You were very focused."

"Unfocused has never been an option for me." I accepted the glass and sipped my seltzer, enjoying the bubbles and lime.

"No, I suppose not." Barbara poured herself a glass of white wine. "I admired how you cared for your family all by yourself."

I swallowed wrong and coughed. "You admired something about me?"

"Stranger things, right?" Barbara sipped her wine.

Frank was now friendly and talkative, and Barbara had developed a cutting sense of humor. "It's backwards day, isn't it?"

Barbara took a longer sip of wine. "It does feel like it, doesn't it?"

Heavy footsteps sounded in the side hallway seconds before Spencer and Frank appeared. Spencer had swapped his muddy pants and shoes for clean jeans, a flannel shirt, and Docksiders.

Barbara poured sodas for her son and husband. "Boys, have a seat at the table."

Frank kissed his wife on the cheek, and she closed her eyes and, for a second, relaxed into his touch. Say what you want about Barbara, but she loved her husband. I shrugged off a twinge of jealousy.

"Olympia, you sit in the chair across from the window. Spencer, you're across from Olympia," Barbara said. "Frank, you're at the head of the table."

"Mom, can I help with anything?" Spencer asked.

"That's sweet, honey, but entertain your guest." How many nouns would Barbara work through before she was forced to call me Spencer's wife?

Spencer sat across from me, smiled briefly, and then took a long drink of soda, as if he was calculating how long this lunch would last. Would this meal end before one of us triggered an argument? I could almost hear the clock ticking in his head.

I glanced to my left. It felt empty, as if a highchair should've been there. In an alternate universe, we'd all be sitting here with Adelaide in that highchair. Barbara would be combing out the tangles from Adelaide's black hair and reaffixing the pink bow her girl had pulled out. Adelaide would pull it out again, and Barbara would put it back in. It would become a game, and we'd all end up laughing about it.

But we weren't in that world. We were in this one, with all its brokenness and flaws.

"I was thinking about your stone, and who could have made it," Frank said.

"He called Henry Bradshaw, but the stone was before his time," Spencer said.

"My father got to know several stonemasons when he was having the addition put on this house," Frank said.

"That was the early eighties, right?" Spencer asked.

"That's right. The summer after I graduated college."

"1982, right?" Spencer asked.

"That's right," Frank said.

"Mom, did you see the house before the addition?" Spencer asked.

"It was all before my time," Barbara said. "I didn't meet your father until he was twenty-five."

"How big was the addition?" I asked. If I handled it right, we could all milk this discussion on the stones for the entire lunch.

"Five thousand square feet," Spencer said. "Basically, the back portion of the house."

The apartment I'd shared with my mother and sister had hovered around one thousand square feet. "Impressive."

"That was a bold move," Spencer said. "I've been reviewing the company's books, and the economy took a big downturn about 1982. Times were tough for us."

"Dad and my older brother, Robert, wanted to keep the company men working," Frank said. "He hated the idea of layoffs. Probably the main reason he decided to build the addition. I don't think he planned on it being so big."

"Was there a woman working on the project?" I asked. "You said something about a woman carving the lake stone."

"That was Adelaide," Frank said.

Barbara dropped a fork. The clang cut the thick sudden silence.

My heart stilled, and I didn't dare look at Spencer. "Adelaide?"

"That was Robert's first wife," Frank said. "He met her at the quarry."

"Dad, Uncle Robert only had one wife. Her name was Harriet," Spencer said.

A moment's confusion on Frank's face hardened to clarity. "No, his first wife was Adelaide. She was a German immigrant. Her father, Hans, was the master stonemason working on the addition project."

Barbara set a platter of meats and breads in the center of the table. I'd been hungry when I'd sat down; now, not so much.

"I remember Harriet, but we never really got a chance to know each other," Barbara said. "Frank and I had just been married when Robert and Harriet died in the car accident."

Frank grabbed two thick slices of sourdough bread before stabbing his fork into thinly sliced pieces of roast beef. "Harriet was Robert's second wife. Adelaide was his first."

"First wife?" Barbara asked. "I never heard that story from anyone."

"A bit of a family scandal," Frank said, chuckling. "I found out by accident, and my father swore me to secrecy. I suppose I've just spilled the beans. But it really doesn't matter now, does it?"

"What do you know about Adelaide?" I sounded unreasonably calm. But I liked hearing the name and wanted to know more about this mystery woman.

Frank layered cheese and mustard over the beef. "Adelaide was so beautiful it took everyone's breath away. She was impossible to ignore. First time Robert saw her, he knew they were going to marry. I admit, I had a bit of a crush on her too."

"I've seen the family Bible," Barbara said. "There's no Adelaide."

I wondered if I was in the family Bible. Somehow, I doubted it.

"Because it was a family secret," Frank said.

I reached for a slice of bread but didn't bother to load it with anything. "What did Adelaide look like?"

"Tall, with long legs. Blonde hair that skimmed her shoulders. She learned how to carve stone from her father."

When I'd gone into labor, I'd begged my Adelaide to hold on. Initially, I hadn't loved the name, but it became a talisman as I gripped my belly. Spencer kept saying modern medicine could do miracles. I'd feared differently. Medicine had conjured no miracles for my mother or my girl.

I raised my gaze to find Spencer staring at me. My voice was barely a whisper. "I always wondered why your dad suggested the name Adelaide."

"I looked it up, and it means 'gift from God.'" Spencer looked at me as if I were the only person in the room. "It made sense."

Unshed tears burned. All I could do was nod.

Barbara cleared her throat. "Your Adelaide was a gift from God. I only wish we'd been able to keep her."

I blinked as I stared at Barbara's glistening gaze. I'd been so lost in my grief it had never occurred to me that Barbara would be hurting too. Unspoken words swirled inside me, but I didn't trust myself to speak.

Spencer cleared his throat. "Dad, what can you tell us about Uncle Robert's first wife?"

"She was young when they met and was barely eighteen when they married. He said she had an independent soul. Frustrated him to no end."

"Not an easy feat in the 1980s," Barbara said. "The world has changed a lot in forty years."

"Why did she carve the stones?" I asked.

"I don't know," Frank said. "Be curious to know why she'd bother with such a silly pursuit during such difficult times."

"What happened to the girl?" Barbara asked.

"She couldn't have children. And Robert wanted children, so he divorced her."

Barbara's back straightened. "How very charming of him."

I nodded and, before I thought, said, "I already don't like him."

"He was a great guy," Frank said. "Don't be hard on him. He'd always imagined having a huge family and carrying on the Stockton name. In the end all that fell to me."

Barbara rose, took her wineglass with her, and refilled it.

I didn't know anything about Barbara and Frank's marriage, but Spencer was an only child. Maybe they'd wanted more children and couldn't have them.

"Dad," Spencer said.

"What did I say?" Frank said.

I could almost hear the snap of a third rail sparking.

"We will discuss it later," Barbara said.

Sipping my seltzer, I wondered how an old stone could trigger this kind of tension. I glanced at a clock on the wall. We'd been eating for fifteen minutes. Not bad, considering.

Barbara ate in silence, while Spencer tried to make conversation with his father about golf. Frank answered the first few questions, but his responses soon grew shorter and a little less connected.

Several times Barbara corrected his answers, suggesting he meant something else. She was gentle and careful with him, and it was clear that despite her annoyance, she was protecting him.

I hadn't really paid a lot of attention to Frank the few times we'd met last year. But now, I understood why Spencer had given up his pro golf tour and moved back to Blacksburg. It wasn't a desire to return home or to take over the family business.

The spark that had ignited our relationship came into sharper focus. Spencer was as hungry for a distraction as I was a year and a half ago. We'd both welcomed the great sex, hikes, and conversation because our own lives were adrift and lonely. A few months of sex would likely have run its course, but neither one of us counted on a pregnancy, quick marriage, or the gut punch of losing our child.

When the meal came to a merciful end, I helped Barbara clear the table. "Thank you. It was kind of you to include me."

She accepted the platter. "Looks like we both survived."

"Until the next meal?" I joked.

Barbara chuckled, but her smile faded when she looked past me. I turned as Spencer helped his father up.

"Thank you," Frank said to him. "Lovely to see you again," he said to me.

"Take care, Frank," I said.

Spencer met my gaze, and though dozens of unspoken words swirled in the gray depths, he nodded and silently left the room with his father.

I glanced at the dishes. "Let me help you."

"That's not necessary, Olympia. I have this. But thank you."

"Right. Well, I'll get going." I didn't waste words about life having a way of working itself out or rainbows after a storm. We both knew it was bullshit. I hoisted my backpack on my shoulder. "I wish you well."

"You too. You too."

As I moved toward the front door, tension pinched my chest. The Stocktons were far from perfect, but they were a unit, and I envied that. Sure, I had Eve, but Eve had a new husband and a child on the way. If I got sick, like Mom or Frank, I couldn't imagine Eve juggling her life and taking care of me.

Outside, I barely noticed the warm afternoon sun as I hurried to my van. Behind the wheel, I arrowed the vehicle down the driveway and then toward town. I wondered if TJ would let me pick up a shift today.

CHAPTER NINETEEN
SPENCER

Wednesday, October 30, 2024, 5:15 p.m.

Spencer sat in the study, staring at the flames crackling in the fireplace. As far as grand plans went—golf, his father, the baby, and now Olympia—it had all crumbled to dust.

He reached for his phone and opened Olympia's Instagram account. He'd been following her travels since the day she'd left Blacksburg. At first, her journey was anything but charmed. She joked about food poisoning from a gas station hot dog. She let the camera run on time lapse for long stretches as she drove over the flat planes of Kansas. She showed the world what it was like to bed down in the back of her van on a futon.

He scrolled down to the start of Olympia's journey and watched as her sallow complexion grew tanner and her cheeks regained their rosy glow. The light in her eyes flickered from time to time, and when she reached Wyoming this past summer, she was grinning from ear to ear when she caught a bass in the Snake River. She sat cross-legged and gutted the fish on a flat stone. Her dark hair draped over her shoulders, but one single strand kept tipping forward into her eyes. How many times had he pushed back that soft hair?

Next in the video, Olympia seasoned the fish and dropped it on a sizzling-hot cast-iron pan. He could almost smell the scents of the cooking fish, the smoke from the fire, and the fresh open air.

And then he'd heard a man's voice in the background. He must have made a joke, because her laugh was infectious. Spencer would have enjoyed that smile if not for the lurking man in the shadows.

"What the hell did you expect?" Spencer asked himself aloud. "She begged you to come. And you said no."

A knock on the study door had him turning to find his mother. She was carrying a plate of cookies. "I thought you might like a snack."

"Thanks, Mom."

She set the plate down gently on the coffee table. "Olympia looked good."

"She did."

"I'm glad. I want her to do well."

"Just not with me, right?"

Mom's frown hardened. "I didn't say that."

"You didn't have to."

"Are you telling me that you're having second thoughts about the divorce?"

He sighed. "No."

"Then what's your point?"

Spencer ran his fingers through his hair. "Is Olympia listed in the family Bible?"

Mom was silent for a moment. "No."

"Why not?"

"I don't know. You two married so quickly, and then you separated. It didn't make sense to backtrack and add her."

"We're still married, Mom."

"If you want me to add her, I will, Spencer. That's something I can fix."

He shook his head. "Never mind. I'm just having a bad day."

"Can I do anything?"

"No. But thank you."

His mother hesitated and then left, closing the door softly.

He walked to the large bookshelf and removed the family Bible resting on its side. It wasn't a lavish book but was bound in a faded black leather binding. He carried it to his father's desk, sat, and carefully opened it.

The first name was Edward Stockton, born in 1865. He'd married his wife, Grace, in 1885, and their first child was born in 1886. The child lived less than a year. The couple would have three more children before Spencer's great-grandfather, Joseph Sr., was born in 1898.

Uncle Robert's marriage to Harriet was recorded for June 1984, and their deaths were recorded three years later. But he didn't see a mention of a marriage to Adelaide. He skimmed down to his name and reached for a pen on the table. Carefully, he recorded Olympia's name and the date of their marriage. He left the end date open and closed the book.

Olympia was back in town, and he could see she'd survived, and she would find her second chance at life. She'd never been the kind of person to ask twice. She'd laid out her first offer of travel with pleading eyes, and he'd said no.

The reality was he didn't have a second chance, even if she asked him to leave with her again.

After his father's Alzheimer's diagnosis and Olympia's positive pregnancy test, he'd undergone genetic testing to determine if he had a predisposition to Alzheimer's. He'd done the test more out of due diligence to the unborn baby. He'd wanted to be certain he'd be there for her and their child.

That clean bill of health he'd expected quickly muddled when he discovered the day after the miscarriage that he carried two genes for Alzheimer's—one from his father and the other from his mother. The doctor's prognosis had been quick and cutting. He was ten times more likely to develop the disease.

So yeah, if he had a second chance with Olympia, he wouldn't act on it. The move would be totally selfish on his part because he'd be condemning her to a dim future. And he loved her too much to ever do that. Better to set her up financially. That was one thing he could fix.

@ThePizzaTraveler

Missing Demons, More Rocks, and Cowboy's Chaps
Delicate Arch, Utah

The hagstone works. The demons don't seem to like it or Utah,

so I'm free to finish the bucket list.

The Delicate Arch, a domed vaulted rock formation, has nicknames: Cowboy's Chaps, Old Maid's Bloomers, Salt Wash Arch. It's almost a two-mile hike up the rocks to the base of the arch, and cold weather has chased away most tourists. But that's okay. Seems the last stop on Mom's list should have reverence.

I've learned three things at the base of the Delicate Arch.

A: It's big, but not delicate.

B: Required all my hiking skills.

C: Mom would have loved this.

#NEWTRAILS #CELEBRATE #BUCKETLIST

CHAPTER TWENTY
OLYMPIA

Wednesday, October 30, 2024, 10:15 p.m.

Exhaustion strained my muscles as I rang up an order for three cheese pizzas, two pitchers of beer, and three colas. After leaving the Stocktons' house, I'd driven straight here, needing work to fill my brain with mindless details while exhausting my nervous energy with physical tasks.

When the lull in traffic finally came, I hunted for other chores. Sitting meant thinking, and thinking never ended well.

Bells jingled seconds before a burst of cold air rushed the open front door. I checked my watch. Tony's didn't close until eleven, and the kitchen accepted orders until 10:30 p.m., but there was always someone who skated in under the deadline.

Grabbing a couple of menus, I turned toward the late-night dinner guest and stopped midstep when I saw Caroline waiting to be seated. If Spencer were here, he'd see his past and future standing feet apart. Caroline, his future, looked neat and bright. I embodied his messy past. Message to future Spencer: it's okay to have chosen peace over chaos.

I smiled. "Dinner?"

"Yes, I'm starving."

I would never have picked Late-Night Carbs on Caroline's bingo card. Glancing around at the empty tables, I walked her to the one farthest from the door. "Does this work?"

"Perfect."

She shrugged off a pink leather jacket, draped it over a chair, and sat. I handed her a plastic-coated menu. "The kitchen takes orders for another fifteen minutes, so you're in luck."

"I've always had great timing."

That made one of us. "Can I get you something to drink?"

She flipped over the menu and scanned the drinks. "Diet Coke."

"Coming right up."

"Before you go, I'll take the personal pan pizza, thin crust. Light on the cheese, onions."

"Perfect."

I put the order in with Buddy, the evening cook, and filled up a red plastic cup with diet soda. After grabbing a straw, I set both in front of Caroline. "Pizza should be up in about ten minutes."

"Excellent." The remaining customers shrugged on jackets, waved to me, and left. "Looks like it's just us."

"I suppose."

"Why don't you sit? I would love the company."

"I'm working."

When she smiled, her nose wrinkled. "It's just us girls. I don't think anyone will mind." Her smile was genuinely warm, and I wasn't immune.

I pulled out a chair. "What's on your mind?"

Caroline sipped her soda. "Spencer."

Not a surprise, but still annoying. "Okay."

"He told me about the high school students visiting the lake today. Quite the adventure, no?"

"It was fun."

"'Tomorrow, I do.' What do you think that means?"

"'Make hay today'? 'Don't delay'? Who knows?"

"Exactly. Which is why I'm here."

"You're going to have to fill in more pieces," I said. "I'm not seeing the picture."

"Spencer and I dated in college. But I guess you know that."

"I remember."

"You do?"

"You might remember Bat Girl."

"That was you?"

I nodded.

She blushed a little and then chuckled. "I was in such shock that I didn't see past the bat. What a night. Spencer and I were both horrified."

"Me too."

"Like I said, we dated all through my sophomore year of college. We were talking about getting married. I'm not too proud to say I was buying bride magazines and ready to start shopping for dresses and venues."

"But . . ."

"He wanted to make a run at the pro golf circuit. We promised to keep in touch, set a wedding date in a year, but it didn't work out."

I shifted in my seat. "Sounds vaguely familiar."

"I know. Funny about the parallels."

Not the ha-ha kind of funny. "What's your point, Caroline?"

"I don't regret finishing college, of course. It would have been silly for me to drop out."

"If you were my sister, I wouldn't have let you."

She moved the straw up and down in the soda. "But I wish I'd tried harder to keep up with Spencer. By graduation, I wanted him to come to me. I wanted him to ask me to marry him. But he didn't, so I waited and watched us drift apart." She sipped her soda as if the confession had left her drained.

"And I don't regret traveling this past year." It had been a matter of survival. And yet here I was, waiting for what? Spencer to run to me and declare his undying love? Shit. "The big takeaway here is that

Spencer isn't going to ask me to come back to him. We aren't riding off into the sunset."

"That wasn't my point," Caroline said.

Buddy, a tall man in his late fifties, carried out Caroline's personal pan pizza, along with napkins, utensils, and two plates.

I moved to stand. "I'm sorry, Buddy. I'm sitting down on the job."

"You earned it, kid. Stay put. I'm shutting down the ovens. Eat."

"The pizza looks amazing," Caroline said to Buddy.

He nodded and walked back to the kitchen.

"Please take a slice," Caroline said.

"Thanks." I didn't touch the pizza, and neither did she. "You're here to tell me you're going after Spencer with all that you're worth, right? You want me to know I had my shot, blew it, now it's your turn again."

Caroline's brow wrinkled. "It sounds a little more cutthroat when you put it that way."

"But that's the gist of it."

She sipped her Diet Coke. "I think Spencer and I might have finally grown up enough to really be good for each other. We're no longer kids who are slaves to hormones and ambitions. We're ready to settle."

If the truth be told, I could've grown to like Caroline in an alternate universe, though in that world, I'd still be married to Spencer and our daughter would be thriving, so in that world, I'd have to kill her if she made a move on my husband.

But again, it was this world, and I'd bet Caroline didn't have a mean bone in her body. And Spencer was a big boy; he could figure out what he wanted for himself.

I wondered if Spencer had told Caroline about Frank's illness, which wasn't my business to share. Would Caroline be able to roll with a punch like that? Growing up easy didn't generally build calluses.

"Why are you here?" I asked.

Her smile looked a little pained, but her eyes glistened with intent. "I don't sneak around behind anyone's back."

A primal urge edged out of my shadows. "You know the divorce papers aren't signed yet, right?"

She didn't blink. "But they will be soon, correct?"

I had always wanted Spencer to be happy. That was what made all this so hard. If he'd been an asshole, I might have even taken the check he'd offered. But he'd been a stand-up guy every step of the way, and I wanted the best for him. My sloppy, messed-up life was not in his best interest.

"Yes," I said.

She leaned forward. "You're cool with me?"

"Yes. Rekindle away with Spencer."

"You make it sound easy."

"You're a smart woman. You'll figure it out."

Caroline relaxed as she stared into my steady gaze. "Thank you."

"Sure."

"No, really, thank you." On the heels of her words was a sigh of relief.

There was no reason everyone had to be alone. "Spencer's not mine to give."

Caroline grabbed her jacket. "I'd hug you, but that would be weird, wouldn't it?"

I rose. "Yes, it would be very strange."

"Okay. Okay. Good." She fished two twenties out of her purse and dropped them on the table. "I've been practicing this speech ever since I saw you at Eve's party."

I pictured her standing in front of a mirror, her shoulders squared and her eyes narrowed. *You did just fine. Practice makes perfect.*

"Thank you again, Olympia. I really do wish you well."

The pizza and drink cost less than ten bucks. It wasn't every day that I got a 300 percent tip, but then I suppose Caroline was buying some goodwill to offset some guilt. "You don't want change?"

"No. No."

Everyone was trying to pay me off. "Thanks."

Caroline opened her mouth as if to thank me again but seemed to realize she was stuck on repeat. Without another word, she left.

I glanced at the uneaten personal pan pizza, grabbed a slice, and took several bites.

"Is that girl making a move on your man?" Buddy said.

Turning, I found him staring. "You have the hearing of a bat, you know?"

He shrugged and smiled. "Amazing what I hear back here."

I wiped tomato sauce from my fingers with a paper napkin. "Wonderful."

Buddy came around the counter. "Are you giving up on Spencer?"

"You can't release what you don't have. He's not mine to keep or hand over," I said. "We had our chance, and it fizzled."

"You two got hit with too much shit too fast. You didn't have a chance to see what you had."

"Maybe."

"No maybe about it. I remember how you'd light up when he came in here. Blushed like a little girl."

"Bullshit. I did not."

Buddy batted his eyes and held his meaty hands to his heart. "And he was pretty smitten with you."

"Hormones." Mixed with loneliness and fear. They were two perfect storms that collided and exploded.

"Don't be in such a rush to write him off, Olympia." Buddy never minced words.

I'd lived this movie before, and I wasn't interested in the sequel. "We're water under the bridge, Buddy. And there's no getting it back."

I'd stay away from Spencer and his family for the next few days. I wouldn't think about angel stones, or a woman named Adelaide whose namesake had never lived.

@ThePizzaTraveler

Bozeman, Montana
8 Lessons Learned This Week

• The T-Rex skeleton proves we live as long as a cosmic finger snap.

• Do what you love as often as you can.

• Gas stations sell fishing licenses.

• The state is big, gas up.

• Hiking the Two Sisters mountains stole my breath.

• Even cute bears bite.

• Huckleberry ice cream rocks.

• Mom was right. The world is a big place.

#LESSONS #MOMSKNOWBEST #LOST

CHAPTER
TWENTY-ONE
OLYMPIA

Thursday, October 31, 2024, 5:15 a.m.

Keeping my distance from the Stocktons was turning out to be a challenge.

I sat at the breakfast bar in my favorite diner. I was ready for a real breakfast and didn't want to wake up Eve and Brad with clanging pots and pans. A waitress with black smudges under her eyes set a cup of coffee in front of me without even asking. I understood her kind of fatigue. There were weeks when I'd logged so many hours at Tony's that I didn't know up from down. "Thank you."

I poured in cream and sugar, ordered the All-American breakfast, and pulled out my broken necklace and wound it around my neck, knotting the ends. The necklace secured, I pulled out my phone. After reading a few news sites, my daily astrology, and the local online paper in Bozeman, I searched the name *Adelaide Stockton, 1982, Blacksburg*, and for good measure I added in *stonemason*.

Nothing came up, which wasn't a surprise.

Next, I searched for Frank's brother, Robert Stockton, and a dozen pictures appeared. The first was taken in 1977. He was an attractive man, and I could see a lot of Frank and Spencer in his features. They all shared the same nose, gray eyes, and strong chins. The next image was his wedding portrait with Harriet in 1984. She was a striking woman, but her jaw was square and her nose larger than the standard of beauty.

"I feel ya, Harriet."

Subsequent pictures of Robert and Harriet followed them over the next couple of years, and then there was the article detailing their car accident. Robert was driving in pouring rain. They were coming home from a party when they crashed into a semi. They were both twenty-seven. I used to believe money insulated you against pain, but that wasn't true. Money greased the wheels, but it wasn't a guarantee.

My phone rang, and Spencer's name appeared. Did the man have radar? "Hello?"

"Have you ordered yet?" His tone was brusque.

"Good morning to you, Spencer." I lifted my coffee cup to my lips. "What do you need?"

"I want to talk. Stay at Danny's Diner."

I glanced around, half expecting to see him, but when I didn't, I remembered Find My Friends. "I'm going to have to disable that."

"Don't. It's handy."

"Stalking me? Not too creepy, Spencer."

"I'll be there in five minutes."

"Why?" I shifted the call to speaker and glanced at the pictures of Robert and Harriet and then closed the window, feeling a little like I'd been caught snooping.

"I'll tell you when I see you."

The call ended. I finished my cup, asked for a refill.

I was halfway through my breakfast when Spencer slid onto the barstool beside me. Disheveled hair mutinously grazed his forehead as if defying finger combing. He didn't speak until coffee arrived and he'd taken several sips. Our brief marriage had taught me that he hated noise and chaos before coffee.

"Why aren't you at Eve's?" he asked.

"It's not my place, and it feels weird being there. I'm more at home in my van."

"Couldn't sleep either?"

I smiled. "Nope."

"Thanks for coming to lunch yesterday," he said. "It meant a lot to Dad."

"Sure. Thanks for letting the kids see the lake."

"Mom was glad you came too."

I raised my coffee cup and paused. "Barbara didn't poison me, so I guess that's all the endorsement I need."

That teased a little smile. "She can be prickly."

"So can I," I said.

The smile widened and tugged the edges of his lips. "I never noticed."

"Good." I furrowed my brows, feigning concern. "I do try to hide it."

He set his cup down. Turned the handle to the left and then back to the right. "You noticed Dad was a little off yesterday."

"I did," I said softly. "Is he okay?"

"No." He waited until the waitress had moved on to the customers at the end of the bar. "He was diagnosed with Alzheimer's two years ago. It's early onset, and it's very aggressive."

I opened my mouth to say something, then closed it. People had tossed platitudes at me when my mom was sick, and even though they meant well, the words always rang hollow. "Is there anything I can do?"

"Yes."

"Sure, name it."

"Don't tell anyone. Mom and Dad are trying to keep this quiet for as long as they can. We're in discussions to sell the company, and this information could affect the negotiations."

"Of course, I won't say a word." I glanced at his crooked collar and resisted the urge to straighten it. "You're selling? I thought the company was a family legacy."

"Dad can't run it, and Mom doesn't want the burden."

"What about you?"

"It was never mine. I came in to keep Dad's chair warm until we figured out what was going on."

"And now you know."

"Basically. It'll be at least another six months before there's a complete transition, but we're on track for change."

"And then what? I mean after the company is gone."

"No idea. I've lost a couple of years on the golf circuit, but I'm young enough to get back in the game."

"That'll take you away from your father."

"In a year, he won't even know who I am, and I'll have convinced Mom to embrace assisted living."

"He's going to go that fast? He seemed really on it when you two arrived at the lake."

"He was having a great morning. That's why I brought him. But you could see he was fading by the end of lunch."

"I did." I shoved out a breath. "I'm sorry. I really am."

A muscle pulsed in his jaw. "You've been down this path with your mother."

"And it sucks."

"What's your advice?"

"Take the moments when they appear," I said. "I wish I'd taken more with Mom."

His eyes turned glassy as he shifted his gaze back to his coffee. "Seems like time won't end. And then suddenly there's none."

"Yeah." I cleared my throat.

He laid a ten-dollar bill on the counter. "Thanks again for yesterday."

"Of course."

I watched Spencer walk out. It broke me a little to see him in pain. But I knew better than most that some problems couldn't be fixed.

I stared at the half-eaten eggs and the buttered toast cut on a diagonal. I wasn't as hungry as I thought. Still, I made myself eat the eggs and nibble on the toast. If I'd learned anything on the road, it was never to turn down a hot meal. Who knew when the next one would come.

I reached for my phone again and this time typed in *Montgomery County, Virginia history*. Most of the world lived their lives without ever seeing their name mentioned in a paper, but birth, marriage, and death certificates were almost always registered, and I remembered Eve saying something about digitized local records.

But as I scrolled through the different databases, I realized this was going to be a bigger job than a quick search. I accepted a refill on my coffee and dove into marriage records. Since Stockton was the only surname, I typed in Frank's name. Dozens of pictures popped up. Images appeared of his parents, of Barbara, and of his brother Robert, but there were no pictures of Adelaide.

According to a few articles, Frank had grown the Stockton Quarry threefold, turning it into the most sought-after stone business in the state. He'd been active in Rotary and a local golf club that taught the sport to kids with "unserved needs." Eve and I could have been the poster children for his organization.

The Wi-Fi in the coffee shop was slow, and several times my phone stopped, forcing me to refresh. As I clicked newspaper links, I found nothing unexpected or anything about Adelaide.

I switched to the Office of Vital Records. Requests for marriage and birth certificates required my identification and a twelve-dollar application fee. I passed on the application fee and ID entry. I checked the time on my phone: 7:30 a.m. Still an hour and a half until any library opened.

Knowing more about Adelaide wouldn't make my divorce easier, nor would this knowledge put money in my pocket or make my return trip to the West easier. But I still wanted to know more about the woman who hadn't mattered enough to be listed in a family Bible but who'd made enough of an impression on Frank that he'd remembered her name despite his disease.

I doubted he wanted to know more about her, and I was certain bringing her up to Barbara would not win any popularity contests for me. Still, I couldn't resist knowing more.

@ThePizzaTraveler

Magic in the oddest places
Bozeman, Montana

A shaman and The Pizza Traveler each were hired to work at a resort hosting a women's spiritual retreat. I served food. The shaman balanced chakras. On a break, the Shaman told me:

All you do, eat, or say can destroy you from within.

You are out of balance.

Your heart chakra is clogged with unsaid words.

You are living for a life cut short.

#MAGIC #SECONDCHANCE #BALANCE

CHAPTER
TWENTY-TWO
OLYMPIA

Thursday, October 31, 2024, 8:59 a.m.

I shifted from foot to foot to keep warm as I stood outside the library. When I spotted a librarian moving around inside, I stared at her, knowing my gaze hovered between glaring and pleading. The librarian peeked in my direction a couple of times before she looked at the clock, and, shaking her head, moved toward the door a minute before opening.

I blew on my chilled fingers when the lock clicked and the door swung open. A slim middle-aged woman wearing a navy blue dress, a white sweater, and clogs stepped to the side. "Good morning."

"Hey." I stared at the endless bookshelves and the multiple computer stations. "I don't suppose you could help me."

The librarian leaned down and unlocked the second door's latch. "What can I do for you?"

I dug out the rumpled napkin covered in scribbled notes. "I'm trying to find information on a woman who lived in the area in 1982."

"1982? That's taking it back a little while." Her eyes sparked with the challenge. "Do you have a name?"

"Adelaide. Bauer." I didn't mention Stockton because the last thing I wanted to do was out Robert's secret first marriage.

"Let's have a look."

"I tried to search her name online but didn't have much luck."

"Online is effective, unless you need information that's buried in old books, newspapers, or city directories. You've come to the right place."

"I'm Olympia Hanover."

"Claire Welch." Claire led me to the front desk and took a seat behind it. "I'm assuming Bauer is her maiden name."

"Yes. She was born in Germany."

Claire eyed me. "Do you work at Tony's Pizzeria? I could swear I've seen you there."

"I did work there for years. I'm putting in a few hours for them this week."

Claire wagged an index finger as if conjuring a thought. "You started an Instagram page, right?"

"That's right."

"The Pizza Traveler. Your travels ended?"

"The plan is to return to the road next week. I'm only back for a quick visit."

"Well, we're glad to have you. And I can't wait to see where you travel next."

I smiled. "Me too."

She pulled the glasses perched on her head down over her eyes.

"Adelaide Bauer. Her father was Hans, and he was a stonemason who worked on the addition to the Stockton house in the early 1980s. She would have been born about 1964, give or take. And I believe Hans died in 1982."

Claire studied me. "You married Spencer Stockton, right?"

I hesitated because I'd never been totally comfortable saying this out loud. But what the hell. "I did."

Claire stared at me for a beat. She was connecting dots about Spencer's and my separation, but thankfully she didn't dig into the whys. She dropped her gaze to the computer and started to type.

"What are you searching for?" I asked.

"There'll be no birth certificate, but if she moved there before 1980, she might be listed in the 1980 census."

"Seriously?"

"The census is always a good starting point."

After a few minutes of searching, she found the handwritten census for Montgomery County in 1980. She scanned the list quickly, seeming to analyze the names with a surgeon's precision.

"There," Claire said. "Bauer, Hans, age forty-five, stonemason. He had one dependent, Adelaide, fifteen."

I leaned in and stared at the name that had been charged with so much sadness and loss for me. "Adelaide Bauer. She was real."

"Very real." Her eyes narrowed. "Do you have any other information on her?"

"Not really. She seems to have vanished in the early eighties. There's got to be more out there about her than the census."

"You think like a woman who lives in the social media age. In 1980 to '82, it was easy to go unnoticed or disappear." Claire drew in a breath. "We do have the yearbooks for the high school in the reference section. And I have digitized records of the local newspaper."

I pulled out my phone. "I took this picture of a stone sculpture. It was in Stockton Lake, which is very low right now. I think Adelaide carved it."

Claire enlarged the image with the swipe of her fingers. "'Tomorrow, I do. 1982.'"

"According to my sister, similar stones were found along the New River, but the water has covered them up again. Those stones were dated 1982, and they all had sayings and an angel figurine."

"An angel?"

"Yeah."

Claire switched databases and keyed in the words *Adelaide Bauer*, *stone*, and *angel*. "I'm in the newspaper database now."

"Okay."

Claire adjusted her glasses. "I remember something about stone angels from my time in high school."

"Really?"

"I'm a decade younger than your Adelaide, but like I said, I remember something about angels." She pressed return. The computer hesitated as it assembled data. An article appeared. She pushed the print button, and the printer spit out an article. "Here we go. Social media, 1982."

June 1, 1982
Local Artist Getting Noticed

Adelaide Bauer is not afraid of taking chances. The high school Junior's stone sculpture took top prize in the Montgomery Student Art contest.

But the local teen doesn't limit her creative expression to the art studio. She routinely leaves her edgy, sometimes graphic stonework all over Montgomery County. However, the teen ended up in hot water in recent months when she turned her chisels to public walls and structures.

The 17-year-old high school student was arrested last month for trespassing and defacing concrete walls near the 118/Christiansburg Exit as well as Blacksburg High School. She claims she was creating art. At the time of her arrest, the teen possessed a chisel and hammer and was notching angel symbols into the school's exterior.

I met up with Adelaide in a local Blacksburg eatery, Tony's. As she ladled teaspoons of sugar into her black coffee, she explained that she saw endless stories in blocks of stone.

"I'm unable to resist," Adelaide said. "I see stone, and I see what it could be."

Adelaide's father, Hans, was a stonemason who immigrated to this country from Germany three years ago with Adelaide. He died in a construction accident last month.

After her vandalism conviction, Adelaide was ordered to perform community service. The teen has been commissioned by the city to recarve the oldest, most worn headstones in the local cemetery. So far, she's re-created five headstones that date back to the 1820s.

What has this community service project taught her? "That we are blips in time. It's motivated me to carve as much as I can in the time I have left." When I pointed out she is only 17, she laughed and snapped her fingers. "That's how fast human life comes and goes."

Adelaide's other stonework will be on display next weekend from 9:00 a.m. to 5:00 p.m. at the Art Studio on Main Street.

"Adelaide was an artist." I tried to imagine how she could have met Robert Stockton. "I guess she's done some of the headstones in the cemetery."

Claire scrolled down the hits. She produced an image featuring a collection of six headstones leaning against the Stockton Quarry corporate sign. Behind the stones stood a young couple. The woman wore a full peasant skirt, an off-the-shoulder blouse, sandals, and a dozen beaded bracelets. She was tall and blonde and had a fresh-faced grin that was both playful and infectious. Beside her was a taller young man dressed in khakis and a button-down. His thick dark hair was brushed off an angled face. His thousand-watt smile projected youth and excitement. The caption read "Adelaide Bauer and Frank Stockton."

"That's Frank Stockton," I said, more to myself.

I studied the image and noted the way Frank looked at Adelaide. It was hard to miss the adoration in his gaze. He'd said he had a little crush on her.

It made sense that this was how the rich young man from a prominent family would've met a tradesman's daughter. As I stared at Adelaide's smile, I noted a light in her gaze as she looked at him. These two were into each other. "They look electric."

"They?"

I shrugged. "Yeah."

Her gaze lingered on me for a moment. "Let me grab the high school directory from 1981 to 1982. I'll be right back."

"Thank you."

"No, thank you. This is far more interesting than shelving books." Claire followed the signs to the reference section.

I studied the young couple. It wasn't too far out there to see these two hooking up, maybe getting married, and the parents obtaining a quiet divorce for Adelaide and Robert in another state. Frank had said Adelaide was Robert's wife, but this picture suggested otherwise.

"I have the yearbooks." Claire held three large yearbooks as she moved toward me. She set all three on the table and opened 1981 to 1982. She flipped to the index in the back. Her finger started at the top of the *B*s and skimmed down to *Bauer*. Adelaide was pictured on four different pages.

The first entry was Adelaide's formal senior portrait. Whereas the other kids around had fixed, posed smiles, Adelaide had a wide grin, and she was winking. Blonde hair draped her pale shoulders, but instead of a single strand of pearls around her neck, like many of the other girls wore, she wore a black cord threaded through a stone. It looked a little like my hagstone.

"Can I take a picture?" I asked.

"Sure."

Only after I'd snapped an image of the photo did I notice the description under her image. "Girl most likely to road surf, carve angels and smash all the rules."

"A free spirit," Claire said. "The art teacher that year was a new teacher. She's still at the high school. Her name is Cathy Rux. She would've known Adelaide."

A father's death would explain why Adelaide had acted out. She'd been so young, and being left untethered would have undermined her life. If I'd been younger when my mother died and had been all alone, I might have acted out too. But with Eve to look after, I felt like I couldn't do anything but work.

"His obituary says he left behind one daughter, Adelaide, who'd been her father's apprentice."

"A girl stonemason." I was impressed.

"By the looks of those gravestones, I'd say she was a very good one."

I pulled up the images of the lake stone. "She easily could've done something like this."

Claire leaned in and studied the image closely. "I don't see why not. Do you have any evidence suggesting she did?"

"The stone was found on Stockton land. She got her stone for her community service projects from the Stockton Quarry."

"It's intriguing."

"How would I find out what happened to her?"

"I can dig through the digital files. It might take me a day or two."

"Really, you'd do that?"

"I'll give you my phone number."

"Okay." I dug rumpled dollar bills from my backpack. "How much do I owe you?"

"Nothing. Like I said, this is interesting."

"And Cathy Rux is at the high school?"

"She is."

She handed me the printer-generated picture of Adelaide. "Why are you interested in Adelaide Bauer?"

The last thing I really needed to do was an ancestry deep dive into my ex's family. And yet, here I stood studying Adelaide's smiling face. "I found that stone, and I've been curious about the mason ever since."

"Want me to keep searching for media references?" the librarian asked. "I can also search major events in the area about that time."

"That would be great. I'll be in town until Monday, but after that you can still reach me."

"Sounds like a plan."

"Thank you."

Outside, I hurried to my van and sat behind the wheel. Again, I stared at Adelaide's face. In 1982, Adelaide wouldn't have been biologically connected to my Adelaide, but she'd clearly made an impression on Frank and possibly Robert. In the chaos of his fading mind, Frank had summoned Adelaide's name and wanted to give it to his first granddaughter. He had to have been more connected to her than he either was letting on or remembered.

She was the forgotten wife. Like me. "Maybe I'm just bonding with another Stockton family outcast."

❧

After I left the library, I drove to the high school. I had no idea when Ms. Rux had a planning period, but it didn't hurt to ask. I parked in a visitor space and walked through the front doors, just as I had in high school. I'd dreaded coming to school. There was always an unfinished assignment or a test I hadn't studied for that was weighing on me. When I'd dropped out after the holiday break during my senior year, it had been a relief.

I walked to the front office and moved toward the long counter. A woman sitting at a reception desk looked up at me. "May I help you?"

"I was hoping to speak to Ms. Rux."

The woman, Mrs. Brady, studied me a beat, and her gray eyes narrowed as she processed my face. She managed late arrivals and absences, and we'd crossed paths a few times. Her expression suggested she remembered me, likely guessed I'd been a student, but the dates escaped her. Seeing thousands of students could get confusing over the decades.

"Your name?"

"Olympia Hanover."

"Hanover?"

"I'm Eve Hanover's sister."

The woman nodded slowly. "Olympia."

"That's right."

"Did you ever get your GED?"

"I did."

"Good for you." She reached for her phone and dialed. "Cathy, I have a former student who would like to see you. She's Eve's sister. Okay. Great." The woman looked at me. "She'll be right up. It's her planning period."

"Terrific."

I wasn't sure if I should sit or stand. I had a few too many memories of sitting in this office waiting to explain why I had to leave school early or had arrived late. I opted to stare into a tall trophy case, as if I cared about the golden awards won by the football and basketball teams. The phone rang, students came and went into the office, and a parent arrived with a forgotten lunch.

The door opened, and this time I heard, "Ms. Hanover?"

I turned to see a tall, thin woman in her midsixties. She had long gray wavy hair that brushed her shoulders and wore a peasant dress and clogs. I'd never had one of Ms. Rux's classes because when I'd been here, art was a luxury I could not afford. Eve had taken her photography class, and I remembered signing a permission slip for my sister to attend an art exhibit.

"Ms. Rux."

Green eyes brightened. "What can I do for you?"

I opened my phone and scrolled to the image of the stone. I explained when and where I'd found it. "I think a former student of yours, Adelaide Bauer, might have made it. Do you remember her?"

Ms. Rux studied the image, nodding. "I do remember her, and this is her work. The 1981–82 academic year was my first year of teaching. Adelaide set a high standard that's rarely been matched in my classroom since."

"What was she like?"

"The girl had such a wild and restless spirit. Her laugh was infectious. She was so very talented."

"I hear she tried to sculpt a portion of the school."

Ms. Rux smiled. "She did. She also carved angels into a concrete drainpipe that was slated to go into the new stormwater system."

"She re-created several gravestones as a community service project?"

"That was right after high school graduation. But yes, she spent the summer carving stone. It was meant to be a punishment, but it wasn't much of one. I went to the graveyard that fall and saw her work. The detail was incredible. That level of work conveys love."

"Where are the stones?"

"At the city cemetery. In the northeast section."

"My mother is buried there." So were Tony Sr., his wife, and his daughter.

"Then you might have noticed the large oak tree."

"I did."

"Just beyond that, near the chain-link fence."

I made a mental note. "Where was she living?"

"There was a house on the mountain near the Stockton Quarry. Her father had use of the house while he worked for the company, and Mr. Stockton said she could stay until September."

"Who was she dating? I've heard rumors it was a Stockton."

Ms. Rux handed me back my phone. "That I can't tell you. I do know she met him before school let out for the summer. She used to sketch his face a lot."

I pulled out the printed picture of Frank and Adelaide. "I found this at the library."

She took the printout and studied the faces. "That's her. And that's him."

"That's Frank Stockton."

"Is it? They all run together to me."

"You are certain this is the guy she sketched? I mean, it's been forty years."

"Her work was stunning and hard to forget. Let me show you." Ms. Rux guided me out of the office down the hallway to her art room. It was a large open space with six-foot worktables smudged with a rainbow of paints. Colored pencils sat in cups in the center of each table, along with small jars filled with papier-mâché flowers.

At the back of the room, a collection of framed art hung in a kaleidoscope-like pattern. "When a student allows, I save the best of the best each year." She pointed to a charcoal sketch enclosed in a simple black frame. "Adelaide's sketch was the first I framed and hung."

I studied the picture of the smiling young man. His dark hair was swept over sparkling eyes, and creases around his mouth suggested he liked to laugh a lot. He looked like Spencer. "Frank Stockton."

"I've seen pictures of Frank Stockton, but he was much older. I wasn't that tuned in to the community in the early days because I was more focused on my painting."

There was no denying that Adelaide had been very talented. "Can I take a picture of this?"

"Sure."

I snapped several images. "Ms. Rux, thank you."

"Of course. And congratulations on your sister's marriage. She's been the talk of the staff lounge."

"She's very happy." I studied the images on my phone. "Any idea where Adelaide might have gone?"

"None. She simply vanished."

❧

When I pulled up in front of the Stockton house, I was certain I'd lost my mind. Barbara had tolerated me yesterday because that impromptu lunch was a one-off. My mother-in-law wasn't planning on making a habit of seeing me. And I was sure she wouldn't have appreciated me sharing what I'd learned about Adelaide and Frank. Had the two married and then divorced? Or was I simply reading what I'd seen wrong?

I knocked on the door.

Familiar heels clicked in the hallway. I shifted my stance, tightened my grip on my backpack strap. When the door opened, Barbara did not look amused. She'd never been a woman who liked interruptions.

"Olympia. Twice in two days. How lucky we are."

A grin tugged at the corners of my mouth. If I didn't know better, I'd say Barbara could grow to like me. "I know, right?"

"What can I do for you?"

"I was hoping I could see Frank. I have information about the stone I found in your lake. I think I found the artist."

Her lips flattened. "He's resting."

"It's eleven thirty in the morning."

"He didn't sleep well last night."

"Okay." I might've known what was going on with Frank, but I'd promised Spencer I wouldn't speak about it with anyone. It didn't take a genius leap to know Spencer hadn't consulted his mother before he'd talked to me. "I was at the library this morning."

"The library? That's a novel way to start your day."

"It was a first for me." My slight wry smile did not coax any reaction. "I found a picture of a young girl who lived in the area about 1982. I think she was your stonemason. Her father, Hans, worked on your addition."

"Right."

"I thought Frank would like to see what I found."

"Maybe another time."

I sensed that if I gave Barbara the printer-generated picture, it'd end up in the trash before I cleared the driveway. "Okay. I'll try back later."

Barbara shook her head. "Don't feel like you must. I know you're busy."

"Olympia? Do I hear Olympia?" Frank's voice echoed from the house.

Barbara turned, opening her mouth, but I spoke first. "It's me, Frank. I brought a picture for you."

He rounded the corner. His hair was damp but combed, and he wore a blue pullover sweater and khakis. Now that I realized how sick he was, I could see signs all over him. The thinness. The semivacant eyes. The poor skin coloring.

"A picture?" he asked.

I could almost see him searching for a conversation that he feared he'd lost. "We talked about Adelaide yesterday, remember?"

"That's right." His face brightened. "I remember."

"I went to the library and asked the librarian to search her. She found a picture."

He accepted the page and stared at the face for a long moment. Even Barbara leaned in, her plucked brow raised in curiosity.

"That appears to be a high school picture," Barbara said.

"Adelaide moved to this country in the late 1970s with her father, Hans. He worked on the addition to this house. He was killed in 1982 in a construction accident."

"I remember Dad talking about a man dying at the quarry when a chain failed and stone fell on him." Frank studied the creased image and frowned, as if sensing old memories stirring just out of reach. How often did he have that sensation these days? How many times did he reach for a word, the location of his keys or his glasses? "She married my brother, Robert."

"How did she meet Robert?" I asked.

"She was at the quarry several times that summer. Hard to ignore her."

"She was married to Robert?" I pressed.

"Sure, of course."

Was this the truth? Or was it a tale repeated so many times that the echoes of the original fable still lingered in his mind?

Barbara drew in a deep breath. "We know she's not in the family Bible, so if Robert married her, the marriage didn't last long."

Like me, Barbara couldn't resist poking at a mystery. "She was arrested for carving angels into the walls of the local high school. She was sentenced to community service."

"Carving gravestones," Frank said.

"Stockton Quarry donated the stone."

Frank nodded. "I'd just graduated college and had started working at the company. Dad put me on the project."

"Do you have proof she carved your stones?" Barbara asked as she accepted the pages from Frank.

"Her former art teacher at the high school recognizes her work. And it kind of makes sense that a teen who's just lost her dad would be channeling her grief. Maybe she felt like she needed to leave messages to the world."

"A message to the world?" Barbara said. "I'd say your trip out west has expanded your imagination."

"I know, sounds like I've spent too much time with shamans and spirit healers. But there are some who believe our dead family speaks to us in the oddest ways when we need to hear their messages most."

"I dreamed about my brother last night. He was showing me how to wield a chisel. We were carving his gravestone."

"Oh, Frank," Barbara said. "That is morbid."

Frank shrugged. "My father wanted me to learn the basics of stone carving. He was a start-from-the-bottom-up kind of guy. Turns out I liked working with stone. That summer I made a few gravestones for families who couldn't afford to have one made. Never charged them a dime. Most of the stones were for children."

I stared at him, waiting for him to say more. When he didn't, I asked, "Have you always done that?"

"No. I stopped by the time I met Barbara," Frank said. "I guess I just ran out of time, like we all do."

"'Tomorrow, I do.'" I immediately caught Barbara's confused expression.

"What happened to Adelaide?" Barbara asked.

Frank frowned. "That's still a mystery. She just kind of vanished."

"No one just vanishes," Barbara said.

"Forty years ago, it would have been easier for people to move away and reinvent themselves," I said.

Frank nodded. "Time swallows us all up eventually."

Time might have blotted out most of Adelaide, but like her stone hidden under the lake waters, I had found traces of her. "Would there be any record of Hans Bauer working for your family?"

"If he worked for the quarry, we still might have employment records," Frank said. "My grandfather and father were sticklers for employment records."

"Could you look or ask Spencer?"

"Why the curiosity?" Barbara asked.

"Maybe because her name was my daughter's name. Frank remembered the name for a reason."

Barbara cleared her throat. "I'm sure I could call the office and have Spencer's secretary pull the man's records."

"Thank you."

Footsteps echoed from the kitchen seconds before Spencer appeared in the hallway. "Olympia, what are you doing here?"

I stood a little straighter as he strode toward us. He was wearing a dress shirt, black dress slacks, and polished loafers. He carried a red tie but hadn't put it on yet. Spencer hated ties. When we'd met, he was loosening a red silk tie while he placed his order for a beer and the number thirteen pizza, the meat lover's special.

He kissed his mother on the cheek, clapped his father on the shoulder, and then glanced in my direction. He didn't smile, and a wariness lingered in his gaze.

"Spencer, what are you still doing here?" Barbara asked.

"My meeting was canceled. I have a little time before I need to get to the office."

"I brought your parents a picture of Adelaide," I said.

The name threw him off for a moment, and then he seemed to remember. "Robert's first wife."

Frank handed the picture to his son. "Olympia is a real Nancy Drew."

Spencer glanced at the picture. "Ring any bells, Dad?"

"Not a one," he said.

"Mom?" Spencer asked.

"Your father knows more about his family history than I do."

Frank took the picture back. "Hans and Adelaide lived in the Mountain House," Frank said. "Dad often found housing for the most skilled workers."

"It burned about that time," I said.

"Early eighties," Barbara said.

I thought back to our first date and the hike to the ruins. It had all seemed like such an adventure, and when we'd arrived, the area had felt so charged with energy. I'd chalked that up to my attraction to Spencer.

"I saw it when I was hiking on Sunday," I said. "The chimney and foundation are still there. An angel was carved in the hearth."

Spencer caught my gaze, and I sensed he was mulling over memories of our first hike there, but he gave no indication.

"I'd love to see it again," Frank said. "But my knees aren't up for the hike."

"Frank, you're not going into the woods," Barbara said. "It's too dangerous."

"I understand that, dear," Frank said, winking. "But maybe Olympia can take Spencer up there. I'm sure he'd like to see it again."

Spencer shook his head. "I can find the place by myself."

"Why not just go with Olympia," Frank said. "Go up there today and take a few pictures. I bet I'll remember more about this Adelaide if I have pictures of that old house."

"Dad, why would the house help you remember?" Spencer said.

"Frank," I said, "Spencer and I don't need to hike there together."

"Why not?" Frank challenged.

"Are you up to something?" I asked.

He laughed. "Not at all. But it's a beautiful day, and there are two young hikers here who should take advantage of it."

"No," Spencer said.

"No," I said.

Barbara shook her head. "Frank, Spencer will get to the old cottage in the next few days, and he'll take lots of pictures and video, won't you, Spencer?"

I watched Spencer shift, searching for the right words that would get him out of this bear trap that was grinding into his ankle. For some reason, I liked watching him sweat, so just to add salt to the wound, I said, "It's supposed to rain at the end of the week, and now that I think about it, today would be a good day. I'm game if you are, Spencer. I could use the exercise."

"Not a good idea," Spencer said.

"You aren't afraid of being around me, are you?" The dare crossed my lips as easily as it had when we were together.

Spencer's mouth pursed. He was competitive to the bone, and he loved a challenge. "I am not afraid, Olympia."

"Then let's go. We're burning daylight, baby," I said.

Barbara folded her arms, but she was wise enough to know when not to put her hands too close to the whirling blades of a saw.

"Barbara, maybe we could pack them a lunch," Frank said. "They'll be starved by the time they get there."

"Frank," Barbara said. "This is none of our business."

"Properties on the Stockton lands are my business," Frank said.

"I didn't mean for this to be a thing for you two," I said. "I didn't mean to stir the pot. I just wanted to show you the picture of Adelaide. But if you grant me access to the land, I would love to hike to the stone foundation one last time. I don't need Spencer to show me the way."

"Spencer, are you going to let your wife go alone?" Frank asked.

"I can go first thing tomorrow," Spencer said. "I really do have lots of paperwork this afternoon."

"So tomorrow then," Frank said. "We'll make lunch for you two to take." He took his wife's hand and guided her out of the room.

When we were alone, I said in a low voice, "Seriously, you're off the hook. I was just razzing you. I can do this alone or not at all, if it's a problem."

Spencer looked toward the kitchen, his expression softening when he saw his father kiss his mother on the cheek. "Dad's been more engaged in the last two days than he has in the last year."

"That's a good thing, right?"

"Yes, it's good," he said. "In moments like this, I can almost believe that the doctors are wrong and he'll be fine."

"Denial. I know the river well. I sailed it plenty of times when my mother was first diagnosed. Your first stop on this journey will be Bargaining. Next there's Anger. And finally, there's Acceptance. It's a real shitty trip. And I'm sorry you're taking it."

Spencer cleared his throat. "I'll pick you up at eight a.m. sharp tomorrow."

CHAPTER
TWENTY-THREE
SPENCER

Friday, November 1, 2024, 8:00 a.m.

When Spencer pulled up in front of Eve's house, Olympia was sitting in her van parked out front. Her engine running, she was reading on her phone and sipping coffee. Finger-combed hair was arranged into a loose ponytail haloed by escaped strands. She looked as if she hadn't slept well.

When she saw him, she nodded, set her cup aside, and shut off the engine. Out of her van, she moved toward its sliding door and opened it.

"Tell me you didn't sleep in the damn van last night." Whispered words hissed over his lips as he put his car in park.

The idea of Olympia sleeping in that box had never sat well with him. The images it conjured had stalked him over the last year. She was an adult and could do whatever she wanted, but that didn't mean it was safe. Or that he had to like it.

Dressed in jeans, hiking boots, a flannel shirt, and a down jacket, he strode around to the rear of his car and opened the hatch. "Why aren't you waiting in the house where it's warm?"

Spencer had been annoyed with Eve since early on in his relationship with Olympia. Olympia made it so easy for Eve to skirt her obligations, but Eve was also a grown woman. She could have taken the initiative and pitched in more after Olympia lost the baby. Maybe if she had, Olympia would have stayed.

"Eve offered, but when she left for work, I came out here to inventory my hiking gear. Then I started responding to direct messages. And then the cat videos. They always get me."

Knowing she deflected with humor, he asked, "You get a lot of direct messages?"

"Surprisingly, yes. People have plenty of comments about my very mundane life."

"Most are positive?" She'd been active on social media when they met. He never understood why she wanted to document her life, but she never missed a day of posting. She'd talked about her mother's illness, her work at Tony's, hikes, football games, you name it. But she'd never discussed her pregnancy or their marriage.

"For the most part. A few are annoyed that I haven't announced my next adventure."

An irrational irritation grated under his skin as he thought about strangers tugging her away. "There aren't enough adventures here?"

"So far, this area is proving to be fruitful. Quite a bit of discussion about the stone."

"Any theories?" He met her at the open van door.

"Plenty, but nothing we haven't heard yet. Most are linking the stone to the hunger stones in Europe. They might have inspired this stone, but I think these messages are meant to be positive."

She opened the van's sliding door, and he peered inside. The shelves on the other side were neatly packed with clothes, dishes, a few pots and pans, and camera tripods. The futon was open and covered with a pile of quilts and pillows. He'd seen several posts of her sitting in this space, looking out over the Grand Canyon.

"Was Stephanie pissed when you left her in Missouri?"

"She's a car, and cars are practical. She was okay with it," Olympia said, smiling. "We had a talk, and she understood. Plus, she wasn't up for the long trip. But Gertie wanted an adventure."

"Gertie?"

"Gertie, a hardworking van. Very excited about seeing the West. She'd never had a trip beyond the soccer camps, grocery stores, and malls."

He shook his head, a smile tugging the edges of his lips. "Do you know how crazy this sounds?"

"Spencer, when did I not sound a little eccentric?" She grabbed her backpack, shouldered it, and shut the van door. "You left brain, me right brain."

Their fierce attraction had tethered them, but their baby had bridged the remaining distance for him.

Spencer spooned close to Olympia's pregnant body as she drifted off to sleep. He'd moved into her apartment a couple of weeks after they'd married, fully understanding it would be temporary, until he could buy them a house with a yard.

As his hand rested on her belly, he willed the baby to kick and send a signal to her old dad. But his girl was very quiet tonight. "She's not moving."

"She moved all day long, jackrabbiting ribs and punching my bladder."

"When are you going to resign from Tony's?" He'd been encouraging Olympia to quit ever since they'd married.

"I'm working up to it. One major life change at a time." She yawned and snuggled her butt closer to him.

Their girl must've been as exhausted as her mother. He'd bet the Stockton Quarry that Peanut would be just as hardworking and focused as her mother.

Ever since Olympia told him she was pregnant, he could feel his brain shifting every day. He was becoming more alert to the hours he logged at the office, the timetable tracking his return to the pro circuit, and his father's declining health. Peanut wouldn't be here for another few months, but she had already changed him. A strong sense of pride warmed him as he drifted off to sleep. It was easy to close his eyes and let the moment go because the future was so full.

That night at 2:06 a.m., Olympia woke him, crying out as a sharp pang racked her belly.

He startled awake. "What's wrong?"

She rolled on her side, curling into a ball, cradling the Peanut closer. "Pain. It hurts so much."

When he clicked on the light, her breathing was labored, her belly drum tight. "We're going to the hospital."

She didn't argue, and that scared the shit out of him.

He pulled on pants and his shirt, his hands shaking as he swiped his keys off the dresser. He feared this wasn't going to end well, and the sooner his girls were at the hospital, the better.

When he pulled back the comforter, blood stained the sheets. Hands still shaking, he slid a coat on her shoulders, picked up Olympia, and carried her down the stairs to his car. His heart pounded in his chest as he set her gently down on her feet and opened the car door.

She doubled over. "This really hurts. This can't be good."

"I know, baby." He lowered her to the car seat, swung her legs around, and fastened her seat belt.

She gripped his hand. "I'm scared."

"I know. Hang tough."

Olympia was hemorrhaging when they arrived at the hospital. Her large T-shirt was soaked, and her skin was so damn pale.

He parked in front of the emergency room, and with the car still running, he ran inside and corralled two nurses and a stretcher.

Olympia was whisked away. As he paced the waiting room, he tried to remember the last time he'd felt Adelaide move. He flexed his fingers, mentally scrambling back for the last moment his daughter had fluttered sometime the previous day.

His girl had slipped away without him realizing it. If he'd been more on the ball, maybe he would have noticed and insisted they see the doctor.

Spencer cleared his throat. "Your right brain ready to hike?"

Olympia stared at him as if his thoughts had grown so loud that she'd heard them. They'd never talked about that night, but it had left indelible scars on them both. "It is."

He accepted her backpack, which felt surprisingly light. "Doesn't feel like you packed much."

"Just a day hike." Her gaze drifted to his pack, which was three times the size of hers. "Expecting a long hike?"

"I remember you mocked me once about overpacking and then took it all back."

She chuckled. "Hoping it's another great lunch."

Smiling, he unzipped the pack's top, revealing two large bento-boxed lunches his mom had handed him as he was leaving.

"Barbara doesn't skimp on food," Olympia said.

"Dad thinks you're too thin." He shrugged. "It smelled great when she was cooking it."

"It's cooked?"

"Parts of it—some are cold, hot, sweet, savory."

"Looks heavy, so be careful of your back. You don't want to mess up your golf swing."

That silenced his next statement. "You had me at 'golf swing.'"

He moved toward the driver's side of his sedan, and she took the front passenger seat. When they were settled, he turned on the engine, and they pulled away.

"Are you excited about Eve's marriage?" Lame question, but it was as neutral as he could come up with.

"Surprised. But Eve likes surprises better than me."

Spencer didn't mention that Eve was pregnant. Brad had told him last week. His friend had been a bit sheepish, almost apologetic. But Spencer had shaken his hand and congratulated him.

Olympia stared ahead when she said, "Has Brad told you?"

It always unnerved him how she could sense his thoughts. "Yes."

"Didn't see that one coming, did ya?"

"No, I did not."

"A spring baby girl."

"Yes."

"Eve seems to have it all under control. And any fears I had of wearing a pink ruffled bridesmaid's dress have been put to rest."

Again with the jokes, but he knew her sister's pregnancy had to sting. For her sake, he chose to keep things light. "I'd pay money to see you in pink ruffles."

"I can almost hear you laughing as I stumble into the church."

He chuckled. "I wouldn't laugh."

"You wouldn't be able to resist. And I wouldn't blame you."

He pulled out of the neighborhood and headed west, back toward his property with the Stone Cottage. "I wouldn't."

"When you marry Caroline, I'm sure it'll be a big event. It'll be the perfect storm of pastels, flowers, organza, and traditions."

He shot her a glance, hoping he'd heard her wrong. "Who told you that I'm marrying Caroline?"

Sharp eyes glistened with interest. "Come on, she's perfect for you. You used to date her, and she's clearly into you."

"Who said?"

"No one needs to say. I saw the way she looked at you at the party. And Barbara couldn't have designed a better girlfriend/daughter-in-law." She shook her head as she stared out at the strip malls giving way to rolling hills marbled with oranges, yellows, and green.

"Did my mom tell you this?"

"No. But I've got two eyes. Caroline gave you multiple I-could-eat-him-up-with-a-spoon looks at the party."

The Look. Yeah, Caroline had gone out of her way to visit him before the party. Her meetings were always professional as she discussed party details that he didn't care about. However, *professional* summed up the total of his current relationship with Caroline. "I hired Caroline to plan the engagement party. She and I dated in high school, as you clearly remember, but nothing since. Except I did kiss her after the party." He needed to be honest with her.

An easy smile curled her lips. "Was it a good kiss?"

He shrugged, hoping she was a little jealous. "I've had better."

"Well, she's got you in her sights, buddy. And she likes what she sees."

"Not in the market for a wife, seeing as I still have one." That was another distinction he wanted to make.

"A matter of paperwork now, right?"

"Is it that simple for you?" Annoyance elbowed past his good mood.

"Life's never simple. Sometimes it's easy, but most times it's hard. This divorce isn't in the 'easy' category."

He didn't speak for several minutes. He'd never seen Olympia back down from a fight, but when it came to their marriage, she didn't go to battle. "I've taken the postnuptial agreement off the table. I'm trying to make it easy."

"Maybe I'm a terrible quitter."

In a perfect world, she'd tell him the divorce was off and she wanted them to try again. And that would be awesome in the short run.

But saving this marriage would one day saddle her with an illness he wouldn't wish on his worst enemy. If he told her the truth now, Olympia-the-terrible-quitter would stand by his side. She'd rise to the occasion and put herself on hold again.

Life had thrown enough pauses in her direction, and she didn't deserve another.

@ThePizzaTraveler

Parts Unknown
Taking chances, getting lost and then found.

The desert roads all look alike to an eastern gal. They seem interchangeable. But each turn or curve in the road is different and unique. While one might be a shortcut, another might screw up your day. Choose wisely, Grasshopper.

#CHANCES #CHOICES #LOST

CHAPTER
TWENTY-FOUR
OLYMPIA

Friday, November 1, 2024, 9:00 a.m.

The morning climb dripped with silence. I knew Spencer well enough to realize the info dump on Caroline's long game had blindsided him. I'd be lying if I said I didn't enjoy the confusion knotting his brow. I didn't want him to want Caroline. But Caroline was a force of nature wrapped in polite smiles and shades of pink. Spencer, or any man in her sights, didn't have a prayer. She'd win him in the end.

The Stone Cottage stood nestled in the woods, surrounded by neatly trimmed bushes, and it was sheltered by the orange and yellow leaves of an oak tree that had been here longer than the house. "You brought it back from the brink."

"Barely. A few contractors wanted to demolish it."

"It's a cozy spot to spend the night."

Out of the car, I glanced at the blue sky dotted with thickening plump clouds. It wasn't supposed to rain today, so I was confident we wouldn't have any trouble with the weather if we didn't linger long.

As Spencer hoisted his pack and mine out of the car, his muscles strained enough to stretch his flannel shirt over a broad chest. He'd always had a great body, and if anything, he was more fit than he had been a year ago.

I accepted my pack. "It should be fun."

"Lead the way."

I started walking, aware of the steady thud of his feet behind me. Dried leaves rustled in a gentle breeze. We fell into a steady pace. Neither of us spoke as the ground grew rockier and the mountain incline increased. My legs strained against the climb, but my breathing was steady. Sweat glistened on my neck and back, grabbed the chill lingering in the air.

"When did you buy back the land?" I asked.

"About two years ago. My grandfather sold it off thirty years ago."

"Why?"

"I assume he needed the cash."

"Were Naked Guy and his girlfriend trespassing on this land ten years ago?"

"Technically speaking, we were."

"Right." I glanced back at him. "Why'd you buy this property again? You're selling the company, right?"

"I like the land," he said, meeting my gaze. "I like the quiet up here. And no matter where I go, I'll always be home."

"That's why you renovated the cottage."

"The master plan is to make the Stone Cottage my home base."

"Keeps you close to your parents." I looked back as his gaze rose. A half dozen emotions swirled in his eyes, but they were too knotted to tease apart.

He nodded.

"I get it." I started walking again, pushing through thickening, overgrown branches and bramble. Several times, the trail vanished, but instinct guided me until I picked up the narrowing path again, as I'd done on Sunday.

Finally, the trail opened into the small clearing. In the center were the remaining burned rafters, the stone fireplace, and the foundation. A breeze brushed over my skin. My nerves tingled.

It was cooler up here, and the moisture in the air was thicker. I looked up across the blue expanse and to white clouds knitted into a blanket. "Life is a series of one-in-a-millions."

"How many do you think we'll see in a lifetime?"

I felt my shoulders loosen. "Depends. If it's the good kind, I'll take as many as I can get. The bad kind, well, I've reached my quota."

"Roger that."

I cut through thick weeds, hoping to find the path I'd created on Sunday. But the earth had already erased all traces of my presence. I moved toward what had been the front door and stepped into the old house.

"Good to see the chimney is still standing," Spencer said.

"Looks like a hard wind could blow it down."

He crossed the small room and pushed against the fireplace. "It's pretty solid."

"Who built this house?"

"My great-grandfather, Joseph. This was the first structure on Stockton land."

"Why so far away from the quarry?"

"The original rock vein is on the other side of the mountain. At the time, the house would've been close. But the vein proved worthless, so he built the Stone Cottage and then the main house. We have several generations of men who love to build."

"And not you?"

"I want to build, but not with stone."

"Your golf?"

"That was the plan. I had several more decades ahead of me."

We'd never talked about dreams or grand plans last year. We were putting one foot in front of the other and not thinking too far ahead beyond the birth of our daughter.

"If your father wasn't sick, you wouldn't have come home, and there'd have been no Adelaide."

His gaze rose to mine. "Are you sorry we made her?"

"I'll never regret having her. My only wish is that we had her now." Saying the words out loud lifted a weight from my shoulders. I'd wanted to tell him this for a long time.

"I would've given anything to have kept her."

"Many times, I imagined getting Dad settled, the business sold, and the three of us going on tour."

"Diapers and cribs on the road."

"Yeah. We wouldn't have been the first family to do it. That's why I was harping on you to quit Tony's."

The cruel beauty of that alternate life would stick with me for a long time. "I wish I had. Maybe if I wasn't so determined to keep standing on my own two feet, she'd still be here."

"You can't play that game," he said softly. He took a step toward me.

I veered out of his grip, tears clogging my throat and forcing me to push away the sadness.

"Does your dad have any idea how this fire started?"

"If he did, he doesn't remember now." The tension eased from his shoulders as if he'd set down a burden. "Two days ago, I caught him, keys in hand, ready to drive here by himself."

"Why would Frank want to come here?"

"I have no idea. He and his father used this cottage when they were hunting. Maybe he thought he was living in the past. Old memories are still the strongest for him. He spent a lot of happy hours up here when he was young."

"I can't imagine how terrifying it must be to feel your mind disintegrate."

Silence snarled around him. "Neither can I."

I looked up toward a gray-white sky, remembering moments like that when I first pulled onto the road. Neither my body nor my brain could engage. It had been terrifying, and I couldn't picture facing decades of that in my future.

"That's got to be frightening for you too," I said.

He flexed his fingers. "As you predicted, I'm working through the stages of grief. Today, I've advanced from fear to anger. When I see him, it's all I can do not to tear the room apart. My father was one of the sharpest minds I've known, and now he's losing it."

"I am more comfortable with anger than fear. The anger permits moral outrage, and I can get a lot of work done when I'm juicing on fury. But fear is a different beast. It consumes and paralyzes me."

"When does bargaining arrive? I'm good at wheeling and dealing."

I shrugged. "Who can say? Grief moves at its own pace, and sometimes it loops around and revisits its previous stops."

"Terrific."

I moved toward the singed west wall and ran my fingers over the hearth's uneven stone. I'd been married to Spencer long enough to learn the basics of stone carving, and I marveled at the craftsmanship. Whoever carved these stones knew what they were doing. "You think this place could be saved?"

"No. The foundation is cracked in too many places."

Cold rocky ridges trailed under my fingertips as I glided my hand along the face. "You should save the stones," I said. "It's a heck of a legacy from your grandfather. One of your guys could make something out of the stones. A shed, a patio, and I don't know what. I do know it's cut too well to waste."

He eyed the fireplace. "Getting it out of here will be a challenge. I can't imagine how the builder transported it up here. But you're right. This is the work of a master builder."

"One stone at a time."

"It'll take months, if not a year."

I shrugged. "In the grand scheme of things, that's not much time. I mean, after you sell the company, you'll have more time, so you could focus on saving this place."

"Why this place? Why is it so important to you?"

"There's an energy up here." I traced the outline of the angel on the hearth.

"Energy?"

"Sounds like too much time with shamans, right?"

He shrugged, smiled.

This was where we'd begun. And in my memories, it would always be special and magical. "From the moment we first visited here, this place grabbed me. Maybe it was Adelaide, who knows? Either way, this place feels like it's crying out to be saved. You saved the Stone Cottage, so now you can save the Mountain House."

A chuckle rattled in his chest. "I was thinking after the company sold, I'd play more golf. I'm ready to retire from manual labor."

A breeze feathered through my hair as I faced him. "Hard work is good for your soul. And this place is not finished with you."

His wry expression reminded me of the guy I'd met last year. "I told myself that when I was gutting the Stone Cottage."

I pictured him shirtless and sweating as he wielded a hammer. God, so hot.

Warmth spread through my body, and I turned toward the view so he wouldn't see the rosy hue spreading up my cheeks. "This view is stunning, and I guess that was reason enough to haul up the stone."

"Joseph was a trailblazer." His voice sounded rougher.

I looked out over the valley, now covered in a heavy gray mist. Where had the rain come from? So much for my weather app. A raindrop fell through open rafters and hit the mud by my boots.

"The house burned in the summer of 1982," I said. "Right after Hans died. Adelaide would've been living here."

"How do you know that?"

"A newspaper account in the paper. A nice librarian showed me the article. And Adelaide's art teacher told me she vanished that summer. What started the fire? What happened to her?"

"Why the interest?"

I moved back toward the hearth. Black scorch marks climbing up the stone suggested the fire had started here. A stray ember onto carpet or a dry wood floor would quickly grow into an inferno. "So many times, I thought about this place when I was on the road."

"Did you?"

I traced the angel. The cherub's graceful wings were delicate, open, and inviting. "Did you see the angel on the hearth?" I asked.

Spencer moved toward me, standing so close I could feel the heat from his body. He traced the outline of the winged figure on the side; he nodded. "Like your stone."

"Adelaide."

"Ah."

"I didn't tell your parents everything I learned about Adelaide."

"Really?"

I drew in a breath, taking in his scent. "I feel as if I'm outing something I shouldn't."

A brow arched. "I doubt you could surprise me with much."

"Well, this might do it."

"Out with it."

"I think your father was married to Adelaide."

He stilled, staring at me as if he was waiting for the punchline. "You're not joking."

"No. I went to the library and found the newspaper picture with the two of them together. Like I told your parents, she met him while she was working off the vandalism conviction. She liked to carve figures into stone, including the local high school."

"She wasn't married to Robert, but Dad?"

"Yes. I think your dad's memory loss has jumbled a lot of the facts. A part of him wants to protect your mother. But another part of him is reaching out to Adelaide." I found the sketch of a young Frank on my phone. "Adelaide sketched this of your father forty years ago. The art teacher was so impressed with it, she's saved it all these years."

Spencer studied the picture. "This is hardly proof."

"No. But it's clear she cared about your father."

He handed the phone back to me.

"I'm assuming your mother doesn't know about the first marriage."

"I'm fairly certain she doesn't." He shook his head. "I'll need more proof."

"Maybe you can find the marriage certificate."

He swallowed. "I was wrong. You did surprise me."

"Sorry."

"Don't be. You can tell me anything." He laid his hand on my shoulder, sending warmth and energy through me.

I shook my head. "Let's not get carried away."

"I'd like to know what happened to Adelaide."

"Me too. Your father was clearly fond of her and likely still is; otherwise he wouldn't have suggested her name for our baby."

"Yeah. Do me a favor and don't tell my mother until I can do a little research."

I laid my hand over my heart. "I don't have a death wish, so I won't be the person who tells Barbara."

"Thanks."

Another raindrop dripped on my shoulder, and a few more hit the top of my head. "We never took pictures for your dad, and the sky is about to open."

He'd forgotten about the pictures. "I'll get pictures another time. Better we make it down the mountain."

"Right."

Fifteen minutes down the trail, the skies unloaded.

@ThePizzaTraveler

On the road

Can a girl unmake a mistake?

I don't fret about most of my blunders, but a few, I discover, still stalk me when I slow down enough to think. So, my solution is to press the accelerator. To the floor. There are trails up ahead, pizza to be made, and distractions to be found.

#BLUNDERS #OVERSIGHTS #GAFFES

CHAPTER
TWENTY-FIVE
OLYMPIA

Friday, November 1, 2024, noon

By the time we reached the Stone Cottage's porch, we were both drenched. My jeans and jacket had soaked up at least ten extra pounds, and my shoes sloshed with each new step. As I wiped off the rain from my coat, Spencer brushed water from his face.

"Bet you wished you hadn't packed so light," he challenged.

"Are you made of soap?" I asked. "A little water never hurt anyone."

"Laugh all you want," he said as he shook his coat and splashed water on me. "But warm clothes are pretty damn appealing right now."

"I can take a little chill." Cold tightened my lips.

He unlaced his boots and toed them off before entering the code into the front door lock. "I'm going inside and changing into dry clothes and getting warm. Care to join me?"

"I could be persuaded." I shrugged off my jacket, leaving it draped over the back of a front porch rocker. Inside, Spencer turned up the thermostat, and the heater kicked on.

I remained by the front door, worrying about my wet clothes dripping water on the wood floor. I knew I should undress. And then I'd be wet, naked, and alone with Spencer. Consequences ticked through my brain. Tracking water on his floors was the least of my concerns.

"Come inside," he said.

"I'm dripping."

He shrugged off his shirt. "Then strip. No mysteries between us in that regard, Olympia."

I had paraded in front of him naked more times than I could count. Even when my body went pear shaped, I never hid it from him. I'd been proud of my changing shape. But now as a shiver settled in my bones and I caught a glimpse of his muscled back, I was suddenly shy. My body was back physically, but it showed signs that I'd been pregnant, including faint stretch marks on my breasts and the C-section scar on my lower belly. I turned and removed my shirt.

"I'll grab you a robe," he said.

"Thanks."

Seconds later, terry cloth sailed across the room and hit me in the back of my bare legs. I grabbed the robe and slid it on. The rough cloth warmed my skin, but the deep chill in my bones persisted. I carried my wet clothes to the laundry room, tossed them in the dryer, and set the dial to hot. Clothes tumbled over and over.

Spencer had changed into a blue flannel shirt and fresh jeans. He knelt in front of the fireplace, arranged smaller pieces of wood in a pyramid shape, and from a wooden box grabbed several sheets of newspaper. He crunched the paper into a tight ball and shoved it between the wood. A strike of a match, and paper and kindling ignited. Soon, well-fed flames crackled.

Yanking the band from around my ponytail, I finger combed my hair, trying to add a little volume and undo the drowned-squirrel look.

He squatted in front of the fire and fed it a medium-size log. His wide, muscled back was hard to ignore.

I liked watching him. He always moved with precision and care, whereas I felt like an octopus juggling multiple tasks at once. I could do a lot of things well enough, but I'd never mastered any one task because there was always another brush fire to extinguish.

I sat on the couch and curled up my feet. Outside, the rain and wind pelted the house. "I thought the polar vortex wasn't supposed to be here until next week."

"Looks like it's early." He dusted off his hands, turned, and sat on the stone hearth. His shirt gaped open in a deep V and revealed more lean muscle. "What made you go to the library?"

"Feels like Adelaide has been sending me signs."

"Signs?"

"Our daughter's name. The lake stone. Your father mentioning her at lunch."

"Coincidence."

"I don't believe in coincidence. Signs appear for a reason. It's up to us to see or ignore them."

"More shaman talk?"

I chuckled. "Maybe. But I need to find meaning in the chaos."

"And?"

"No meaning yet. But the universe sends clues, and it's up to us to notice and decipher them."

Spencer shook his head. "You didn't like the name Adelaide when I first brought it up."

"It sounded old fashioned to me."

He shifted and turned to face me. "Dad had liked it so much."

"I love the name now."

"So do I."

Silence hovered between us. We were on this track for a reason, and I knew enough now to realize the window into those days would one day close for good. "Where were your parents?"

"Both were at the hospital."

"I didn't see them when I woke up. And they never visited me."

"Mom said you would be upset and wanted to give you space."

Maybe that was true at first. And then Eve had arrived wrapped in a hurricane of tears and hugs that drew my remaining energy.

"I was there," Spencer said.

I plucked at a loose thread on the terry cloth sleeve. And, almost too softly, said, "Seeing you made it all worse."

He ran long fingers through his hair. "I know."

"It's not your fault. Nothing could've fixed me in those days. Even if Mom had come back to life, it wouldn't have mattered."

He nodded slowly.

"How are you doing?" I asked.

"Me?"

"I'd hoped your parents would take care of you after I left. I know they adore you."

"Mom's cure for anything is to stay on the move. Golf, club, work, parties. It was chaos for months."

"I invited you on the open road." The words slipped out before I could catch them.

"I know. And I wish I could've gone. But I needed to stay for Dad."

"I thought you couldn't stand to be around me."

He shook his head. "That's not true."

Maybe it was selfish, but I resented that he'd chosen his family over me. But given the same choice, I could easily have done the same. "Your family needed you."

He moved toward me and knelt, resting steady hands on my thighs. "I never wanted you to leave."

My heart stumbled as warmth from his fingers seeped through the terry cloth into my skin. "I get it. Rock and a hard place."

His eyes glinted as his hands remained steady. "Do you understand?"

I cleared my throat. "Yes."

His hands slid close to my knees. "I thought you hated me."

"No. Never."

He swallowed as if these raw emotions scraped his throat bare. "You still look cold. Can I get you a drink? Wine. Bourbon."

"Bourbon. Chase the chill from the bones."

Nodding, he rose and moved to the small minibar created from a reclaimed barn table. He poured liberal portions into two crystal glasses and handed one to me.

"Thanks." I held up the glass, marveling at the craftsmanship of the tulip-shaped crystal, funneling aromas of black pepper and clove. I sipped. "Tastes amazing."

He drank. "Dad gave it to me. Called it a housewarming gift."

"When you finished the house?"

"I did a lot of the grunt work. Hauling out debris, demo, sanding floors. Paid the professionals for the important stuff. Roof, electrical, plumbing."

"Few would've tried to save this place."

He shrugged. "I am king of the lost causes."

I swirled the glass. Bourbon cycloned slowly. "Like me?"

"No, I never have seen you that way. You're a force. Fearless."

I traveled in a whirlwind of furious energy, but I was rudderless. Only raw nerves kept me putting one foot in front of the other. I'd learned at age twelve that people who stopped moving were swallowed whole by the universe.

A slight smile tipped the edge of my lips. "A cook in Bozeman called me a Tasmanian devil."

"Fits." The deep tones of his voice made the semi-insult almost charming.

I took another sip of bourbon, welcoming the warmth spreading through my body. "The last time I was here with you, the roof was barely in place. We basically camped out under the stars."

"Thankfully, not raining."

Sex on a first date wasn't generally a recipe for success, but neither one of us had been worried about the long haul.

"No, not raining." Tension banded his vocal cords, forcing him to clear his throat.

I walked to the fireplace and set my glass on the mantel. The heat quickly soaked into my skin, leaving me flushed. But maybe that was the bourbon. Or Spencer. He'd always made my skin glow.

At our closest, we had moments when we could almost read each other's thoughts. Threads of that severed connection itched as if they were growing again.

"What was your favorite moment on the trip?" he asked.

"There were a few." I faced him and stepped away from the fire. "What struck me was how nice everyone could be. When I got food poisoning, I stayed in my van, parked close to the gas station bathroom. I was pretty sure I was going to die. An old man knocked on my window and handed me a cold can of ginger ale. An hour later, a woman with deep lines etched in her face brought crackers and more soda. I don't know where they came from, but I guess they saw me."

A frown furrowed his brow.

"Don't blame yourself. I should've known better than to accept a free hot dog that came with five dollars of gas."

"How long did you sit there?"

"Twenty-four hours, maybe. When it was over, I felt as if I'd purged more than my guts. I felt lighter. Though I don't recommend the method."

"I'll keep that in mind."

I moistened my lips. A week ago, I was in western Montana, dreading the trip home. Now, here I was. I glanced at his left hand and his wedding band. Without a thought, I crossed to him and took his left hand in mine. I ran my fingers over the shiny gold band. It was so smooth, but by rights it should've had more patina to mirror our storms.

"I'm surprised you still wear it," I said.

"I noticed you don't wear yours."

I reached for the cord around my neck, and the gold band and stones slid up from between my breasts and out for him to see. "Restaurant work. Better to keep it on a chain so your hand doesn't catch."

A skeptical brow arched. "Catch on what?"

"Sheeters that thin the dough. Tony Sr. always kept his wedding band on a chain."

He captured the rings, tilting my wedding band so he could read the engraving inside. I didn't have to see it to know it. *Forever*. Maybe if we'd also included our initials, the universe might have realized *Forever* referred to us.

"Where did you get the stones?" he asked.

"Roadside vendor. Supposed to ward off evil spirits."

Nodding slowly, he gently tugged the cord and drew me toward him. I could have taken a step back, reminded him of the legal ramifications of nearly divorced people having sex. And I knew myself well enough to know that was exactly where this was headed.

But I didn't resist. I allowed the soft pull to move me closer until our lips were an inch apart. I swallowed. "I don't have protection."

"I do," he said.

I almost wished he hadn't said that. I touched my lips to his, gently, carefully, hoping touching him would douse my attraction with a cold bucket of reason.

But tasting him focused and narrowed my attention to his mouth. I grabbed a handful of flannel in my hands, pulled him toward me, and teased his lips apart with my tongue. He opened his mouth as he wrapped his arm around me. I rose on tiptoes, sliding my fingers through his thick hair.

His other hand slid down my back, cupped my buttocks, and squeezed gently. Breath caught in my chest.

Time stopped.

Suddenly the past and future didn't exist. There was just now. And the flood of sensations I'd denied for a year rushed over me with no thought to my delicate composure.

His fingers unknotted the robe's belt, and the front opened. For the first time, I hesitated. He hadn't seen me since I'd lost the baby.

"You don't have to hide from me," he said.

"I don't look exactly the same."

His fingers slid to my waist. "I like what I see a lot."

This was who we were. The same. And different.

His hand moved up to the side of my breast. His thumb teased my nipple. "I want to be inside you," he whispered.

My flawed body no longer seemed that important. I nodded. "Yes."

He cupped my breast, leaned in, and kissed me on the lips. The rush of sensations was so delightfully painful and exciting. I leaned into him, deepening the kiss.

He pulled back. His eyes were wild with desire and too many unnamed emotions. If I was expecting a reasonable thought from him to end this, I didn't see one. Neither one of us was going to save the other.

He took me by the hand and led me to the same bedroom I'd slept in on Saturday and Sunday nights. I'd stripped the sheets, washed them, and remade the bed before I'd left. I didn't want to leave any traces of me behind.

In the bedroom, he kissed me and then slid the robe off my shoulders. Terry cloth pooled around my bare feet. He cupped my breasts, kissed my stretch marks and then my nipple.

Nerve endings danced, and whatever had been incinerated last year clawed through the ashes. Tears pooled in my eyes. I arched and pulled him closer to the bed. "Is the condom close?"

His gaze determined, he reached into the bedside table and fished out a condom. He tore open the package with his teeth as he unfastened his jeans with the other hand. Denim slid down his legs, and he stepped out of them. When he slid the condom on, his hands shook just a little. I moved toward him and helped steady his fingers.

He shook his head. "Don't touch me. I'm too ready."

"Me too."

I scrambled into the middle of the bed and propped myself up on my elbows as he shrugged off his shirt and climbed onto the bed. If there was any hesitancy between us outside the bedroom, it had taken off with reason. But that was the way it had always been with us. In the bedroom there were no barriers, no sickness or troubles. It was just pure, raw energy.

His lips met my mouth seconds before he shoved inside me. My body was tight, and he hesitated as I stretched to accommodate him. As the tension faded, he moved inside me. As I raised my hips toward him, he pushed harder and pumped faster. Raw sexual desire fused with emotions, creating a combustible moment. I moaned and arched against him as I teetered toward the edge.

Spencer touched my center, finding the spot as if no time had passed. I called it the magic button the first time he'd grazed it. He certainly hadn't forgotten about it or how to caress it just right. I groaned his name, lifted my hips higher, and gripped his back. Energy filled me up so fully that I could barely draw in a breath. And then I snapped, and spasms rippled over my body. He thrust inside me one last time and came. Once the explosion had cleared, he fell against me, his weight pressing me into the sheets. For a moment, neither of us moved as our hearts crashed against our chests.

"Fuck," he whispered against my ear.

"You're not kidding," I said, breathless. I'd forgotten how right the world could feel in this moment.

Finally, he rolled onto his back, pulled off the condom, and carried it into the bathroom. When he returned, he hesitated. I could see his mind working. Should he get back into bed with me to linger so we could savor each other's warmth? Or maybe he should dress and leave the room so I could dress alone?

He did neither. Instead, he sat on the side of the bed as I rolled onto my side toward him. He didn't hide his curiosity as he stared at my breasts, my narrow waist, and the scar on my belly. He leaned forward, traced the scar, and then kissed it.

I threaded my fingers through his hair as the tears pooling under my lids spilled.

This moment was personal only to us. No matter who he married or spent his life with, he would only share this pain with me. I was glad there was no one he could ever experience this pain with. This was ours alone.

He drew back, ran his hand through his hair, and stood. He reached for his pants, slid them on, and pulled them up with a jerk.

The fragile connection between us shattered, and I could hear the outside world beating against the front door. I rolled onto my back and stared at the ceiling. As my brain cleared, I could see the tension returning to his shoulders. Like me, he knew we'd made a mistake.

I needed to chock this up to a final goodbye or a last burst of emotion before our star flared out forever.

I sat up and moved around the bed until I found the bathrobe, slid it on, secured the flaps, and tied the rope belt.

As he buttoned his shirt, he turned toward the door. "Your clothes should be dry by now. I'll check."

"Thanks."

When he was gone, I moved into the bathroom and stared into the mirror. My eyes radiated the wild desperation of a trapped animal who couldn't go backward or forward. "Stupid is as stupid does."

We didn't speak as Spencer drove me to Eve's house and my van. Both of us were lost in our own confused thoughts. Our relationship had been drifting toward the end, and now it had been jerked back toward a toxic gray zone where mud sucked in around with such ferocity that moving forward was impossible.

He threw the car into park, and I got out, opened the back hatch, and grabbed my bag. "You can tell your dad that you saw the foundation."

"Right. Top priority." His surly edge suggested this was the very last thought on his mind right now.

"Don't worry, I won't tell anyone," I said.

His eyes were as brutal as the thick rain that had closed in on the mountain. "What are you talking about?"

"Eve. Brad, your lawyer. They don't need to know. We can move forward as if nothing happened."

"It did happen. I'm not sorry, and it's none of their business."

"I get it. We're both trying to rebuild our lives, and what happened at the cottage was more like echoes of the past. I understand it's not a promise or suggestion of the future."

Frown lines deepened.

"We closed the loop." I was struggling to keep my voice light. One more minute and I was going to break into tears. "Live well, Spencer. Have Brad call me. I'll sign whatever I need to sign. Even the postnuptial."

"Olympia."

I held up my hand and closed the back hatch. Stepping away from his car, I opened my van door and tossed the backpack onto the front passenger seat. I pretended to be fumbling in my purse for my keys and didn't raise my head until I heard his car pull away.

I laid my head on the steering wheel as a sigh ripe with sadness, loss, and love shuddered from me.

In this moment, I realized I could move to the other end of the world, and it wouldn't be enough to distance myself from this damn town and Spencer.

I started my engine, checked my face in the mirror. Nose red. Eyes watery. Cheeks flushed. Cold water and a soda would take care of that. Time to get my shit together, work the shifts I owed TJ, and leave town for good.

@ThePizzaTraveler

I-90 East, Montana
Three things I hate.

Blisters.

Sitting for long stretches.

Asking for help.

#HATE #DESPISE #DETEST

CHAPTER TWENTY-SIX
OLYMPIA

Friday, November 1, 2024, 4:45 p.m.

I didn't notice the text on my phone until I parked behind Tony's Pizzeria. It was from the producer I'd DM'd two months ago with links to my page. He wanted to set up a phone conversation today, and he'd given me a five o'clock deadline. I glanced at the time. It was 4:45 p.m.

I ate up another five minutes, staring at the text and trying to convince myself that this was real. Could the golden ticket to my next life just find me this easily?

"Hell, he's probably a serial killer," I said to my phone.

Headlines would tease the story of a woman lured to an abandoned airport hangar or a remote location. It would be too late, of course, when she discovered she'd made a terrible mistake, seconds before the axe fell.

Still, I dialed.

Serial killer or not, this could be an opportunity. Today had proved to me I needed to get the hell out of Dodge. My phone call went directly to voice mail. Calling with ten minutes to spare didn't exactly scream *eager.* I cleared my throat twice and sat up a little straighter. "Pete, this is Olympia Hanover. You emailed me about a possible development deal. Call me anytime at this number. I'm ready to get going on this project."

I ended the call and lingered in my car up until 5:00 p.m. It wasn't like he was sitting around waiting for my message. Likely, he'd already written me off because I'd delayed eight hours returning his call. I'd bet hard money everyone else he'd contacted had gotten right back to him, and I was last in line.

When five came and went, I changed my phone settings to ring and vibrate. I climbed out of the car, shouldered my backpack, and entered the restaurant's rear entrance, as I'd done a million times.

The scents of tomatoes, garlic, and basil greeted me as I moved to my locker, hung up my backpack, and donned a clean apron. I checked my phone before tucking it in my back pocket.

TJ was talking to himself when I stepped into the kitchen. When he saw me, his expression was a mixture of relief and maybe a little annoyance. "You're late. I thought you'd left me again."

"I said I'd be here." I washed my hands in the sink and then grabbed a couple of slices of pepperoni.

"You used to arrive earlier."

"I went hiking today."

"In the rain?"

"Not my first brush with bad weather." I glanced at my phone, double-checking to make sure it wasn't accidently on silent mode. Turned up and ready to receive. But no Pete. No calls.

I could feel TJ's gaze, but when I looked up, he refocused on the mound of dough he was kneading. "Do you know what you're going to do? I mean, after this week?"

I couldn't figure out if he was annoyed or reconciled. "Still working on it."

His meaty fingers dug deeper into the dough, pulling and yanking at the mixture as if it had offended him. "What does that mean? You always have a plan."

A smile teased my lips as I thought about today. It had not gone according to plan at all. "I've never had a plan. I've been running on nervous energy since I was twelve."

"That's not what it looks like. Seems like you always have your shit together."

"It's all smoke and mirrors, TJ. But what the hell, right?"

Once, it had bothered me that I didn't have a life plan. I saw myself as a failure. But now, I kind of liked that I didn't have it all mapped out. You can't be open to greatness if you're mired in plans, right?

He muttered an oath, his temper sliding from his grip. "You need to have a plan, Olympia. If you don't have a plan, life will make one for you, and you might not like it."

"Are we still talking about me?"

"Of course we are. I care about you, and I don't want to see you get hurt."

"Plans don't prevent hurt, TJ."

"No, but they can buffer you from all the shit that's out there. Plans are important."

"How exactly do they keep us safe?"

He looked at me as if searching for words suitable for a child. "If my father had not planned for me to take over this restaurant, I don't know where I'd be."

"Well, you wouldn't be here, but would that be so terrible? You had big dreams when we were kids. You wanted to open your own place in another city."

He tapped his index finger against his temple. "I didn't have enough brain cells to know I had a good gig right here."

"I remember a boy aching to find a life that was all his own."

He looked upward and shook his head. "He was a fool. Don't be a fool."

I crossed my arms. "Your point?"

"You have a good thing here."

Life tended to get comfortable over time. Before, even with all the pressures on me with my mom and sister, I found comfort in routine. Even when unexpected bills arose, they had a sameness I understood. It was easy not to raise my head and see what else was possible. Eve had managed it, but not me.

"It took an earthquake and total destruction for me to realize I needed a change."

"And you had a change for an entire year." He wiped his hands off, faced me, and laid his palms on my shoulders. "You got all that out of your system. Now it's time to settle down again and build something for yourself."

"Build what?"

"Maybe, stay here," he said softly. "Maybe we could see if we can find what we had again."

"Us?" I watched his gaze drift to my lips.

He closed the distance between us and pressed his lips to mine. The contact conjured countless memories of a young woman who had depended on TJ as if he were a life raft. At one point our dreams had merged. And then Mom became so sick, and I had no time for him. And he'd drifted away into Gina's arms.

I pulled back, moistening my lips.

His voice was heavy with desire. "We were good together."

I smiled. "Maybe at one time. And then you went down on Gina in the pantry."

He winced. "I was young. Foolish. I didn't realize what I had in you until you left town."

"What's going on with you and Gina?"

He traced circles on my shoulders. "She's tired of working here. She's been begging me for a vacation for a couple of years, and I kept putting her off. She announced she was going to do what you'd done, and she took herself on a vacation."

I hadn't been on vacation. I'd been running for my life. "Have you called her?"

"A few times. She's asked me to join her."

"Then join her."

He removed his hands from my shoulders and shifted his attention back to his dough. "And leave the restaurant? Impossible."

"It won't go anywhere. And you have Buddy cooking for you part time. I'm sure he'd take the extra hours for a few weeks."

"Buddy is a cook, not a manager. I'd rather close than screw up my reputation. If the restaurant is closed, it won't make money, so the money I burn on vacation will leave a mark."

My eyebrow rose. "Last year you bragged about doing so well financially. I think there was even talk of opening a second location."

"That was last year. I wasn't as profitable after you left."

"You got to make hay while the sun shines." His pouting lips—yes, pouting—annoyed me. "My house was on fire, and it needed all my attention."

He shook his head. "I would take time off and travel with my wife if you agreed to run the place for me. You're the only person I trust with Tony's."

I had made life easy for him. Back when I carried half his load, he would take time off—at a time when I couldn't afford to miss a day of work. He'd known I was desperate for money and had let me wait tables until I could barely stand. "I promised you two more days, TJ. And then I'm leaving."

A frown furrowed his brow. "You were never selfish. And now you are."

"I'm long overdue." I glanced out toward the restaurant. A couple had entered and were waiting to be seated. "Speaking of business."

I greeted the couple, seated them, and took their order. As the place filled up, I forgot about TJ's offer, Spencer, and the producer who still hadn't returned my call. Nothing was a sure thing. Except, of course, if I stayed here, then it would be a lifetime of the same.

TJ retreated to the kitchen, sulking as he slammed dough on the counter and banged oven doors closed.

It was past seven when Eve and Brad came into the shop. I was a little surprised. This wasn't their kind of place. I seated them and handed each a menu.

Eve accepted hers easily, but Brad looked uncomfortable. Was it because I was Spencer's wife, or was seeing me here reinforcing Eve's roots? My sister might've been able to dress the part, but Eve was no country-club kid.

"The meat lover's pizza is on special tonight," I said.

Eve wrinkled her nose. She understood that *special* meant TJ had meat in the refrigerator that was going to go bad in a day or two, and he was trying to move it. "How about the veggie lover's with extra cheese?"

Brad handed me back his menu. "Sounds good. I'll also take a beer."

"Soda for me."

"Right."

"It's weird to see you here again," Eve said. "You were such a fixture. But it's like you were never gone. Does it feel odd to be back?"

"It feels like a paycheck," I said, smiling.

"I wish I had a nickel for all the pizza boxes I folded," Eve said.

I arched a brow. "You wouldn't have gotten rich. That job was not your forte, Eve."

She shrugged as she smiled at her husband. "I was slow. So Mom took me off box duty and put me on napkin rolling."

"Again, not a superstar," I said.

She laughed. "All part of my evil plan."

Brad looked around the dining room, and I wondered how he saw it. How did he see the worn floors, chairs covered in red vinyl, and framed posters of Italy? I saw home. Eve, as she'd once said, saw a trap to be escaped.

"You've been here before, right, Brad?" I asked.

"A few times during my high school summers. It wasn't for me."

When he'd rolled through here in high school, Eve would have been doing homework in the back booth or napping in the back room as the night wore on. I'd have been rolling napkins and folding pizza boxes while Mom waited tables. "Why not?"

"Pizza isn't my type of food," he said. "But the Yelp reviews for this place have always been terrific."

Ever the diplomat. "We do hear a lot of nice comments about the pizza. Let me put in your order."

Minutes later I served up their drinks and promised pizza soon before I moved to another table and took orders from three college-age girls dressed in oversize sweatshirts and jeans. Next, I pocketed a tip from another table as I cleared it. I'd been on my feet for six hours straight, and after the hike and sex, my legs felt like lead. I was ready for this night to be over.

When I returned with their pizza, Eve's smile looked uncomfortable. It occurred to me then that it had not been her idea to come here but Brad's.

"How many hours do you think you've logged here?" Brad asked.

"Thirty thousand, give or take." I'd run that little math assignment when I was camping in Utah and bored.

"Could it be that many?" Eve said.

I shrugged. "When you're on the road, you have time to think."

A frown furrowed Eve's brow. "Olympia saved the family."

The resentment simmering under the words didn't surprise me. Eve had always hated where we came from. "One pizza at a time."

I left Eve and Brad to their meal and checked back once, but by then there were enough people in the restaurant to keep me far away. When I looked over, Brad and Eve were standing, and he was tossing three twenties on the table. Half the pizza remained.

I caught his gaze while he helped Eve with her coat. "You guys want a to-go box?"

"No, thanks," he said. "We're fine."

The forces that had pulled Spencer and me apart existed for my sister and her husband. Marriage was hard enough, and when you tossed in different backgrounds and future priorities, it became more difficult to maintain. "Have a good evening."

"Thanks, Olympia." Eve's gaze flickered toward me, but it didn't linger a beat.

When they left, I had the feeling that I'd done something wrong.

By eleven, the last of the customers had left, and I locked the door behind them. I was wiping down the tables when TJ brought me the bucket and mop—something he'd never done before.

"What, no flowers?" I asked.

"Just helping."

"Thanks."

"I'm sorry," he said. "For the kiss."

"Don't sweat it."

TJ lingered. "Your sister still hates this place. She was never happy here."

"It's not this place. It's all the sad memories embedded in the floor and walls."

"There were good times too." He brushed flour from his apron.

"There were. We had some laughs."

"Think about my offer, Olympia. I know I can come on strong, but if you stayed here at Tony's, I'd make you a partner."

I flipped over the chairs and set them on the tables. "A partner?"

He set four inverted chairs on a table. "A partner. Forty-nine, fifty-one."

I grabbed the mop and slopped it on the floor. "I get the fifty-one?"

"Very funny. No, I do."

It was a generous offer. I would always be comfortable if I stayed here. Forty-nine percent wasn't a small offer. But it didn't tempt me. "Maybe give Gina the fifty-one percent. Maybe she'd come back if she didn't think she was free labor."

"What are you saying? We're married. We're a team."

"This place was your father's dream and then yours by default. She's basically an unpaid employee. At least I got paid."

"I take good care of my wife. And the credit card she's currently using is covered by Tony's profits."

"Sounds like a kept woman."

"I don't think of it that way."

"Take a couple of weeks, join your wife, and then put half the business in her name, TJ. You might be surprised."

"She doesn't love this place like you."

Had I ever loved Tony's? It had offered security, it kept my family together, and I would forever be grateful I'd had it. But love? No. "Call Gina."

I finished up the floor, dumped the mop bucket and then the trash. I washed my hands and grabbed my backpack. "See you tomorrow, TJ."

He was polishing a stainless steel worktable. "Thank you, Olympia."

I left through the back door. The cool night air rushed me, and I turned up my collar and burrowed deeper into my jacket. In my van, I switched on the engine and willed the heater to work faster. I checked my phone for about the seventh or eighth time tonight. Still, no calls. No texts. No Pete.

I tossed the phone on the passenger seat and backed out of the parking lot. The drive to Eve's took less than fifteen minutes, and when I parked in front of her place, I hesitated as I stared at the perfect Pinterest house. A neighbor dressed in a bathrobe was walking an old dog, and he paused to stare at me and the van in a not-so-welcoming kind of way. The van or me didn't fit the neat, normal vibe surrounding the cute little homes with manicured lawns and fall wreaths hanging on the doors.

"Just a couple more days," I said as I got out of the car.

"What?"

I rolled my head from side to side, working out the tension, and then walked up to him. "The van will be gone in a couple of days."

He looked taken aback, as if the cone of invisibility that had protected him had shattered. "Why are you telling me?"

"You were wondering, weren't you?"

"No. Maybe." He hadn't expected his silent daggers to be shot back at him. "Vehicles are supposed to be parked in the driveways in this neighborhood."

"And then I'd block in my sister and her husband, and they couldn't get to work in the morning."

"Those are the rules."

"Two days. I'll be gone in two days."

"Good." He took his dog inside, leaving me alone under the moonlight.

I locked the van, crossed back to the house, and reached for the front door. Suddenly, I missed having my own bed in our family apartment. I missed routine. TJ was right: I knew this world well. And at moments like this, the comfort of the mundane was so seductive.

"Stockholm syndrome," I muttered.

I let myself inside the dark house and closed the front door as quietly as I could. Closing my bedroom door, I moved to the adjoining bathroom, brushed my teeth, and peed. I stripped, then climbed under the covers and plugged my phone into the charger. One last check of the phone.

Still no call or text from Pete.

But there was another text, from TJ. Offer still stands. this is where you belong.

Not exactly the cavalry to the rescue, if there was such a thing. But I knew he meant well. How appalled would Eve or Spencer be if I became part owner of Tony's? That simple woman who'd barely graduated from high school but who could outwork anyone was baaaack.

I closed my eyes and shook the phone a little as if it were a Magic 8 Ball. "Stay or go? Stay or go?"

One.

Two.

Three.

When I opened my eyes, I studied the empty screen, waiting for: *Without a doubt.*

Most likely.
Concentrate and ask again.
Reply is hazy. Try again.
But there was nothing.
Nothing from the universe, Spencer, or Pete.
Like it or not, there was no magic riding to my rescue. If anyone was going to save me, it was going to be me.

CHAPTER TWENTY-SEVEN
SPENCER

Saturday, November 2, 2024, 7:30 a.m.

Brad was waiting for Spencer at his law offices when he pushed through the front door. He didn't like to call in favors, but today he required one. He hadn't slept most of last night, and he needed to understand the depth of the quagmire his dick had dug.

Brad was dressed in jeans, a thick sweater, and athletic shoes as he drank a cup of coffee out of the US Open mug Spencer had given him. One look at Spencer, and Brad filled a second cup and handed it over.

Spencer took a sip. This was his fourth cup so far this morning. "Thanks."

"Is your father okay?"

"Yeah, Dad is fine," Spencer said. "Other than he had his keys and was ready to go on a drive."

"Damn. I assume you stopped him."

"I did."

"And you didn't sleep through the night, did you?" Brad said.

"I did not."

Brad nodded to his office, and they went inside, both taking one of the two leather chairs in front of the desk. "Eve and I had dinner at Tony's last night. Olympia keeps that place humming. I've never seen anyone juggle like that woman."

"She's good at what she does. I'm surprised the place survived without her."

"Pizza was good."

"Great."

Brad sipped his coffee, giving up on small talk. "Spill it. You're not here because your dad tried to go for a drive."

"What?"

"Why are you here?"

Spencer drew in a breath. "I had sex with Olympia yesterday."

Brad's cup paused inches in front of his lips. "Okay."

"You once said the divorce could go through easily because we've been separated for twelve months. Did I literally screw up the clock? Do we have to wait another year?"

Brad set his cup on his desk. "Depends. Where were you two?"

"We hiked up to the ruins of the old cabin north of the Stone Cottage. That's the property my father was interested in visiting, by the way."

Brad rolled his head from side to side. "This happened at that burned-out foundation?"

"No. It rained. We returned to the Stone Cottage."

"Okay. Now tell me why you were hiking with Olympia."

"Because we were checking out the ruins for Dad. He's kind of fixated on them now."

"Again, why?"

"Why did I have sex with Olympia, or why does Dad have a thing for the property?"

"Let's start with the lesser of the two. Why is your dad obsessed with the remains of a house?"

"According to Olympia, Dad was married before he met Mom."

Brad's eyes widened. "You're shitting me."

"He was right out of college, and his bride had just graduated high school."

"Why would Olympia even care about something like this?"

"Because Dad's supposed first wife was named Adelaide."

Brad's head tipped back. "Your father suggested the name for the baby."

"Dad says Adelaide was married to his brother, Robert, but now I'm not so sure."

"Do you know what happened to this woman?"

"No. But if Olympia is correct, this Adelaide Bauer was the daughter of a stonemason killed on a Stockton jobsite in 1982. She'd have been living in the house about the time it burned."

"I can look into that, if it helps."

"I'm not sure why it really matters at this point. It won't be long before Dad has forgotten her completely."

"Doesn't hurt to find her. I hate it when the dots don't connect."

Spencer rubbed his hand over his face. "If all this is true, it's a textbook case of like father, like son. The Stockton men tend to marry women who don't meet the family standards, whatever the hell that means."

"Which brings me back to Olympia."

Spencer's eyes narrowed. "What I liked best about Olympia was that she didn't fit the family's model of the perfect wife. I find perfect very boring."

Brad folded his arms. "This brings me back to . . ."

Spencer muttered an oath. "The hike seemed innocent enough."

Brad shook his head. "Tell me you aren't that naive."

"Okay, but I thought I could swim around the sharks. I thought we could really control ourselves."

"You see Olympia as a shark?"

"No, of course not. But my attraction to her has always been hard to control." He pressed fingers to his temples. "It was foolish to think

Olympia and I would be able to keep our hands off each other out there." He ran his hands through his hair. "Is this going to be a problem for me?"

"Depends on Olympia. Technically, she could petition the court to start the divorce clock over again. Would she do that?"

He shook his head. "I don't think so."

"But?"

"But nothing."

"Then why are you here?" Brad asked.

"I just wanted to cover my bases, just in case." He swirled the coffee. "Has Olympia said anything to Eve?"

"I doubt it. She certainly didn't give any hint of this development last night at the restaurant. She didn't come home until after midnight, and she was still sleeping when I left to come here. Which begs the question: Did she really tear up the check from you?"

"I don't know."

"Eve said Olympia has a lot of pride."

"There's pride, and then there's stupidity."

Brad arched a brow. "Let's get back to yesterday. Was it a booty call or the beginning of a reunion?"

"It can't be a reunion," Spencer said.

"Why not?"

Helpless rage scraped under his skin. "I've told you my test results."

"You're talking about something that might not happen, and if it does, it's decades into the future. You have no idea what therapeutics will be available in thirty years. Don't let this ruin what you have now."

"My grandmother said something like that to my mother when my grandfather died. Everyone knew my grandfather was getting very forgetful, but my grandmother was certain Dad didn't have anything to worry about."

"You haven't told Olympia, have you?" Brad asked.

"About Dad, yes. About me, no. And I'm not going to. She needs to get on with her life."

Brad shook his head. "Sounds like you're in deep with her still. One month ago, when you mentioned divorce, it was all very cut and dried. I'm not getting that vibe now."

"I know. I *know*. But I'm determined to see it through. It's the right move. I'm here just to make sure the paperwork can go through."

"Do you think Olympia would really contest the divorce?"

"No. She said she'll call you and set up a time to sign the papers."

"What do you really want?"

Spencer had made this decision months ago and had been so sure of it. "It doesn't matter what I want. It's what's best for her."

"Then what was yesterday about?"

Spencer glared at his friend. "It's not like I planned this."

"I don't believe in accidents, Spencer. It's nice you sponsored the party for Eve and me, but let's face it, you knew Olympia would attend and you'd see her."

"I didn't know that." But he had. Olympia was Eve's only family, and even though she'd never RSVP'd to the invitation, he knew she'd come.

Brad's eyes narrowed as if he were dissecting a bug. "I'm paid to spot this kind of bullshit. You had a damn good idea she'd come to the party, and subconsciously you were hoping something like yesterday would happen."

Annoyance fisted in his chest. Nothing had been straightforward since he'd met Olympia eighteen months ago. "Just get her to sign the papers."

Brad sipped his coffee, letting the silence linger. He had always rocked the pregnant pauses and could make anyone across the bargaining table squirm. "Think you can stay out of the sack with Olympia until after the ink is dry?"

"Fuck you."

Spencer wasn't sorry they'd slept together. Christ, it had felt so good to have her in his arms. In those moments, his troubles had fallen away. But this wasn't about making him feel good. It was about doing the right thing.

A smile tipped the edges of Brad's lips. "I'll reach out to Olympia and ask her for another meeting. If she agrees and signs, then you're off the hook."

Off the hook.

He needed to be free. He needed to get on with his life, find his way back to the pro tour, because right now he was dangling on a metaphorical fishhook, and it was torture. Better to be alone than trap Olympia into a marriage that wouldn't end well in the long run.

@ThePizzaTraveler

On the road

Scraps and leftovers will keep you alive.

And sometimes they taste good.

But in the long run, no one thrives on the unwanted.

#CRUMBS #REMNANTS #HUNGRY

CHAPTER TWENTY-EIGHT
OLYMPIA

Saturday, November 2, 2024, 8:30 a.m.

I had made eggs, pancakes, and bacon by the time my sister stumbled into the kitchen.

Eve shoved back her hair, glaring at me through narrowed eyes. "What's wrong?"

I poured my sister a cup of coffee and dressed it with fake milk. "What could be wrong?"

"Please." Eve sipped her coffee before carefully setting the white mug down.

I rolled my shoulders, unknotting the tension. As much as I wanted to tell my sister about Spencer, I didn't want her sharing my news with Brad.

Brad seemed like a good guy. He was patient with Eve when she was tense or snapping at people. In many ways, he'd taken over the caregiver role I had filled for most of my life. And his father had helped me save my family.

But he was Spencer's lawyer. And getting too personal with him put him in a bad spot.

I sipped my coffee. I owed TJ one more day. I'd have about a grand in my pocket by Monday, which was enough to fund gas and food money all the way to Arizona. "Never mind."

Eve sat back, her eyes narrowing as they had when we were kids and I insisted that our mother was fine. "You had sex with Spencer."

Color warmed my cheeks. "What are you talking about? Of course I didn't."

"Oh, shit!" Eve shouted. "You're lying. I can see it in your face."

"I'm not lying."

"You lied to me most of my teen years, Olympia. Every time you said we were going to be okay, I knew you were choosing between paying for groceries or electricity. But I was so desperate to believe it, I did."

"We were okay, weren't we?"

"Because of you."

"Which means you can trust me now. Don't read anything into my expression."

Eve shook her head. "Nope. I'm not buying it. Why? Where? When did the deed happen?"

"Eve, don't worry about it."

"Are you kidding? It's all I can think about now."

"Whatever you think happened, even if it did, doesn't matter in the grand scheme of things. Can we change the subject?"

"You used to say that at the end of each month before payday, when we were eating tortilla-and-mayo sandwiches," Eve said.

As I readied to toss another bucket of excuses on this flaming truth, she held up her hand, silencing me.

"Tell me you were very careful and won't get pregnant this time," she said softly.

I didn't answer. However, knowing we'd taken precautions and I wouldn't get pregnant made me very sad. If I'd gotten pregnant this time *and* stayed pregnant the last time, I'd have two babies by next summer. I would've landed right in my mother's shoes when she was close to my age. Didn't matter that I'd sworn over and over I'd never live my mother's life. Which technically I wasn't. But I was a little jealous of Mom now.

"You and Spencer barely looked at each other at my party," Eve said. "How did it go from *meh* to sparks so quickly?"

My sister would keep at this until I cracked. But I wouldn't break. I checked my phone for messages. Nothing from Pete.

"Where were you yesterday?" she asked.

"I hiked up to an old house that burned a long time ago. Frank was curious about it."

"I thought Frank never liked you."

"He seems to like me better now that I'm on the way out."

"But you're not exactly on the way out, are you?"

"I am leaving. Regardless of whatever you think did or did not happen. Spencer and I don't do marriage well."

"You two were pretty united when you were pregnant."

"That time has passed." My phone rang, and I immediately checked it. Spam.

"Have you two spoken since the dirty deed?"

I rolled my eyes. "There was no dirty deed."

Eve shook her head. "Okay, soul-searing and uplifting deed."

"Shut up."

"Why do you keep checking your phone? Waiting on Spencer?"

"I had an email on Monday from a studio producer. He liked the reel I sent him. He asked me to call by five yesterday. I called him right before five and left a message. He hasn't called me back."

She squealed. "That would be a fantastic opportunity. Unless he's a serial killer."

I laid my phone face down on the counter. "Believe me, I've considered that."

Eve grinned. "But it would be cool if he were legit."

Excitement flickered, and I didn't extinguish it this time. A grin tipped up the edges of my mouth. "That's what I think."

"So, what are you going to do if this producer doesn't get back to you?"

"I'll keep doing my thing," I said. "I'm leaving on Monday, one way or the other."

"I was hoping you'd stay," Eve said more softly. "You could hang out with me some more."

"I'm not into torture."

She laughed. "I can be fun. And we do okay together."

"Just the idea of getting pedicures and manicures and trying on dresses makes me want to cry."

"We'll only look at black dresses, and you can have your toes painted with clear polish."

"'It'll be fun!'" I imitated Eve's high-pitched, excited voice. "How many times did little Eve utter that fib?"

She laughed. "Okay, I know walking around a mall is agony for you. But seriously, we'll pick out an activity you like."

"I like hiking."

Eve winced. "Something indoors, maybe?"

"Eve, I love you, but let's face it, we aren't wired very much alike."

"I wish I were more like you," she said. "I'm going to need to be more serious and focused when this baby comes. I'm worried I'm too selfish to be a mother."

"You'll be fine." I set my coffee cup down too quickly and splashed caramel liquid on the white counter. I wiped it off with my fingers and smeared my damp hand over my jeans.

"Mom didn't spend as much time with me," she said. "You were her favorite."

"I was older and was a workhorse like her. You're much smarter than Mom and me put together."

"I was always the odd man out with you two," she said.

"Why do you say that? Mom loved you. I love you."

"I irritated her. I know she was trying to keep her head above water, but I just needed her to stop working sometimes and see me. And you were so stressed I don't think you even saw yourself."

"Mom and I were very proud of you. And I don't remember Mom bragging about my report cards." I was signing my name on Eve's report cards by the time I was in eighth grade.

Eve shook her head. "When Mom got sick and we realized she was going to die, I felt so cheated. Whatever I thought we might get to do one day just vanished. It felt like the universe blew a hole into my life." Her voice halted a fraction as she raised her cup to her lips.

"I'm here for you, even though I won't be in town. We can talk every day. You can send me pictures of the baby bump as it grows."

Eve shook her head. "I don't get you. You were so rooted in this town, and now you can barely stand to be here."

"Roots have a way of going bad, I guess. When I lost Adelaide, none of this made sense."

"She and Mom are here."

"I know you'll look after both their places."

When my phone pinged with a text message, this time I didn't look. I'd been too focused on the phone and its disappointments.

"Aren't you going to look?" Eve asked.

"No."

Eve snatched the phone off the counter. She read the text, raised her brows, and smiled. "Interesting."

My sister had mastered the art of teasing even before she'd gotten out of diapers. When she was four, I found her floating face down in the bathtub. I'd panicked, dashed toward her, and jerked her out of the water. She'd spit water in my face and laughed. Another time, while I was jogging, nine-year-old Eve rode ahead on her bike and hid it in the bushes. Certain that someone had snatched my sister, I'd fought back panic until I heard giggling from behind a stand of thick bushes. Yeah, Eve's teasing always led to an adrenaline rush.

"Not taking the bait," I said. "You've fooled me too much."

"I'm not kidding." A smile tugged at the edges of her lips. "Do you want this text to be Spencer or the producer?"

What a choice. I wanted to hear from both. "I'm going to murder you."

Laughing, she lifted the phone and read, "Olympia, sorry for the delay. Can I call you this morning? Pete."

Pete. My heart kicked inside my chest. I hadn't told my sister the producer's name. I reached for the phone, but Eve held it back. Jesus. Did my little sister ever grow up? "I will break you if you don't give me that phone."

Eve laughed, stood, but shook her head. "Say please."

"Eve!"

She tossed me the phone.

I caught it inches above the counter. "Bitch."

Laughter bubbled out of her. "You pretend you don't care, but you care so much it hurts."

My sister's words washed over me as I typed my response and then read it back to her. Pete, good to hear from you. I'm available anytime!

"You sound a little desperate. And please tell me you didn't use an exclamation mark."

I swapped it for a period.

Eve shook her head. "And don't be that available. Tell him you can be reached until seven p.m. EDT."

"You sound like Sylvia."

She rolled her eyes. "You're stalling."

"What if he can't talk until later?" My sister rolled her eyes heavenward as if she were dealing with a child. I deleted *anytime* and replaced it with *today*.

"Good. Now you may send it back," she coached.

I stared at the cracked display as my thumb hovered over it. Shit. I didn't want to care so much about this. If it didn't pan out, I didn't know what was next.

"Press the magic button," Eve said.

I hit send and then set the phone on the counter as if it were radio-active. We both stared at it. The clock ticked. And nothing.

"He'll get back to you," Eve said.

"I hope you're right."

"When he does call, let it go to voice mail. Make the fucker work for it."

I laughed. "Easier for you to say."

"Olympia, I've spent a lifetime making people work to please me. Am I a master manipulator or not?"

"You're an artist when it comes to persuasion."

"Don't be like Mom and be grateful for the little scraps that life tosses your way. You deserve so much more."

"You make me sound like a doormat."

She shrugged. "You were, kind of. But I don't blame you. You took anything to keep us going and didn't have choices. Now you have them."

"I got plenty in return," I said.

"Like what?"

"The family stayed together. Mom was cared for until the end. We didn't have to go into foster care. You graduated college with undergrad and master's degrees. All big wins in my book."

"Life has already taken too much from you."

My paychecks made me solvent for a little while. I'd had a good man for a little while. I'd had a baby growing in my belly for a little while. I'd traveled the country for a little while.

And for the first time, I was tired of having the good stuff for just a little while.

The phone rang.

@ThePizzaTraveler

Bozeman, Montana

When Elsa sings "Let it go," I try,

But it's never as easy for me as it was for the cartoon heroine.

A party invitation found me working in a Montana pizza shop.

My sister is getting married.

Time to go home.

Home. I used to understand the word. Now I'm not so sure what it means.

Either way, time to go back for a little while.

#RELEASE #NEWLIFE #TOMMORROW

CHAPTER
TWENTY-NINE
OLYMPIA

Saturday, November 2, 2024, 9:00 a.m.

The phone rang once, then twice before I reached for it.

"Voice mail," Eve cautioned.

"My ass." I accepted the call. "This is Olympia."

"Olympia, it's Pete. Sorry to miss you yesterday." His voice was deep, upbeat, as if we'd known each other for a lifetime.

Had he missed me, or had he dodged me? I'd almost convinced myself that he had decided I wasn't worth the effort. I turned my back to Eve's anxious face. "No worries."

"I'd like to run an offer past you." A chair squeaked in the background, and I imagined him leaning back. "We're doing a food/travel show. It's in the pilot stage right now, but we're testing five applicants."

There were four others. Of course. "Okay. Sounds intriguing."

"But we loved the Pizza Traveler hook."

"Terrific."

"Can you be in Bozeman next Thursday so we could meet in person? I can't send you a ticket. We're still very low budget."

Thirty hours of driving. Two hard days. If I left on Monday morning, I could make the trip with a day to spare. If there were no delays, the van didn't break down, and I didn't lose my nerve. "I can do that."

He detailed the payout (more than I was making at Tony's), and he explained they'd put me up in a hotel and cover my meals during the seven-day test. "Do you have an agent?" Papers shuffled in the background as if he was already moving on to the next task.

Eve, who'd sneaked up behind me, handed me a note that read *You have a lawyer*.

I stood a little straighter. "I have a lawyer."

"Excellent. I'll send you a copy of the contract. Have your lawyer look it over, and if it works, I'll generate a DocuSign agreement."

Eve started dancing in circles and fist pumping.

"Sounds good. I'll speak to my lawyer today."

"Talk to you soon." The line went dead.

When I hung up, Eve cheered: "Well played."

I faced my sister. "Does Brad know contracts? He's the only lawyer I know. Even though he's my husband's divorce attorney."

"This has nothing to do with the divorce. He likes you and he owes you. And he would never say no to me."

"Saying no to you is dangerous. But he owes me?"

"Please. If not for you, there'd be no me and no baby."

"I didn't think about it that way."

"You need to start thinking big, Olympia. I'll text him now."

"I'll bring it to him as soon as I can print it out. The sooner I can sign, the better. It's going to take me two days to drive to Bozeman."

"Bozeman?"

"That's where the journey begins."

Eve reached for her phone. "Okay."

An hour later, I stood in the lobby of Brad's office. It felt awkward tossing work in his direction, but desperate times.

I rang the bell on the reception desk. *Order up!* danced on the tip of my tongue.

Brad appeared. He was wearing jeans and a sweater. "Olympia."

A sigh underscored my rattled nerves. "Thanks for helping me with this. I don't know contracts, and it would be nice not to get scammed."

"I'm happy to help. Come on into my office."

I took a step toward him. "Do you always work Saturdays?"

"I try not to, but lately there's been a lot of work. A good problem to have."

"I know the feeling."

The space still had the oppressive feel it had on Monday, but I could tolerate it today. It was no longer the end of the line but the beginning of a new adventure.

He gestured toward a chair in front of his desk, and he took his seat behind it. I handed him a copy of the contract I'd printed out at the office supply store on the way over. "I've glanced at it, but most of it's Greek to me."

A half smile tweaked his lips. "Contract law is my thing."

He slid on tortoiseshell glasses that added a few years to his slim face. He had one of those faces that would age quickly. The lines around his mouth and across his forehead were already visible and destined to deepen.

"I can leave it with you or wait while you read."

"It'll take me a couple of hours," he said. "I tend to reread and take notes."

"That's excellent."

"If this pans out, you're on the road for good?"

"I suppose I am."

His gaze held mine. "I heard you and Spencer hiked to the ruins."

It didn't take a huge leap to realize Spencer had told him. Likely he was trying to figure out how he was going to unwind the mess we'd gotten ourselves into. "It was something to see. Then we got caught in the rain."

"I heard." I'd never been good about talking around subjects. Growing up on a diet of poverty, a mother's illness, and a younger sister's teenage hormones, I'd learned extra words were usually an unnecessary waste of time. "I'll sign the divorce papers and the postnuptial agreement on Monday, if that also works. Might as well tie up all the loose ends at once."

"Sure, it works. Is that what you want?"

"It's what must happen, right? Time for Spencer and me to move on."

He leaned back in his chair, threading his fingers together over his chest. "What's it like just dropping everything and leaving?"

I'd expected judgment, not curiosity. "Scary. A little exciting. Terrifying."

"I remember when Spencer left for the pro golf circuit. The chances of him making it were slim. But he didn't seem to care. I admired the hell out of that. I've always taken the path laid out in front of me."

"That's not a bad thing."

"No. It's not. But still, I've always wanted that feeling of the unknown."

"You've got a baby on the way. That's an adventure."

He smiled. "It is."

"Is that conviction I'm hearing?"

Clearing his throat, he sat forward. "Yes, it is."

"Good. Because if you aren't one hundred percent in with Eve and the baby, I'll come back to town."

His chuckle sounded nervous. "And beat the hell out of me?"

My shoulder lifted with a shrug. "Yes."

He held up his hands in defense. "I'm never leaving Eve. I adore her."

"Good answer." The knot of tension in my back eased. "You and Eve still have time to travel before the baby comes. And travel with a baby is very impossible."

"Think your sister would consider a camping trip with me?"

I found a smile. "You two can go anywhere you want, Brad." I pictured his dad sitting behind this desk, looking so rock solid and sure. "There are some pretty fancy places out west."

"I don't get that much time off."

"You can make the time. You can see a lot in two weeks. And she's a teacher and student. Big holiday break and summers off."

"Maybe. Hard to sacrifice all those billable hours. Maybe when I'm older."

I shook my head. "That's what my mom and I used to say. I saved money, and when it came time to book our trip, Eve needed tuition money. And the next year, Mom's car transmission fell out. And then Mom got sick. We never made it out of the town limits."

"That was bad luck. I never met your mother, but Eve speaks so well of her."

"We can't have it all, Brad. I mean, some of the very lucky few can, but most of us must choose. Take two weeks, pick a spot, and go. Eve's holiday break is coming up soon."

The pained smile on his face told me he still believed he could have it all. "You make it sound easy."

"Death simplifies everything. You will or you won't."

He cleared his throat. "Right."

"I'm not barking at you, Brad. I'm talking to Olympia 2015. She and her mother thought they had the rest of their lives to do the fun stuff."

"Spencer used to call me when he was on the road playing in Florida, South Carolina, California, or Hawaii and ask me to join him. I never found the time."

"Because there was always something that had to be done."

"Yeah."

"'Tomorrow, I do'?"

"Come again?"

"The stone I found in Stockton Lake."

"Right. Eve mentioned it."

I smoothed my hands over my knees, stood, and swung my backpack onto my shoulder. "Tomorrow isn't a guarantee. Don't wait too long." I shook my head. "I'm convincing my lawyer not to work."

He breathed deeply as he stood. "I'm not going anywhere until Monday."

"Thanks." I'd lit a tiny fire in Brad. Who was to say if it would hold. Little fires could be blown out with a few strong gusts of practical air. And Eve could be ruthlessly practical when it came to keeping her world stable. "What time would you like me here on Monday?"

"Nine too early?"

That would give me time to get the van packed. As soon as the divorce papers were signed and the development deal reviewed and hopefully secured, I'd be on the road. One way or another, I was leaving Monday morning.

"No, that's perfect."

As I moved toward the door, Brad said, "Spencer told me about Adelaide. I told him I'd try to find her."

"That would be nice." I did feel a connection to her. "Someone has to remember her."

"Spencer won't forget," Brad said softly.

@ThePizzaTraveler

Letting go is hard . . .

Traveling is magic,

but magic runs out, if it's not refreshed from time to time.

I've never found the refresh button.

#LEAVING #MAGIC #NEWSTART

CHAPTER THIRTY
OLYMPIA

Saturday, November 2, 2024, 10:15 a.m.

There were no customers in Sylvia's when I arrived in a rush of cold air. I quickly closed the door and rubbed the chill from my fingers.

Sylvia looked up from a pink cashmere sweater she was folding. "Olympia, I was hoping you'd come see me before you left."

"I'm sorry I haven't had you to Eve's for dinner. I've been working so much."

She smiled. "That story sounds familiar. You're always working."

There was a time when I didn't notice the weight of responsibility. Now it rested heavily on my shoulders. "I think sometimes I was born to work."

She shook her head. "That is not true. At least not anymore."

"I'm going to learn that lesson. One day. Soon."

Sylvia neatly laid the sweater onto a stack of the same, crossed the store, and kissed me on the cheek. Immediately she rubbed off a smear of lipstick. "When?"

"Soon."

"Have a cup of tea with me."

"I'd love that." I hugged her tightly, pretending just for a moment that my mother would have hugged me like this if she hadn't been so busy or worried about paying the monthly bills or sick or dead. My mother had smelled like oregano and garlic but never Chanel.

"I've seen your van parked in Tony's lot. You've logged a few hours," she said as she guided me to the break room behind her counter.

"I needed to replenish the cash flow," I joked.

Sylvia paused and regarded me. "If you need money . . ."

I shook my head. "I do not. In fact, I might have a new job."

"Really?" Sylvia filled an electric teakettle with water and pressed the button.

Speaking about my new job felt a little bit like a jinx. I crossed my fingers. "Maybe a travel/cooking show. We'll see."

Eyebrow arching, Sylvia set up two mugs with tea bags. "Sounds fascinating."

"I took a huge chance last year. It didn't work out so well."

Sylvia shook her head. "I wouldn't say that. Have you and Spencer resolved your future?"

"Do you mean divorce?"

"Not necessarily."

"I told his attorney I'd sign whatever papers he had for me on Monday."

The kettle clicked off, and she carefully poured hot water into each cup. "You're at peace with your decision?"

"Is there such a thing?"

Sylvia's shoulders lifted in a shrug. "It's there, but I've found it's fleeting. One door closes and then it opens another, leaving space for more joy or tragedy."

"I suppose."

"Any luck with your stone?"

"I think I identified the girl who carved it."

Sylvia arched a brow. "A girl? How intriguing. I pictured a gray haired old man with a ponytail leaning over a rock with a chisel."

"Her name was Adelaide Bauer."

Sylvia drew in a breath. "Adelaide? What are the chances? I knew of her in high school. She was a senior, and I was a sophomore."

"You knew her?"

"It was hard not to know of her. She was a bit eccentric. So beautiful. Every girl wanted to be her. Every boy wanted her."

"What was she like?"

"She never minded drawing on public walls. Once she rode a skateboard on the interstate while holding on to the back of a truck. Her laugh was infectious." She traced the rim of her cup. "I envied her willingness to take chances."

"Her father died right before graduation. A construction accident. Maybe that changed her."

"She was wild before he died. Worse after he was gone. Once I heard her say she wasn't destined to live a long life."

"Were you friends with her?"

"No. Sophomores did not mix with seniors, who were gods and goddesses to the underclassmen. As much as I envied her freedom and wildness, I was also afraid of it. Her flame burned so hot it wasn't sustainable."

"After she carved her designs into the high school, the courts mandated she re-create gravestones for the oldest weathered markers."

"And the stone she used for her sculpting came from the Stockton Quarry, from what I remember."

"Yes."

Sylvia set the tea mugs on a small round table and then placed creamer and sugar beside them. "A female stonemason. That certainly fits the girl I knew. She would not be afraid to chase an avocation dominated by men."

I sat and picked up the warm mug, cradling it in my hands. "Adelaide lived in a cottage on the Stockton land."

"She drove an old red Ford Pinto to school every day. It was covered in peace sign stickers, and there was a huge dent on the side. I don't know how she was able to keep it on the road." Sylvia sat. "I remember seeing her the day before summer vacation. Her blonde hair was so bright and her skin as smooth as silk. I never saw her again."

"Did anyone say where she went?"

"No. She vanished. And by fall, school was in full swing, and she was forgotten. I haven't thought about her in decades."

"I can't find any traces of her."

"Why does this matter to you?"

"I guess it's her name. Adelaide. It feels a little like my Adelaide is reaching out to me through this girl."

Sylvia's expression softened. "Why would she do that? She knows you loved her and still carry her in your heart."

I paused, acknowledging my sadness and then allowing it to pass. "It makes no sense. But ever since I returned to town, I wake up hearing my baby daughter crying." Unshed tears clogged my throat. I cleared it.

Sylvia's gaze softened. "Have you talked to Spencer about this?"

"We did. It was a very raw, emotional conversation, but we did talk."

"If I had my way, I'd lock you two in a room without clothes and keep you there until you remembered why you originally connected."

The comment coming from a prim woman made me laugh. "It takes more than chemistry."

"It was more than that."

All traces of humor faded. "The *more* is gone."

"I don't know about that. I see a bit of extra color in your cheeks, and unless I'm getting too old, I believe that's a love bite on your neck."

I tugged up my collar.

"I don't picture TJ as a biter."

I laughed at the suggestion.

Sylvia regarded me over her raised cup. "Blushing?"

"No."

"You are."

"The tea is hot."

Sylvia set her cup down, and the humor drained from her face. "Maybe Adelaide Bauer is helping you with your unfinished business with Spencer. Maybe that's why she's captured your imagination."

"It's finished."

"I will take that bet."

When I arrived at Tony's, TJ was wearing earbuds as he set saltshakers on the tables. I could tell by the way his body was swaying that he was listening to his favorite song. His white T-shirt fit across his broad shoulders, showing off his muscles. He'd always been proud of his body and kept a set of weights in his office so he could work his shoulders or biceps in the small breaks he took. I had to admire him. No matter what he'd said, he loved this life. Sure, he'd like more waitstaff, but he took his legacy from his father very seriously. If he'd kept it in his pants, I likely would have married him out of loyalty. We would've taken a long weekend honeymoon and returned to the place where we'd met. Maybe we'd have had a couple of kids by now.

But it takes loss to tip out all the neatly stacked apples in a cart onto the ground. Loss of TJ to Gina. Loss of my mother. Loss of Adelaide. Each time I gathered a few apples and put them back in the cart, something upended it again. Now, I was afraid to count on the screen test. What if I lost this chance too?

And then Gina came in through the front entrance as if she'd never been gone, and TJ froze as she walked toward him. I wasn't sure if she was going to slap him or kiss him. That was the way it was with those two. He let the mop drop and closed the distance between them. For a moment, they both stood stock straight, inches apart, neither touching.

Then Gina took his face in her hands and kissed him. Hard.

He wrapped one arm around her and cupped her ass with the other. She ground full hips against him.

Okay, well, this was awkward.

I backed up into the workroom and slid off my apron. I wasn't due here until four, and I guessed TJ and Gina would be headed up to the storeroom for some privacy.

Good for them. I wasn't jealous of them but of what they represented. They might not have had all the answers, but they had enough to be happy.

Outside in the cold, I shrugged on my coat and slid behind the van's steering wheel. I turned on the engine and cranked the heat. I drove to the cemetery, knowing this could be the last visit for a long time.

I parked near the spot and sat in my car for at least ten minutes before I summoned the courage to get out. Would this visit ever get easy? Would I finally accept Adelaide as a tragic time in my life? Maybe one day, I'd settle down and have another baby, maybe two. "I won't forget you, baby girl. I won't."

In the cold wind, I crossed the cemetery as brittle brown leaves crunched under my boots. I found Adelaide's and my mother's places easily this time. No searching or hoping somehow the graves didn't exist and it had all been a terrible mistake.

When I knelt in front of their spots, I noticed immediately that the flowers were fresh. White orchids. Extravagant and unable to withstand the winds.

I touched a white petal, still delicate, warm, and soft. The stones I'd left were arranged in a very straight line.

"I suspect your daddy's been here," I said. "I'm glad he comes to see you. Even if I'm not here, he'll see that you have your flowers." Tears glistened in my eyes. "Your daddy is a good man. He and I didn't do a lot right, but we made you, and that made it all worthwhile."

Tears swelled in my eyes and spilled down my cheeks. Sadness and grief rolled over me, and I didn't resist them. I let them wash over me and saturate every cell of my body.

I lost track of how long I sat, but finally I noticed the chilled ground and cold seeping into my bones. I stood, stamped my feet, ready to get the blood flowing. I kissed my fingertips and pressed them against the stone.

As I turned toward my car, I realized I still didn't have anywhere to be for a few more hours. Shoving my hands into my pockets, I savored the warmth as the feeling came back to my fingertips.

I moved toward the old section of the cemetery, where the stones dated back a couple of hundred years. The metal modern nameplates slowly gave way to graying headstones. Time had left the oldest ones so weathered that it was hard to read the names.

I scanned the stones, hoping to see one that might make sense to me. Most of the people had died over a hundred years ago, and I didn't recognize any names.

Shifting deeper into my coat, I continued walking, reading names, noting that a few had lived long lives, but many died young by today's standards.

As I moved down the row of the oldest stones, I came to a section of ten that appeared new. However, the dates were older than on the stones I'd just seen.

I ran my fingers over the arched tops, marveling at the smooth texture. The etched names and dates were crisp, sharp, and straight. And at the base of each was an engraved angel with open wings.

Adelaide. "Are these yours?" I said to the stones.

Cold emanated from the stones into my fingers. "Are you here to help me with unfinished business?"

Wind whistled through brittle leaves barely clinging to their branches. Several fell around me.

"Or maybe you need me to help you? What can I do for you?"

My phone rang, and I glanced at the display. When I saw Barbara's name, hope gave way to curiosity. Why would Barbara call me?

"Barbara?"

"It's Frank."

"Frank? What's going on? Are you all right?" I turned from the stones and started back toward my van. Frank couldn't be okay if he was calling me.

"I think I'm lost." He laughed, but it sounded ragged and nervous. "I shouldn't get turned around so easily, but there you have it."

I fished keys from my pocket. "Can you give me an idea of where you are?"

"I'm not exactly sure."

I kept my voice calm, but I started walking quickly across the cemetery toward my van. "What did you see last?"

"The Stone Cottage."

I opened my car door and slid behind the wheel. "You're at the Stone Cottage?"

"I was. Now I don't know. Spencer showed me the pictures and told me about your visit yesterday to the Mountain House. It sounded amazing, and I could see it all so clearly in my mind. I wanted to see it for myself. I wanted to remember."

I started the engine. "Remember what?"

"Someone I loved."

"Who did you love?" I glanced back toward the cemetery's arching gate.

"I don't remember." The admission sounded as if it had been wrenched from him.

"It's okay. I'm more worried about where you got turned around. When did you enter the woods?"

"It feels like forever."

"It's easy to forget." Frank could be anywhere in the woods, and there were dozens of places where he could stumble and fall. "Have you called Spencer or Barbara?"

"No." He dropped his voice into a stage whisper. "I was hoping to fix this without causing an issue. I know you know this area well."

"How did you know my number?"

"I can still work a phone and find names under contacts."

"Right. Sorry." I fired up the engine, drove out of the cemetery, and nosed the car toward the mountains. "I'm glad you called. Let's see if I can figure out where you are. What do you see around you?"

"Woods. Lots of woods. It's so overgrown. Christ, this area has changed so much, and the bare trees look exactly alike."

Traffic was light, so I moved through town easily. "What about the horizon? Can you see it?"

"I do. I see my favorite mountain."

The area was surrounded by mountains. "Do you remember which one?"

"Damn name escapes me."

"Okay." I pressed the accelerator and raced through a yellow light. "What's it shaped like?"

"A bald head."

"I know the one." He was deep on the trail near the Mountain House's ruins. "You park by the Stone Cottage?"

"I did." He sounded proud, relieved even. "I can walk back to the Stone Cottage."

"No, don't do that. I have an idea of where you are now, and if you keep moving, I might not be able to find you. Is there a place you can sit down?" It wasn't too cold right now, and I could reach him in less than an hour if he had indeed parked at the Stone Cottage.

"There's a big stump on the side of the trail."

"Is there a big tree lying over the path?"

"There is."

"I think I know where you are. Go ahead and sit for me, and I'll come and get you."

"I could use a rest. My feet are killing me."

"Then sit. Hang tight, Frank. I'm on my way."

"Good. See you soon." He ended the call.

I was tempted to call him back to make sure he was okay. I took a left and started following the winding road into the mountains. I called

Spencer. The call went to voice mail. "Spencer, this is Olympia. Can you call me? It's about your dad."

As I continued to drive, I scrolled through my contacts and called the Stocktons' home phone. Barbara answered on the second ring.

"This is Barbara." Her voice sounded edged with worry.

"Barbara, this is Olympia. Frank just called me from your phone."

"Oh, my God. Where is he?"

"He said he was hiking near the Stone Cottage and got lost."

"Hiking! Why in God's name would he go hiking?"

"I'm not sure. But he's lost."

"Why didn't he call me?"

"He's embarrassed and confused. I think I know where he is, but I'm not a hundred percent sure." I pulled onto the small road that twisted up toward the Stone Cottage.

"He has nothing to be embarrassed about."

"Games aren't my thing, Barbara, so I'm going to be straight. Spencer told me about Frank's diagnosis."

Silence settled on the line.

"Have you called the police?" I asked.

"No. Not yet."

I drove up the gravel road. As I drove toward the barn, dust kicked up around my tires. As I passed the barn, the Stone Cottage came into view. And near the cottage was Frank's white Cadillac, parked at an odd angle. "I see Frank's car parked at the Stone Cottage."

"Thank God. Can you find him?"

I parked beside the Cadillac. "I'm headed into the woods now. I'll call. Can you get hold of Spencer?"

"He's been at the quarry all day. The reception can be terrible there, but I can get a message to him."

"I'll call when I find Frank, but if you don't hear from me in the next half hour, call the police, Barbara. Keeping this secret is not going to help Frank."

More silence. "Thank you, Olympia."

"Sure." I ended the call and got out of the van. Grabbing my backpack, I loaded it with water bottles and an extra blanket. As I moved past the Cadillac, I realized it was still running. I opened the door, sat behind the wheel, and pressed the brake. I shut off the engine.

On the passenger seat was a gossamer red scarf with a fringed edge. It wasn't anything I pictured Barbara wearing. Lifting it, I inhaled, drawing in a musty scent created over decades.

"Adelaide." I carefully folded the scarf and replaced it on the seat. "I'll find him."

Pulling my knit hat from my pocket, I got out of the car and angled toward the path in the woods. The sun was overhead, and where it breached the trees, it was warm. However, in the shade the air felt cool. I knew that once the sun went down, the temperature would drop thirty degrees.

I was rushing, my gaze scanning the woods, so I didn't see a fallen branch. I tripped on it and had to take several large, awkward steps before I barely caught myself. Heart beating faster, I steadied my breathing and slowed my pace.

"Frank!" Irritation rattled in my voice. I stopped, listened, but didn't hear anything. I continued up the path. "Frank!"

Nothing.

When I rounded a wooded corner, I saw a golf hat lying on the path. It was new and clean and clearly belonged to Frank. Why take off his hat?

As I climbed the narrowing mountain trail, I spotted the large tree stump, but there was no sign of Frank. Sitting on the stump was a cell phone. I pocketed the phone, fighting back frustration.

"Frank! I told you to stay put! Where the hell are you?"

I looked up to the clearing ahead. If he'd made it to the top, there were three other paths he could have taken down the hill. I jogged up the trail, and when I reached the top, sweat pooled between my shoulder blades, and I was breathless.

"Frank!" I drew in a breath, doing my best not to sound panicked. Wind trickled through the trees. "Frank!"

For several beats, the woods filled with silence.

"Frank, if you don't answer me now, I'm calling Barbara."

"I'm here." The words came out on a sigh.

I scanned the area and found him standing by the stone hearth. I rushed toward him. "Frank, are you okay?"

His hands and his face were covered in scratches, and the knees of his pants were smeared in mud. "No worse for the wear. I tripped. Stupid mistake. No reason to fuss."

Taking his chilled hands in mine, I rubbed them until they started to warm. "You're so cold."

He shook his head, his initial ease vanishing. "I thought it was supposed to be warm today."

"In the valley. Not here. I have a blanket." I pulled it out of my pack and wrapped it around his shoulders. My relief was palpable, and slowly the surge of adrenaline faded. In the absence of fear, annoyance bubbled closer to the surface. "Why are you here, Frank?"

He withdrew his hands from mine. "You sound like Barbara."

The comparison sharpened my tone. "I do not."

He shook his head. "If she were here now, her voice would have that same biting quality, and she'd be giving me that same look." He scrunched up his face. "If you aren't careful, that frown will stick."

I softened my scowl. "Frank, that is not helping."

He straightened his shoulders as if I'd made a mistake. "I'm not a child."

He wasn't. He was a grown, accomplished man who was losing his independence. My temper cooled. "I know. But I'm also not Barbara."

He held up his hands, his index and thumb an inch apart. "Maybe a little."

I nudged his shoulder. "Very funny. Let's get out of here."

"She's not all that bad," he said. "She's tense because she's always worried."

"I understand that now."

He shook his head. "I never intended this to be such a drama. I just wanted to see the house."

"Why?"

"Because I owe it to Adelaide."

"That was her scarf in your car?"

"It was."

"What do you owe her?"

"She asked me to come here once. She begged me. But I didn't come. And then she was gone."

"What happened to her?"

He studied the streaks of soot on the foundation. "There was a fire here."

"I can see that. It destroyed the house."

"It was a cold night, and she liked having a fire in the fireplace."

"Did she build a fire?"

A frown furrowed his brow as he stared at the hearth. "I warned her about not banking the flames too high. Embers could spark so easily."

"Did she burn down the house?"

"She didn't mean to."

I checked my phone and realized I didn't have service up here. "We should get down off the mountain before it gets dark."

"I'm not ready to go yet."

"Frank, we can't stay."

"I can't leave yet."

Until his curiosity was satisfied, getting him off this mountain was going to be tough. "Well, we're here. Have you had a chance to look around?"

"I only just arrived. Took me a while to find the path up here."

"We can take a quick tour, but I need to call Barbara soon or she's calling the police."

"She'll be mad if we go now or in fifteen minutes."

"Maybe she won't be as upset as you think." I followed and watched as he studied the blackened stones.

"I remember the night this house burned." He traced an angel etched into the cornerstone of the fireplace. "We were in a drought, just as we are now. The lake was low, and the ground was so dry." He shook his head. "I told her not to build the fire too high."

"Why didn't you join her up here?"

"The memories come and go so often now," he said, looking down at me. "I try not to let it show, but it's getting harder to hold on to the past. My memories are turning to water, and they're slipping through my hands." He curled his hands into fists.

I took his hand in mine. "Why weren't you here?"

He frowned, glaring up the path toward the mountaintop. "My father. He insisted I forget her. He wanted to end my marriage. Said it was the dumbest thing I'd ever done."

"How did the house catch fire?"

He shook his head. "My father and I fought, and I finally left. I saw the smoke trailing up through the trees when I arrived at the Stone Cottage. I panicked. I needed to find Adelaide and apologize and tell her I loved her."

"What happened?"

"When I arrived, flames were eating through the house." He knelt by the hearth and gathered a handful of ashy dirt in his hand. "The heat was so intense. I rushed toward the door, but the heat drove me back."

"Was Adelaide in the cottage?"

"This house had been her home," he said more to himself. "She and her father had lived here for a few years. When her father died, my father said she could stay until September. She'd wanted to go to dinner in town. She wanted people to know about us. I kept putting her off." He dropped his gaze as if he were swimming through the choppy waves of the past.

"Did you call the police or fire department?"

"There was a landline at the Stone Cottage. I called from there. The police contacted the forest service, and they dropped water on the blaze." He rubbed his blackened hands together. "It took days for the house to cool. My father hired a team to search the site."

"Did they find her?"

Tears glistened in his eyes. "He said they did. But he never would let me see her. He took care of her funeral and had her buried at the city cemetery."

"Did you ever tell Barbara about this?"

"I didn't meet Barbara for several more years. Adelaide was almost forgotten by everyone but me by then. I wanted to save her. I tried. But I wasn't enough."

I knelt beside Frank and wrapped my arms around his shoulders. "I think Adelaide knew you loved her."

Tears fell down his face as he stared at his hands. "She didn't know."

"She left the stone for you."

He raised his gaze and looked at me.

"I don't believe in accidents, Frank. You remembered her name and asked Spencer to name our baby Adelaide for a reason. I found that stone in the lake bed for a reason. I'm here now for a reason."

CHAPTER THIRTY-ONE
SPENCER

Saturday, November 2, 2024, 4:30 p.m.

Spencer's mother was in a panic when he returned her three missed calls. She hadn't left him any messages. But she'd called when she knew he was on the job, and that translated into a red flag.

"Finally!" His mother sniffed and drew in a ragged breath.

"What's wrong, Mom? Is it Dad?"

"Your father decided to drive to the Stone Cottage and go on a hike."

"What?" He shoved hands through his hair as he started his car. "I took the car keys from him the other day."

"He found them."

Spencer cursed. "Where is he? Is he all right?"

"I don't know. He called Olympia, of all people." No missing the anger and frustration. "Did you tell her about your father?"

"I did." He started the car.

"Why would you do that? I told you I wanted to keep this quiet until the company sold."

He pulled out of the parking lot onto the road. "She's not going to tell anyone."

"How do you know that? She has every reason to hate us."

"I know, but she doesn't." He gripped the wheel so tight his fingers ached. "I'm not having this conversation with you now, Mom. I'm headed to the Stone Cottage to see if I can find them. When's the last time you talked to Dad or Olympia?"

"About ninety minutes ago. I've been calling, but the calls are not going through. She told me to call the police, but I haven't. Why hasn't she called me?"

"There's no cell service on the mountain."

"Which makes all this so terrible! What if he's hurt?"

"Olympia knows her way around the woods."

"You're assuming she's found him. What if he's fallen and she doesn't see him?"

"I'm fifteen minutes away, Mom. Hang tight. I'll call you as soon as I get to the Stone Cottage."

"Promise me."

"I promise." He heard the desperation in her voice. He'd heard it when Olympia cried out in pain and started bleeding. He'd heard it in the emergency room as she was wheeled into the operating room. He'd made his share of bargains with God, but they'd all gone unheard. Now, he didn't attempt any deals. He drove faster.

When he pulled up the long driveway and saw the Cadillac and Olympia's van, he allowed the breath he was holding to ease over his lips. Out of his car, he moved toward the path in the woods. Shit. He'd dealt with his share of scenarios over the last two years. Taking over the company, removing his father's access to the bank accounts, and taking his car keys . . . each marked a step closer to a future neither of them wanted. However, in all that time, he'd never been faced with his father wandering off.

He'd been on the trail ten minutes when he heard Olympia's voice. The relief was so acute his eyes stung with unshed tears.

"Olympia!" he shouted.

"We're here," she said.

We. He jogged up the hill, jumped over a log, and rounded a corner when he saw his father sitting on a stump drinking water while Olympia supervised.

Olympia's body language was relaxed, and Dad, keying off her, didn't look as if he had a care in the world. "Dad."

He looked up and grinned. "Spence."

Olympia laid her hand on his dad's shoulder and smiled. "Frank went for a bit of a walkabout, got a little turned around, but all is good now. No need to worry." Her pointed gaze served as a warning for him to remain calm.

"Dad, you picked a chilly day," he said, easing the edge from his voice. "Did you make it to the old cottage?"

"We did," he said. "It was something to see. Been a long time since I've been there."

Spencer glanced at his phone. No service. "We might want to get to the cars so I can call Mom. She's a little worried."

A slight smile tipped the edges of his dad's lips. "Your mother does worry."

"I tried to call a couple of times," Olympia said. "We took so long because Frank needed a break."

Spencer knelt in front of his father. "If you aren't used to these hills, it can be exhausting. Dad, if you can stand, let's try to get a little farther down the hill so I can call Mom."

"I need a couple more minutes," he said.

"I'll hike down to the cars and call Barbara," Olympia said. "You and Frank can follow."

Spencer looked up at Olympia, noting the scratches on her hands and the dirt on her shirt. "Thank you."

"Sure. No worries." She kissed his dad on the head and continued down the hill.

"You two should try again for another baby," his father said.

Olympia hesitated but kept walking.

"Where'd that come from?" Spencer asked.

"I like Olympia. She's a good person."

"I know she is. But remember, Olympia and I are getting a divorce, Dad."

He shook his head. "Why would you do that? I can see she makes you happy."

Spencer glanced ahead and hoped Olympia was far enough down the trail not to hear. "It's for the best."

"What the hell does that mean?" His dad shook his head. "That's what people said to me when they found out about Adelaide. I let my family pull me away from her."

"Nobody is pulling anyone," Spencer said. "We just drifted apart."

Spencer swallowed. Olympia was sailing out of his life, and he didn't know how to stop this action he'd put in motion last year. "Are you ready to go home, Dad?"

"I need to rest."

He was starting to feel like the old man was playing him. "You can only lecture me if you keep walking."

"I don't want to go back home."

"Why not?"

"Because I don't want to go back to my life. It's fading, and I don't recognize it anymore. I'd forgotten about Adelaide. How could I have forgotten her? I loved her so much."

Spencer took hold of his father's arm. "If we go now and settle things with Mom, I'll bring you back here. We'll hike as much as you want. You just have to promise me you won't try this alone again."

"You'll bring me back?"

"I will." As he tugged on his father's arm, the resistance melted. His dad stood and followed him down the path.

When they reached the clearing, Olympia was on the phone. She was nodding, speaking quietly, but her cheeks were flushed. No doubt his mother was venting her fears and worries onto Olympia.

When she saw them, she moved toward them quickly and handed the phone to his dad. "Speak to your wife."

He grimaced. "Is she mad?"

Olympia nodded. "Oh, yeah."

"Time to pay the piper," he muttered. "Barb, baby. How are you?"

Spencer could hear his mother's voice through the phone. She was asking him if he was okay and if he was hurt. She was holding off on the third degree, but that was coming.

Olympia ducked her head, slid her hands in her coat pocket, and walked toward her van. Spencer followed, all the while looking back and keeping an eye on his father.

"Thank you," Spencer said.

Sweat had created a ring of curls around her face. "No worries. Glad I found him."

One lock drifted over her left eye, and he wanted to brush it aside. "He's never done this before."

"When my mother was sick, every day brought a new limitation. Some were very small. She'd try to cross a room and trip. And some were very large, like a fall downstairs or another collapsed vein. The harder she clung to her life, the more bruises and the weaker she got. Slowly but surely, our world narrowed until it was just her, me, and the disease."

Spencer looked back at his father, who was now smiling. "He's still a charmer. If anyone can calm Mom, it's going to be Dad."

"She clearly adores him. I'm a bit jealous."

He was so hungry for peace, for the times he laughed easily. "Seriously, thank you. After the way Mom behaved, you didn't have to do this."

"Barbara has been decent. She's scared. I get it now. I know what it feels like to see the world crumbling. It's not fun."

"I mean before. When we were first married. She wasn't kind."

Sadness knotted her brow as she looked at him. "She was protecting you."

As he watched his father laugh, jealousy knifed him. Dad was losing his life with his wife, but at least he'd had a life. Spencer couldn't say the same. He'd thought about Olympia all day. How could they be so good in bed and so wrong in life? "Brad called me."

"You two chat often, don't you?" she asked.

Her cheeks were flushed from the difficult climb and descent. "He said you're coming by the office on Monday."

"Once I jot my name on the dotted line, I'll be leaving."

"That's what he said."

"Did he tell you I have a deal to maybe work on an adventure/cooking show?"

"He did not."

"I was checking my phone for service when I saw his text come through. He's looking at the contract for me. He said it's a solid offer."

Last year she'd begged him to join her on her trip, but she wasn't asking him to join her this time. Maybe she saw he was needed here. Maybe she just wanted to move on. "He'd know. The man knows contracts."

"Does he like what he does?"

"He's good at it."

"I'm good at waiting tables and making pizza. Doesn't mean I love it."

"Why are you asking about Brad?"

"Because he's married my sister, and they're going to have a baby. I got the vibe that he's not thrilled with his life."

"He's crazy about Eve."

"I'd like to believe Brad won't have a life crisis as she's giving birth."

"He wouldn't do that."

"I hope so."

Olympia stared at him, slowly drawing in a breath. "What aren't you telling me?"

"I've been straight with you about Brad."

"I mean you. What aren't you telling me?"

"My father's disease is likely my future."

"How long have you known?"

"I had tests done shortly after you got pregnant."

Frown lines around her mouth deepened. She was furious. "And you never told me."

"It didn't matter. You had enough on your plate."

"Eve, now you, using my circumstances to keep me out of the loop."

"No, that was not my intention."

His dad approached them and handed the phone to Olympia. "Barbara wants to talk to you."

"Okay." She drew in a breath and found a smile. "Barbara."

"How is Mom doing?" Spencer asked as he watched Olympia turn from them.

"I smoothed it out." He winked. "She's fine."

"I don't know how you do it," Spencer said.

"A gift," his dad said, grinning.

Olympia ended the call and returned to them.

"All good?" Spencer asked.

"Yes. She wanted to thank me." She slid her phone in her back pocket. "Fellas, I need to go. I'm already late for my last shift at Tony's."

He'd told her the worst, and she hadn't reacted. But that was what she did when times got tough: she lowered her head and worked. Spencer didn't like the idea of Olympia working there. He wanted to pull her into his arms and hold her close. "Okay. Call me if you need anything."

"Will do." Olympia hugged him. "If we were still together, none of what you told me would have mattered, Spencer."

He squeezed her tighter, struggling to keep his voice even. "I know, Olympia."

She pulled away, blinked, and then hugged his dad. "Stay out of trouble."

"Can't make any promises," Dad said.

"Don't eat any truck stop hot dogs," Spencer said.

She chuckled. "You don't have to tell me that twice."

He resisted the urge to pull her back into his arms. He didn't want to let her go. But he didn't reach out as she moved toward her van, her shoulders back. She didn't turn around, but when she drove down the driveway, she waved at them both.

He loved his family. But right now, he resented the hell out of them.

@ThePizzaTraveler

Dreams come true, second chances, and other lies.

#CINDERELLA #HEA #UNTRUTHS

CHAPTER THIRTY-TWO
OLYMPIA

Monday, November 4, 2024, 9:30 a.m.

I'd spent Sunday hiking, hoping physical exhaustion would make this meeting easier. But signing the divorce papers and postnuptial agreement was difficult. As ink from the Montblanc pen slid over the linen paper, the weight of failure settled on my shoulders. It wasn't the most painful moment in my life. But it hurt.

The development deal had been drawn up into a simple contract that Brad had read and amended. The new version had arrived early this morning. I signed my name on the computer and pressed send. The contract softened some of the sting of leaving but didn't erase it.

Brad stacked the documents. "Did you see Eve this morning?"

"She was gone before I got up. She hates goodbyes."

Brad frowned. "I love Eve, but I don't understand her."

"She'll call me on the road. That way she can pretend I'm down the street and haven't left."

"If you say so?"

I hugged Brad. He smelled of Old Spice, just like his father. "Thank you. Good luck with the baby. FYI, Eve had colic as an infant."

He chuckled. "Not surprised."

I pulled back. "She's not always easy, but I think all that bluster is to hide her fear."

"Fear?"

"I have it too. She gets dramatic and dresses over the top, whereas I work. We're both trying to keep the tough times at bay."

"She never talks about all that."

I sighed. "I tried to hide all the really bad things from her, but I don't think I did a good job."

"You did a great job."

"Thank you for saying that."

"I'll take care of her."

"It might take her a little while to get comfortable with all that."

"When are you going to slow down?"

"Someday."

He shook his head. "That sounds a little like never to me."

"Maybe." I paused. "Look out for Spencer."

"I will."

"Thanks."

"What if you invited him on the road this time?"

"It's got to be his idea. And after today, I'm not sure it matters."

I left the office and slid behind the wheel of my van. This was my safe space. It felt familiar and had served as my rolling home. When I left last year, I'd been broken and shattered. Now I wasn't celebrating, but I knew I'd be fine.

As I turned on the engine, a hand banged against the driver's side window, startling me. A quick look to the left put me almost face to face with Eve.

I got out of the car. "I thought you were at work."

"I was. I struck a deal with two different teachers to cover my next classes. I'll have bus duty for the next month, but it'll be worth it."

I hugged my sister. "I'm glad you came."

Eve's grip tightened around my neck as a sigh shuddered through her. "I'm not. I hate goodbyes. I don't want you to go."

Sadness coiled around my throat. "I must give this new job a decent shot."

Eve sniffed and drew back. "Did you sign the contract?"

"I did."

"Did he call?"

"Pete?"

"No, Spencer."

"No calls from Spencer, but it might be a little weird if he did."

Eve's frown deepened. "He should've called."

I laid hands on my sister's shoulders. "There's not much else to say." I hadn't told anyone about Frank being lost in the woods. And I understood if Spencer and his mother were consumed with figuring out how to go forward. "It's okay."

"Do you want me to blow up his mailbox or put a bag of dog poop on his doorstep? I can do that."

"You've done it before."

"I know."

I chuckled. "No. It's fine. No stalking or sabotage necessary."

"Air out of his tires? Pizza deliveries at two a.m.? Or I could put him on a blood donation list. You know how they like to call."

"It's okay."

Eve's expression sobered. "I'll keep putting out flowers."

I didn't have to say where. We both understood. "Thank you. Tell them I'll always love them."

Eve sighed and relaxed into my embrace again. "You need to become a content-creator superstar, okay? Don't half-ass this opportunity."

"I'm not planning on it." I allowed my sister to cling until I needed to pull away. "I'll work like it's the Saturday-afternoon rush at Tony's on a home football weekend."

"Perfect." Eve swiped a tear. "You're going to call me each day, right?"

"We've never talked daily."

"Maybe we should. Maybe we should be more connected. I'll give you updates on the baby, if that's okay."

"It's more than okay."

Eve's hand slid to her belly. "I love her so much already."

"I know."

"I'm so sorry about Adelaide."

The lingering pain was a tangible reminder that my girl still had a place in my heart. "I'm grateful for the time she was in my life."

"I admire you."

"Don't. I'm making it up as I go along."

"I'll be calling you with pregnancy questions, if that's okay."

"Of course." My eyes dampened with tears. "Take care of yourself. Try not to wear Brad out. And if he ever wants to camp in Montana or Utah, hear him out. This marriage isn't the Eve show."

My sister chuckled. "It's all the Eve show."

I kissed my sister on the cheek, squeezed her tight one more time, and climbed into my van. Eve stood on the street, kissing her fingertips and pressing them to the glass.

CHAPTER THIRTY-THREE
SPENCER

Monday, November 4, 2024, 5:30 p.m.

"It's been quite a week," Mom said.

Spencer looked up from the glass of bourbon he'd been nursing for the last hour. He set the glass on the table. Brad had called him at eleven this morning and told him Olympia had signed the divorce papers and left town. "It was."

His mother came into the study and sat across from him. "Olympia made quite an impression last week."

"She did."

His mother smoothed manicured hands over her thighs. "She's leaving?"

"She's gone. She signed the papers and is back on the road."

"Have you signed?"

"I will tomorrow."

His mother rose, crossed to the bar, and poured herself a liberal glass of bourbon. She took a long sip. "I'm calling the agency in the morning. We need full-time care now for your father."

He shoved out a breath. "What changed your mind?"

"I can't take care of him properly. What happened over the weekend is going to happen again. It's only a matter of time."

"I'm glad you see it that way. It'll take a weight off your shoulders."

"I'm not sure if this weight will ever be lifted, Spencer." She took another sip. "I can't do it alone after you're gone."

He stood and crossed to his mother. "I'm not going to abandon you."

She shook her head as she met his gaze. "I don't want you to see me through this. Because there is nothing you can really do for me or your father. This is our journey. I want you to live your life while you can."

He cleared his throat. "I made you a promise."

"I'm unmaking it, Spencer." She set the glass down. "You're going back on the tour. You're an excellent golfer, and you should get the most out of your talent. I know you love the game."

Her words unlocked something in him. "Are you sure?"

"The company will be sold soon. There's no reason for you to be here. And last I checked, we have a local airport, and you can return anytime."

"You're sure?"

"More than ever." She picked up her glass and took another sip. "Your father talked about his Adelaide today. He said loving her was like trying to cup water in his hands. No matter how hard he squeezed his fingers, she slipped away."

That was how he felt about Olympia. She had fallen through his fingers again. "I understand that."

Brad had hired a detective today to find out all he could about Spencer's father's lost wife. She'd been important to Olympia and his father, so she was important to Spencer.

She shook her head. "I also want you to talk to Olympia. Be honest with her. Tell her how you feel."

"I can't do that."

"Give her the chance to decide. She could turn her back on you, but I suspect she won't."

"She wouldn't for any health-related reason. But she might ignore me because I've been an ass."

"You are a stubborn man. Just like your father. But I've forgiven him more than once."

"He's lucky to have you."

She raised her chin. "I wrote Adelaide Bauer Stockton's name in the family Bible."

"You did? Why?"

"There might have been a time when I'd have been angry about a secret like that. Or even jealous of her. She sounds like a free spirit, something I've never been. I think that's why I resented Olympia at first. She was so strong, so self-assured, so ready to take a chance. If you haven't noticed, I'm not terribly exciting."

"I disagree."

"Now, when I think of Adelaide, Olympia, or Olympia's mother, I picture all the women that are alone in the world. None of them should be forgotten."

He cleared his throat. This year had changed his mother, but also him. He no longer wanted to focus on what he'd lost, or might lose, but on what he could still have. "Thank you, Mom."

She kissed him on the forehead. "You're young. Live your life."

@ThePizzaTraveler

A Lot Can Happen in a Year

Behind the wheel of my faithful steed Gertie, I roll out of Virginia, the nose of my van pointed west. I'm lighter, better, but not on my way to Perfect—a destination that does not exist. Maybe I might have a second chance or two in my future.

#TRAVEL #365 #IMPERFECT

CHAPTER
THIRTY-FOUR
OLYMPIA

Friday, November 15, 2024
Bozeman, Montana

It was negative ten degrees. An early snow had delayed production, though the locals said this wasn't the worst fall cold snap on record, not by a long shot. No, sir, it could get mighty colder here.

But I didn't care about the past. I only cared about now, and the fact I was freezing my ass off as I smiled for the camera. Of the five applicants who had made it to this stage, one had already quit, and another had gotten appendicitis. That left three remaining applicants.

I had no idea how my recording had gone. I was nervous and giggled when I was making pizza dough, which I dropped in the open flame. I quickly recovered and formed a new disk, and this one successfully hit the cast-iron pan. The dough sizzled in the hot grease. Making thousands of pizzas in my life had finally paid off.

I flipped the pan pizza and smeared crushed heirloom tomatoes and roasted garlic on the top. Next, I sprinkled fresh mozzarella, and then I placed a lid on the pan. While my pizza cooked, I told a kitchen-nightmare story—one of many I hoped to tell. It was the day TJ had mixed up the salt and sugar bins, and the sauce and all the pizza that night tasted like candy. Slightly amusing now, but it was not funny that day.

I grabbed an oven mitt and raised the lid from the cast-iron pan and then, gripping the handle, slid the perfectly cooked pizza onto a bright-blue plate. Touchdown. I grinned at the camera until the producer yelled cut.

The producer told me I'd nailed it, but he'd said that to the last two applicants.

The drive from the site to town took twenty minutes, and when the driver dropped me off at the hotel, I was grateful it was done. Whether this gig worked out or not, I would be fine, but I knew I'd done a fantastic job.

Stepping into the hotel lobby, I drank in the warmth and the hum of conversation. The production crew would pay for my hotel room for two more nights, and then I was on to the next stop. I'd been considering south, maybe Southern California.

I moved into the small bar and found a seat at the end. The air had a leathery Wild West scent. I'd been around food all day and hadn't eaten a single bite.

The bartender's name was Sam. He was in his midfifties and had skin weathered by years in the sun and salt-and-pepper hair tied back with a strip of rawhide. Very Montana.

"How did it go today, kid?" He called everyone *kid* because, I suspected, he wasn't good with names. He set a cold bottled beer in front of me.

"Not bad." I took a long sip.

"You called home yet?"

"What?"

"The other two contestants phoned home from this bar. They were excited. Said they were sure they'd won."

I could call Eve, but I'd need to summon more energy. Eve would want all the details, and then she'd press me for emotions and feelings. Too much right now.

Beyond my sister, that was it. I'd cut ties with Spencer two weeks ago. I thought about him often. I wanted to tell him his future health didn't matter. But I didn't call. I'd accepted the fact that he didn't want me enough to try.

His signature line was still blank on the divorce papers when I'd signed my name, but he'd likely closed the deal by now. Brad had no doubt filed the papers in the Commonwealth of Virginia. I could see Caroline circling closer around Spencer. With me gone, she had a clear shot at the guy she'd always wanted.

Chapter closed.

I should've felt relieved. But I didn't. It would take time for my emotions to catch up with logic.

"You want the usual burned burger?" he asked.

"Yes. With extra fries."

Sam nodded and moved on to another patron, leaving me alone to scroll through my phone, read the latest on social media, and drink my beer.

Contemplating the next stage of my life was too much for today, but tomorrow I'd be refreshed and ready to go again. I was a survivor. My life was shifting into phase II—or was it III?—and it would be better than the past.

Sam set the monster burger and fries in front of me. "Shame to overcook a good piece of meat like this. There should be a law."

My first burger order with Sam had required serious negotiations. He hated overcooking meat. I was now suspicious of any meat that wasn't well done. "You are an angel."

"Damn near dry as a bone."

"Perfect."

My stomach grumbled. I took several bites of burger and could feel systems coming back online. I took another big bite.

I was midchew when someone took the seat by me. Raising my napkin, I wiped my lips and checked my phone for a text from the producer. Nothing. The other two contestants had been sure they'd won the part. Me, I wasn't sure about anything.

Sam asked the guy next to me what he wanted, and when he said, "Beer, thanks," the familiar voice drew my attention up.

Spencer sat beside me, reaching for a handful of peanuts as if he were sitting in Tony's, waiting for me to finish my shift. "I was wondering when you'd notice."

I picked up a fry and took a bite. At a loss for words, I realized I'd never noticed his very piercing gaze. Had it always been filled with questions and hope?

"Fry?" I asked.

"Sure." He took one, unmindful that his fingers brushed mine, and ate it in one bite.

"They make the best fries here," I said.

"That so?"

"Burgers are great too. But don't tell Sam you want your burger well done. He won't like that. Out here, meat's ruined if it's not twitching on the plate."

"I trust you ordered yours well done."

"Yes, and I gladly took the heat." My laugh was quiet. "Food poison me twice, shame on me."

He grabbed a few more fries. "I'll keep that in mind."

I took a long drink from my beer. I wasn't much of a drinker, but this moment seemed to warrant liquid courage. "Frank and Barbara okay?"

"Same. But doing fine. Dad is in a good routine now. Mom hired a full-time caregiver. We sold the company. Transition should take a few months; then I'm off the hook."

"Wow, that's amazing. I'm glad to hear that."

Sam came up and set an iced beer in front of Spencer. "Looks like you like the fries."

"I do," Spencer said. "Is there a rare burger to go with them?"

Sam's deadpan face sparked with approval. "Coming right up."

When we were alone again, Spencer asked, "How did it go today on set?"

"*On set.* Still feels weird to hear those words associated with me." I shook my head. "I don't know how it went. The other two applicants told Sam they'd knocked it out of the park. I, on the other hand, dropped the first pizza but recovered on the second."

"People like recovery stories. They'll see themselves dropping the pizza and then making a second one that was better than the first."

"Well, if the producers don't want slick and packaged, then I'm their girl." But if I was honest with myself, I really wanted this new challenge.

"Did you tell any stories?" he asked as he took another fry. "I think these shows like the cooks who tells stories."

"I told them about the time that I mixed up the salt and sugar bins."

"Makes you sound vulnerable, human. Nice." He leaned toward me. "They'd be crazy not to hire you."

"Thanks." I took another bite of my burger and took my time chewing. "What brings you out this way? Is everything all right with you?"

"I found Adelaide Bauer Stockton."

"Seriously?"

He drew in a breath. "Dad was right. She died in the cabin fire. My grandfather had her remains buried in the cemetery about fifty yards from our girl."

Our girl.

"My grandfather wielded a lot of influence. It wouldn't have taken much for him to shut all that down." He pulled out his phone and showed me a picture of her grave. There were fresh roses on her spot. "Dad put the flowers there."

"How did your mom take that?"

"She bought the flowers for him and drove him there."

"Wow. That couldn't have been easy for her."

"She didn't seem to mind at all."

I handed his phone back. "You could've texted me that."

"I considered it. But if I texted, I wouldn't be here and seeing your reaction for myself. And you have a terrible record of responding to texts, from what I remember."

"True."

"Nothing's changed with me, and I recognize it's selfish being here," he said. "It's not going to end well for me."

I shook my head. "It never ends well for anyone, Spencer. No one gets out of here alive."

He shook his head, as if he had to line up all the facts on the bar in front of me. "My risk factors are high."

"My mother's were low. My chances of a stillbirth were very, very low. No one has a lock on the future."

Resistance still lingered in his gaze.

"This is a beautiful hotel, and we are young." My words dangled. "I didn't make my bed today, but I don't think rumpled sheets are going to be a problem."

He straightened his shoulders. "Dismissing the future is easy when we're on top of our game."

"I've traveled through the valley of illness and loss. I'm no tourist. And I still insist that borrowing trouble is pointless."

"It still doesn't feel right."

So stubborn. "Well, if you feel that way, then go. You've delivered your news, and you've seen for yourself I'm fine. Go home to your parents, find Caroline, and rejoin the golf tour. Last I checked, we're divorced, or well on the way, so you're free and clear."

He shook his head. "That's not exactly right."

I raised a brow. "I signed the papers."

He met my gaze. "That's the thing. I never signed."

"Why not?"

"I went by Brad's office, and he had the papers ready. I must have stared at that blank signature line for ten minutes before I told Brad to hold off."

"Why?"

"I spent most of last year missing you. And the idea of endless tomorrows without you was too bleak to consider." His Adam's apple bobbed as he swallowed. "And again, for the record, Caroline's not on any list of mine. But if you want me to sign them, I will."

I pushed my plate away. I'd been so hungry five minutes ago. "What do you want?"

"You said once that I should follow you. I'm hoping the offer is still open."

Carefully, I wiped fry grease from my fingers. Out of nowhere, icy fear jabbed. I stood at a crossroads. I could keep running or stand my ground with Spencer. "I made that offer a year ago."

"I don't remember an expiration date." He took a sip of beer and carefully set the mug on the bar. "Hoping 'better late than never' is applicable in this case."

Anyone else would see a buff, chill guy trying to pick me up. But I saw the warmth and worry in his gray eyes. When I imagined my tomorrows with him, the tension balling in my chest eased. I wasn't afraid of being alone or forging my own path. But when he was with me, the world felt fuller. "Okay."

He shifted his gaze and sipped his beer. "Okay what?"

"If I get this cooking gig, I'd be traveling too."

"We'll find the balance."

Balance. I'd never quite had that. I'd lived in the extremes for so long, I wondered what it would be like to feel steady and on track.

I caught Sam's gaze as he came toward me with Spencer's plate. "Can you make that burger to go?"

Sam eyed Spencer. "Sure."

Spencer barely moved. But his gaze lingered on me as Sam slid cling wrap over the plate.

"Thanks, Sam," I said.

"Sure thing, Olympia."

Sam set the bill in front of Spencer. He scrawled in a generous tip and signed.

"Get your plate, Spencer," I said. "And let's go upstairs."

Desire darkened his eyes.

I slid off the barstool and left a ten-dollar tip. Leaning close to him, I whispered, "Time to saddle up, cowboy."

Chuckling, he stood, cupped my face, and kissed me. He tasted of salt and beer, and he smelled of faded citrus aftershave, dust, and travel. Why did he always feel so good against me?

"I have a room here too," he said.

"Take your pick." Impatience buzzed under the words.

"I don't care." He kissed me again. "Which one is closest?"

"I'm on the second floor."

"First. I win." He took my hand and turned toward the lobby.

"Hamburger," I said, giggling.

Spencer grabbed his covered plate without looking and pulled me toward the hallway leading toward the guest rooms. I had no idea where his room was in the sprawling lodge, nor did I care. We were together. Our life wouldn't be perfect; no one's was.

ABOUT THE AUTHOR

A southerner by birth, Mary Ellen Taylor has a love for her home state of Virginia that is evident in her contemporary women's fiction. When she's not writing, she spends time baking, hiking, and spoiling her miniature dachshunds—Buddy, Bella, and Tiki.